*Epona's Gift* is *National Velvet* AND *Twilight* combined! Having lost so much . . . hardworking, horse-loving Eppie navigates what she can control in her life with young horse Legend while dealing with boys, going to school, looking for a safe home-life, and creating friendships in California.

~Tiffany Chiu, Owner and Trainer, Mystic Canyon Stables ~ Tiffany's Red Barn

What a great book! *Epona's Gift* reminded me of my lifetime love for horses and the companionship they have brought me and the lessons that they have taught me throughout my life.

~Meredith Whitney, Animal Communicator/Intuitive/Medium

Anyone who has loved a horse, yearned for a horse, kept secrets, lost a loved one, felt alone, had moments of triumph, or feared losing what is important to them will find themselves in *Epona's Gift*.

~ Stephanie Dietz, Horse Rescuer/Proud Horse Mom of LaRoux

*Another Book by Cat Spydell*

## *Other Books You May Enjoy by Cat Spydell*

The Time Traveler's Apprentice at Hollywood High

The Fairies of Feyllan

The Wolfpack Guide to Dog Training

## *Coming Next*

On the Road with Rad the Peacock

Jenna's Rave

The Planted Seed

Epona's Gift
Cat Spydell

The characters and events in this book are fictitious.
Any similarity to real persons, living or dead,
except historical references
is purely coincidental
and not intended by the author.

Cover design and photography by Gineve Rudolph

Mischievous Muse Press
ISBN: 9781938208423
Printed in the United States of America

*For Dale the Big Red Pony,*
*who reminded me how*

# Epona's Gift

# Chapter One

Eppie Wills took the wad of twenty dollar bills from inside her jeans pocket and counted. *Eighty bucks,* she thought, crossing the small room over creaky wood floors. Under the daybed mattress she retrieved a manila envelope and pulled out $260 more dollars. At the green scratched desk, she placed all the bills neatly in the top drawer, double checking the door was closed in case anyone walked in. Hurriedly she filled out the wrinkled bank deposit slip. *$340 more dollars,* she told herself. *Getting there.* Her temptation to keep a twenty lingered only a moment before she wrapped notebook paper around the money and put the whole amount in an envelope, added the deposit slip, and sealed and addressed it to the secret credit union account in Colorado she once shared with her mother. She hid the envelope again in the top drawer under a folder until she could deliver it to the post office personally tomorrow.

"You in there Pauline?" Tracey's voice lilted down the hallway of the small Bungalow-style house.

"I just got back," Eppie, who hated the name Pauline, replied. She straightened up and ran her hands down the front of her jeans to check her pockets before picking up a book from the bookshelf as Tracey Dursom, her legal guardian and distant relative, poked her head in the door. Eppie quickly picked up her cell phone and pretended to text.

"You been at the stables?"

"Yeah, I smell like horse. I was gonna take a shower," Eppie said to the friendly-faced woman peering in.

"You don't have time, dinner's on in a few minutes. Just sponge it off real well, I'm sure it's not too bad."

Eppie sniffed her pits and arm. "It's bad."

"Just do your best," Tracey repeated with a smile before she went down the hall to roust Jim and Lonny for dinner. Lonny and Jim were blood brothers, and Tracey was their adoptive mom who had taken them in as foster kids five years ago with her husband Rich. Eppie was family too now. Sort of.

Eppie put down the phone and looked in the mirror over the dresser. *That was close.* Tracey was nice enough, and often Eppie wished that she could just relax and be open with her. But she knew the drill . . . this was home number three, and while she'd been here longer than the others, she knew at any moment some weird thing could happen and she could end up someplace new. All of her plans could be destroyed. Eppie sighed and tried to smooth her flyaway hair. Even in two braids, bits stuck out wildly, and she found a few pieces of hay stuck in. *I look like a country bumpkin and I'm living in Los Angeles*, she thought, pulling the alfalfa from her locks. Her mind wandered to the stables even as she went into the cramped turquoise-tiled bathroom and washed her face, hands, and arms, and spritzed on some Hawaiian Ginger Mist spray all over her body to mask the horsey smell.

Her mind wandered back to her day: Today she'd cleaned out several stalls; and it was payday, so that was nice. The best part was when she'd seen the Friesian that she'd seen only once before. The horse was a stallion, she was pretty sure, and his gait was forward, his black back rounded and baroque, his head tucked in an elegant way while his long mane seemed obscene compared to the hunter/jumper Thoroughbreds in the stable stalls she cleaned, all trimmed and pulled and shaved. When she caught a glimpse of him, she'd stopped cleaning the stall she was in, frozen with the manure rake in her hand, as she watched the horse's muscles flex in the sunlight. His rider expertly guided him on the trail that led by the stables up to the riding ring. To her the Friesian was a real horse, like the kind she'd grown up with, like the kind she'd ridden when she was little, back before mom died; before Colorado was a memory, before her life had taken a wrong turn from which she still, now at age thirteen, had yet to recover.

Pushing the horse from her mind, Eppie wandered down the narrow hallway to the open living room that had a corner area for the dining table. Tracey, Jim, Lonny, and

Rich all waited for her. Jim was sixteen about to turn seventeen, and starting to get mad about not being able to take driver's ed (*there's no money for extras right now, Jim, we're sorry*) and his strict curfew of 10:00 pm, Lonny, who was eight, was easygoing as long as he could get a ride to the beach to surf, or if he could skateboard whenever he wasn't surfing. Since Eppie's "pretend" dad, Rich, surfed, those two were like buddies, always together and talking waves.

"She doesn't smell too bad," Jim said, sniffing the air as he passed a casserole dish full of au gratin potatoes.

Rich shelled out pieces of pork chops. "And we," he pointed to Lonny with this thumb, "we smell like the ocean, so that just shows how well-rounded we are as a family."

"I don't get it," Lonny added. "Who wants to be shoveling horse shit when you can go to the beach?"

"Lonny! No cussing at the table," Tracey said. "In fact, no cussing at all."

Jim, Rich, and Lonny laughed, and Eppie hid her smile. She was used to Lonny's use of bad words, because her room was right next door to the one Lonny shared with Jim and she often overheard snippets of their discussions.

After dinner Eppie helped clear the plates, and then retreated to her room. She stared at her desk and muttered "homework" as she put her notebooks and Language Arts book on the wood surface. Opening everything up, her mind wandered. Next door, the ongoing screech and buzz of the boys' video game reverberated in her room. Distracted and just wanting to sleep, she reached up underneath the desk where she'd duct taped a big envelope to the underside. She reached inside by feel and pulled out a paper. The breeder's letter greeted her eyes like an old friend.

*Congratulations!*
*SOLD!*
*Yearling stallion, Warlander:*
*Friesian/Andalusian*
*$8500, monthly payment plan accepted.*

And there it was, beneath the words, the picture of her stallion, of her very own horse: Legend. In the picture of the day-old colt running with his mother, his dark eyes seemed to search into the depths of her soul, if only on paper. Eppie pulled out a second photograph, taken a month ago, that had arrived in Eppie's email with this note:

*Eppie,*
*Legend is getting so big! We hope you can move him home with you soon. Janine.*

There Legend was: grayer now, his mane thickly grown down his well-sloped back, his intelligent eye staring at her with such intensity that Eppie felt as if she had already met her young horse. She still owed just over two thousand dollars, to get her horse delivered to her. Then she had to find a way to pay the $500 per month stable fees. But she knew in her heart that buying Legend was the right thing to do. The proof was in her hand. With shaking fingers Eppie pulled the final piece of paper from the envelope. There it was, her horse's bloodline. Two horses listed behind the sire, or father's side, was the black Friesian horse Onyx, her mother's pride and joy. And two back on Legend's mother's side was the dam Pixiedust, her mother's favorite Andalusian mare. Her mother's horses were still out there somewhere, their bloodlines all Eppie had left in the world.

Eppie needed to get back some of the things the universe had stolen from her already: her mother, her life, her ranch in Colorado, her . . . everything. Gritting her teeth, she wiped a rogue tear away, determined not to cry. She slipped the precious lineage paperwork back in its hiding spot and tried to refocus on homework.

*A horse would heal so much, a horse that came directly from the bloodlines Mom started over twenty years ago, before I was even born,* Eppie thought as she made herself focus on the task at hand.

## CHAPTER TWO

School: Unbearable. Eppie hated school, and while Lomita wasn't the worst town in the world, it wasn't Palos Verdes, the majestic green hill a mile above her where all the horsey girls she mucked stables for lived. Palos Verdes reminded her a bit of Colorado, as it was rural, with horse trails, and hills, but with the ocean surrounding it. Lomita was quaint, with railroads and trains, and little sidewalk cafes, and her favorite shop in the world, the feed store, with its cool horse products and fancy halters and bridles that reminded her of home, all right within walking distance. School was just the thing she had to get through to get to the Lomita Feed Store or the stables at the end of the day.

Today sucked more than usual.

"Class, today we'll begin our oral reports. Justin, would you start?"

Eppie's heart leapt. She hadn't done her oral report! By the time they'd eaten dinner last night, and she'd looked at Legend's papers, and then done her Language Arts handouts, she'd forgotten all about the damn oral report. She looked over at Maggie, the one girl she could sort of call a friend at Narbonne Middle School, and gave her a desperate stare. Maggie's eyebrows shot up in a sympathetic but I-can't-help-you way. Eppie slumped down in her seat, hoping-hoping-hoping that Mrs. Marston wouldn't call on her. Next to her Lexel and her groupies were primping, putting on lipstick and laughing at Justin as he tried to stutter out his report on the book on dragons that he'd read that week.

"Lexel, please sit quietly," Mrs. Marston said. Lexel stood and gave an exaggerated hushing motion to her friends, sticking out her butt, trying to look cool. They all tittered as Lexel settled into her seat again, smirking. Eppie glanced over at her: mistake. Lexel glared back in a menacing way. Eppie edged even lower in her chair.

"Pauline, would you like to go next?" Mrs. Marston asked. Eppie's heart beat even faster, and the butterflies began their flight. Next to her Maggie raised her hand.

"Um . . . Mrs. Marston?" Maggie said.

"Yes, Maggie?" The teacher gazed mildly at the interrupter.

"I'm feeling ill, may I use the restroom?"

"Go ahead. Take a hall pass."

"Thanks." Maggie got up and her knees buckled as she walked by Eppie's seat. Eppie, her Thoroughbred-quick reflexes intact, reached up and grabbed Maggie's arm to steady her.

"Pauline, why don't you escort Maggie to the nurse's office," Mrs. Marston said, her eyes conveying that she knew exactly what was going on: Obviously *Maggie* hadn't written her oral report. Eppie jumped up and helped Maggie with her books, and grabbed her own backpack too. They'd just bought fifteen minutes of precious free time, hall passes in hand.

"Wow, that was stunning," Eppie said, shaking her head.

"Well, I couldn't let you struggle. I know how hard you work, what did you do, pass out at your desk again last night after mucking twelve tons of manure til dark?"

Eppie smiled, glad Maggie "got" her. "No, I just forgot this time."

"It's the poop from the barn, I think it's affecting your brain." Maggie rolled her eyes upward.

"I think you're right," Eppie giggled, glad to be free of the classroom with Maggie as they walked down the hall.

They walked very very slowly to the nurse's office, and reached it just as third period was ending.

"I think she's dehydrated," Eppie said as they went into the office. Maggie sat down and let the school nurse give her a chilled bottle of water. All the kids at Narbonne knew that to get free bottled water, all you had to do was go in the nurse's office and say you were dehydrated. Nurse Davis was a huge advocate of drinking a lot of water and kept dozens of little bottles on hand in the medicine fridge.

When Nurse Davis went into the main office to get something, Maggie handed Eppie the bottle and she waterfalled some into her mouth. It dripped coldly down her chin and she wiped it, smiling.

"I feel much better," Maggie called to the nurse.

"I didn't take your temperature or make a chart, sit," the nurse replied just as the bell rang.

"I'd better get to class, thanks for the save. Sorry you're stuck here!" Eppie whispered.

Maggie shrugged. "I don't mind, I really was thirsty. Wanna meet after school and walk home together?"

Eppie remembered her important errand to go home, get her envelope to send to the credit union, and walk to the post office to mail it. Then Tracey was giving her a ride to the stables to work at 4. "Okay. After school I'm going to the stables but I have to run an errand first, can you come with me?"

"I have violin at 5, I have to practice right when I get home, I can't go with you for errands. But I'll see you at lunch!"

Eppie left with a small wave, feeling weird about leaving Maggie alone. In the hallway she saw Lexel and her popular friends lording over the students who were walking to class. She ducked down and headed the other way, glad gym class was meeting out by the field today so she didn't have to have another run in with Queen Lexel of NMS. As she headed outside and saw the green playing field spread out before her, she imagined how the other kids would react if she brought Legend to school with her, and if he'd enjoy running loose on a field like that, his mane and tail flowing freely behind him.

# Chapter Three

Tracey's old red SUV was in the driveway when Eppie got home from school. *Damn.* It would be tricky getting her envelope in the mail to the horse breeder Janine. She'd have to come up with some kind of lie.

"Hi, Pauline! How was school?" Tracey asked as she scrubbed one of last night's dinner pans over the sink. Tracey worked at a preschool in the mornings after she got all the kids to school, but was always home by the time everyone got back in the afternoon.

"It was good, thanks," Eppie said. She wished she could tell Tracey about how Maggie had rescued her when she didn't have her oral report ready, but Eppie knew stories like that . . . they just made people like you more, and they made people want to get closer. Eppie now knew that sometimes people who were close to her went away. She wasn't about to risk it.

"Good," Tracey said, facing her, disappointment in her eyes at the short answer. "Oh, hey, I thought we should visit your grandma Sunday, you haven't seen her in a couple weeks."

"Good idea," Eppie said dully. Grandma Emmaline was her only family left, the one who took care of her after her mom died, the one who sold the horses and their Colorado horse ranch, and moved Eppie in to Grandma's California neighborhood four years ago. It could have been okay, Eppie thought, her fist tightening at the memory of Grandma collapsing two years ago. The ambulance, the hospital, the whirlwind of suddenly losing the only adult in her life. The stroke.

Now Grandma, once full of energy and fun, was half the woman she was before. She was barely able to talk to Eppie when she visited her in the depressing dark nursing home, with her numerous caregivers always lurking around. Eppie liked to remember her grandma how she was back when she was little, when Eppie and mom would come to California and stay in a nearby hotel. They would visit Grandma and chat on the big soft couch, when Grandpa Bud was alive and they had lemon and tangerine trees in their backyard and a dog named Spoof (whatever happened to that Schnauzer?). Grandma cooked delicious meals and they walked on the strand by the beach. Eppie rode a scooter.

That woman melted into her wheelchair under that musty old knitted blanket in that wretched home was not the grandma she wanted to visit. A guilty lump formed in her throat. "Sunday is good," she managed to squeak out.

"Okay. Are you ready to go to the stable?" Tracey asked.

"Um . . . not yet. I have to . . . do something." Eppie's mind raced wildly. "I have to give Maggie her notebook, I carried it for her to the nurse's office and forgot to return it."

"Nurse's office . . . did something happen to Maggie?"

"Um . . . she got dehydrated, that's all. She's fine now. I'll be back really quick." Eppie was amazed how with every breath, her lies deepened.

"I could drive you," Tracey offered.

"Um . . . no, that's okay, because I'm not one hundred percent sure where she is, but I know her friend who lives next door I can give it to if she's not where I think she is, it's just quicker if I just run. Gotta pee first though."

Eppie clamped her mouth shut so no more of her cockamamie story would come out. She sprinted away, because she really did have to pee now, the only true part of her story. She did so super fast before she rushed into her bedroom. She felt in the desk drawer for the addressed envelope full of cash and stuffed it into her underwear, not trusting her jeans pockets. She grabbed a yarn necklace with a small key on it and shoved it over her head as she raced outside, the cooling October air fanning her face as she took two shortcuts to the post office. There she handed the woman behind the counter the envelope addressed to the credit union, which already had the correct postage plus two extra one-cent stamps, just in case.

"Hi there, how are you today?" the woman asked, her eyebrows raised. "Checking your mail for your mom again?"

“Yeah,” Eppie lied, pulling the little key she wore out from under her thin Roxy T-shirt. “The usual.” Her eyes burned as she held in tears.

How she wished that were true! Eppie had gotten the secret mailbox online by using her mother’s social security number, and putting it in her mother’s name, just like the bank account that Eppie shared that was still in her mother’s name. The same bank account that Eppie was using to buy her horse on the Internet using PayPal.

So what if the account read Evangeline, not Pauline, Wills? It was Eppie’s money, money her mother had given her, money from the credit union account that somehow had been overlooked in the shutting down of the farm, a small bank in Colorado that didn’t know that Evangeline Wills was dead and that her thirteen-year-old daughter was using the account now. And, as her mom Evangeline herself many times had done, buying a horse with the money. It was Grandma who had kept the bank book and added to it on birthdays and holidays, telling Eppie each time, “now here is more dosh for your future!” Eppie found and kept the bank book as she helped clean out her Grandma’s house, a ridiculous task for an eleven year old kid. She had slipped it into her pocket and that bank booklet was her one connection to her past that meant something.

Eppie checked the mailbox, which was empty, and ran home, her fugly discount sneakers pounding out her pain with each thump on the sidewalk.

The hay and horse smell of the stables instantly calmed Eppie. Tracey pulled up and began negotiating the U-turn in her big car as Eppie checked her phone.

“Either I’ll pick you up or Rich will, at 6:30,” Tracey said as Eppie tossed her cell in her bag and opened the door.

“Thanks!” Eppie said as she hopped out, her eyes taking in the hunter/jumper horses being led around by girls in tan riding pants and knee-high black boots. The horses all looked spectacular to Eppie, who was used to horses fuzzing up for the winter and getting mucky and muddy until the snows came. These horses had clean sawdust-filled stalls, insect masks, and gloss sprays that offered a showtime sheen every day of the week, regardless of the weather, which was mostly the same all the time in Southern California. Cashmere, a leggy blonde with a small prim nose, waved Eppie over.

"Pauline!" she called, her bay Thoroughbred, Cesar, calmly following alongside of her. "I'm so glad you're here! Can you take him? He needs to be walked, I had a lesson and don't have time to cool him down." Cashmere handed the leather bridle rein over to Eppie, who took it and patted the tall horse on his sweaty neck.

"What's the matter?" Eppie asked, not understanding why the high schooler, only a couple years older than her, didn't have time to care for her own animal.

"I have to meet my boyfriend Bo at Lamppost."

"The pizza place?"

"Yes, there's a lacrosse dinner or something, pre-season meet the team. He wants me to come."

Eppie had no words but merely nodded, glad to get some real horse time in. She led Cesar back to the front of his stall and tied him out on a lead line there, removed his saddle, then took off his bridle and exchanged it for his halter and lead rope. Clucking, she pulled the horse to walk him around to cool. She wished she could just hop on him but she wasn't allowed to ride these horses. They weren't like the ones she'd known before at her own ranch. These horses were more like conglomerations. Each one had a lot of people attached: a groom or stablehand or stallmucker like herself, or the barn worker guys in the little tractor who fed them hay and pellets twice a day, a trainer or two, and an owner, and each inevitably had the man behind the wallet: Daddy. The horses seemed conformed to their owners and trainers and even groomers and muckers. To ride someone else's horse here was unthinkable. To pull on a horse's mouth too hard, to post incorrectly, give the wrong cue for a jump, allow the horse to continue on a wrong lead . . . these were the potential no-nos of time-sharing any of these beautiful creatures.

Eppie leaned her face against Cesar's damp neck and breathed in. More than anything, Eppie missed riding. She missed throwing her leg over a horse, pulling herself up, getting to know the animal underneath her, sensing its mood. Would it buck, get nervous, want to run? All of those possibilities were there, but she sensed them in a horse, could understand its needs, its fears, even its desires. It's what her mother had taught her, using her own wits and a lot of different training methods. But no one here knew that she had all that inside her. To them, she was just Pauline, the poor girl from Lomita who liked horses but couldn't afford one, and would muck stables for cheap just to be near them.

Little did they know that she had one coming soon, a horse of her own. As Eppie walked Cesar, she closed her eyes and for a moment, pretended she was walking her own horse Legend. The heavy hoof fall thudded behind her and the smell of horse sweat heightened her inner tale. Opening her eyes, she realized she would still be spending a lot more time walking horses than riding.

Legend was young, just over three years old, and she wouldn't be able to ride him for a while, but she would still be able to train him. He would be only hers, and when she did finally ride him, he would gallop on the trails with her hands in his mane, and they would become one. It was just how she, and in some ways, her mom, had planned it.

She couldn't wait.

# CHAPTER FOUR

Dusk came all too quickly, as it always did. Eppie heard Rich's car horn as she was giving a big roan quarter horse named Mr. Bill a hug. The horse seemed affronted as she pulled away, but she patted his neck reassuringly. "I'll be back tomorrow, Billy. Don't worry."

Eppie put the rake away, made sure the halter was hung correctly on the hook by the stall (her mother's voice always came into her mind as she worked: *Don't let your tack touch the ground, Eppie. That's just lazy horsemanship!*), then she headed toward the wide dusty driveway. It was that voice that comforted her and made her know that her mother was still with her somehow, at least in her mind while she worked with horses.

Seeing Rich's minivan, she sprinted toward him, a fine layer of dust covering her shit-kicking boots that Tracey bought her at a thrift shop that were too big but functional. She hopped in the back seat next to Lonny, whose hair was soaking wet.

"How was the barn?" Rich asked, smiling back at her as he turned the van around.

"Great," Eppie said, returning the smile. It was all she could give him, but she was always bursting to say so much more.

"Aren't you going to ask about the waves?" Lonny asked in his cute-but-aggressive way.

"How were the waves, Lonny?"

"They freakin' sucked! Man, yesterday we got some two to three foot sets with an occasional three and a half foot outsider, it was epic! Today: Toasted, all under a foot."

In spite of herself, Eppie giggled. "I have no idea what you're saying."

That made Rich, Lonny, and the usually quiet Jim in the front seat laugh. Eppie kind of liked having brothers, even if they were pretend brothers in a pretend family. She laughed with them, and could see Rich watching her in the rearview mirror. His eyes softened and she smiled at him again. She wondered if he'd run home and tell Tracey they'd made a breakthrough with poor Pauline.

It was late at night when Tracey and Rich finally quit wandering the halls, brought the white cat, Lacey Bell, inside, and went to sleep. Eppie did her homework, Snapchatted, and started watching videos about horses but had a hard time staying up and even dozed off twice waiting for the family to get to bed. Once the house was quiet, she pulled her phone from the bedside table and turned it on. She found the email icon and Eppie typed in her mom's address: *HorseLoverr.* Up came the screen of her mother's old email account. When she put that first fateful deposit of $5000 down to buy Legend, she'd let it slip to the breeder that her name was Eppie, even though the breeder Janine thought it was Evangeline Wills, not her underage daughter, buying her horse. Eppie explained to Janine it was her nickname after the slip up, which was true. Any Google search would have told Janine, who lived on the opposite side of Colorado from Wills Warlander Farms, that Evangeline Wills had died in a tragic car accident, but Janine was old-school, and her daughter Janis had emailed Eppie once to tell her in a businesslike way that she handled the Internet transactions because Janine "doesn't do computers." Eppie was glad the breeders didn't bother with the details of researching their horses' new owners. It was even more of a sign that Legend was meant to be hers.

She typed in her mother's old email password, *myboyonyx*, and composed an e-mail to Janine.

> *Hi Janine,*
> *I am sending another $340 by PayPal next week. This will bring my balance on Legend to $2,285, including the transportation fees. I can't wait for Legend to come home! How is he doing?*
> *Eppie*

If Janine had only known how much the updates meant to her, how her heart swelled up to normal size again whenever Janine sent her a picture of Legend, or shared a story about his antics at their stables. Janine . . . or probably Janis . . . shared a story about how he was grumpy about being left out of the herd, but as a young ungelded male would be competing with his stallion father, the beautiful Onyx son, Aloha. Often Legend would pull some crazy antic like yank the metal stripping off the stable roof, or knock over his sawdust bags, or throw the rakes around to show his discontent, and while the breeders weren't necessarily charmed by the scenario and just wanted to offload their rowdy second stallion, Eppie lapped up these Legend stories that filled her soul with the closest thing to happiness that she'd felt in a long time.

Eppie typed in *Warl* . . . in Google. Warlander horse pages came up; Warlanders, that horse with the rounded form, foot "feathers," and tons of hair like their black Friesian half, but also with a delicate air about them, an athletic build from the Andalusian side. They were rare, a new sport horse, sort of like Labradoodles in the dog world, that mix between Labradors and Poodles, but Friesians and Andalusians. In Eppie's mind, it was the perfect horse breed.

Creating amazing Warlanders was her mother's forte. Mom was one of the pioneers in the Warlander breeding field, helping decide which horses would make the perfect pair, which attributes of the horse were correct for passing on the genetic details that made the breed so special.

Feeling parched, Eppie climbed out of bed and used her phone flashlight to find her way to the cold dark kitchen. She got a glass of water, setting the phone down as the Warlander page glared, lighting up the room enough so she didn't have to turn on a light.

"What are you doing up?" came a voice very near, a deep voice that shook her to the core. *Jim.* How did he get in here without her even hearing him? Lacey Bell darted in through the swinging door behind him, a white blur under the table.

"Shiz! You scared me!" Eppie clutched her heart. "What are you doing up, sneaking around. Spying on me?"

Jim opened the fridge, grabbed some OJ, and gulped it straight from the bottle, ignoring Eppie's horrified expression. "I saw a light when I got up to piss, thought we had robbers. Had to come see. What are you doing, looking at porn?"

"Ew! None of your business!" Eppie's hand reached for her phone, but Jim was fast. He grabbed her cell and held it aloft, examining the images on the screen.

"What's a . . . Warlander?" he asked, squinting in the darkness at the bright screen.

The word, spoken aloud, stirred up Eppie's senses. It dawned on her that her plan was so secret that she had never even said the word to anyone since she put down the last $5000 of her mother's hidden money to buy the horse a year and a half ago when she moved in with Rich and Tracey, and started working at the stables to earn the rest. She probably hadn't said the word Warlander since before her grandma had her stroke. Jim looked at her strangely, pulling her into the present moment. He set the phone on the counter.

"They're . . . they are the horses my mom bred," Eppie said, snatching up her cell. "They're rare, they use two other breeds put together to make a Warlander."

"Is that the kind of horse you take care of at the stables?" Jim asked, rummaging around in the fridge for a snack.

"No . . . I mean, they're really rare. There are none around here. Most of them are in Colorado, but there are some north and south of here in California too, just none in L.A." *Yet*, she thought.

"How do you know so much about these special horses?" Jim asked, opening a jar of peanut butter. Eppie squirmed in her thin nightshirt but used her phone and found her favorite photo of a Warlander named Dominator to show Jim the fine details of the horse. Dominator was one of Onyx's offspring.

"I was a like a breeder, with my mom. This is what I did all my life until she died." The last word came out a whisper.

"I thought you were just a horse-girl wannabe," Jim told her, spreading peanut butter on a piece of white bread. "So you actually know what you're doing?"

"Yes. I can ride any horse. I've shown in Western riding, barrel racing, and even English Hunter/Jumping, and Dressage."

"I have no idea what you're saying!" Jim chortled.

Eppie laughed with him. "I guess we just all have our own little worlds," she said.

"Well, you have yours, and Lonny has his. I'm not so sure about me."

"What do you mean?" Eppie asked, but a blinding light hit her eyes, causing her to jump.

"Is there a party going on that I should know about?" Tracey asked as she stood in the doorway, arms folded after snapping on the kitchen light. Her look said, *you'd better have a good reason for being up.*

"Oh . . . sorry," Eppie quickly shut down her phone. Tracey walked over and held her hand gently over Eppie's to stop her.

"Show me what you were looking at?" Tracey said. Eppie reluctantly pulled up the screen, where Dominator stood proud in his photograph.

"Pauline, this is a beautiful horse," Tracey said, sounding relieved.

"That's the kind of horse that her mom bred," Jim told her.

"Is that right, Pauline? You used to have horses like these?" Tracey stared in wonder at the screen, the picture of the gray stallion majestic before them. "I knew Grandpa Bud's new wife came from a horse family, but I never heard any of the details." Tracey was talking about Eppie's Grandpa Bud; she and Tracey sort of shared the same Grandpa but he'd been dead a long time, almost seven years now. The "new wife" was Eppie's grandma, Evangeline.

"This is one of the colts from my mother's stud horse," Eppie whispered.

"You've met this horse?" Jim asked, looking astounded.

"Um . . . no. Live cover."

"What's that?" Jim asked.

Tracey grinned. "It means that her mom's stallion got this horse's mother pregnant through stuff sent through the mail, is that right?" Tracey asked. Eppie blushed and nodded.

"Ew. Okay, now I really don't know what's going on here, I just know I'm going back to bed," Jim announced, a disgusted look on his face, but his eyes twinkled as he looked back at Eppie before leaving the room.

"Sorry if I woke you up, I couldn't sleep," Eppie told Tracey, who was pouring two small glasses of water from the fridge door. She handed Eppie one, not noticing Eppie had an empty glass in front of her already.

"I guessed what was happening when I heard voices in the kitchen." Tracey pulled up a stool and straddled it in her soft pink Victoria's Secret pajamas. She pushed a strand of her auburn hair behind her ear. "These horses are amazing, Pauline. How come you haven't shown me this before? I love horses."

"You do?" Eppie was surprised. Tracey had never mentioned it.

"Well, yeah. Grandpa Bud and your grandma had a couple of horses when I was growing up. They were more like nags, actual work horses, not like this . . . but I got to ride them once around the pasture, up in Central California, when they lived on that ranch up near the wine country, with your mom. That was a fun time."

Eppie couldn't believe it, that Tracey knew anything about her life. That she'd ever even ridden a horse. And with Eppie's mom?

"Did you ride Western or English?" Eppie asked.

"Well . . . more like with a halter and bareback. You know, just hanging out on a horse."

"That's my favorite thing to do," Eppie said, nodding, excitement filling her up inside. Never mind she hadn't actually been on a horse since her grandma had her stroke, and her weekly dressage lessons at the stables were cancelled. It cost over $200 per week for those lessons, and that was more than the Dursom family could afford.

"Well, you ride at the stables every day, don't you?" Tracey asked lightly.

Eppie wanted to say yes, so Tracey wouldn't be able to see how much the horses meant to her, but she shook her head.

“I just clean out the stalls, you know, and groom and walk the horses. All the horses there are in training, and the owners don’t like other riders on them.”

Tracey stared at the horse on the screen and then at Eppie.

“You mean . . . you work there?”

“Yeah. Sort of.” The danger zone flashed a mental warning. If she had a job, would she have to give Tracey some the money she earned? Quickly she added, “I volunteer. I’m too young for a real job, you know.”

Tracey’s shoulders relaxed. “Oh. You must really love horses to volunteer to clean up horse poop!”

“It’s what I know,” Eppie shrugged, shutting down. Tracey patted Eppie’s shoulder. “Well, let’s get to bed, you’ll be too tired to do anything tomorrow, it’s nearly one in the morning!”

Eppie followed Tracey down the hall, her insides churning. Had she said too much? Would Tracey try to stop her from “volunteering” at the stables? What if she found out Eppie really got paid to work there? Worse, what if she found out that Eppie had already paid more than $7000 in the past year to buy a horse in Colorado?

“Goodnight,” Tracey said as she entered the master bedroom. Eppie gave a little wave and went into her room and climbed in bed. Long after the house was dark and quiet again, Eppie stared into the dark of her bedroom and agonized over letting Tracey know so much about her secret world of horses.

# ~CHAPTER FIVE~

Sunday arrived, and Rich took Lonny and Jim to the batting cages. Eppie and Tracey sat at the kitchen table eating a breakfast of cantaloupe and scrambled eggs. Eppie helped Tracey clean up the dishes afterward. As she put the last glass in the dishwasher, Tracey stretched her arms up over her head.

"I love Sundays! Sleeping in is the best. I'm going to go shower, Pauline. Then we'll visit your grandma."

"I took a bath last night, I'll be ready," Eppie assured her. As soon as she heard the shower running, she picked up her cell. Eppie had learned all of the pertinent numbers in her life: her mother's social security number, the credit union account, her PayPal password . . . all of it was embedded in Eppie's mind. Quickly Eppie checked in to Janine's horse breeding farm site, Mohican Ranch. She went to the sales page, found Legend's picture and the *Congratulations Eppie!* note, and clicked on *Pay with PayPal.* Double checking the account number that connected to her mother's old credit union, Eppie paid $340 toward her purchase of Legend. She wished that there were new pictures. Under comments she wrote:

"Sorry this is taking so long Janine. I'll pay more next month. Eppie."

Then she hit *Send*, quickly exited the account, and then went to her cell's history page and erased any evidence that she'd ever visited the Mohican Ranch Friesians Website.

The drive to San Pedro from Lomita wasn't far, but Eppie dreaded it. Grandma Emmaline had always been a fun and feisty woman. Mom used to tell stories about Grandma and Grandpa's California ranch, but they'd retired and moved to Los Angeles after Grandpa Bud had his first heart attack. The second one killed him years ago, but Eppie could remember the jolly, red-nosed man fondly, and even had a vague long ago memory of riding one of his Shire horses when she was two; she remembered being so high up on that huge work horse, and Grandpa Bud being so far below her she could see the red circle of his bald head surrounded by a ring of white hair. It was a slim memory, like hearing about someone else's dream. Grandpa Bud was just a warm feeling that she had in her heart now.

Grandma Emmaline was another matter. The three of them were inseparable; Mom, Eppie, and Grandma Emmaline. Grandma was always visiting their ranch in Colorado after Grandpa died, and she spent a lot of time telling Eppie everything she knew about horses, which was a lot. When they visited Grandma Emmaline here in her San Pedro home, they went to Disneyland, the beach, Universal Studios, Hollywood Boulevard, and Beverly Hills. Grandma took Eppie to theater plays and horseback trail riding in Palos Verdes, and showed her scrapbooks that she'd made over the years with all the pictures of Evangeline on her horses, winning ribbon after ribbon in shows. There was even one photograph that Eppie remembered, with a man Grandma accidentally said was a trainer named Paul standing next to Evangeline's horse, holding the lead. Paul . . . could that be her father? Maybe. It was an answer she'd never gotten, nor had she ever found out what happened to her father. Her dad was just another missing person in her life.

Now as Tracey pulled her SUV into the small driveway at the private home where Grandma was being cared for, an angry knot tied itself up in Eppie's belly. Why did Grandma have to have a stroke? If she hadn't, Eppie would still live with her. She wanted to care for her and live with her again, but it was gone: Everything. Mom, the horse ranch in Colorado, Grandma's house with the lemon and tangerine trees in San Pedro, Grandpa Bud, Eppie's life. Eppie stomped up to the front door while Tracey lingered near the car, locking up.

"I'll be right there."

Eppie rang the doorbell and a friendly lady with a name Eppie couldn't pronounce opened the door. A buzzer rang, the home's little version of a prison bell. Eppie nodded at the Filipino woman and went down the hallway to the bedroom where Grandma always sat in her leather recliner. Grandma's eyes lit up when she saw Eppie. Eppie went over and gave her a hug, holding her for a longer moment than she should: tears welled up in her eyes.

"Hi Grandma," Eppie said, looking around the small room with its dark green carpet, pale pink walls, and flowery art prints on the wall. Not at all Grandma's taste. Grandma had a real bull's skull on her glass coffee table at her old house, a rawhide rug in the den, and white-washed pine floors with knots that looked like faces in the wide planks.

"Hi . . . b . . . beautiful girl," Grandma managed to say, and the struggle she had getting just those small words out angered Eppie all over again. Tracey still hadn't come in. She did that sometimes, she waited outside for a while so Eppie and Grandma could be alone together. Eppie felt wild with the unfairness of it all. She went close to Grandma and leaned in near her ear.

"Grandma, I have a secret. I'm buying a horse. One of Mom's horse's offspring, Grandma. It's out of Onyx and Pixiedust, Onyx is the grandsire, and Pixie's the granddam. I'm going to have a piece of Mom again soon, here in California."

Grandma's eyes were reeling as she took in this information, but Eppie could see she'd only confused the old woman. Grandma didn't always understand where she was, or what had happened to her daughter, or sometimes, what had happened in their lives before the stroke. Sometimes she couldn't talk at all.

"B . . . beautiful," Grandma repeated. It was like it was the only word in her that wasn't stuck. Tracey had once said that it was lucky that Grandma knew who Eppie was, that it was obvious how important Eppie was to her. But Eppie thought that if she was so important, Grandma should have taken better care of herself and not had a stroke in the first place.

The front door jangled its warning bell and seconds later Tracey came in and sat on the bed next to Eppie. Grandma seemed fidgety, not her usual quiet self, and Eppie looked at Tracey.

“I was just telling Grandma about school,” she said quietly.

“Damn,” Grandma said. Sometimes she cussed for no reason.

“My girl,” Grandma said. She was more talkative than usual today. “My girl. Yes. Horse. My girl,” Grandma said.

“Did she just say horse?” Tracey asked, looking astounded.

“Um . . . I told her about the stables too,” Eppie said, excitement welling up. Had Grandma, who hadn’t said a full sentence for over two years, just told Eppie to go ahead and get her beloved Legend? A wide grin stretched over Eppie’s face.

“That was unusual, I’m going to see the nurse about her medication,” Tracey said. Eppie could hear them talking in the hallway, using words like “recovery,” “aphasia,” “non-cognitive,” but Eppie tuned it out and held Grandma’s hand, feeling like she had a true friend in the world after all.

## Chapter Six

Lexel stood in the main hallway when Eppie attempted to run by as she arrived for school.

"Excuse me, Miss T-Shirt, who told you it was dress-like-a-boy-day?" she called out to Eppie. At first, Eppie didn't realize that Lexel was talking to her. Then she realized that it was a mistake to not pay attention to the most popular girl at Narbonne Middle School. The NMS Queen was on her.

One of Lexel's right-hand girls, LiLi, grabbed Eppie and wrangled her in front of Lexel. Lexel was tall with big curly black hair, dark chocolate skin, and attitude. Her pink shimmery lips were suddenly in Eppie's face.

"What, you're too good for me, white girl? You don't hear me asking you a question?"

"Um . . . no?" Eppie tried. Lexel glanced back at the seven girls who now were interested, rising up from their seats on the benches by the main office.

"No?"

"No, I didn't hear you."

"I see. So you're all up in your own world, and I'm nothing to you?"

Eppie knew there was no right or wrong answer, and she was suddenly surrounded by other eighth graders who looked like an ad for the United Nations. She had never felt so white, or so in the wrong place before in her life.

"What was the question?"

Lexel laughed, and her cronies joined in. Lexel held the collar of Eppie's "boy shirt" with her long red nails, looking offended.

"Take some pride, my woman. You're not a fifth grade boy, you know?" she said, turning away. Eppie rushed off, trying to figure out what had just happened, and realized that wearing the hand-me-down skater clothes cast-offs from Jim wasn't going to cut it at NMS. She hurried into the nearest bathroom, even though she heard her name being called from a distance. Once inside, she leaned her hands against the side of the sink and looked in the mirror.

"Paulie?" a voice said. Only one person called her that, it was Maggie. Eppie looked up at her.

"You okay?"

"You saw that, huh?" Eppie felt like punching the mirror. She knew from experience, after her mom died, that punching inanimate objects did more damage to her hands than to the object. She shook with anger.

"Just ignore Lexel. You know, now that we're in eighth grade she's worse than ever. She's going to be fifteen, at the end of the school year. She's like some hormonal teenager. She was held back. For stuff that happened at home, not grades. She's super smart too."

"Really?"

"Swear."

Eppie looked in the mirror and stared at her reflection. She was tan . . . more than she thought, from being outside all the time. Her hair, normally long, brown, and wispy, was bleached from the sun and pulled back into a hasty ponytail, and Jim's old shirt caught her at the neck, making her look boxy and turtle-like. She sighed.

"Well, she's kind of right. I do look like a boy."

Maggie stepped closer as if she'd been waiting to hear these words for decades.

"You know, it's not that hard to dress like a girl," Maggie said. She tugged on her turquoise Hollister tank top with its empire waist flattering her slim frame, the deep blue color amazing against her pale freckled skin. "See this? It was more expensive, about twenty bucks on sale, but these?" She tugged on the form-fitting lace lined tanks underneath. "Two for five bucks. And the jeans . . ." she did a model turn. "Those you can't skimp on, you've got to pay at least $35 on sale."

"I don't have money for clothes." Eppie washed her hands and splashed cold water on her face. Maggie handed her a paper towel.

"What? You work five days a week after school! How can you be broke?"

Eppie hesitated, about to tell a lie about having to give the money to her guardian family to earn her keep, but Tracey and Rich were nice people. She didn't want to dis them. She turned and faced Maggie, ready to tell her secret.

"Well, the truth is . . ."

Several of Lexel's girls burst into the bathroom, but luckily Lexel wasn't with them. They laughed when they saw Eppie.

"Hey, Skater Boi," one of them, LiLi, said.

They swarmed the stalls and Maggie grabbed Eppie's hand and led her outside. They walked across the lawn to a bench under a tree. Eppie kicked the scrabby dirt under her flip flop sandal. She couldn't decide whether to trust Maggie or not, but remembering that Grandma approved gave her courage.

"I have a secret, Maggie, but you have to seriously promise not to tell anyone, ever."

Maggie's eyes grew wide, and she stared at Eppie, nodding. "I swear."

"No matter what?"

"No matter what."

"K." Eppie took a breath. "K. I bought . . . a horse. An expensive, good horse. And I'm bringing him to live here this summer, but it's a secret. He's going to be the way I make money, you know, put myself through school and stuff. He's like . . . the key to my future."

Maggie opened and closed her mouth. She stared at Eppie. "What? How do you make money on a horse? Horses are really expensive!"

"He's a stallion, that means that he can be bred, with mares . . ." Eppie saw Maggie's lost look. "With girl horses. He's a boy horse I can breed with girl horses, and I get like over $1500 every time."

Maggie sat back, a smile hovering near the corners of her mouth, but then she frowned.

"You're buying a horse . . . to make it have sex with other horses . . . for money?"

Eppie's eyes grew large and she laughed. Maggie laughed too. Somehow when Maggie said it, it was all so simple and plain. In her own mind, it was a complex, convoluted mess.

"Yes."

Both girls laughed and were still giggling when the first bell rang.

"Okay, so you have no money because you're gonna be a horse pimp," Maggie said as they walked to class. Both girls held in the ongoing giggles. A cute boy that Maggie liked, Eric, waved at the girls. Maggie waved back and looked Eppie up and down. "I'll give you the no money thing then, but I do want to give you a make-over. You know, dress you up, make you look like the superstar I know you are under that T-shirt."

"Okay."

"K, how about if my mom picks you up at the stables after work and you come home with me for dinner and a make-over? Would your fakey mom be cool with that?"

"I'll ask her," Eppie said.

"Okay, so we'll call at lunch to find out. See you in third period!" Maggie turned left as Eppie turned right for their first period classes, and Eppie felt freer having shared her secret about Legend with Maggie . . . even if she didn't really get it.

Tracey was not only on board for Eppie to go to Maggie's when she heard about the make-over party, but she even offered to take both girls shopping on Saturday (Eppie's day off) to buy Eppie some new jeans.

At 6:30 the Peterson's Voyager pulled into the stable lot. This time Eppie cleaned up a little at the drinking fountain. She knew she smelled like horse, and felt bad getting into a stranger's car with her dusty clothes and stable stench.

"Wow," Maggie said, looking at the scraggly Eppie in wonder. "Um, Mom, this is Pauline, I call her Paulie. Paulie, my mom."

"Thanks for picking me up," Eppie said.

"You're welcome, Pauline. It's nice to meet you."

Maggie's place was a large new two-story house where an old one . . . probably one a lot like Tracey and Rich's house . . . had been. They had a pool in the back yard and Eppie would have loved to swim in it ("The heater's off until next spring," Maggie said) and they had two cute little Pomeranian dogs, Frick and Frack, running around barking at her and nipping at her heels. Maggie's older brother Kyle, who knew Jim from their high school, was there with his friends in the large den, playing Grand Theft Auto and yelling and punching the air. Eppie liked being there. The grand scale of the house reminded her of her home in Colorado with its ceiling-high windows framing the Rockies. The girls went upstairs to Maggie's bedroom.

The room was straightened and neat with just a couple of corners of clutter, but the blue, gray, and green bedspread, white dresser and desk, and cool accessories looked like a Pottery Barn ad. Maggie swung open two large shutter doors to reveal an overstuffed closet.

"Let's get to work," she said.

By the time dinner was ready at 7:45, Eppie had showered, had used a face mask and deep conditioning treatment, and had her hair blow dried and flat ironed. She had never felt so clean. They had to break for dinner and Eppie walked down the staircase wearing Maggie's off-cast Abercrombie shorts, a sexy polka-dot button-down Hollister tank, her hair had sparkling barrettes in it, and she was wearing mascara and lip gloss, and Maggie had even applied pancake make-up to her arms to hide her "cowboy tan," that white vs. dark line where her T-shirt sleeve ended.

The reaction from the boys said it all. One of them even whistled.

"Who's that?" she heard someone whisper. Smiling nervously, Eppie took her seat next to Maggie. Both girls giggled together as Mrs. Peterson doled out delivery pizza and sodas to all the kids.

Regardless of the initial complements, Maggie was still the middle grade younger sister, and the Sophomore boys talked among themselves, with Kyle occasionally doing something gross to offend the girls and make them squeal, like letting his soda drip from his mouth onto his pizza and then eating it. Eppie was having fun though. One boy in particular, the one who had said "who's that?", caught her eye. He had shoulder length brown hair and a perfect white grin. And she caught him looking at her a couple of times too. His name was Brian and he went to Western High with all the others.

By the time Eppie got back home that night ("Thanks for the ride, Mr. Peterson!") she had an arsenal of last year's clothes saved from the charity box at Maggie's house. Maggie was shorter and slimmer than Eppie, so the tops fit snugly and the shorts were shorter than they were supposed to be, and none of the jeans Eppie tried on would even button, but still Eppie had a whole new wardrobe, and some of Maggie's old make-up to boot. For the first time in a long time, Eppie felt pretty.

❧♦❧

Cashmere was facing the Thoroughbred Cesar as he leaned back against his bridle rein. She yelled at the horse, who had stalled at a jump which sent her flying over the fence. Cashmere was mad and dirty.

"You stupid ass!" she screamed at Cesar. Cesar leaned further back, and Eppie couldn't stand the sight. She ran over and took the reins from Cashmere. Eppie turned away from Cesar, clucked gently, and led him away from the scene. The horse was shaking, and so was Cashmere. She looked ready to cry.

"Shhh," Eppie whispered to Cesar. "You're alright." Cesar followed willingly, glad to be free of his irate owner. Cashmere's trainer, in a lesson in another ring, was rushing over. Eppie led the horse to the far side of the ring, away from Cashmere's wrath. She ran her hands down Cesar's legs to make sure he wasn't injured, and checked his walk. He seemed okay. She walked him slowly around the ring to calm him down, and as Cashmere walked over to meet her trainer on the path between rings, Eppie brought Cesar back over to the offending jump. It was a low cross-bar, two foot, something he could jump no problem. Cesar pulled his head up as they neared the jump, and Eppie made soothing sounds to him.

"C'mon, Cesar. It won't bite. Shhh."

Cesar snorted and made a grunting sound, and Eppie made him circle the jump. He side-trotted nervously at first, but after the second round settled down a bit. Then he stopped and wouldn't budge. Something was spooking him. Eppie led him away from the jump and looked at it from the angle he'd been heading in from, and saw it . . . a loose piece of duct tape flapping in the slight wind. Eppie went over with Cesar, who stopped and snorted again, and she talked gently to him as she ripped the tape off. She stuck it in her back pocket and shhhed the horse again, and led him around the jump one more time. He looked for the offending monstrous snake, as that was what it was in his mind, but it was gone now. He relaxed and finally sniffed the jump, proclaiming it safe again. Cashmere and her trainer were hurrying over to retrieve Cesar.

"You should get right on, have him jump it again so he won't associate it with a bad experience. Give him lots of praise when he does it too," Eppie said, forgetting that no one here knew she had any experience with horses.

"That's right," the trainer said, appraising Eppie. "Go on."

"I'm not riding this stupid horse! No way!" Cashmere pouted. She looked at her trainer, Andrea. "You do it!"

"I'm in a lesson," Andrea said mildly, obviously used to Cashmere's tantrums. "And you are going to ruin this horse if you don't start thinking of Cesar first, Cashmere."

"Then you do it," Cashmere said, ignoring Andrea, and handing Eppie the reins.

"Me?"

"Yeah. You know so much, you do it!"

Eppie looked at Andrea, who shrugged and walked away.

"Really?" Eppie asked.

"Yes, really! For Christ's sake, do you think I'm kidding? I'm not riding that jerk!"

Eppie nodded, not willing to argue the point for another second, and led Cesar to the mounting block. Cashmere took her helmet off her head and handed it to Eppie, who snapped it on quickly. She stepped up onto the wooden box and put her foot in the stirrup, held the rein, and climbed onto Cesar's back. He was thinner and taller than her Friesian dressage horses that she was used to, but still, he was a horse, and Eppie knew instinctively what to do.

She guided Cesar with a delicate tug of the rein and a gentle nuance of pressure from her legs and got him to trot around the ring. She posted, moving up and down in the saddle, until she could feel his perfect gait. She designed a quick course in her mind and got him to canter, and began the sequence. She would put the scary jump in the middle so he wouldn't have to think about it right away.

Everything left her. She was no longer at a stable in Palos Verdes but she was a girl on a horse, at one with Cesar, as she leaned forward anticipating the first jump. Cesar flew over it effortlessly, and landed smoothly. Cesar was a much better jumper than Eppie would have guessed, having seen Cashmere riding him. He could do so much more than she asked of him. Eppie knew she'd probably never ride him again so she took him to his fullest range, taking even the largest jump at the end of the ring. Cesar didn't hesitate. Finally it was time for the scary jump. Cesar rushed toward it, all muscles moving, his ears perked forward. He sailed over it, as if not even remembering what had haunted him mere minutes before. Eppie felt exhilarated and she nearly cried with happiness as she slowed Cesar to a trot after two more jumps. Trotting, she guided him back over to Cashmere, who was staring at Eppie in awe. So were several other girls who had stopped what they were doing to watch. Eppie patted Cesar high up on the neck (*always reward your horse, Eppie, then they feel really confident about themselves*), her mother's voice said in her mind.

"Wow, thanks," Cashmere said sheepishly as Eppie handed her the reins. Every cell in her being was quaking with adrenaline and happiness. She smiled.

"Where'd you learn to ride like that?"

"I grew up on a horse ranch," Eppie told her. She was wearing a pretty shirt, thanks to Maggie, but was still wearing her boy jeans, and still looked like a bumpkin compared to the other girls surrounding them, she knew. To compensate she held her head high.

"I had no idea," Cashmere said. The trainer, Andrea, was coming over to them, her lesson over. She approached the huddle of girls and patted Cesar's neck.

"You take this horse and cool him down, Cashmere. And clean out his stall," Andrea ordered.

"I already cleaned it," Eppie said.

"You've done a lot for Cashmere today, then," Andrea said fiercely. "If you hadn't just given that horse back its feet, we'd be retraining a two foot jump for the next month!" Andrea stormed off, and Cashmere seemed to forget about her within a moment.

"Hey, Pauline . . ." Cashmere said as she walked back to the stables leading Cesar. "Would you be interested in riding Cesar for me sometimes? I mean, like this Christmas break I'm going away, so while I'm gone, but also maybe once a week?"

"Is it okay with Andrea?" Eppie asked, having learned from listening around the barn that it was a bad idea to do anything without your trainer's permission.

"I promise you, Andrea won't mind. I'll pay you, of course."

"You . . . would give me money to ride your horse?" Eppie stopped walking, afraid moving would change the deal.

Cashmere shrugged. "Sure. I mean, you're obviously better with him than I am, and my boyfriend is getting mad about all the time I spend here. He wants to hang out with me on Wednesdays, the only day he doesn't have lacrosse after school."

Eppie grinned. "Sure, I'd love to. I really like Cesar. He's a great horse."

"Whatever," Cashmere said, handing Eppie the rein. "Then would you mind putting him away for me too? I want to go home." Cashmere was already pushing send on her cell to call for a ride before Eppie could reply.

Eppie spent extra time with Cesar, knowing she was behind on her stall cleaning (she still had Mr. Bill and the Morab mare, Veronica's, stalls to clean) but she cooled Cesar down, hosed him off, walked him to dry, groomed him, then fed him treats in his bucket and got him a fresh bucket of water, although he had an automatic waterer (Eppie could tell he didn't like to use it from watching him once). She patted and hugged him, glad to finally have a horse to ride, even if it was just once a week.

# Chapter Seven

Saturday was the perfect day to the hit Del Amo Mall, which was partially outside. It was cool and sunny with high clouds and a surreal blue sky. Tracey even looked stylish in her Capri jeans, gold top and Roman sandals. Eppie and Maggie held onto each other and giggled every time a cute boy walked by. A pack of cute boys, and forget it . . . they were goners.

Tracey was in her element, and Eppie had no idea. She was a bargain shopper extraordinaire, and she could walk right past the world's most adorable pair of shoes if they were overpriced. Maggie had a wad of cash with her "just in case", and Eppie had even withheld twenty precious dollars from her horse fund for the occasion.

"Jeans. This girl seriously needs jeans," Maggie said in a comfortable way to Tracey.

"Oh, tell me about it! I have tried to drag her to the mall a million times, but she always tells me she's fine with what she has! I've been itching to shop with Pauline for over a year!"

Had she really been with Tracey for over a year? It seemed like she'd just moved in a month ago. Eppie enjoyed hearing their banter and wished she could be so open with Tracey. They seemed more like mother and daughter than she and Tracey did, that much was for sure, even Maggie's pale red hair complimented Tracey's dark red locks. Eppie walked a little way behind them, drinking her old-fashioned lemonade they bought at a stand, listening to them talk.

"No, not Sears . . . definitely not for Pauline's new style. We have to try someplace new and cool, this is a fashion crisis, after all," Maggie was saying.

"Hollister?"

"Shirts only. How about Anthropologie?"

"Way expensive! But we can look in there for ideas, it's great for that. Target?"

"OMG, get real! And it's across the street. American Outfitters?"

"Good idea."

The two of them marched directly to the store (Eppie had never heard of it before). Once inside, Eppie felt like a princess with people hired to dress her. Even the salespeople and nearby shoppers put in their two cents.

For each pair of jeans, she had to model them in front of her dressing room.

"Too low cut!"

"Too short. She's tall, isn't she?"

"Too faded. They look old. Who wants to pay $75 for faded jeans?"

"Hey, those are nice, what about those?"

Finally two pairs of jeans, both on sale, were selected and bought, and Eppie wore one pair out of the store, shoving her boy jeans in the Outfitters bag. Now with her wispy and colorful hand-me-down tanks, curvy jeans, and wearing Maggie's Power Peach lip gloss, she was on her way to definitely *not* looking like a boy. Then she bought shoes (cool plaid Vans and a pair of pink Rocket Dogs), and Eppie was glowing with confidence. She was having fun. For a moment, she almost forgot about all the crappy stuff that was wrong with her life. It dawned on her that shopping was better than therapy.

"Oh no, it's Kyle!" Maggie groaned, pointing to her older brother. That boy she liked, Brian, was with him.

"Isn't that Brian?" Eppie asked, trying to sound casual, but she saw Maggie and Tracey smile knowingly at each other. Eppie was glad she had her new jeans on . . . Brian had never seen the "old Eppie" with the big boxy boy shirts and horsey jeans.

"Hi Brian!" Maggie called in a singsong voice. She waved. Eppie grabbed her hand but it was too late. Brian and Kyle were walking toward them. Tracey quickly moved away from the girls so they could pretend they were shopping alone at the mall. Brian smiled at Eppie.

"Hi, Paulie," he said, using the nickname Maggie used.

"Hi," Eppie said shyly.

"What are you doing here?" Kyle demanded of his sister.

"We're shopping, duh, whaddya think?" Maggie replied.

"Get anything nice?" Brian asked, still smiling at Eppie. Eppie blushed.

"Just, you know . . . girl stuff," Eppie said. Kyle laughed and punched Brian on the arm. Brian blushed and smirked. Eppie turned bright red, realizing it may sound like they were buying tampons. Maggie saved the day.

"Yeah, you know . . . clothes?" she said, raising her eyebrows at them in case they were thinking anything else. Eppie wanted to die right there on the spot.

"I got some new shoes," Eppie said to cement the fact that they were indeed buying clothes, only clothes. She modeled her pink and bling Rocket Dogs.

"Cool," Brian said with a grin, but Kyle grabbed the Outfitters bag out of her hand. Eppie reached for it, but too late. He pulled her boys jeans she'd worn earlier from the bag.

"Who do these belong to, your dad?" he asked.

"No, they're my brother's," Eppie said, flushing. It was partially true; they had been Jim's once.

"Why do you have them then?"

"I wear them to work," was all Eppie could come up with.

"You work? Where?" Brian asked, interested.

"At the Academy Stables in Palos Verdes," Eppie said, as Maggie wrestled the bag and jeans from Kyle.

"Oh yeah?" A curious look passed over Brian's face. "I've been there before. What do you do?"

"I . . . I'm an assistant. I help out, you know, ride, groom, that kind of stuff," Eppie said vaguely.

"You get paid?"

Eppie glanced around, looking for Tracey. She was far out of earshot, looking at sunglasses on a mall cart parked in the walkway. "Yeah, I do."

"Cool," Brian said. "I work too, I bag groceries at Trader Joe's on Sundays."

Eppie smiled at him, glad that he was more down to earth than most of the boys she'd met. "Cool," she said. She wanted to ask Brian why he'd been to the stables, did he ride, too? Wouldn't that be the most perfect thing, if they could ride together someday? But Maggie slammed into her as Kyle playfully pushed her, and Eppie fell over. Embarrassed, she started to get up. Brian's hand was there to assist her.

"Thanks," she said, her face red again.

"OMG, I'm so sorry, Eppie!" Maggie squealed. She punched Kyle on the arm and held her hand out. "Give it back!"

Kyle meekly handed Maggie the bag and then put his arm around Eppie. "Sorry, Paulie," he said. Eppie managed to nod.

"It's okay," she said.

"Are you all right?" Brian asked as Kyle pulled him away from the girls.

Eppie smiled her thanks. "I'm fine," she said.

"Good." Brian gave her a long look. "See you around, Paulie," he said, waving at her.

"I think he likes you!" Maggie whispered when they were out of earshot. Eppie couldn't help but watch Brian as he walked away.

## ~Chapter Eight~

Eppie felt great on Monday as she hit campus in her new clothes and well-conditioned shiny hair. She noticed several boys look her way and elbow each other, and she ducked her head and tried to keep from smiling. Her smile was cut short by Lexel's sing-song voice.

"Hey, looky here. Skater Boy is a girl!"

Eppie kept her head low and tried to swish past Lexel, but those long red nails caught the flowing hem of her shirt. Eppie stopped and looked up; today's Lexel lip gloss was purple.

"Hey, what's your hurry, Skater Girl? Can't you sit a minute and take a compliment?"

"What is it?" Eppie said in a quiet voice.

Lexel looked Eppie up and down in a dramatic way and nodded so her friends gathered around.

"I have to give you serious props, you took my advice, and you look good. I admire that. What's your name?"

"Pauline."

"Yeah, right. You're in my Language Arts class, right?"

"Yes."

"Well, Pauline . . . you've got a free pass from me today, because you respected what I was saying to you. I tell you you look like a boy, and you come back looking like a girl. Good. Now run along, Little Pauline. You don't wanna hang out here with us, those boys are checking you out!"

Eppie didn't look up to see if boys were really checking her out but said quickly "thanks" and rushed past the group. Lexel's gang laughed as she left. Eppie breathed a sigh of relief. A Lexel 'free pass' was a good way to start the day.

Soon Maggie arrived and she squealed when she saw Eppie. "OMG, you look so good!"

"Thanks. Lexel even thought so."

"What? Lexel was impressed? Damn, I'm good!"

"Oh, so you get all the credit?"

"Hey, I'm the one who saw the diamond in the rough."

"I guess. Thanks, by the way, for all the cool shirts."

"Seriously! They were in the cancer bag, going to charity. No big deal, really."

Two boys from their PE period walked by and gave them both approving glances. Eppie smiled. School was miles better today than usual! But she couldn't help but think about Brian. These boys seemed so young. She wanted to ask Maggie more about him, but didn't know how to go about it without seeming obvious.

"So how's it going with Eric?" Eppie asked.

"Nothing's going! Boys are so lame. It's like, we hung out at Katelyn's 4th of July party, totally hit it off, he texted me until September, and as soon as we get back to school, he ignores me. Whatevs!"

"I know it, believe me. I think older boys are the way to go."

"Older, like as in high school?"

"Well, sure."

"Like as in . . . Brian?"

Eppie looked up and Maggie was grinning. *Busted.* Eppie blushed. "Yeah, like as in Brian."

Maggie's smile ebbed from her face. "Paulie, he has a girlfriend."

Eppie's senses reeled momentarily as her dreams of getting to know Brian better flushed away. "I just think he's cute."

"I can tell you like him, Paulie. What's worse, I can tell he likes you too."

"Why is that a problem?"

"His girlfriend is some big hotshot at some private school, with money, all that. You know, rich bi-otch. It's hard to compete with that."

Eppie thought a moment. So Brian was taken. She should have known. He was too cute to be free. And she was just some dumb eighth grader, how was she supposed to compete with the rich biotch? Ironically if it wasn't for buying Legend, Eppie would be in great shape financially. Maybe then she could compete. She sighed.

"I don't know what I'm thinking anyway, really, Maggie. Yes, he's super hot and toasty, and I need a drool bucket when I see him . . . but I'm too busy to have a boyfriend. And I have to focus on getting my horse here! Now I have a riding job too, so I'm working even more! And he's too old for me."

"So you don't want to know that my brother is having a pool party next Saturday night and I'm allowed to invite one friend and you're it, and Brian will be there?"

"With his girlfriend?"

"I doubt it, no one's ever met her. She doesn't hang out in Lomita."

"Wait, I thought you said the pool heater wasn't coming on again til next year?"

"Dad's making an exception! He turned it on last night."

Eppie smiled again, her grin wide. "I suppose . . . since Saturday IS my day off . . . ". Eppie started clapping and jumping up and down. "Yes! I totally want to come!"

"Please tell me you have a super hot bikini to wear."

Eppie's expression sank comically, giving the answer. Maggie sighed too.

"No worries, we'll raid my closet, yet again."

Eppie air clapped as the two of them laughed.

Cesar perked up as they aligned with the jump, and they flew over it, his body high over the rails, upon landing continuing into a canter. Eppie marveled at how well he responded to her lightest touch; he was an expensive horse, $75,000 before he had even started training, Cashmere had said, but it was as if he had been waiting for Pauline: Someone to guide him, who was confident, who could challenge him. They flew around the course and he was perfect. She patted him high up on the neck to congratulate him and slowed him to a trot. After posting around the ring a couple of times, she brought him down to a walk and gave him his head by loosening the reins. She could tell he was happy. Soon she dismounted and led him out of the ring.

“That’s really something,” a tall lady with a fancy bouffant hairdo said. She wore English riding pants and boots, but had a crisp button down shirt that said ‘someone else handles my horse.’

“Thanks,” Eppie said as the lady shut the gate for her so she didn’t have to turn Cesar around. “He’s a great horse, really eager to please. I’m enjoying my time on him.”

“Oh, I know he’s great,” said the lady. “I’m Beth Krause.”

“Hi,” Eppie said, unsure if that was supposed to mean something.

“Cashmere is my daughter.”

“Oh!” Eppie blushed. This was the woman paying her to ride Cesar! “Sorry, we’re mostly first name around here, I didn’t know Cashmere’s last name. I’m Pauline. Sorry.”

“Don’t apologize, Pauline. I came here to see if Cashmere was just wasting my money by hiring a barn rider, but you ride more like a trainer. How old are you?”

“Thirteen.”

“Where do you go to school?”

“Narbonne Middle School.”

“So you’ll go to Western High next year?” Mrs. Krause asked.

“Yes,” Eppie said, ready for the grilling to stop.

Mrs. Krause wrinkled her turned-up nose, similar to Cashmere’s, in a distasteful way. “I see,” she said, her cool brown eyes searching for an answer to an unfathomable question as she looked at Eppie.

“Where’d you learn to ride like that?”

Eppie wasn’t ready for her story to become barn gossip. “In Colorado, at Wills Warlander Farms,” she said.

Mrs. Krause paused, as if she was going to ask more questions, but she whipped a crisp hundred out of nowhere. “Well, here you are. Cashmere said you prefer cash, which I thought was a bit shady, but if you’re only thirteen it’s probably easier than checks, I’d imagine.” She handed the money to Eppie. “This is payment for this week. Next week, I’ll give you the same.”

Eppie stared, and opened and closed her mouth. “A hundred . . . a week?” she said quietly.

Mrs. Krause stared again with her eagle eyes. "Her other trainers make twice that for riding him half the time and the horse doesn't perform nearly as well for them. It's money well spent, believe me."

Eppie shoved the hundred into her front jeans pocket. "Thanks," she said.

"But . . ." Mrs. Krause looked at Eppic carefully. "I'm going to buy you an outfit to wear while you ride Cesar. You look like a cowgirl in those jeans. What's your size?"

"Twelve juniors, tall." She was glad she knew the answer from her weekend shopping spree.

"Shoes?"

"A nine boot." Her tens were too big.

"And Cashmere's old helmet fits you well, I see, so a medium." Mrs. Krause typed a note into her phone. "Cashmere says you're here every day, correct?"

Eppie nodded.

"Okay then, I'll bring your jods and chaps tomorrow. If you're going to be on Cesar's team, you need to represent, Pauline." Mrs. Krause gave the faintest twinkle of a smile and turned back to her parked Bentley. Eppie stared after her. A hundred a week! She was only making about $300 a month now! At this rate, she'd have Legend in two months and still be able to board him at the stables. Shaky breaths welled up inside of her as she finished putting away Cesar. She couldn't believe her luck. Things were finally turning around for her now. Legend would be coming home soon, she was earning more than twice what she'd gotten before, and she looked good, and she'd see Brian again on Saturday night. Her tears were hot but full of gratitude as Cesar nuzzled her sides, checking for hidden carrots.

# Chapter Nine

Eppie stashed her jodhpurs, button-down riding shirt, a new velvet helmet, and the field boots and half-chaps (those leather leg pieces that made the boots look knee high but were for gripping the saddle) in the backpack she'd gotten at the beginning of the school year and hadn't used yet. How to explain all the expensive new gear to Tracey? The jodhpurs were tan slim-cut pants that made the body more form-fitting on the horse, and the leg chaps were to keep her leg grip steady against the leather saddle. The shirt was maroon and looked great on her, and apparently Cesar really did have a team, and apparently everyone on the Cesar team wore these same maroon shirts with a gold stitched logo of a horse and the word Cesar embroidered across the back. Eppie felt "owned" somehow but decided it was a small price to pay to get the answer to all of her dreams. Owning Legend was becoming a reality!

She'd hurried through her stall cleaning and horse walking today, and talked to Mrs. Krause about the care of the new clothes (she was only required to wear them on Wednesday, when she rode Cesar, and Mrs. Krause requested that she NOT muck other horses' stalls in them, please). Eppie had to get over to the barn offices before 6:00 so she could talk to the owner about renting a stall for Legend. This was the tricky part of her plan, trickier than getting Legend from Colorado. A horse moving company was doing that part for her, it was already paid for as part of the purchase fee, but could she pull off renting a stall without an adult helping her?

Eppie pulled the backpack onto her back, put away the manure rake and locked the gate to Veronica's stall. The dark little mare whinnied at her as she left, and Eppie happily blew her a kiss. "See you tomorrow Ronnie!" she called, running toward the offices, which were really house trailers set up at the front of the well-manicured stables.

Eppie knocked tentatively at the tinny door and a booming bark rose from within.

"Just a minute!" a woman's voice called. "Howser, get back!" she said, and the dog barking stopped, there was a shuffling noise, and then the door creaked open. "Come on in."

Eppie went up the flat wood step and entered the "office," which had hardwood floors and nice furniture, and was surprisingly comfortable, and was more like a home than an office. The woman who opened the door, Marta Greeves, motioned for her to sit. Eppie knew who she was and had seen her from a distance but had never spoken with her before. Eppie could hear a large dog sniffing around in a closed off room behind her. She was glad she wasn't too dirty today as she sat on the floral couch, dropping her backpack full of new riding clothes to the floor. Marta sat in a leather chair across from her. A tabby cat leapt from the back of the couch into Eppie's lap, startling her.

"I know you, seen you around. Pauline, is it?" Marta said.

"Yes."

"You're a stall mucker, right? For Szechwan, Thunder, Mr. Bill, and Veronica. And I saw you on Cesar. Did you join Team Cesar?"

"Yes."

"Probably the best move they've made in a while," Marta muttered under her breath. "What can I do you for?"

Eppie petted the cat in her lap and it purred. "I've been saving up for a horse," Eppie said nervously. "I'll need to rent a stall and wondered if you had one opening up."

Marta looked at Eppie and then pointed to the cat. "That's Miss Tibbles. She likes her throat rubbed."

Eppie rubbed the cat's throat and it shot its nose to the ceiling in appreciation, purring louder.

"There's a contract, it's $500 a month, includes feed twice a day and the stall, not mucking, as I'm sure you know. You know the drill, leave the poop in the big plastic bins and our guys will take it away every day at 7 pm. Rent's due by the 5th. Every late day is ten bucks extra." Marta leaned over and fished around in a blue accordion file on the dark teak table. She wrangled out a form and handed it to Eppie. "Here's the contract. Just get your mom and dad to sign it, and have them write out a check to Academy Stables dated the first of next month. That'll be your last month's deposit. Then there's the first month, you pay that at the same time with a separate check."

Eppie's heart sank. "So . . . it's $1000 up front?"

"That's right."

Eppie panicked. She had to be careful or it could tip off Marta, who was already checking her out in a beady way. "I'm not getting my horse right away, I'm just finding out everything, you know, how much it all costs," she stammered.

Marta's shoulders sloped down slightly. "Well, how soon do you think it will be?"

Eppie calculated. "Three months."

"Then keep that form. Three months goes pretty fast."

Marta stood up and so did Eppie. Marta held the door open, a sure invitation for Eppie to leave. "Get back to me when you know for sure, since you work here I can hold one for you if I know you're coming in the following month."

Eppie nodded and mumbled "thanks!" while trying to seem cheery as she grabbed her backpack and exited.

Rich drove into the driveway and locked up his brakes when he saw Eppie coming out of the trailer. She was usually waiting for him at the other end of the long stable driveway. He rolled down his window. *Go back inside*, Eppie willed Marta, but she stood out on the front stoop, and for a horrifying moment it seemed as if Marta was going to go over and talk to Rich herself. Marta stooped a bit and waved to Rich, and Rich smiled, looking puzzled, and waved back. Eppie raced to the car, yelling "goodbye!" to Marta. Marta started to follow Eppie toward the car but Eppie was fast. She jumped into the back seat and told Rich, "Let's go!"

"That lady is coming over here," Rich said, and he leaned toward the open passenger window where Jim sat.

"Oh, I think she's just saying goodbye," Eppie said, her head spinning. *Go go go!*

Marta did amble over to the minivan. She leaned her arm on the open window of the car door and peered her gray head inside.

"This girl of yours here, she's a good one," she said to Rich.

Rich looked flustered but smiled. "Thanks. We're fond of her too."

"She's a good worker, a conscientious rider, and we'll be glad to have you folks on board in a couple of months," Marta said. She reached her hand inside the car, right across Jim's chest, and shook Rich's hand. Rich smiled wider, as he did when he was nervous. "Thank you," he said. "Appreciate it."

Marta turned and slowly walked back to her trailer. Rich looked at Eppie in the back seat through the rear view mirror. "Who was that?"

"Marta, the manager." Eppie said as she slapped Lonny, who was cracking up in an exaggerated way in the seat next to her. He punched her back in the leg.

"Ow. Rich, Lonny hit me!" It was lame, but it changed the subject. Or Eppie hoped it did. Wrong.

"What did that woman mean, we'll be glad to have you on board in a couple of months?"

Eppie sighed as Lonny tried to grab her fingers to bend them backward. "Oh, the stables are having a 'bring your family to work day'. You know, for fun. Just for you all to see what we do here," Eppie lied, hating the sound of it. Even lamer! But Rich laughed as he turned the van around.

"Uh, Pauline . . . we know what you do here, and if it's okay with you, we'd rather not come see the horse poo personally."

Lonny and even Jim laughed at that one, and Eppie blew out her breath in relief. *Close one.* Two steps forward, three steps back. A thousand bucks up front! That would add too much time, she'd have to wait even longer to get Legend! And how was she going to get an adult signature on that form so she could finally bring Legend home?

# Chapter Ten

Saturday didn't come fast enough. That day of the week was usually hard for Eppie; all of the horse owners took care of their own horses on Saturdays and Sundays so Eppie didn't go to the stables on weekends. But today horses weren't even on her mind. She woke up early and started counting down the minutes until the high school party at Maggie's house.

After breakfast she was so excited that she couldn't even focus on reading the horse training books that she usually studied, or on her next week's oral report (as if!), or any of the other stuff she usually did when she wasn't at the barn. Instead she laid out the clothes she would wear that night on the bed. Maggie gave her a skimpy hot pink bikini that she'd barely worn (her mother didn't like the color with her red hair). It was a bit snug but Maggie said that made it look even better. Maggie had even come up with a darling miniskirt that she'd gotten for her birthday last year that was too big (*my Aunt Lorraine thinks I'm fat*). It was even a little bit loose but Tracey stitched a quick seam in the back, and now it fit her fine. Her bright yellow top and headband, and she was ready to go. But it was only nine in the morning.

By eleven she was pacing in the kitchen and Tracey, who was working on the computer, rolled her eyes.

"Pauline! Why don't you go help Rich and the boys in the back yard if you have so much energy?"

"Aren't they fixing that cement wall out there?"

"Yes, and they can use an extra pair of hands. It's hard work."

Eppie held up her hands, showing Tracey her perfect manicure that she'd stayed up late last night polishing. Tracey sighed.

"Okay, well, what time is the party?"

"Seven."

Tracey checked the clock. "Oh."

Luckily her cell phone rang in her room and Eppie raced for it. Maggie. "Hello?"

"Paulie?"

"Hi! OMG, I can't wait for tonight!"

"Me too. Mom says you can come early and that you can stay over tonight. Wanna come now?"

"What? Really? Sure, let me ask!"

Tracey looked up expectantly.

"I'm invited to come early to Maggie's and to spend the night. Please, can I go now?"

Tracey smiled in a relieved way. "Sure! Let me just finish this up. You go pack and I'll give you a ride."

"I'm on my way!" Eppie squealed, noticing that the more she dressed like a girl the more she sounded like one.

"Yay! I'll tell mom. Hurry! See you soon! Bring your clothes and bathing suit, and don't forget your hair stuff, makeup . . . all of it."

"K, I know . . . bye!" Eppie hung up the phone and danced around, going into the kitchen to grab some food first, just as the boys came inside. Jim looked at her and then looked at Tracey. "What's with her?"

"She's excited because she's going to Maggie's party."

Jim's eyes narrowed. "Maggie's party? You mean Kyle's party, right? It's a high school party."

"She kno-o-ows," Eppie said. "But I get to come too, as Maggie's sleepover guest."

Jim made a breathy noise. "You know what Tracey, those guys . . . I don't know if Pauline should be hanging out with those guys."

"Jim, shut up! I'm not hanging out with any guys, I'm hanging out with Maggie!"

Jim gave Tracey an expectant look.

"Jimmy, it's nice that you want to watch out for Pauline, but I've talked to Maggie's mom. The girls are not really 'going to the party'. They're going to occupy themselves upstairs while the party is happening."

Eppie didn't know that she wasn't technically invited to the party but she huffed. "See?"

"Whatever," Jim said. "It's your life, Pauline."

"Drama King!" Eppie said. Tracey stood to intervene.

"Pauline, please go get ready, okay?"

Eppie didn't need to be told twice. She left the kitchen and zipped down the hall to her room to pack up for the big night.

The Petersons really knew how to throw a party. The sliding screen doors were removed so that the house flowed into the backyard pool area, and lights were being strung in an "X" shape high above the pool to make a lighted "tent" overhead that at night would reflect across the steaming aqua water. Tall outdoor heaters were rented and lined the pool area. A bar, serving mocktails and soda, was being set up, and Maggie told Eppie that a bartender would come later to make the drinks. Large tables with luau tablecloths were ready for the platters of food in the kitchen, and two helpers were hired for the occasion as well.

"Wow!" Eppie said, looking around at the display. "This is awesome!" She remembered that once Maggie had told her that her family would be considered poor in Palos Verdes, but in Lomita they were well-off.

"Yeah, everyone's talking about it. I'm so glad we're able to go, Kyle's having a stinkin' fit over us being there."

"Because we're girls?"

"Because we're eighth graders."

"We're not that much younger than them," Eppie said as the two ran upstairs to spend the rest of the day getting ready for the big event.

Seven o'clock came quicker than it would have if Eppie were home waiting, and the girls were decked out. Eppie thought she looked better than she ever had in her life. Maybe not her whole life but at least better than she'd looked since Grandma had her stroke and she got sent to the foster home system. She admired herself in Maggie's full length mirror.

"Yes, you're fabulous," Maggie said.

"So are you!"

Maggie was stunning in her sky blue checkered Ralph Lauren bikini that poked out from underneath her soft teal blouse, making her eyes look icy blue. Of course they had no intention of swimming; that would mess up their hair. The bikinis were for show only.

A loud squeal erupted from the pool area and Eppie ran to the window to see. A girl, a high schooler, had been thrown in already. She was squalling like a baby about her cell phone. Eppie could see a big cluster of femme fatales standing by, huddled together to protect themselves from the same fate.

"Girls?"

"Naturally, there are girls. What did you think?"

Eppie shrugged. Somehow when Maggie had told her Brian's girlfriend wasn't coming, she got it in her head the party was for boys, but then she realized that high school boys probably didn't have boy-only parties anymore. Of course there was competition. Oh well. They would still look hot at the party, and that was worth a lot.

Eppie and Maggie made their planned entrance, walking down the stairs with a strut in time with the dance floor music that played throughout the house's built-in speakers, but there was only one person there to witness it. It was the bartender, looking lost.

"The bar's out back, right?" he asked.

"Yeah," said Maggie, looking deflated. "C'mon, let's go see what's happening,"

Eppie followed her out the door.

They stood apart from the other guests at first until the party got too crowded and people started to come near them. A couple of high school girls came over and talked to them, telling them they looked cute and asking whose little sisters they were. Eppie was sipping her mock apple martini when Brian came outside. He was with a group of other guys, and two girls mixed in, but he definitely didn't have any rich biotch hanging on his arm. He was flying solo. Eppie started smacking Maggie's hand excitedly.

"I see him," Maggie said with a giggle.

It only took about ten minutes of helloing for Brian to find Eppie and Maggie.

"Hello, ladies," he said, coming up to them. He smiled at Eppie. "How are you doing?"

"Good," Eppie said. Silence. Maggie nudged Eppie. "Um . . . how are you?"

"Great. Better now. What are you drinking?" Brian motioned toward her electric green drink.

"Mock apple martini."

"Is it good?"

Eppie paused. "Not really. The lemon one is better, tastes like lemonade."

Brian laughed. "Wanna go with me to get one?"

Eppie handed Maggie her drink. "Sure!" Brian led Eppie by the hand to the bar area.

He ordered two lemon fizz martinis, and handed the fake cocktail to Eppie. She sipped it. A nearby heater was warming the area but Eppie thought the warm feelings she was having had nothing to do with the propane device.

"Thanks, Brian." She meant for him paying attention to her as much as for the mocktail.

"Hey, no problem, Paulie. You know . . . the drinks are free." He laughed. She laughed too.

"Brian!" A group of newcomer boys swept Brian away from her, and his look was apologetic as he got led to the very edge of the pool (but not in it). Eppie shrugged and returned to Maggie.

"I think I'm in love," she said, watching Brian struggle to stay dry.

Things began to change by ten. It was becoming obvious that there was real alcohol mixed in with the fake cocktails, and that some kids were drunk. They had apparently brought their own stash and were adding it in to the virgin drinks being served. Some of Jim's crowd were among the drunk boys, and they were stumbling around and laughing, and trying to push girls into the pool. Things were getting out of hand.

"Should you get your parents?" Eppie asked as a boy crashed into the heater pole, which luckily didn't topple.

"Yeah . . . those jerks! They're gonna ruin the whole party."

Maggie went inside to find her parents, who were hiding upstairs in their master suite. Eppie felt very alone with the rowdy boys as two girls went into the pool, and a chair got knocked over.

"Hey!" yelled the bartender, as one of the boys took an unopened bottle of soda and shook it up hard. He unscrewed the cap and unleashed the brown fizz all over the crowd, but most of them were wet already and they jumped back in the pool. Eppie took the brunt of it, all over her cute yellow outfit. She was drenched. She gasped, horrified.

"Sorry!" the drunk guy called. Eppie could feel her mascara streaming down her wet face and she turned to run inside. She was furious and hoped Brian hadn't seen.

Once inside she went down the back hallway, away from the rest of the party, and ducked into a small bathroom by the garage door. Her make-up was ruined, her hair wet and sticky. Her clothes stained. Frustrated at being cold and wet and sticky and stained, tears welled in Eppie's eyes. She grabbed a handful of tissues and began dabbing her eyes, and then took a towel from the rack and pushed it against her hair to dry off. She heard someone coming down the hallway and thought it was Maggie.

"That sucks," came a deep voice. "That guy shouldn't have done that."

Eppie looked up and was surprised to see Jim standing in the doorway. Not standing, leaning, as if the doorway was holding him up. She hadn't seen him all night and didn't even know he was at Kyle's party.

"Jim?" she said, looking into his face. He was drunk. Really drunk.

"That guy, he sucks," Jim repeated. He took his hand and tried to wipe some of the soda off Eppie's arm, and then looked at his wet hand as if not knowing what to do with it. It made Eppie uncomfortable to see him like this. She'd overheard Tracey telling Rich once that they had to lock the alcohol cabinet, and now she understood why. Jim was a drinker. Eppie tossed him a hand towel. Jim wiped his hand and then came into the bathroom with her.

"Need . . . help?" he asked, and Eppie smirked. He was the one who needed help!

"I'm fine." She continued to mop herself up, annoyed. "Why don't you go get some air, Jim?"

"I . . . need to help you . . . Pauline. . ." Jim leaned over toward her, and for one horrible instant Eppie thought that he was going to be sick in the sink. She was shocked when he grabbed onto her and wrestled her against the wall and tried to kiss her, his mouth all over hers. Repulsion wrenched through her as she pulled away from his awkward grasp.

"Oh my God! Get off me! Get out of here!" she shrieked.

"I'm sorry! I just . . . I just . . ." Jim started, and he lunged at her again, his hands groping for her. Eppie was able to get away because he was so wobbly, but she burst into tears, unable to cope with the fact that someone she thought of as her brother had just kissed and grabbed her like that. She heard someone come down the hallway.

"Go," she hissed to Jim. But Brian was right there, coming in.

"What the hell is he doing to you?" Brian wanted to know. He saw Jim retreat into the corner. Eppie was crying too hard to tell him, but her missing shirt buttons that were now on the floor gave Brian the answer he needed. He punched Jim in the nose.

# CHAPTER ELEVEN

It wasn't a brawl, because Jim was too drunk to defend himself, and Brian figured that out after the second punch. Jim was now sprawled out in the hallway with a bloody nose and people were starting to gather in the hallway to see what was happening. Eppie grabbed Brian's arm.

"Brian . . . please . . . swear, don't say anything," Eppie said fiercely, her fingers digging into his arm. "Brian. Please. Just don't. I mean it, I'll explain later."

"All right, let's break it up," Mr. Peterson said as he pushed through the crowd, Maggie behind him. He looked at Brian for an explanation.

"This guy was drunk and started swinging at me," Brian said, pointing to Jim.

"Okay, everyone out of here. Party's over," Mr. Peterson said. As everyone groaned and began to clear out, Mr. Peterson pulled Jim up to his feet. Eppie gave him some tissue for his nose.

"Can someone get this guy home safely?" Two friends volunteered and grabbed Jim and helped him down the hall. Eppie stood there, looking a mess. Brian's face searched hers, trying to figure out what was going on.

"I was helping her get cleaned up," Brian told Mr. Peterson.

"Oh my God, Paulie, what happened to you?" Maggie asked, pushing through the lingering guests toward Eppie.

"Wrong place, wrong time, exploding soda," Eppie said, glad the soda and tears were mixed together so no one could tell she was crying. She was shaking, not believing what had just happened.

"You, outta here," said Mr. Peterson, pointing to Brian. Brian high-tailed it down the hallway. "This has gotten out of hand. Maggie, get your friend upstairs. This party is over!"

Later Eppie was still damp from her shower but wearing fresh pajamas (Tracey's cute hand-me-downs) and feeling cleaner, but her insides were all twisted up and she was shaking.

"Why are you so freaked out still?" Maggie wanted to know.

"They were fighting right in front of me!" Eppie said, not wanting to tell Maggie about the disgusting thing that had happened with Jim. It was her fault, she knew . . . she'd started dressing cute, showing off her body more, and Jim had reacted in the way any boy would react. But he was not just any boy, he was practically her brother! Eppie felt nauseous just thinking about it. She clutched her stomach. A loud bumping sound on the wall came from the neighboring room and she jumped.

"That's just Kyle, Dad let a few of his friends stay if they are quiet in his room."

"Oh." Eppie climbed into bed next to Maggie, careful to lay her towel out flat on the pillow to not stain the pillowcase with wet hair.

"You're okay. It was just a little fight."

"I know." She'd been around a lot of fighting in those dark days after Grandma's stroke, she even spent a week in a half-way house where the girls were way meaner than Lexel. Those girls were mad at the world and they meant business. She shuddered to think what would happen if she ended up back there now. It would mean she'd lose everything: Legend, Maggie, Grandma, Tracey and Rich and Lonny . . . her mind reeled and she shook.

"You're still really upset."

"I'll be all right."

A small knock came at the door.

"Come in!" Maggie called. Brian walked in, alone.

"Hi," he said quietly, looking at the two girls in bed. "I guess this is a bad time. I'll talk to you later."

"I was just going downstairs for a food run," Maggie said, hopping out of bed superfast. Eppie sat up, pulled her legs out of the covers, and stood.

"Hi! I didn't know you were still here." She sat down on the edge of the bed as Maggie left the room.

"Yeah, I started helping with the clean up and they let me stay. I wanted to see if you were okay."

"I'm fine," Eppie lied. Brian gave her an appraising look.

"That guy, he drinks too much."

"I know." Eppie realized that Brian didn't know Jim was her relative. "He lives with me. I mean, he's . . . kind of like my brother. It's complicated."

"Jim Halloway is your brother?"

"Not really. He's my guardian's adopted son. We're not blood related."

A relieved look came over Brian's face. "Oh! I thought—I thought that he was—well, never mind what I thought." Brian visibly relaxed, and Eppie knew what he was thinking. He was thinking Jim had tried to maul her, which was true. No one knew what really happened but Jim and Eppie, and Eppie wasn't about to tell anyone. If she told, she'd be the one moved out of the Dursom's house. They wouldn't separate the two brothers, they'd just get rid of the newbie trouble maker: Eppie. Jim would probably forget it happened. Eppie would take it to her grave.

Brian reached over and took Eppie's hand. "I'm glad you're okay," he said. She stared at his hand holding hers, and couldn't believe it. The boy she liked was holding her hand! A thrill raced through her and she squeezed her fingers around his, glad to have someone there to comfort her. Brian reached over and pushed her wet hair away from her face and kissed her lightly on the lips. Eppie didn't even flinch. She would call this her first real lip kiss, and forget that the other thing ever happened. She felt warm and jittery as Brian's soft mouth touched hers. Eppie kissed him back. She could hear Maggie making obvious noises, clearing her throat, in the hallway, and they broke apart, still holding hands.

"I'm back!" Maggie said, bringing in a big tray of party food leftovers: cheese, crackers, chips, cookies, pineapple and apples, humus and pita bread, and a tote bag full of ice cold sodas.

Brian didn't even try to hide the hand holding.

"I'd better get back next door," he said, motioning toward Kyle's room. "I'm glad everything's all right."

Eppie smiled up at Brian, struck by how good looking he was as his dark hair framed his face, making his green eyes stand out. He held her hand until the last possible moment, then dropped it just as he walked out of arm's length. Maggie stared open-mouthed as she put the food tray on the bedspread. When the door closed he rushed over to Eppie.

"OMG!" she whispered in a high voice. "He held your hand!"

"He kissed me!" Eppie mouthed, and the look on Maggie's face was priceless. Her mouth formed a perfect 'o'. Eppie giggled, and Maggie began laughing. Suddenly they were in fits of laughter but trying not to be heard. They were spasming under the covers and exaggeratedly rolling around the bed, knocking the food off the plates and laughing even harder, all in a whisper.

# CHAPTER TWELVE

Eppie didn't want to leave the Peterson's house the next day. She didn't want to face Jim. The night before had been the best and worst party she'd ever been to, and her stomach was still a jumble of nerves when she thought of it. But Tracey was there honking in the driveway at eleven.

"How was the party?" she asked as Eppie got in the car. Tracey looked like she'd been up all night herself.

"Good. We were mostly upstairs pigging out."

"I heard things got a little crazy," Tracey said as she backed out of the driveway and headed toward San Pedro.

"I guess that some older kids were getting wild and Mr. Peterson shut the party down."

"Did you see Jim there?"

Eppie hesitated. Finally, "No. Was he there?"

"Yes." Tracey looked over at Eppie as if trying to discern what to tell her. "Two of his friends brought him home last night."

Eppie didn't like where the conversation was going but tried to stay aloof. "That's nice that you didn't have to come pick him up," she said. "Saves a trip."

"No, I mean . . . look, you may as well know. Jim's been drinking lately. Last night was the fifth time he's come home drunk. That's why he can't get his driver's license permit. Rich won't let him until he shapes up."

"I thought you couldn't afford driver's ed classes?" Eppie said, this new information sinking in. She'd been feeling guilty about spending 8K on a horse while Tracey and Rich couldn't afford driving classes for Jim.

"They're expensive, but that's not the real reason."

"Oh."

"So you really didn't know any of this was happening?" Tracey asked. Eppie hesitated only a nanosecond.

"I haven't known at all that Jim was drinking," she said. Mostly true: she'd just found out last night. The hard way.

"Well, let's go see your grandma, and then we'll get some stuff done today. It's been a long weekend."

*Yes, it has*, Eppie thought as they drove toward Grandma's assisted living home.

Eppie's mind pingponged back and forth between Brian and Jim, but she didn't even know how to reach Brian and she didn't see much of Jim at all for the rest of the week. He was staying with older sober living friends of Tracey and Rich's for the time being until Jim's fate was decided. Family dinners were a quiet withdrawn affair, with polite "please pass the salt" and "this tastes great." Only Lonny was his usual boisterous self, and he took the edge off the rest of the family's woes.

Eppie was driving herself crazy by thinking too much so she turned all of her focus on the stables and was ready for action on Wednesday. She took the transit bus directly from school and changed into her Team Cesar gear in one of the empty enclosed stalls. She turned Cesar out in the big corral and he rolled in the warm sand, itching his back, his hooves up in the air. He stood up and shook off as Eppie got into the ring with him. She imagined herself with Legend, and how she'd be letting him run soon in this very spot. She could imagine him rolling the same way, excited to be in the turn out with her every day. Eppie clucked and got Cesar to trot around the ring, then canter. He bucked a few times, throwing his head, and got silly and started running at a full gallop. It seemed to Eppie that Cesar was enjoying himself more now that she was riding him.

"Whoa, Cesar," Eppie said. "Come here." She held out her hand and Cesar trotted to her, his hooves up high, looking like the show horse he was. Eppie slipped the leather halter over his nose and patted him, and led him to the tie outs to groom him and get him ready to ride. In her new Team Cesar riding clothes and with Cesar behaving like the perfect horse, Eppie felt like she fit right in.

Tracey found Eppie's carefully folded riding clothes in the backpack that night and Eppie explained that she was now riding for Team Cesar. She left out the part about being paid.

"It's not costing you money, is it?" Tracey asked. "I don't want them taking advantage of you."

"Absolutely not," Eppie confirmed. "They just need extra riders, and they like how I handle him."

Tracey looked at the jodhpurs and fancy jersey folded in the backpack. "These look expensive."

"They are. But I didn't pay for them, honest. Mrs. Krause did. She said she 'wants me to represent'. Her real words."

Tracey looked Eppie up and down as they took the riding clothes and put them in the laundry basket (Tracey washed Eppie's laundry on Thursdays).

"So here you are, finally riding again . . . why didn't you tell me?" Tracey asked.

Eppie paused. Why didn't she tell her? Was it because she had so many secrets now that she was afraid to say anything at all, for fear of slipping up? Or was it because she was afraid of leaving the Dursom's and she didn't want to get any closer to Tracey than she had to? All of the above? Eppie shrugged.

"Pauline," Tracey said. "Listen. We took Lonny and Jim in after their dad went to jail, you know. He was trying to raise the boys alone as best he could but he got involved with drugs and robbery." Eppie was surprised. It wasn't what she expected Tracey to say. "Rich and I always wanted kids but it never happened, so we thought, let's start a foster family, and that way we can make a difference in some kids' lives. So we agreed to take the brothers so they could stay together. That was about four years ago."

Eppie nodded.

"But Rich was getting the most from it. I felt a little left out; I don't surf, play baseball, skateboard . . . Rich was having this second childhood with the boys and I was sort of like a scullery maid, cleaning up after them all the time but not really having any of the fun. Since Lonny and Jim's dad is in prison, he was willing to sign away his parental rights, and we adopted them, and we love them like our own."

For some reason Eppie felt tears welling up behind her eyes. She braced herself.

"I wanted the same thing Rich got from the boys. And then we heard what happened to Grandpa Bud's wife, your grandma, Emmaline, and that you were living with her when she had the stroke and you were in the foster system too, and we finally tracked you down. We didn't even know you lived here before that, and now here you are, a lost part of our family, for over a year now, and I have loved every second of having you here, Pauline. It's been so nice to have another girl to share things with. I love your work ethic, how you stay focused . . . you're a great kid."

Eppie could feel the word "but" enter the room before she heard it.

"But I feel like you're holding back. I know I can't replace your mom, or even your grandma, but I'm here for you. I want to be a part of your life. But you seem so . . . shut down. Secretive. I can never say for sure what's going on with you."

Eppie nodded again. Words jumbled up in her throat but didn't come out right. She wanted to say so much, but the truest thing rose to the top.

"I've been scared," she said finally. "Afraid that this wasn't my last home. I've been to two foster homes . . . and they weren't that great . . . and . . ." Eppie stopped, thinking of the halfway house, the other place she stayed just three months and shared a room with five other girls with a family in Bell, and the one in Pasadena where the foster mom took gas money from Eppie's babysitting jobs for driving her to San Pedro to visit Grandma. Eppie left there owing her money, according to that woman.

"And you're afraid that we're going to let you go back to the system? Pauline, that won't happen! You're part of our family, and you're here to stay. I plan on dancing at your wedding and being at your child's first birthday party, all of it!"

"You do?"

"Of course!"

"I . . . didn't know," Eppie said. She reached up and gave Tracey a hug. Tracey held her tightly back, and Eppie could feel her holding in tears. Eppie felt better, but the truth about what happened with Jim haunted her. What would Tracey do if she found out?

## CHAPTER THIRTEEN

Eppie sat on her bed alone in her room the following Sunday looking at Legend's picture. She wanted to ask Janine for a new photo of Legend but she knew it was really the daughter she'd be emailing, and that lady was sort of crabby. She wanted to breathe Legend in, to pat his neck, give him a horse hug. Szechwan, one of the horses she mucked every day, was a hugger, more even than Mr. Bill. Whenever Eppie went into his stall he would come over and put his head over her shoulder and pull her into his chest. She loved that, horse hugs. They were the best. Almost as good as Brian kisses.

Being distracted about Brian again (it was the weekend, no horses) made her feel squirrely inside. She slid the horse photos into the envelope and flopped backwards on her comforter. Tracey was with Lonny and Rich was at work, unusual on the weekend. Jim had been staying with the sober family friends for the week so he wasn't even around. She was home alone and bored. Even Maggie was gone to some family function until late tonight. Eppie had nothing to do and no one to talk to. Sighing, she reached for her school bag to start her homework when the door to her room opened.

It was Jim.

She shrieked and grabbed a pillow to cover herself, even though she was wearing clothes.

"What are you doing in here?" she asked. "You're not allowed in here!" She was home alone with Jim! They hadn't even talked since the party.

"Don't worry. I haven't been drinking," Jim said. "Can I come in?"

"No," Eppie said quickly.

"I'll just stand here then. I won't come in, promise."

"Go away!"

"We need to talk, Pauline."

Eppie's heart raced. That was the last thing she wanted to do, but Jim launched.

"It's been eating me up . . . what I did. I'm sorry. I was drunk and acting stupid."

Eppie listened but didn't know what to say. She didn't want to say "that's okay," because it wasn't okay. It would never be okay.

"You shouldn't drink so much."

"I shouldn't drink at all. It makes me have weird thoughts. Rich is taking me to a place . . . a rehab place . . . tomorrow."

"You're leaving?"

"Just for thirty days. But I wanted to set things straight with you, Pauline. I'm so sorry about what I did. I won't do it again. I haven't slept . . . I have barely eaten . . . I'm just sick about it."

"Who knows about it?" Eppie asked, her voice sharp even to her own ears.

"Just us."

"Then let's keep it that way, because I don't even like thinking about it."

Jim paused and shifted from foot to foot in the doorway. "Okay."

"You swear you won't tell, Jim? Because I won't. Not ever, not to anyone. I didn't tell Maggie or Kyle or anyone."

"What about Brian? He must have guessed something was up, he punched me pretty hard."

"He only thought he knew what happened, but when I told him later that you were my brother, he assumed he was wrong about the whole thing."

"Oh. Wait, you know Brian like that? I mean, well enough to talk to him?"

"Yeah. Sort of."

"Oh."

"If anyone finds out, Jim . . . we could lose our place here. You could be separated from Lonny and I could lose everything; my grandma, my horse . . ."

"Horse?"

"Horse job," Eppie added quickly. "Riding. Everything that matters."

Jim looked at Eppie in a strange way. “Well, I won’t tell anyone either. So it’s a deal.” He held out his hand but didn’t come in the room. “Most people shake on a deal.”

Eppie felt repulsed at even touching him. “Let’s not push it, okay? But yes, deal.”

Jim looked offended but didn’t say anything more. He turned and went out the door, leaving Eppie wishing Tracey would hurry up and get home soon.

At school, word got out that Maggie and Eppie “hung out with high school kids” and were at that wild party everyone had heard about, and so suddenly their social status raised a few notches to the point where Lexel and her gang even gave them the time of day. Maggie and LiLi were starting to chat in the halls since they’d worked on a science project together in class. Lexel didn’t exactly befriend Eppie, but she wasn’t stopping her and harassing her either: a big improvement in Eppie’s days.

Cesar was the best part of Eppie’s week. Wednesdays didn’t last long enough. Eppie loved changing out of her shit-mucking jeans for the day, into the Team Cesar garb. People treated her with respect now, she noticed, as she rode Cesar around the ring. They stopped to watch her. Sometimes she’d see Mrs. Krause with other people, talking about her, pointing. Cashmere’s trainer Andrea would have nothing to do with her, though, she found out later.

“Hi,” Eppie said to Andrea one day after she’d cooled Cesar down.

“You shouldn’t work him before you ride him,” Andrea said. “In the turn out. You shouldn’t run him. He works hard enough.”

“He just likes to get his sillies out,” Eppie said casually, not really meaning to start an argument. That’s how she saw it . . . you turn the horse out to stretch, and to roll, and to have some fun before working in the ring. Her mom had always done it that way.

“You’re just a kid. What can you possibly know?” Andrea said, looking affronted. Eppie’s eyebrows shot up.

“Oh . . . no, I don’t mean anything by it. That’s just how I do it.”

"You're practically an infant! How can you have a 'way of doing it' at all? You come in to clean out stalls for other people's horses, and now suddenly you're the barn's top trainer?"

Eppie got it right then. Somehow she had stepped on Andrea's toes by taking the job to ride Cesar from Mrs. Krause.

"I'm just riding Cesar so Cashmere can take a day off, Andrea. I'm not trying to take over. In fact, I have a horse coming in a couple months that's green and I'll be busy working with him."

The lightning that flashed behind Andrea's eyes was a warning signal that Eppie may have said too much.

"You have a horse coming here? What kind, a Thoroughbred? Warmblood?" She named the obvious hunter/jumper choices.

"No." *Here we go*, thought Eppie. "A Warlander."

"There's no such breed of horse," Andrea retorted.

"It's a newer sport horse breed. Half Friesian, half Andalusian. For dressage." Now Eppie knew she'd said too much. To let on that she knew dressage, the complicated technique of using the horse's beautiful movement to complete different challenges in the ring, would spark a discussion that could spill way too much information. Eppie bit her lip.

"You know dressage? What level are you?"

Eppie sighed. She knew any answers she'd give now would only lead to more questions.

"I was working on my first level tests, okay?" She nearly said 'before my grandma had a stroke,' but she stopped herself.

Andrea appraised Eppie, but her look was less hard. "The trainers who work here, myself included, pay hundreds per year to the city to have a license to train horses, Pauline. You can't just come in here and start training other people's horses for money without going through the proper channels. You'll make too many enemies, and that's something you can't afford to do right now."

Eppie could tell there was a threat in there somewhere. "I'm not training. I'm riding. End of story," she said, trying to be firm but not too rude. Andrea knew what she was doing and Eppie respected that.

"I've been working with Cesar and Cashmere for a long time now, Pauline. Just don't undo what I've spent so much effort on." Andrea started to walk away.

Eppie knew she should let it go now but she couldn't help herself. "Is Cesar better or worse in his lessons since I started riding him?"

Andrea stopped and turned back. "Truthfully, he's wonderful. When I ride him. Better than ever. And he seems happier. But when Cashmere rides him, he's confused and doesn't understand her cues anymore. So while you and Cesar could probably go far together . . . " Andrea's visor shaded her eyes as she looked hard at Eppie, "Cesar is not your horse. So the way I see it, you're not doing Cashmere any favors."

Andrea huffed off, and Eppie's cheeks burned at the back-handed compliment. So she was still a good rider. Missing two years of lessons hadn't set her riding skills back as far as she feared. Eppie clamped her mouth together to keep from crying. She wanted Legend to come now more than ever so she could be free to train her own horse however she wanted, without all these opinionated people getting in her way.

## Chapter Fourteen

Mrs. Krause was waiting for Eppie the following week when she brought Cesar in his halter to his stall. Cesar was ready for dinner and paced impatiently, and Eppie made him stop, hold still, and then she let him inside.

"You handle him well, Pauline," Mrs. Krause said, handing Eppie her weekly money. Eppie calculated quickly; she had sent in a large payment on Legend and she was down to $700 that she still owed on him. Just a few more weeks and she'd bring him home.

"Thanks," Eppie said, for the compliment and the money.

"I've overheard a few things I wanted to talk to you about," Mrs. Krause said. "I heard that you are bringing a dressage horse here?"

Eppie was stunned. *Wow, that went around fast.* How the heck could Mrs. Krause, who came to the barn once a week that she knew of, find that out?

"Yes," Eppie said cautiously.

"Yes." Mrs. Krause repeated, mimicking Eppie's weak tone of voice. She stared deeply into Eppie's eyes. "Pauline, please be blunt with me. I may be able to help you, but you need to talk to me."

Mrs. Krause seemed to be on to her entire secret, and it made Eppie uncomfortable. Could she somehow use what Eppie told her against her? Could she keep it from happening? Eppie was afraid to open her mouth.

"Look," Mrs. Krause said. "I don't like to fool around. I will tell you what I know. I know that you need to pay for a monthly stall here for your horse. I know you haven't turned in your paperwork yet to reserve a stall. I know that you are buying a Warlander dressage horse and that you need to somehow pay for all of that. From what I've heard, your parents have never been here before and don't seem to be at all interested in your horse hobby, so that makes me think that you could use some help." Mrs. Krause looked at Eppie expectantly.

"That's all true," Eppie said in a small voice, and tears shook inside of her. Could this woman somehow kill all of her plans and hard work in a single afternoon? "But there's more to it than that. A lot more." The tears defied Eppie's wishes and trickled down her cheeks.

"Pauline, are you done here today?"

Eppie nodded.

"Do you have a ride home?"

"I need to call someone in a half hour."

"Call and tell them I'll bring you home. We need to talk."

Mrs. Krause parked overlooking the ocean as Eppie sipped on the caramel Frappuccino Mrs. Krause had bought for her at Starbucks. Eppie had told her everything, and now she felt vulnerable but also somehow relieved as she poked at her frothy drink with the green plastic straw.

"So, you are in a financial bind," Mrs. Krause said. "But I really admire you, Pauline. You've been through a lot and you've worked really hard. And even at your young age, you seem like the kind of kid who could really make it in the horse world. Cashmere isn't, you know. She's got her head in the clouds when it comes to horses."

"Why does she do it then?" Eppie asked.

"I make her." Mrs. Krause said matter-of-factly as she looked over at Eppie. "I thought that being in charge of the well-being of a horse would give her the discipline and courage she needed. It didn't change her much though."

Eppie stared at the bay stretched out below them. The sun was lowering in the sky, bathing the beach cities with a golden glow. She couldn't believe it. Mrs. Krause was *making* Cashmere ride, when all Eppie wanted was to ride her own horse and couldn't? How could life be so unfair?

"I'm a rider, Pauline. I've always been one, and my happiest memories are of my times on horseback. I broke my hip a few years back and have been afraid to ride since then, but I still enjoy it all; being at the stables, being around horses. It is my life." Mrs. Krause sighed.

"I want someone to mentor, and obviously Cashmere isn't interested. You seem like the perfect candidate. I understand you, Pauline. More than you know. And, you need me. For your plans to succeed, you need an adult on board. I know you've struggled to do this on your own . . ." Eppie held back a sob. "But I can have your horse here by the end of the week and we can begin a training program. Everything would be above board, and I would inform your parents . . . your legal guardians . . . about the situation. Are you in?"

Eppie couldn't believe what she was hearing. Was she in? Legend could be hers by next week? But what would Mrs. Krause really want from her? Would Legend still be her horse, to do with what she wanted? Or was she signing a contract to be the newest member of Team Legend, one of many people involved in his training and upkeep? Eppie's brain raced wildly.

"So . . . Legend would be my horse, right?"

"Absolutely. You've paid most of his fees already."

"And I can train him myself, muck stalls, all of it?"

"Of course. Your horse. In exchange for your help with Cesar, more riding than you're doing now, I'll pay all of Legend's expenses, including his shoeing, and vet bills. All of it."

"I'm keeping him barefoot . . . no shoes. Just hoof trims." All of Wills Warlanders Farms horses were barefoot. Mom always said horseshoes made the hoof too narrow and unstable.

Mrs. Krause paused. "It's your horse."

"What about my guardians, especially Tracey? I don't know that they'd understand that I bought a horse, especially when they're having trouble paying the bills right now."

Mrs. Krause nodded. "We can arrange it so that they are aware that you are working for me, riding Cesar, and working with Legend, but that you aren't getting paid. Maybe we'll just say that in exchange for your help, the horse will be yours when you turn eighteen? Then you'll no longer be under their custody, right?"

Eppie looked at Mrs. Krause. That felt wrong somehow. "But he's still my horse now, as of this minute, right?"

Mrs. Krause laughed a little. “Of course.”

Eppie paused. “Can I get that in writing?” she asked in a small voice.

Mrs. Krause laughed again and finished her decaf non-fat latte. “It will all be legal and the documents will be signed, Pauline. I’ll even arrange for a mediator to go over the paperwork with you so you completely understand the contract. We will need a guardian signature as well.”

Eppie melted, her hard steely surface dripped away and she burst into tears of happiness. “Yes!” she half-shouted. “I’m in! Thank you so much!” She reached across the front seat and hugged Mrs. Krause in spite of herself. Mrs. Krause gave her a hug back, and when they pulled away, there were tears in both of their eyes.

“When I drive you home, Pauline, run in and get your paperwork on the sale. I’ll buy Legend for you tonight.”

Eppie let herself cry, sobs wracking her body. She was finally getting Legend!

A piece of her mother’s life was coming back to her.

# CHAPTER FIFTEEN

Eppie thought about Brian and Legend as she mucked out stalls the next day. She and Maggie had talked about Brian all during lunch. Veronica, the small bay Morab, the Morgan/Arabian, was in the turn out corral. Eppie could hear "Ronnie" snorting as she ran around loose, running over to the fence occasionally to talk in a nicker to Eppie as she worked, reminding her she was still there. Eppie waved her hands at Ronnie to run and went back to raking. She thought of school, knowing she had monopolized most of the lunch conversation, telling Maggie about Legend and Mrs. Krause, sharing how she finally spilled the beans by sharing her big secret. Maggie looked stunned and congratulated her. Eppie felt relieved she could share her good news.

"Wow! A lot has happened since yesterday. Including the fact that . . . I talked to Brian!" Maggie burst out, biting into her packaged apple slices.

"You did? When?"

"He was at our house last night doing an assignment with Kyle. I pulled him aside and asked him if he liked you."

Eppie's mouth opened wide. "You did not!"

"I did."

Eppie didn't know if she should hug or slug Maggie. "Really? What did he say?"

Maggie smiled as Eppie's insides churned.

"He does like you. A lot."

Eppie felt warm all over. "I thought he had a girlfriend?"

Maggie shook her head. "No, not anymore. They broke up."

"The rich girl? They aren't seeing each other anymore?" Eppie was stunned. Now what? A sixteen year old high school boy liked her? She had no idea what to do with that. Her stomach butterflies stirred awake.

"That's what he said. He says he wouldn't mind seeing you again. He really likes you, Pauline. Like I said, a lot. He thinks you're way more mature than some girls his own age."

Eppie blushed deeply and nervously moved her hair from her face, tucking it behind her ears.

"Wow." She remembered the kiss, delicate and soft, and his warm hand clutching hers. "Should I give him my number?"

"He asked for it but he wanted your cell. He said since he knows Jim it would be weird to call your house. I gave it to him, I knew you wouldn't mind, but he said he may want to message you online instead. Time to finally get on Facebook Eppie!"

Eppie nodded. "Okay," she said. She didn't usually chat online with anyone, since she was too tired at night to talk to Maggie, her only real friend, but she could stay up late and talk to Brian if he wanted to talk. She shook with excitement.

"Pauline!" a voice shook her from her memory of the day. It was Mrs. Krause, walking quickly up to her. She glanced over and checked Ronnie, now rolling in the turn out, before looking at Mrs. Krause. Did she now own Legend? Was he on his way here? Eppie uncharacteristically dropped the manure fork and ran out in front of the stall.

"Hi, Mrs. Krause!" she called.

Mrs. Krause stopped in front of her, carrying the manila envelope Eppie had given her, along with some loose papers. "Hi Pauline. First of all, you can call me Beth. Mrs. Krause sounds like my mother-in-law," Beth said.

Eppie nodded.

"Secondly, Legend is paid for!" Beth held up the PayPal receipt. "But there's a small problem," she added quickly, seeing Eppie jump up and down, clapping. Eppie stopped and froze.

"What is it?"

"You didn't mention that he was a stallion," Beth said. "They don't allow stallions here, or at any public stable in Palos Verdes."

Eppie's heart sank. "What?" She didn't know.

"You'll have to geld him, Pauline. Handling a stallion in a barn full of mares is a bad idea. And it can't happen."

Eppie felt like crying. What about her future, her dream to breed Legend to other Warlander mares?

"I had planned to make money breeding him," she said.

"You'll have to revise those plans if you want to bring him here, and to be honest, you don't have the transportation required to keep a horse someplace else, if you can find a place willing to take a stallion. Not if our agreement holds for you to ride Cesar three days a week."

Eppie looked up at Beth. There was no hope for it, she could tell. She nodded glumly. "I'll geld him. How much is it?"

"It's only a few hundred more, Pauline. I'll make the arrangements, Janine has a good vet she's got ready to go. But now he'll have to recover from his surgery for a couple of weeks before we can bring him here. The timing is set back."

Eppie nodded again miserably, wishing she had more time to think. But she knew the deal. If she wanted to keep Legend at the barn, which was her goal, she had to follow the rules. Her heart twisted up. Now she would have a gelding, and he was going to be a hobby horse. She couldn't make a career with a gelding, except maybe to show him occasionally, and there was no way to make a living doing that. She'd have to find another way to make money for her future with horses. But she couldn't get him at all if she didn't do it.

"Okay. Go ahead. Let me know how he is doing after the surgery," Eppie said with a sigh. She heard Veronica whinny at her from the turn out. "I've got to go get Ronnie," she said, motioning with her chin toward the public corral. She turned and ran toward the mare, hot tears streaming down her face.

The house seemed somehow quieter without Jim there, or at least, less crowded. He was in his rehab program and dinners were animated again, with Lonny clowning around more to mask the fact that he missed his brother. Everything felt relaxed, and Lonny and Eppie got closer than ever before. They started playing Yahtzee before bed every night, since there was a strict "no television" rule after 6 pm on school nights. Lonny's bedtime was 9:00 pm, and Tracey told Eppie she could have the house computer each evening from 9 til 10 pm, which was her bedtime.

"I can't believe you got two Yahtzees!" Eppie complained.

"That's because I rule the world," Lonny said, his white-blond hair twisted in salty curls around his face. If Tracey didn't make him shower every morning, Eppie suspected he'd be like a little bronzed wild man, unbrushed and covered in salt and seaweed from the ocean, never to bathe or brush his teeth again.

Once Lonny went (complaining the whole way) to bed at 9, Eppie dashed for the computer. First she checked her email messages on Evangaline's email account. Janine, or maybe her daughter, had sent a message.

*Legend is doing well, though he's not eating as well as we'd hoped. It will be at least two more weeks until we will ship him out to California. We have the company standing by for an October 26 ship date, for him to arrive in California on October 27. -Janine.*

Eppie noticed that the email was cc'd to Beth. It was weird having her secret plan exposed and shared, but in a way, the pressure was off. Legend was coming, and nothing could stop her from finally having the horse she'd worked so hard to get. She sent Legend a mental hug, something she did often, and imagined soothing him with her hands, petting up behind his ears, patting his big circular cheeks. She couldn't wait until it was real.

Eppie checked her message app and found Brian easily.

Pauline: *How are you?* she typed.

Brian: *Good to hear from you! I'm doing homework. Watching the game.*

Pauline: *Game?*

Brian: *Football.*

Pauline: *Oh. Just found out my horse is coming October 27.*

Brian: *Oh yeah? Cool. There's a party the 30th. Halloween bash. Wanna come?*

Pauline: *With you?*

Brian: *Of course.*

Pauline: *Sure! Should I dress up?*

Brian: *Of course.*

Pauline: *Where is it?*

Brian: *Friend's house. Beezer. I don't think you know him.*

Pauline: *K.*

Eppie smiled as she typed. Brian asked her to a Halloween party! She had a date, a real live date with a high school boy. She wondered if she could somehow bring Maggie to the party, but knew that would look lame to ask. And what about Tracey? Would she let her go? Her mind reeled as she and Brian messaged until exactly 10 pm.

## ❧Chapter Sixteen❧

Tracey let Eppie miss school on the 27th, since it as such a big day. Eppie paced the barn after doing her mucking and turning out chores early. Legend's stall was immaculate . . . there was a fresh layer of sawdust shavings on the ground, a brand new plastic water pail (flat on one side) hanging on the wall, a treat of oats and alfalfa pellets in his rubber horse feeding trough, and a brand new rhinestone-studded red halter with matching red lead, a gift from Cashmere, hanging on the saddle box hook. The only thing missing was the horse.

"They're an hour out," Beth said after checking her cell.

Marta Greeves wandered up. "Hello," she said. "Your horse is coming today, is he?'

Eppie smiled at Marta, though she felt faint with excitement. "Yes."

"Be good to see this mystery horse," Marta said with a wink. She nodded toward Beth. "Nice thing you've done for the girl."

"She deserves it, Marta. She's for real. One of us."

Marta nodded knowingly. "I'm gonna ride Big Red. Eppie, I have another horse that hasn't been out on the trail all week. Would you join me?"

Eppie was torn between waiting at the barn and riding, an opportunity she never passed up, but Beth urged her on. "The wait will kill you, Pauline. Go ahead."

Eppie nodded and followed Marta down to the lower stables where she ran her Western style private lessons and classes. She pointed to a round Paint mare.

"That's Kachina. She needs a ride real bad, the lesson student who rides her is sick and she's missed three lessons this week."

Eppie went into Kachina's stall and patted the horse, who glanced over with a *who are you?* expression. She put on the halter and led her out to the tie ups and backed her into the rubber matted area, clipping the tie lines on either side of the black headpiece. Eppie groomed the horse and lifted her feet to clean them out with the metal question-mark shaped pick. She was pleasantly surprised to find out that the horse had no horseshoes on her hooves.

"Hey, she's barefoot!" she called to Marta, who was in the grooming station across from her getting Big Red ready to ride.

"All of my horses are barefoot," Marta replied.

"Mine too!" said Eppie, and then she paused and looked at Marta, who had a quizzical look on her face. She giggled. She barely had one horse, and had forgotten for a moment where she was. "I mean, when I had a lot of horses, they were all barefoot."

Marta grunted a reply as she began saddling Red. "Kachina's tack is the tack room."

Eppie went in the spacious barn-turned-tack room with the wrought iron saddle bars and bridle hooks neatly labeled with gold engraved plates, and pulled the Western bridle and saddle bar and hook marked KACHINA. She tacked Kachina up and then led the Paint to the mounting block, climbed up on the block of wood and got on. The Western saddle felt big compared to Cesar's English one, but after adjusting the stirrups she was ready to go. She followed Marta on Big Red out a tiny side gate under a grove that led to a huge hilly open field with trails zigzagging all around. They walked their horses side by side under the eucalyptus trees, the horses perking up their ears with interest at being out in the world.

"She's a nice mare," Eppie said, patting Kachina on the neck. She was talking to Kachina but Marta nodded.

"Great little horse, heart of gold. Very patient. She just gets crabby if she doesn't get ridden every day."

Eppie smiled. "You've got it rough, don't you? Having to ride every day."

Marta's lip stayed stern. "It's getting harder as I get older, believe me."

"I wish I could ride Legend, but he's not old enough, and I want to bond with him and train him on the ground first before I get on him. I want to be the only one who rides him. I've never had a horse that was only mine before."

"I have a feeling he'll be your horse soul mate."

"He already is, and I haven't even met him yet."

After they walked a bit, Marta got Big Red to jog and Eppie followed suit. Kachina had a nice gait; the rocking motion was comfortable as Eppie felt the wind in her hair. She liked riding without a helmet, against the rules at Team Cesar. The cool October breeze picked up and whistled through the trees with a haunting melody. Eppie wished she could be at the stables in the morning every day. This felt like home to her.

Soon they were cantering over the open trails, the horses' running hooves pounding the compressed sand path. Then a jog and a cool down walk and they were done. From the top of the hill Eppie could see the road below. She saw a horse trailer coming up the main road.

"They're here!" she shrieked, and Kachina did a little side dance to protest the unexpected noise. Eppie neck-reined her around, heading back to the stables, and this time it was Marta following her. They raced toward the barn and Eppie jumped off Kachina. She wanted to rush over and greet the trailer but duty wouldn't allow her to leave a horse that still needed another quick cool down and grooming. But Marta understood.

"Go! I'll put them both away."

Eppie hesitated. Marta clucked at her.

"Really, go, Pauline! This is your horse, not Beth Krause's horse. You get over there and get him feeling safe and secure. He's had a rough couple of weeks you know."

Eppie knew, and she nodded and ran as fast as her shit-kicking boots would allow. Legend had arrived!

The sleek aluminum horse trailer was huge, and could fit twelve horses. It pulled into the main stable parking lot and everyone who was there came out from whatever they were doing to watch. The truck was so big that Eppie wondered how it would ever turn around. The driver seemed to wonder that too; his eyes darted around the dirt lot as he climbed down from the tall cab. Beth rushed over to him and went over the paperwork on his clipboard. He handed her a pen and she shook her head and motioned toward the trailer. He nodded and they walked to the rear of the trailer where he opened the back.

Eppie rushed around to see, and there toward the back past a Palomino and a Paint she caught a glimpse of a dark gray-black horse; thick mane, ears flattened in the dimly lit trailer bed. *Legend.* She stepped up into the trailer. The whole thing was covered in safe black rubber, including the walls. The driver pulled the rolling sidebar up and back to open the stall area. Eppie got her first real look at her horse.

He was magnificent. His head was beautifully formed, and he looked at her with a questioning gaze, as if wondering what this newcomer was all about. His neck was tucked and perfectly aligned with his rounded shoulders and back. His mane grew on both sides and flowed down toward his chest, and his legs were sturdy, but not too thick. He favored his mother more than his father . . . more Andalusian than Friesian, and he was stunning. Eppie held her breath when she could see it: Onyx's beautiful roundness and Pixiedust's fine features in the legs and nose. Her mother's horses were both within this one beautiful creature. Tears blurred her eyes; she really did have a small piece of her mother back in this living, breathing horse.

"He's beautiful," Eppie heard Beth say from faraway. Eppie couldn't take her eyes off of him.

Eppie went up to him and held out her hand under his nose. He sniffed it and then nuzzled her fingers with his fuzzy lips. Eppie patted him and he stood stock still; he knew how to stand, that much was for sure. She leaned over and placed her hands around his neck, her fingertips finally, finally, touching that course mane. She hugged him deeply and breathed him in. He rubbed his jaw along the back of her shoulder, itching his face nervously, stamping impatiently.

Beth stepped in and checked him carefully for any injuries, and looked at his mouth and teeth.

"He seems pretty unfazed," she said, and then she signed the paperwork that the driver handed her, pressing a monetary tip into his hand. The driver stepped forward and put a rope halter on Legend with a white rope attached and handed the leadline to Beth.

"He's all hers," Beth said, and the driver gave the lead rope to Eppie. Eppie took it, all instincts intact, and brought the now-nervous Legend off the back truck ramp. Once in the sunshine, she saw how spectacular he really was. Even after his two day ride and recent surgery, he gleamed in the sunlight, the lightening of his babyhood blackness apparent in his blue-gray coat.

"He's going to turn white," Marta said knowingly as she approached.

"Yes, he'll be white," Eppie said. "Just not for a while."

"He's handsome."

Legend's ears pricked up as he surveyed his new surroundings. His nostrils grew wide as he sniffed the air, and the wind in the trees caught his attention but didn't spook him. His hooves were hopping in place on the ground, which must have felt good after being in the aluminum trailer with rubber mats. He pawed the gravel driveway and side-stepped, feeling his freedom from the enclosed truck bed. Another horse in the truck whinnied and Eppie caught sight of a black Friesian in the opposite corner.

"That one's his half-sister," the driver said, pointing over to the whinnying horse. "Same sire. She's going to a riding academy in Temecula."

Eppie felt bad separating Legend from his stall mate. Legend picked up his head and gave a loud answering whinny. The whites of his eyes showed as he seemed to realize his sister wasn't accompanying him. Eppie knew how he felt, having to leave family behind. The mare was still calling to Legend as the driver pushed up the back door of this truck and locked the gate. Legend unexpectedly reared up, the white lead flying free of Eppie's hands. Luckily Marta was close enough to grab it as he landed; he was nearly loose in the parking lot! Eppie's heart pounded as Marta handed her the rope and she flushed. He was more than she expected. *He's still a baby*, Eppie reminded herself. The fact that she had just purchased an untrained horse was hitting her hard. Legend reared again, this time less exuberantly. Carefully Eppie inched in toward him.

When he landed she gathered the lead tight and patted him reassuringly.

"That's a bad habit," Marta noted off-handedly.

"We'll get past it," Eppie said defensively. Beth watched Eppie calm Legend.

"He holds himself beautifully," she said. "You could go far with this horse."

Eppie cautiously led Legend toward his new home, trying to quell the wrenching she felt in her gut as the Friesian in the horse trailer continued to stamp and shriek her goodbyes. Legend pranced lightly on his feet as the truck began the arduous task of turning around in the tight lot.

Eppie decided that Legend needed to get out of there so she walked him up and down all the aisles at the barn. He would stop suddenly, spooking a bit here and there, to look at something that startled him. His intelligent eye would gaze at the offending bag, trashcan, or water hose, and then he would assess, and continue on his way. After two trips through the whole barn he was fine, no spooking, so Eppie turned him into his stall. He went around every inch of the place, sniffing everything. When Legend found the blue water pail he drank deeply, and then ate the treats he found in the bucket. Eppie noticed he liked the peppermint candy the best.

"Don't hand-feed him, you'll spoil him," Marta cautioned as she came over to see Legend again. He was chewing on a carrot, watching as Marta approached. Beth followed.

"I know," Eppie said.

Marta smiled. "I know you know." She handed Eppie a tissue-wrapped rectangle. "I bought you a little present," she said.

Eppie was surprised. "You did?"

"Sure. Open it."

Eppie ripped open the tissue (Legend didn't even flinch) and there was a shiny metal stall marker. Written in fancy letters was the name "Legend". Beneath Legend it read "Owned and loved by Pauline Wills".

Eppie loved seeing that written on metal for the whole world to see. She gave Marta a hug, and Marta hugged her back.

"Thanks so much! It's the best!"

"You're welcome, Pauline. Now I'd better git . . . I've got a lot of horses waiting on me."

Eppie turned to Beth and hugged her too. "This wouldn't have happened if it weren't for you, Beth. Thank you, from the bottom of my heart."

Beth grinned. "You're welcome Pauline. I can't wait to see what you can do with this horse!"

Eppie smiled and turned the name plate over in her hand, letting it catch the sunlight. *Legend. Owned and loved by Pauline Wills.* It was real to her now. She owned a horse! Legend was finally hers, and for the first time since she'd lost so much, her dreams had come true.

## ≪CHAPTER SEVENTEEN≫

Leaning on the metal gate to the turn-out pen had been Eppie's position for over an hour. Legend would explore and sniff around, then come to her, checking in with her for security. Suddenly he lifted his head, the wind catching his mane, and he galloped, tail high, to the far end of the turnout.

"You're lucky no one else is waiting," Marta said, motioning toward the sign that told riders the turn-out corral time limit is 20 minutes.

"He's been cooped up for two days in that trailer," Eppie said. "He needs to run still."

"I can see that."

Legend trotted back, nostrils wide and snorting, and then he whinnied loudly. An answering call came, but not the one he was hoping for. He bucked a couple of times and then resumed sniffing the ground.

"It takes them awhile to forget their old lives," Marta said. "But he's obviously taking to you. He keeps coming back to you."

"That's a good sign," Eppie said, her heart swelling. Marta was right, Legend was sticking close to her. She looked at the horse and felt small and insecure. Did she have what it would take to make him into the amazing horse she knew he could be? Worry furrowed her brow.

"I want to give you something," Marta said. "Back at my trailer. Come around when you're done here, I don't have any lesson kids showing up til 3:00 today."

"I will," Eppie said as Marta limped away. Eppie watched her go and wondered what else Marta might have for her that could top the metal sign proclaiming that Legend was indeed hers.

At Marta's trailer, Eppie watched Marta pull a bent, cracking, paper-filled notebook out from a low bookshelf. "Here," Marta said triumphantly.

"What is it?" Eppie asked, looking at it carefully but not taking it from Marta's hand.

"It's some old school learning, from the professor himself."

Curious, Eppie took it from Marta and opened the heavy blue 3-ring notebook and read the first worn and yellowing page, neatly typed on a typewriter: *Professor Berry's Mail Course in Horsemanship.*

"What is this?"

"It's something given to me back when I first started training," Marta responded. "I was determined to train horses at an early age, like you. Earlier even. My mentor, an uncle who lived on a ranch as a hand, gave this to me. It must have cost him a lot to have someone type it up for him, but he understood that the information was important. You can use it while you train Legend. All the secrets are in there. Mind you, some of this information is outdated and just plain cruel, but look past that and you'll see some real gems of wisdom in there."

"In . . . this book?" Eppie looked at the tired thing incredulously. She scanned her eyes down the page.

*Book Number One. Colt Training.*

Turning a few pages, she read sections on a horse's temperament, on shoe training, on saddle horses . . . the book was surprisingly full with hundreds of pages of typed nuggets of information, with cut-out photographs pasted in. The language was stilted and old-fashioned, like a British person had written it.

"Where is this professor guy from?" Eppie asked.

"Here in the USA. He was considered by many to be the world's best horse trainer in the 1800's."

"The eighteen . . . hundreds?" Eppie shook her head. "Wow."

"Just read it. You may be surprised at what you can learn."

Eppie stared at the book again, and she could sense the amount of times it had been opened and pored over. "Thanks Marta. This is great!"

"You're welcome. Now . . . go on, git. I have lesson kids coming, took you long enough to put that horse to bed."

Eppie grinned. "I'm going to spend a lot of time with him, Marta. That's the whole point."

"Just don't forget what promises you made to get him here, Pauline. You still have to ride on Team Cesar, starting today."

Eppie started. She'd forgotten all about Cesar! Quickly she tucked the unusual notebook under her arm and dashed over to change into her riding gear.

Eppie felt like her world was speeding up, she was so busy now; school, then riding Cesar, and spending every other waking second with Legend. She was staying at the barn until the last vestiges of orange light winked out over the ocean just a mile or two off, until she couldn't see well and she was tripping in the twilight. Some nights she kept a small light clipped onto her riding helmet so she could stay even later, but Tracey didn't like her staying after sunset very much. Nights were dawning earlier and earlier as the darkest time of the year was approaching.

And then, there was the Halloween Party! October 30 tapped her on the shoulder announcing its arrival before she knew it. She woke up Saturday morning in a panic. Somehow in all of the fuss over Legend she hadn't even had time to put together a costume.

"Tracey!" she complained loudly as she stumbled into the kitchen for her morning toast and hot chocolate. "I don't have anything to wear for that Halloween party tonight!"

"Party . . . tonight?" Tracey said. "What party?"

Eppie froze. Had she really forgotten to tell Tracey? Her thoughts raced. Yes, somehow in all of the week's excitement, she'd left out the small fact that she was attending a high school party with a sixteen-year-old boy.

"It's a Halloween Party! All my friends are going. Didn't I tell you?"

Tracey moved to the family's wall calendar in the kitchen. Saturday the 30th was blank except for Lonny's swim team practice and an appointment at Jim's treatment center. Lacey Bell came out from under the table and seemed to look at the calendar too. She gave a plaintive but questioning meow.

"No mention of it here, Pauline. And you know that I would have written it down."

Eppie stared at the calendar square. "Oh. Sorry. I guess I just . . . forgot . . . "

"That doesn't mean you can automatically go, Pauline. I have to clear everything. Like, where is it? Who is hosting it? Who are you going with? Are the parents home? I need to talk to them too. All of that has to be covered in advance. You know that."

Eppie hung her head. Yes, she knew. How had she even forgotten to finish making arrangements? She realized that getting Legend had overtaken her common sense in dealing with her real life.

"I'll get all the info and get back to you, is that okay?" she said quietly.

"Yes, but don't count on anything. This sounds too last-second and sketchy to me."

Upset, Eppie ducked out of the warm kitchen, making a bee line for her room, her stomach growling, loudly complaining about the uneaten toast. She had a lot to figure out: how could she get Tracey to let her go? And she needed a ride to the party. And she needed a costume! And none of her own friends would really be there, so how could she get Tracey to say yes? Her thoughts whirled around the conundrum occupying her brain. She considered her options. She would have to call Brian and see what he knew about the party, as lame as that was. Could she sound more immature, having to ask him about the party details so she could tell Tracey? She picked up her cell and called him, and found herself nervously intertwining her fingers when she heard Brian's voice on the other end of the line.

"How are you?" Brian asked. "Excited about tonight?"

"Yes," Eppie said in a hesitant voice. "I just needed to get the address, you know, so I can get there."

Brian gave it to her. "Let's meet at 8:30. Nothing will be going on until then."

"What was your friend's name again?" Eppie asked.

"Which friend?"

"The one having the party."

"Oh . . . Beezer."

Eppie sighed. That didn't sound like a respectable name, and Tracey wouldn't go for it. "Is that his real name?" she asked.

Brian paused. "Uh . . . no. That's just what we call him. Why?"

"It's just a weird name, that's all," Eppie said. She didn't want to ask any more questions; soon it would be obvious that she was fishing for information to give to a parent.

"His last name is Bemis, don't ask me how we got Beezer out of that," Brian chuckled. Eppie's bad mood lifted. She had a name! And an address. She could fudge the rest.

"Well, I guess I'll see you there at 8:30 then, is that okay?" Eppie asked.

"Sure. I'll see you then. Are you sure you don't want me to pick you up though?"

Eppie could imagine how that would go over with Tracey and Rich, a high school boy picking her up for a date.

"Nah, thanks though, I have some stuff to do first!"

"Okay, sure. See you tonight, Pauline!"

Eppie's heart lifted as she hung up the phone. Now she only needed a costume!!

Eppie pulled the old trunk from the back of the closet. It was the one thing she'd always had with her in all of her different homes. It belonged to her grandmother and held some pretty cool old things in it. Eppie remembered something that might make a cute costume as she lifted open the lid, rusty hinges creaking.

The musty smell of old clothes, photographs, and paper greeted her nose. On top was a tray that fitted into the box that held letters, newspaper articles, and old pictures of her grandma and mom when they were young. Temptation jabbed at her; looking at those carefully arranged photos always made her both happy and melancholy at the same time, but it was after noon already and she still had nothing to wear. She lifted the top drawer out of the box. Beneath it were layers of tissue. She reached in and peeled back the first layer. A tidy dressage costume was on top. It was her mother's when she was training for the Olympics. The top hat was a bit bent and Eppie straightened it before laying the costume aside and digging deeper.

After removing several layers of old memories, Eppie found it. She pulled out the big fancy circle skirt complete with ruffled petticoat and the prim little fringed shirt that went with it. Grandma's old rodeo queen costume. The sequin-covered turquoise cowboy hat was the perfect match to the velvet turquoise skirt and white shirt with sequined pockets and blue leather fringe. It would be a bit big; Grandma had been plumper than Eppie when she was a young woman, but as Eppie pulled it up in front of her she knew it would fit well enough. Excited, Eppie put the clothes on and looked in the mirror. She remembered the picture of Grandma wearing the costume and was surprised at how much she looked like an angular version of that woman from another time, another place. A tear dripped unexpectedly from her eye. She wiped it away and set about the task of making the dress work. What if she wore it to visit Grandma, she wondered? Would it somehow pull her out of the spell that the stroke seemed to have over her? Eppie decided to take it and show it to her at least, and see if it could help Grandma. She did a quick spin and loved the way the kooky skirt moved.

"Cowboy boots. Damn," Eppie said under her breath. She looked deeper in the trunk and couldn't find any. She didn't have any either, just her barn shit kickers. They were a disaster. She couldn't wear them to a party! What about her Team Cesar boots? Eppie fished them out of the closet where they stayed on weekends. She zipped them up; a little weird, but doable. Admiring herself in the mirror, she didn't see Tracey push the door open. Lacey Bell tiptoed in, saw the clothes in the trunk, and made herself at home in the center of the pile.

"Oh, sorry Pauline, I didn't know you were in here," Tracey said as she put some tennis shoes and a hairbrush Eppie had left in the living room on top of her dresser. She smiled when she saw the outfit. "Wow! Is that the one you showed me once from your trunk?"

"Yes, I was thinking of wearing it to the party tonight, I got all the information." Eppie handed Tracey the piece of paper with the address on it. Tracey frowned as she looked at it.

"Who is Beezer?"

"Bemis. The last name is Bemis."

"What's the first name?"

Eppie hesitated. "I forgot."

"Do you have a phone number so I can talk to the parents?" Tracey asked, her voice hopeful.

"Um, just the name and address, sorry."

"Can't you call Maggie and ask her?"

"Well . . . " Eppie paused. She realized that she didn't want to lie to Tracey. "Maggie isn't coming after all. I found out that it's not someone in our grade."

Tracey squinted at the address again. "What grade is this Beezer person in?"

"High school," Eppie said quickly. Tracey's eyebrows shot upward.

"Well, you know firsthand what happened at the last high school party you attended," she said, her voice rising. "That's the whole reason Jim doesn't live with us anymore right now! He was drinking at a high school party! You can't go, Pauline. I'm sorry, but this is not something I can go along with."

Eppie couldn't believe it. Tracey wasn't going to let her go on her very first date? The heat rose to her face.

"But, Tracey! There's this guy who invited me . . . I have to go! I told him I would!"

"Pauline!" Tracey looked shocked. "You especially aren't going anywhere with a high school boy! That's the end of it! You are not allowed to go anyplace if we don't know the parents and we must check it out ahead of time, you know that. Look at what happened when Jim lied to us about his whereabouts! He was brought home, beat up and drunk, and that's just what we know about it . . . who knows what really happened that night? The answer is no! I'm sorry!"

Tracey left the room, shutting the door hard behind her. She had never gotten angry with Eppie before. A hard lump walled up in Eppie's throat as she threw herself on the bed and cried. Brian would think she was such a baby if she couldn't go! He'd probably never talk to her again now. Eppie cried and cried until her empty stomach hurt, and then she fell asleep on the bed, her Grandmother's rodeo queen costume fanned out around her.

## Chapter Eighteen

Eppie felt miserable all morning until Tracey offered to take her to the barn on Sunday afternoon so she could meet Legend. Legend whinnied when she approached, and it made Eppie feel less glum about missing the party with Brian. When she woke up after 11 pm that night, she contacted him to say she was so sorry but she fell asleep. He'd said it was okay, that he'd catch her later, but he hadn't called her back.

It was a different world at the barn on Sundays. All the weekend warrior horse owners were there, and all the lesson students were not. A few people wandered over to see the new kid in town, Legend, and Eppie told his story, leaving out a few parts for Tracey's benefit.

"He's gorgeous," Tracey said after feeding him a red and white peppermint. "I can see why you like to come here so much. Go ahead and stay, I'll run some errands and pick you up in a couple of hours if you want."

Eppie agreed, glad she hadn't unleashed the venom she'd been considering saying to Tracey yesterday. At least Tracey was being nice and apologetic today. Eppie looked up at the turnout; there was a line. It would be an hour til she would get in. She guessed the other two were full as well. She threw the red sparkly halter Cashmere had given her over Legend's head and led him out of the stall. She would take him to the hilly trail behind the stables for a walk.

Wishing again she could ride him, Eppie moved in stride with Legend, who was following along amicably. They fell into a rhythm that she enjoyed, and she held her hand against his neck to comfort him. As soon as it was time to pass through the gate that led to the fields, Legend stopped. He threw his weight back, ready for a fight to see who would win the gate-passing. Eppie turned and faced him and he pulled hard against his leadline.

"Legend!" Eppie said. She backed up, and came alongside him, not looking at him, and tried again to lead him through. He wouldn't budge. She tried a couple more times but he was now prancing nervously, and from her previous experience she could tell he was ready to rear.

"Excuse me," said a girl on a horse who wanted to get through. Eppie pulled Legend out of the way; he willingly went inside the stables, back toward his stall. She let the girl and horse out. *Now he'll follow that horse,* she thought. She tried again to lead him past the gates. Again he leaned backward. Eppie was infuriated. How could he be so stubborn? Hot tears edged the corners of her eyes. Her insides boiled.

"Legend!" she yelled even louder at him, knowing better as the horse, a good 15 and a half hands high and not yet fully grown, skipped sideways. It was like wrestling an alligator trying to make him listen.

"Whoa!" came a familiar voice. Marta! Eppie looked up to see Marta coming in from the trail on Big Red. She felt the warm prickle of shame dot her face.

"Hi," Eppie said glumly.

"Hi yourself, Pauline. What in tarnation are you doing to that poor baby?"

Eppie shook her head. "I just lost my patience with him. He can't do anything!"

"Pauline," Marta said, swinging a bit stiffly out of the saddle. "Honey, this horse hasn't had any training. He can maybe hold still for a farrier and a vet and to be groomed but that's about all he's learned so far. Where do you think you're taking him?"

"The turnout was full so I thought I'd just take him out there . . ." she looked out at the hilly terrain beyond the gate. What was she thinking? On cue, Marta mimicked her thoughts.

"What were you thinking? This is a good-sized horse already. One good rear and your skinny ass would be flying and so would he, far from here. Now lead him gently back in and quiet him down, girl. You've confused him. He doesn't know what you want from him."

Head hanging, Eppie led Legend back to the stall. This he knew, and his pace picked up. He skittered back and forth nervously down the aisle past the stalls of other horses, some blowing out at him as he danced by. Now he couldn't even walk normally! Eppie fumed, mad at herself now as much as Legend. He was no better than his first day at the barn! She was ruining him, ruining a perfectly good horse because she didn't know what the hell she was doing. Damn it!

Marta was leading Red behind her, talking calmly. "Put him away, Pauline. Let's work with him in his stall for a while. He knows enough to feel safe there at least."

"Okay," Eppie said, her throat tight. She felt terrible as Legend about knocked her over to get back to his safe haven. She took off his halter. He checked the rubber bucket she usually put his treats in and looked upset to find it empty. He kicked it with his foreleg, as if punishing it for letting him down. Eppie leaned over the metal stall gate and heaved a sigh, holding in tears.

"Okay," Marta said after she tied Red to a nearby hitching post. "Let's see what this baby knows, shall we?" Marta opened the stall door and then closed it behind her. Eppie stayed put.

"Come on! This is your horse, not mine," Marta reprimanded. Eppie slid sideways through the bars and stood up inside.

"I haven't been able to do that in 20 years," Marta said with a smile, patting her round middle. "But never mind. Okay, talk soothingly to him. Get him to stand still."

Eppie did as she was told, and whispered gently to Legend. His head jerked a few times and he looked away from her, pretending to gaze far off, but Eppie caught him sneaking peeks at her from under his long gray lashes. Her heart welled up again at that; she maybe hadn't done as much damage as she thought by being a complete moron. She reached her hand out and he nuzzled it with fuzzy lips.

"Good!" Marta said. "See, he's responding to you. Now just pet him down; just rub him. These horse people around here are all business. They come in, halter the horse, tie him up, brush him, saddle him, ride him, cool him down, put him to bed. What about just hanging out with him too, Pauline? Just play with him. Have some fun."

Pauline stared for a moment at Marta and for some reason she couldn't even figure out she felt like crying again. *Have fun? Have fun?* She almost felt like laughing like a crazy person, that concept just felt so weird to her. But Marta was right! She'd bought Legend . . . nearly killing herself to do it, for what? To make another robot horse like Cesar? To put Legend through the rigors of training to make him the perfect dressage horse? She couldn't even ride him until he was nearly four years old and his back was strong enough to hold her. She still had a year of this, just a young untrained horse, to deal with. And Marta's advice was to have fun?

Eppie did laugh. She started laughing and it felt so strange to be laughing in the stall with Legend there giving her a worried look, that she laughed more until she couldn't stop. Marta giggled a bit with her, and then more, and suddenly she couldn't stop either. The two of them laughed until their sides hurt. Eppie had tears again, but these were tears of laughter. She wiped them away and drew her hand under her nose.

"Oh . . . my . . . God," Eppie gasped. "I'm a complete mess!"

Marta giggled. "Yes, you are! A complete mess. But you're getting there, Pauline." Marta laughed one more time before containing herself. "Keep this in mind. It may be the key to solving all your problems."

"I completely suck," Eppie went on. "I finally have the thing I've wanted so much, worked so hard for . . . and I'm completely stressing out. I need to relax!"

"If you relax, so will Legend. Remember . . ." Marta smiled.

Eppie giggled. "I know, have fun," Eppie said.

Having fun was harder than it should have been. Eppie didn't really know how to go about it so she did as Marta suggested and used her fingernails to scratch Legend's silvery coat all over. At first his back twitched and he seemed uncertain but after she found a spot on his neck that he enjoyed having scratched, he began to lean toward Eppie. She smiled up at him when he did that, and she was delighted: he was just like a little kid. She was like a mom to him, she realized. She had to show him what to do.

Eppie then practiced picking up his feet, and they began a game. She would bend over and she would tap his hoof and he would lift it up into her hand. Sometimes he'd lift it before she tapped it, but soon he understood it was a game and he waited for the tap. Legend had a mind of his own, it seemed. He made up another game, one not so pleasant. When she went to pick up his back hoof, he lifted his tail and foul-smelling gas drifted into the air.

"Legend!" Eppie shrieked, plugging her nose and pulling away. This seemed to excite Legend, and after the third time Eppie realized by reacting that way, she'd pleased him and she'd just inadvertently trained him to do it every time she went to pick his back hooves. *Damn it,* Eppie thought. *The only thing I've managed to do today is train my horse to fart on me!* Eppie looked at Legend's deep brown eyes, and she could see the smile within.

## CHAPTER NINETEEN

*School equals a whirlwind,* Eppie thought as she dashed from school to the barn. She now did her homework in the car. Tracey gave up on Eppie's bus pass, her usual way home, and was now picking her up directly from school to give her more time with the horses, since nightfall was coming on earlier. Tracey may not have known all the details about Legend, like how Eppie really got him and that he was the grand-offspring of her mother's favorite stallion and mare, but she was smart enough to realize that Eppie's spending so much time at the barn had quelled any issues with boys, parties, and sleepovers, so she became a willing participant in the horse game.

It seemed like Eppie barely had time to turn Legend out, ride Cesar and then play, yes play, with Legend once more before she was standing next to her tack cubicle, the small reading light clipped to her helmet as she stripped off her riding boots, half chaps and jods and changed back into her jeans and lambswool boots. Darkness now tapped her on the shoulder before she was ready to leave Legend. She ran back to his stall for one last look before Tracey picked her up.

As she hurried in the semi-darkness, except for a few far off lights on the barn outbuildings, she was surprised to see Cashmere near Cesar's stall. She was absently tossing carrots into his big rubber feeding trough.

"Hi!" Eppie said, breathlessly approaching. "What are you doing here?"

Cashmere looked up, startled. She relaxed when she saw it was Eppie, and Eppie knew why: Cashmere thought Eppie was beneath her, and didn't care if she was caught in a vulnerable moment.

"Oh, it's you," Cashmere said, sniffing. "I'm just visiting Cesar. I miss him. I miss this place."

Eppie wasn't sure what to say and found herself gnawing on her hangnail.

She quickly put her hand down, suddenly glad for the nightfall so Cashmere couldn't see her face redden. She took the clip light off her helmet so she wouldn't blind Cashmere and held it between them, aiming it on their feet.

"Oh. I'm . . . surprised. And glad. Cesar misses you."

"He does?" Cashmere looked surprised.

"Yes! Aren't you riding him at all anymore?"

"Just once a week, but I missed last week so it's been awhile."

An awkward silence spread over them like the bourgeoning sky above. A honk from the parking lot sounded, but it wasn't Tracey. Two spotlights illuminated them both as the car turned around. Cashmere looked up.

"That's my ride. I'll see you around," Cashmere said, turning to go. "Oh, I saw your new horse. He's amazing. You must be enjoying him."

"Yes, but . . ." Eppie stopped herself, but she decided, what the hell? Cashmere was honest with her. "Actually he's a bit of a brat. Very pigheaded. He's taking some getting used to, to be honest, especially after working with Cesar, who aims to please."

"I always thought Cesar was pigheaded," Cashmere smiled, and Eppie could see her white teeth in the gloom. "I can relate." The horn regaled again. "I have to go."

Eppie wished she could ride Legend so they could ride together. How much fun would that be, to actually go riding all the time with someone out on the trails like she used to?

"See you next time you ride Cesar," Eppie managed. "Oh, and I forgot, thanks for the great halter for Legend. I love it!"

"Mom said you did. I'm glad. You're welcome. See you."

Cashmere trotted off toward the demanding headlights and horn, and Eppie was wondering if the driver was Beth or someone else. As the car turned to leave under the stable sign lamps, Eppie could see it was a minivan . . . she remembered it was their housekeeper's car that Beth had bought for her to use when she ran family errands. Eppie rushed over to say goodnight to Legend and barely had a chance before her own driver, Tracey, arrived.

❧♦❧

Eppie absently tapped her pencil against her book when she looked up at her teacher, now standing over her desk. Mr. Hodgekins reached down, snatched the pencil from her hand, held it up high, and walked back to the front of the room where he was going over some of the finer details of Jack London's *Call of the Wild.* Red faced, Eppie slunk down in her seat as she heard snickering behind her. She scolded herself for her damn wandering mind.

She was a wreck in school now! Every thought was of horses, horses, horses. What plagued her the most was how to train Legend. The "having fun" was working out well, she'd played tag with Legend in the turnout yesterday and he would chase her and gently head butt her and push her with his face and then trot away. But she still worried that she didn't have what it would take to make him into a good strong riding horse. She started carrying Professor Beery's raggedy notebook around with her. She read it so often in between classes that Maggie had started chatting with Alice Lin, also called LiLi, of Lexel's crowd. Eppie liked LiLi so she didn't mind. In fact, reading the notebook so much kept her out of the endless banter about the eighth grade boys, none of whom she was interested in since the only boy she liked was Brian. Now she was thinking of Brian! He hadn't called her since the day of the party, or met her again online. Eppie wished she had gone to the Halloween party with him. Her mind truly tortured, Eppie wished she had the notebook with her now. It was in her locker. If she were reading it in class she wouldn't be tapping her pencil so much and her mind would be racing so distractedly.

"Miss Wills, please see me after class," Mr. Hodgekins said as the bell rang for lunch. Eppie sighed. LiLi was in the same class and saw Eppie's predicament.

"Save a seat for me, will you LiLi? And tell Maggie I'll be late."

LiLi smiled and nodded in a comradely way and ducked out the door. Eppie went to the front of the class to Mr. Hodgekins little-used but overly cluttered desk.

"Am a boring you, Miss Wills?" he asked.

"No," Eppie lied. "I'm sorry, I'm just very antsy lately."

"Others have noticed a change in your behavior as well. Not that I expect an honest answer, but are you by chance using drugs?"

Eppie was so surprised by the question that she blurted out a strange staccato laugh, which probably made it look exactly as if she were using drugs. Mr. Hodgekins' concerned frown made her clamp it down quick.

"I'm sorry . . . no, not at all. I'm just, I just have a lot going on right now."

Mr. Hodgekins looked like he wasn't in a hurry for lunch, even though Eppie was. He motioned for a chair. "Let's talk," he said. Eppie reluctantly sat down.

"Horses!" Mr. Hodgekins said when Eppie explained everything to him, maybe more than she needed to after she'd gone on a small tangent about Legend's parentage. Once she started talking about the stables and Cesar and Legend, she found she had quite a lot to say. "Not drugs. Well, that's a relief. Not at all what I was expecting to hear, that's for sure." Mr. Hodgekins rose from his seat, and Eppie followed suit. "Okay, then, scoot on out for lunch, and I'll report to the counselor and the two other teachers who thought you were using," he said matter-of-factly.

"What do you mean?" Eppie asked, confused.

"Whenever a student's behavior changes significantly, there's usually a roundtable discussion with the teachers and counselors, to see if a pattern is noticed elsewhere." He chortled. "I'll bet they'll be surprised when I tell them it's just a case of a teenaged girl in love with a horse." Mr. Hodgekins handed Eppie back her pencil. She stuffed it quickly in her bag and pushed out of the room. *Drugs!* Eppie thought, mortified. She was going to have to pull her head down from the clouds, she could see, and try and stay focused in school. Reprimanding herself again and thinking of the funny story she'd have to tell Maggie, Eppie went down to the cafeteria.

After going to her locker Eppie rushed to the usual spot where she met Maggie for lunch and was surprised she wasn't there. She hadn't been *that* long. She looked around and found Maggie at Lexel's table instead, pressed against LiLi as if they'd barely squeezed her in. She was laughing with LiLi, their heads together. They didn't even notice Eppie. A thick knot choked her throat and she felt her eyes burn. Maggie was sitting at Lexel's table! And there wasn't room there today for Eppie.

Turning with her home-packed lunch in hand, Eppie made for the only other table where there was room. She and Maggie called it the Dweeb Diner, where the 'dweebs' with no friends hung out, or where kids who didn't do their fifth period homework rushed to finish algebra and biology handouts. Eppie paused at the table with a quick glance around for another option, and finally sat down and bit into her apple. She sighed and began reading Professor Beery's advice on how to calm an unruly horse, but somehow, her heart just wasn't in it this time.

# ❧Chapter Twenty☙

Time flew so quickly that Jim came home and it seemed like minutes since he'd left, yet when he came in the front door from the treatment center there was something different about him. He seemed less arrogant, and more subdued. Tracey threw her arms around him, and Lonny hopped right up on his piggyback spot as if no time had passed.

Dinner was a tight affair as Jim shared what he'd learned in treatment. *Somehow I've missed all of this*, Eppie thought, thinking of the other day when Maggie and LiLi had lunch without her. She knew that Tracey and Rich had been going to meetings with Jim, and had been learning how to cope with having an alcoholic teen in their home over the past month, but Eppie had been oblivious to all of it. She had even been at the barn riding Cesar and taking Legend out when the treatment team had come into the house to talk to the family. *Ieep missing stuff from my real life now that Legend is here*. Not that she minded not being a part of Jim's recovery. The less she had to do with Jim, the better.

Normally Eppie would have showered after dinner and hung out in her pajamas with Lonny or watched TV or checked her very empty messaging account for a word from Brian, but now she felt uncomfortable being in her PJs around Jim. *Why he'd have to kiss me?* she wondered. *Damn it! Should I have told someone? Did he?*

She wanted to know if he'd told but she didn't want to talk to him. She'd managed to put him into the furthest part of her mind for the whole month, and now here he was, right in her face. Eppie decided that since Lonny had missed him so much that Jim and Lonny could hang and she'd stay in her room. Maybe read more of the prof or do some extra credit homework.

After showering Eppie dressed in her jammies and put her feet up on the bed. Her day enveloped her and she picked up her vanilla sparkle body lotion and rubbed it into her sore feet and hands. Those damn riding boots in the metal stirrups took their toll by the end of the day, and now she was walking and running around more than ever. She was exhausted. Her feet felt tingly from the lotion, warm heat was pouring in through the vents, barring the outside cool November night. Eppie's thoughts went to all the usual stops: Legend, Cesar, Maggie, Brian, School, Grandma, Home, and when it came to Jim, she stopped it and went back to Legend. Soon she fell asleep on top of the covers.

When she woke up it was dark and she was freezing. Tracey had obviously come in and had thrown a knit blanket over her, but the heat was turned off for the night and the room was chilly. Lacey Bell was curled up behind her legs, stealing her warmth. The cozy white long-furred kitty purred in her sleep, unaware of Eppie's discomfort as she continued her mouse-chasing dreams. Eppie carefully extracted herself from the sleeping cat and tried to climb into her bed without disturbing her. She managed it and found herself wide awake at 3 am. *Now what?*

Her mind began to wander again into all the usual pockets so Eppie got up for some water. She was startled to find Jim in the kitchen again, his own tall glass of water in hand. Luckily she'd managed a robe and slippers. She couldn't believe her rotten luck.

"Oh, hi," she said quietly. "Just getting some water."

"Me too."

"Oh."

She poured the water from the plastic jug in the fridge and went to dash out the door when she felt Jim's big warm hand on her cold wrist.

"We need to talk," he said.

"I'm really tired."

"It's important."

"Oh. Okay, what?" Eppie felt nervous and sweaty, even though she was cold. The last thing she wanted to do right now was talk to Jim!

"Sit down," Jim said.

Surprising herself, she did as she was told.

"You tell anyone?" Jim asked.

"No."

"Me either."

"Okay."

Silence.

"Not even the counselors, not anyone. No one knows but me and you, and now you don't have to worry, I'm sober, it won't happen again. I'm sorry."

"Okay."

"No really. Sorry."

"You already apologized."

"But you didn't accept it."

"I can't do it just to make you feel better. Just let's move on, k? Forget it ever happened."

Silence.

"K."

"I'm going to bed."

Heart pounding, Eppie hurried through the house, balancing the glass of water and drinking it quickly when she got to her room. She snapped on the bedside light. Lacey Bell looked up and blinked in disbelief as if to say *turn that off!* Eppie let her eyes wander around the room, now covered with small pics of horses; Legend, Cesar, Pixiedust, Onyx, a whole legacy of horses that she was lucky enough to know. She looked at the photos until she fell back asleep with the light on, much to Lacey Bell's chagrin.

## CHAPTER TWENTY-ONE

At 10:00 on Friday night Eppie sat at the family's kitchen computer, playing solitaire. She'd been studying Professor Beery's notebook but all it did on weekend nights was make her antsy, because she wanted to go directly to the barn and try stuff out. *Better to keep distracted,* she thought. She checked her messaging account, but there was still no chats from Brian. He'd probably forgotten all about her by now, she realized, and she was about to go offline when the screen blinked.

*How are you?* Eppie read in the message box. It was Brian! Her insides did a crazy dance.

*Good!* She typed in, her fingers shaking a bit. *Busy. How are you?*

*Good. Busy. Sorry you couldn't make that party, it was fun.*

Eppie couldn't believe it. She was having a conversation with Brian! OMG. Her mind raced wildly, what happened? Didn't he and his girlfriend make up? What was he doing home alone on a Friday night? She had no idea what to ask him, so she typed in:

*I was so sad to miss it! Tell me about it.*

*The usual. A bunch of people dressed up crazy having fun. But it wasn't as fun without you.*

Eppie soared. *That's nice*, she typed.

*I mean that. So what have you been up to?*

She wanted to type in, did you and your girlfriend reconnect at that party? Are you seeing her again? But instead she wrote:

Pauline: *Horses and school. My teachers think I'm on drugs, LOL*

Brian: *What? Y?*

Pauline: *Because I'm so spaced out, the horse thing is overwhelming sometimes & I'm always thinking about it*

Brian: *It's like my sports teams, that's all I do it seems like*

Pauline: *Why are you not out with your friends? It's Friday night*

Brian: *They're boring. I wish I could hang out with you*

Pauline: *Maybe we can arrange it*

Brian: *How?*

Pauline: *Maybe you can come to the barn sometime*

Eppie was afraid to say it, because she was always so focused and busy at the barn, but she was also alone there, away from the prying eyes of adults. It was all she could think of saying. There seemed to be a pause on the other end. *He's typing,* she thought.

Brian: *I'm not really a horse person, I'm allergic*

Pauline: *Oh*

Eppie was sad to hear that bit of news. Allergic to horses? That didn't bode well for their relationship, that much was for sure.

Brian: *But I can maybe come to your school, or meet you after*

Pauline: *I'm always at the barn after school*

Brian: *Weekends?*

Eppie thought. She could get a ride to the barn, and have Brian pick her up there. Couldn't she? That would be risky, but who would know? Only Marta was there on weekends, and she wouldn't know Eppie wasn't allowed to be in a car with a high school boy. She could even say it was her "sort of" brother Jim, for all Marta knew. The plan fell into place.

Pauline: *I'm at the barn tomorrow, but you could pick me up there & we could go get a coffee or something*

Eppie was surprised at her own boldness, and bit her lip as she waited for his response.

Brian: *Can we meet at the General Store up the street? Don't want to drive into the horse parking lot, sneeze cough*

Eppie remembered the little store that sold sandwiches, candy, and horse tack near the stables.

Pauline: *Sure* she typed with a pounding pulse.

Brian: *What time?*

Eppie hesitated only a second before continuing with the arrangements to meet Brian. Was she really going to sneak off and meet him? Apparently she was, as she typed Brian a message and they solidified the plans.

"Pauline, you don't have to look like you're going to prom to go to the stables! Let's go!" Tracey called as Eppie was applying black eyeliner and mascara. "What gives?"

"What do you mean?" Eppie asked, putting away the makeup and grabbing her stable backpack.

"Okay, I'm not stupid. You're wearing makeup, you brushed your teeth twice, and you're wearing your best school shirt to go muck out horse poo. I'm a woman, Pauline. I know when a girl is dolling up for a boy."

Eppie's cheeks warmed as she wrestled with an answer. "There is a boy," she said slowly.

"I knew it! Who is he?"

"Just a supercute guy at the stables, he rides there," Eppie lied. "He's usually only there on weekends."

"So are you going to muck stalls in your good shirt?"

"No, but I'll make sure he sees me in this one!"

"Is there anything I need to worry about?"

"He's just for looking at, eye candy, don't worry. He's much older." Weirdly, Eppie wasn't completely lying: Brian was much older and he would see her in her good shirt.

"All right. Let's not get too boy crazy, okay? Stay focused."

"I will," Eppie lied again.

It was hard not tapping her feet the whole way to the barn and Eppie focused on that, trying to stay still. When Tracey dropped her off, she dashed over to her tack cubical and stashed her horse backpack, taking out the small cute sparkly purse with her money, school ID, lip gloss, and breath mints. She fluffed her hair and headed back toward the dirt path that led to the General Store.

"Whoa, Missy," a voice said. Eppie turned. It was Marta! "Where you off to?  You look fancy today."

"Just getting some snacks at the General Store," Eppie said, wondering at the fact that it was getting easier and easier to lie.

"Why so fancy?"

"Cute boy," Eppie said with a little smile that she hoped looked innocent. "At the store."

"Ahhh. I see. Can I join you? We can talk about some training tips I was thinking might work for you and Legend. And I could use a break, I've given lessons to six riders already this morning. I promise to ignore you at the store, so the cute boy won't think we're together."

Eppie didn't know what to say. Marta was going to join her! How the hell would that work out? How was she going to ditch her to go off with Brian? Eppie nodded, not knowing how to disengage from the invasion.

"Let's go," Marta nodded toward the stable entrance. They walked slowly toward it.

"How's it going with Legend?" she asked.

Miserable at her bad luck, Eppie swallowed hard. "Better."

"I saw you two playing tag. That looked fun."

The lump stayed in Eppie's throat, and she suddenly felt bad for ditching Legend today. He was probably waiting for her, and here she was, sneaking off to meet Brian! She wanted to stop and cancel the whole thing, especially now that she'd have to keep lying to Marta to actually end up going anywhere with Brian.

"It was. He responds better to lessons learned while playing. He doesn't like to be told what to do."

"I've been reading up on Warlanders, since we have one here now. Seems like they respond a little differently, that's true. They are very smart, but playful, according to what I've read."

"That's what my mom always said too."

As they neared the open stable gate, a car pulled in. The driver, a friendly-looking man, rolled down the window.

"Can you tell me where I can find Marta Greeves?"

"That would be me."

"I called you last week, I'm Kevin, we spoke about getting lessons for my girls?" In the back seat two young girls were bouncing up and down excitedly. "Sorry we didn't make it Wednesday. Can we sign up now?"

"Oh, sure! No problem. Park over there by that mobile home, where it says Visitor Parking. I'll be right with you."

Marta looked at Eppie. "Oh well, duty calls. Hurry back from the store and that boy, Legend is waiting for you, you know."

"I will," Eppie said, the guilty throat lump returning, though she was relieved that Marta wasn't going to come with her to see what she was really up to.

Brian was waiting in the lot, slouching against his silver car, his beloved Mustang convertible. His eyes darted around as he greeted Eppie.

"Hi!" He gave her a hug, and Eppie breathed in as her face nestled into his shoulder. He smelled so good, like 41, that Abercrombie cologne. "Wow, you look so cute!"

"Thanks!" Eppie said, feeling in over her head. "So do you." She smiled and blushed. *Did you say that to boys?* She had no idea. But he did look cute; his long zig-zaggy haircut fell over one eye, and his skater-boy jeans were both tight and low. He looked adorable. Brian laughed and swung his arm around her. "Let's go," he said, opening the car door for her. Eppie only hesitated a second before climbing in.

Brian's car was cleaner than she'd expected but then she stole a peek to the back seat and saw a pile of fast food wrappers and some athletic cleats on the floor. She sat quietly while he revved the engine to life and threw the car into gear, pulling quickly out of the parking lot.

"Where do you want to go?"

Eppie thought he, the older one, might have a plan already. She thought of the day she and Beth Krause had driven up to look at the ocean with their designer coffees.

"Want to look at the ocean?" Eppie asked.

"Great." Brian drove a little fast, but he seemed careful enough. After a few minutes Eppie relaxed. Brian drove up over the peninsula and right as they reached the crest, he pulled over into a scenic view parking area. He climbed out of the car and came around, opening the door for Eppie. Spread beneath them was the rugged terrain of the peninsula, hugged by the blue shimmering waters of the Pacific. Across the sea Eppie could see Catalina Island, and other islands whose names she didn't know were visible far off on the horizon. A salty breeze enveloped them and the mid-November sun blazed after a week of fog. Eppie breathed in deeply and closed her eyes. She felt so happy, and the lump in her throat was gone.

Feeling a kiss on her lips, she opened her eyes. Brian was kissing her! Not just a little kiss, but this one was longer, sweeter. Deeper. Eppie succumbed to the sensation and returned the kiss, feeling Brian's mouth on hers. Strange feelings shot through her; she felt like she could do this for hours, just melt into Brian and kiss him all day. After a long time they pulled away, and Eppie felt like a different person. Her senses were tingling. She looked at Brian, who was smiling. *Did he feel it too?*

"Wow," he said, tapping Eppie on the nose with a fingertip. "That was some kiss."

Eppie leaned her head against his shoulder, not trusting her words.

"Wait here, enjoy the view. I'll be right back."

Brian ducked into the car and Eppie for a brief weird second thought he was going to leave her there when he started up the engine, but after a moment she realized, he was putting the top down on the convertible! He opened the door for her.

"Hop in," he said.

She did as she was told.

Later that night Eppie was lying on her bed, phone in her hand. Lacey Bell was a fuzzy white lump asleep against her side.

"You're kidding!" Maggie shrieked. Eppie laughed.

"No, not even," she said, enjoying the deliciousness of all of it: her amazing day with Brian, which ended in more kisses and even a small "feel up" (possibly accidental). Then when he'd taken her back to the barn, or technically the General Store because of his allergies, Marta had been waiting and had asked if she and Cashmere would assist her with a new trail riding class on Saturdays. Marta said she'd pay them to ride two of her Western horses and assist with the kids. Eppie couldn't speak for Cashmere, but she'd agreed in a heartbeat. Then she and Legend had made a breakthrough, as she'd taught him the word "trot," wanting him to understand voice commands, and he'd seemed to understand. It had been one of the best days of Eppie's life since her life went to hell when Mom died.

"Wow Pauline, you and Brian are becoming couple of the year!" Maggie said as Eppie picked the nail polish off her thumbnail. "I guess he must have broken up with his girlfriend again."

"We didn't really talk about that, but that's probably what happened. They maybe tried to get back together and it obviously didn't work out."

"Maybe it's because of you!" Maggie squealed again.

"What do you mean?"

"Maybe he couldn't stay with her because he was secretly falling in love with you!"

Eppie couldn't believe her ears, but it did sort of seem that way, didn't it? He and his rich bitch girlfriend were broken up when she'd met Brian, then they'd met up again at that wretched Halloween party, but now he was back with Eppie! Maybe it was true!

"Wow, I had never thought of that."

"That's got to be it! This is so exciting! Maybe he has a friend for me and we could double date!"

Eppie's throat lump returned as she realized she wasn't allowed to date at all and that she'd had to sneak out just to go for a drive by the ocean with Brian.

"Well, it's complicated. I'm not supposed to be seeing him, you know."

"I know . . . but that makes it even better, doesn't it? A secret love affair!" Maggie rambled on about how Eppie and Brian would remain secret lovers until she turned eighteen, and then they'd suddenly elope. Eppie was glad she'd had such a fun day, but wondered: Could she keep on lying to all of the adults who had been so kind to her and go behind their backs to keep seeing Brian?

# Chapter Twenty-two

Eppie couldn't sleep, even though she was exhausted. Lacey Bell was sleeping smack in the center of her bed now, and Eppie was pushed off to one side, her eyes open in the dark as she thought over and over about her day with Brian. It was nearly midnight and she felt no hope of ever sleeping again. Brian's sweet tasting lips on hers . . . everything inside of her was singing with joy.

She heard a click that sounded like the front door and she stiffened. Who could that be? Jim had gone to bed early, and she knew Tracey and Rich were in bed too. Lonny was afraid of the dark, he wouldn't be up at night on his own. Was someone breaking into the house? Eppie hid her head under the covers, doing a mental inventory of heavy objects to use as a weapon in her room. Why didn't she have a baseball bat in there? Heavy footsteps tiptoed down the hallway, right toward her bedroom door! Lacey Bell woke up, growled, and darted under the bed. Eppie thought she was going to have a heart attack, she was so scared. Her breathing was quick and shallow. *Crap!* She could hear the doorknob turning. She peeked out and could see a man's form illuminated by the porch light streaming through the glass window of the front door beyond. Eppie wanted to scream but she froze. *Pretend to be asleep,* she thought as the man peered into her room. She was going to die!

"Pauline?" came a voice. It was a raspy male voice she recognized. Jim!

Eppie stayed still, hoping he'd go away. He wasn't allowed in her room.

"Pauline!" Jim whispered. "You awake? I gotta talk to you."

Eppie vowed not to move but she could see Jim was stepping inside her doorway. He would keep coming in if she didn't respond.

"I'm awake," she said irritably. "Stay the hell out, Jim! You're not allowed in here." She talked in a normal voice, not caring if Tracey and Rich heard. *Screw him!*

"I just had to tell you some stuff," Jim said quietly. His shadow weaved a bit. "It's private though, can we go in the kitchen, since you don't want me in here?"

"No! Get lost."

"It's about you, and that guy Brian."

Eppie's eyes narrowed in the dark. Now what! And where had Jim been anyway? He'd come through the front door but he was supposed to be home all along. What was going on?

"I'll be there in a minute," Eppie said, feeling irritable. Eppie was fuming as she put on her thick robe and slippers and marched into the kitchen. Jim was eating potato chips and drinking Gatorade when she came in, but she could smell something else . . . alcohol, on his breath. Jim was drinking again!

"You've been drinking!" Eppie glared at Jim.

"Just a drink. Just a little, but I'm not drunk. But shut up! I have to tell you something about Brian."

Eppie stood with her arms crossed, wishing her white nightgown was not so thin, and glad for the robe. "Hurry up, I'm cold and I want to go back to bed. What is it?"

"Brian is two-timing you! I heard about your day today with him, he's telling all the guys that you're all hot with him and that he's doing you!"

Eppie couldn't believe her ears. Sex? With Brian? "That's a lie!" Eppie said hotly.

"No, it's not. I heard it at a party, he was telling his friends. They were asking me if I was getting any from you too!"

Eppie felt nauseous. *What?* "I just went for a drive with him, Jim. Lay off, okay? You're drunk and you don't know what the hell you're talking about!"

"Okay then, how else would I know you were with Brian today if he wasn't talking shit about you?"

Eppie considered. Could it be true, that Brian was lying about what had happened today?

"Brian said specifically that I had sex with him?" Eppie demanded to know.

"Uh, no. He didn't say that, just that you'd had 'a horny day.' He implied."

Eppie relaxed. She almost smiled. That wasn't so bad, really. If she'd had to describe it, she may have even used those same words.

"Jim, stay the hell out of my life! What the freak are you doing, out drinking, and then coming home and harassing me? If you don't leave me alone I'm going to tell Tracey and Rich that you're drinking again! Your ass will be out of here so fast you won't know what hit you!"

Jim leered and lurched forward, grabbing the chair to hold himself up. He leaned his smelly potato chip-crumbed face close to Eppie's.

"Oh yeah? Well, you're not supposed to be driving around in a high school boy's car now, are you? So you'd better just keep your mouth shut! You could lose everything too, you know, including that precious horse you spend so much time with!"

Eppie went cold inside and in spite of herself her eyes welled with tears. *Damn Jim!* Jim looked pleased at her reaction.

"You have no idea what I went through to make this life for myself! Just leave me the hell alone! Don't even talk to me!" Eppie told him.

Jim grabbed her arm and pulled her right up in his face. "So we have something on each other. You behave and I'll behave, got it? Don't you threaten me again, Pauline. You'd better be nice or I'll make sure you lose everything. Everything including that stupid horse, you hear me?"

Eppie couldn't believe that Jim was being so mean, and she didn't like the way he was holding her so close to him, so her body was almost touching his. There was something dangerous and lecherous in his eyes that made her want to run away. Crying now, and unable to control the shaking and sobs that welled up in her, Eppie nodded.

"Promise?" Jim asked, trying now to act like the nice older brother, now that he'd broken her, just like a wild green horse.

"Ye-es," Eppie sobbed.

Jim pulled her close to him, his body rubbing against

hers as he hugged her. “Good,” he said.

The moment he let go, Eppie ran crying out of the room.

~•~

Eppie felt like a blob on Grandma’s couch the next day. Her heart wasn’t in it; she loved Grandma but she was depressed and tired from the night before. Tracey puttered around straightening things and doing all the work to make small talk.

“Pauline’s excited about a new young horse she’s training, aren’t you, Pauline?”

Eppie nodded, and cleared her throat. Even talking seemed so hard right now.

“Yes,” Eppie said. “I told you last time Grandma. It’s a Warlander, like the kind mom used to breed. My mom, your daughter, Evangeline.” Eppie remembered to use the phrases one of the nurses had taught her; when you mention someone, remind the stroke victim who that person is every time. If she’d felt up to it and Tracey weren’t in the room Eppie would have explained again that Legend was actually related to mom’s horses, but she sat quietly instead.

Tracey glanced up at Eppie. “Pauline, why don’t you tell your grandma about how you found her old rodeo skirt and tried it on, and how cute it was.” And so it went, Tracey prompting her, Eppie repeating what was said until Tracey sighed and announced that they should leave.

“You seem kind of out of it today,” Tracey said as they got back in the SUV.

“I’m really tired. I barely slept last night.”

“School problems?” Tracey asked.

Eppie shook her head. “No, nothing like that.”

“Oh.”

They drove in silence, Eppie sighing periodically as she thought about this new situation with Jim. She felt so . . . unsafe. He had her exactly where she wanted her. Now she was in trouble even if she never saw Brian again. And what about Brian? What was he saying about her? It didn’t sound so bad when Eppie had heard what he’d really said, but what was that part about Brian two-timing her? Jim had been gone a long time in rehab, maybe he wasn't up on the fact that Brian and his girlfriend had broken up? Eppie's whole body felt sore and tired. She just wanted to go home and go back to bed.

"Lunch?" Tracey asked as they pulled into the driveway. Eppie was a little hungry but food didn't sound good to her.

"No thanks. I think I'm getting sick. I'm going to go back to bed, do you mind?"

"No, in fact, Jim stayed home in bed today too. Must be something going around."

The mention of Jim made Eppie lose her appetite all together, and she was grateful when she sank down into her bed and quickly fell asleep, leaving the problems Jim was causing behind her.

Luckily the week flew by again and by Wednesday Eppie was back to normal, able to push Jim completely out of her thoughts since she barely saw him anyway. Brian had messaged her every night so she knew that they were okay. He apologized for talking about her when she asked about it, but he'd said he was so happy that he was with her that he couldn't help bragging about it. Eppie had melted at his sweetness but still hadn't been brave enough to ask Brian about the ex-girlfriend. She decided it didn't matter, obviously he wouldn't be messaging her if he was seeing someone else.

Things were good. Even Maggie and LiLi were including her at lunch again, now that she was leaving Professor Beery's notebook at home.

After school Eppie was surprised to see Cashmere at the barn.

"It's Wednesday! Don't you see your boyfriend Wednesdays?"

"Not lately, and I felt like riding. Did Marta talk to you about assisting with her trail riding class on Saturdays?"

"Yes, I'm doing it, are you?"

"Well, I didn't want to, but my mom says it's smart to get in with Marta, and she's making me get a job anyway, she says it will 'build character', so I may as well do that.

It's better than making Frappucinos for a bunch of pimple-faced losers or handing out smelly ice skates at the mall rink."

Eppie laughed, surprised at Cashmere's ability to sum it up, even if she was being rude.

"I'm glad you're riding Cesar today. Are you having a lesson with Andrea?"

"Andrea quit."

"Really?" Eppie had never heard of an instructor quitting a student before! Usually it was the other way around.

"She got all bent out of shape when you came on Team Cesar, then when I missed two lessons, she bailed out."

Eppie didn't know what to say. "Sorry."

Cashmere smiled. "It's not your fault. She was on me all the time anyway. Do you mind watching me for a few minutes though? Maybe you can give me some pointers on Cesar."

"Sure."

Eppie told Cashmere how Cesar liked to be turned out to roll in the sand first, then groomed and readied to ride. Giving her all the hints and tips she could think of, she watched as Cashmere rode Cesar. Cesar threw his head in the air and started charging down the center of the ring. Cashmere pulled the right rein hard to turn him and eventually stop him.

"You need to loosen his rein. He likes a loose mouth," Eppie called.

"Andrea told me to keep it taut so he won't bolt!"

"No, he likes it loose. He only wants to bolt when you tighten it. Trust me!"

Cashmere walked Cesar toward the fence, holding him back. His big legs pranced as he fought her for his head.

"He's going to take off again!" Cashmere said, tears of frustration edging the eyes on her pale face.

"I promise he won't if you loosen his rein. That's what he's trying to tell you, see? He's saying 'I need my head looser so I can lean into the jump'. Listen to him, watch him. He'll tell you what he needs. Try again."

Cashmere loosened the reins, but not enough. Nonetheless Cesar responded to her command and took the jump effortlessly, sailing over it. He tossed his head a bit as they approached Eppie on the fence.

"Even looser. Your hands should not touch any part of the braid on the rein, see?" Eppie showed Cashmere the flat part of the reins, the smooth black leather that led to the buckle. "Hold his reins there," she pointed, "and then hold your hands forward a little before the jump. He needs complete freedom of his head to concentrate. He does really well that way."

"I'm scared! I feel like I have no control of him if I do that!" Cashmere wailed.

"Look, you still have your legs, and your body movement, and your voice. Didn't anyone ever tell you that you don't ride with your hands, you ride with your body?"

Cashmere smiled weakly. "No, no one has ever told me that."

"All cowgirls know it. Try again, and don't you move those hands up on those reins!"

Cashmere was obviously nervous but she did as she was told. Cesar perked up and went around the ring at a canter, taking every jump smoothly with no issues.

Eppie clapped. "Great! See? He loves that!"

Cashmere had a big grin on her face. "Wow! That's the most fun I've had on him in ages!"

"Right, horses like to have fun too. It can't all be about work, you know," Eppie said, sounding like Marta to her own ears.

"I guess you're right."

An awkward silence followed, and Cashmere cleared her throat. "I'm going to give it another go."

"Okay, I'm going to go turn out Legend." She could hear him in the distance calling for her. He'd heard her voice and was demanding a visit. Eppie shuffled over to Legend's stall, glad that Cashmere was back on Cesar. She knew Beth would also be glad that her daughter was taking some initiative. Again it struck her how hard she'd worked to get Legend, and how Cashmere was given everything on a platter and didn't appreciate it. Sighing, she approached Legend's stall. He stuck his head between the bars and turned to face her, a soft nicker of greeting welcoming her.

## Chapter Twenty-three

After school on Monday Maggie walked ahead of Eppie toward the buses, her arm tucked into LiLi's. They were laughing as they paraded down the hallway.

"Hey! Wait up!" Eppie said, rushing to catch them.

Maggie turned and smiled. "Hey Sistah!"

LiLi eyed Eppie coolly. "Hello, Pauline."

"Hi LiLi! Hi Maggie! Where are you two off to?"

"We're malling it, as usual," LiLi sniffed. "Hey, didn't you used to take the bus?"

"My mom is picking me up now," Eppie explained, realizing how complex it was to accurately call Tracey her mom without a long explanation. "I work after school."

LiLi brightened. "Oh yeah? Where, at the mall?"

"She works at the stables, up on the hill," Maggie informed her. LiLi's eyes narrowed.

"You mean, with horses? And horse *poo*?"

Eppie nodded. "Lots of both."

"Ew!" LiLi plugged her nose.

Eppie laughed. "It's not *that* bad." LiLi didn't look convinced. "Mostly I ride horses."

LiLi scrunched up her eyes. "And you get paid for that?"

Eppie nodded, feeling uncomfortable now. What was LiLi getting at?

"Yes. Sort of. Why?"

Maggie shifted uncomfortably as LiLi's eyebrows shot up. "No reason," she said. "I just didn't know you were a horse girl."

By Tuesday a big dark storm had rolled in and rain was pounding the cement. The sky matched the way Eppie was feeling, because now the whole school was calling Eppie "Horse Girl" and laughing about it. Eppie was infuriated and didn't even know why: She WAS a "horse girl." It was the best part of her life. So how come when the boys said it, it sounded lewd, and when the girls said it, it sounded low-class? Eppie saw Maggie heading into the bathroom right before third period and she followed her inside. Luckily they were alone, probably because now they were both late for class.

"What is up with your twit of a friend?" Eppie asked.

Maggie twisted around in surprise. "Paulie! What do you mean?"

"I mean LiLi! What's her problem? She's on me like no other! Everyone is calling me 'Horse Girl' and I know she started it!"

Maggie nodded. "She probably did, but come on, that's just stupid. It's a stupid name. No one cares."

"I care!"

"Hey, you should hear what names most kids at this school get! Horse Girl? I'd take it in a nanosecond."

"Why are you standing up for her?"

Maggie eyed Eppie. "Look, you know how it is, Paulie! It's dog eat dog here."

"What's that supposed to mean?"

Maggie put her heavy bag down on the ground and faced the mirror, fluffing her damp strawberry hair. "It means this: I'm going to high school next year with Lexel and her friends. I can either spend the next four years being miserable, or I can get in with the in crowd. If I get in, I can get you in too. But you have to play it cool, and throwing attitude at LiLi isn't going to help you any."

Eppie stood there a moment before realizing her mouth was open. She closed it, touching her tongue against her chapped lips.

"So you're picking LiLi over me?"

Maggie swung around, staring at Eppie. "Aren't you listening? I'm securing both of our futures for next year! Look, my brother told me in September how to manage it. He said, get a best friend in 8th grade, and then both of you move into a larger popular group of kids all going to the same school. It's winter break soon and we're practically there! That's what I've been doing, and we're not even halfway through the year."

Eppie's head was spinning. "Wait, so I come in where?"

"You're the best friend. Well, except you haven't been around much at all lately. So I have LiLi, you know, as backup."

Eppie's eyes teared up without her permission.

"Don't cry Paulie!" Maggie wailed. "Seriously, this is the best thing for all of us! You have to trust me. But you can't blow it by pissing off LiLi. Just let it all slide, it will blow over soon."

Eppie was mad at the tears that careened down her face. They were hot and angry, the way she felt inside. "So, we were never really friends, in your mind? I was just . . . the girl playing the role of your best friend?"

"Drama Queen! No! Just trust me. I still love you." Maggie handed Eppie a rough paper towel from the dispenser. A yard duty with her hair in cornrows walked into the bathroom as Eppie dabbed at her eyes.

"Ladies? May I ask what you think you're both doing in here?"

"I was just on my way to class," Eppie said, tossing away the towel.

"And I gotta pee," Maggie said, dashing into the bathroom stall.

"Get yourself back to class," the short and wide yard duty told Eppie. She nodded and hurried out the door, the rainy dampness clearing her head, but her heart was still a tight bump.

At least that night when Eppie went to her messaging app, Brian was there waiting. It helped ease the heaviness she felt from her conversation with Maggie.

Brian: *How are you dollface?*

Pauline: *Dollface?*

Brian: *I don't know where I got that.*

Pauline: *Me either! It's funny though.*

Brian: *Weird. What are you up to?*

Pauline: *Not much. You?*

Brian: *Missing you.*

Eppie's heart did a somersault. He missed her! A little thrill went deep inside of her as she thought of their high-voltage kissing date.

Pauline: *Me too you,* she typed.

Brian: *That's sweet. When can I see you?*

Now what, Eppie wondered. How could she arrange to meet him again?

Pauline: *Sunday?* She typed.

Brian: *I can do Sunday. No games. I'll pick you up?*

Pauline: *At the General Store again, if that's okay.*

Brian: *I can do that. Can't wait. I gotta go do homework though, it's late and I've got a million tests this week.*

Pauline: *K. I should get some sleep myself.*

Brian: *Wish I could be there to watch you sleep!*

Pauline: *That's a little creepy.*

Brian: *I meant it in a cute and sexy way.*

Pauline: *Oh. Okay then.* (Smiley emoji)

Brian: *Gotta go. See you Sunday. Same time?*

Eppie had to think about it before she typed *Yes, same time.* She sent the message and Brian clicked off right after he read it without getting back to her. She sat there, feeling strangely alone. At least she had a date with him, but that meant she'd have to tell yet another lie! She heard footsteps in the hallway and froze, hoping it wasn't Jim. It was, but he was just going across the hallway from his room to the bathroom. As soon as she heard the door close, she turned off her phone, glad to be in her own room so she wouldn't have to see him. Her room was her sanctuary now; not only could she have her horse pictures and her own secret world in there, but also it was the only place where she felt truly safe from Jim.

Eppie was so excited about her date Sunday that she almost forgot to be excited about her job on Saturday! It was her first day helping Marta with her trail riding class. Saturday morning, Cashmere arrived, looking exceptionally appropriate in her cute jeans, a light blue button down shirt, and adorable rhinestone-edged cowboy hat and fabulous must-have-cost-a-thousand dollars cowboy boots. Eppie felt humbled in her old shit-kicker boots, her boy jeans, a giveaway faded pink sun visor and an old polo shirt. She sighed when she saw that Cashmere was even wearing makeup.

Marta had Big Red haltered to the tie out for Cashmere, and Kachina for Eppie. She herself was readying Buck, a big challenging Quarter Horse that only she rode.

"Well, girls, nice to see you looking less . . . hunter/jumper," Marta said. Eppie smiled and Cashmere even did too. "This task will make you humble. Now go grab your horses' tack, then each of you need to get seven more horses ready in an hour. There's a list taped up on the tack room door."

"Eight horses, bridled and saddled, in an hour?" Cashmere asked, the smile wearing off. Even Eppie was surprised.

"You thought you had it easy? What, that I would ready seventeen horses by myself and you'd just come for the ride? Hell no. Why would I pay you for that?"

Cashmere's shoulders slumped and Eppie sighed and grabbed Kachina's tack. She showed Cashmere where Big Red's gear was in the big barn that was now the Western Riding Academy tack room.

"It's heavy!" Cashmere complained as she lifted the sturdy leather saddle from its iron cage bed.

"Well, yeah," Eppie said. "You have ridden Western before, haven't you?"

"I've been on a few trail rides and to horse summer camps, so I have." She grunted with the weight of the saddle and threw it over Big Red's back.

"You forgot the saddle pad!" Eppie called after her. She thought she heard a snort come from Marta.

"Oh, right." Instead of being embarrassed, Cashmere stomped to the tack barn and picked up the woven red and black Navaho-looking blanket, as if it were the blanket's fault she'd forgotten it. She marched back and put it on Big Red's back, who was standing patiently, as if waiting for her to get it together.

Eppie lost track of Cashmere and was done readying Kachina and was checking the list when she heard Cashmere scuffling around behind her.

"Damn it!" she swore. "I broke a nail!"

"Let me help," Eppie said, going over to her. She saw the problem; Cashmere didn't understand how to cinch a Western saddle. She'd tied the leathers in a knot on the D-ring and then had tried to buckle it like an English saddle on the right side.

"It goes like this," Eppie said, quickly unhooking everything and starting over. She showed her how to snake the leather of the cinch binding through the ring and tighten it, and showed her how to lean against Red's belly if he bloated out to keep the saddle from being too tight. Once Red released the air from his gut she quickly pulled it tighter and looped it into a neat knot.

"Tell you what," Cashmere said. "I've never really done the saddle thing much. I've always had people for that. I'll bridle, you saddle, and then we can be done quicker. Let's go each get a horse, k? Or better yet, you get one and I'll get the bridle ready, then while you're saddling, I'll go get another horse and you get the saddle, k?"

There was something in the way Cashmere spoke that made Eppie believe at first that they were really a team, until she realized she, Eppie, was hauling all the saddles out of the tack room and that Cashmere was deliberately picking horses nearby to pull, while Eppie's were invariably in the third and fourth aisles over. By the time the first trail riding class student arrived, Eppie was exhausted and sweating, and Cashmere was fresh but still pouting over her broken nail. Marta had a lopsided grin on her face that didn't help matters, but she didn't say anything. Not up front, but as she walked past Eppie she whispered, "I'm paying you two the same, you know." Eppie grimaced.

As the students converged it was pandemonium making sure everyone was on their correct horse, with all stirrups adjusted. Cashmere designated herself as a sort of "spotter" for those using the mounting block, so Eppie ended up doing all the complicated riggings on the stirrups, adjusting each to the proper length. Ultimately she'd retrieved seven horses, put on sixteen saddles, and adjusted thirty-two stirrups. She felt tired and mad.

Eppie was glad to finally get on Kachina when they were ready to ride so she could rest from her grueling morning task. Soon it was apparent that Cashmere took up the rear so she didn't have to talk to anybody, and Eppie ended up running Kachina back and forth along the line of riders, helping all sixteen riders with whatever problems they were having with their horses while Marta led the way.

The large group wove up the hard path to the top of the hill, the dry stalks of once-green and yellow summer mustard flat and brown around them. Spread out beneath them was the cold sparkle of Los Angeles, and the ocean flowed around curved beaches as the Pacific lapped her shores. On top of this hill, they could see everything, including the blue-tinged mountains that shaded the sprawling city. Eppie sucked in her breath in appreciation.

A scream shattered the moment. A scream that she recognized, high pitched, fervent. It was Legend. He'd spotted her and the group from below, or maybe heard them and now could see them from his corral! A loud bang followed, echoed by alarmed calls from nearby riders.

"Legend!" Eppie cried out. Marta looked concerned.

"He's kicking at the bars, girl. You'd better go settle him down."

"But, you need me here!" Eppie looked from Marta to the stalls below them.

"I would consider this an emergency. Go!"

Eppie didn't hesitate. She swung Kachina around and the big Paint trotted down the hillside toward the barn, her feet madly lifting to keep her balance on the slope. Eppie held onto the saddle horn and let her go, though normally she would never allow a horse to run downhill. After a few moments that seemed like a tight-chested eternity, she reached Legend's stall. She dropped Kachina's reins in front of her, ground-tying her, and hurried toward him.

A woman had him shooed into the corner of his stall and pinned him there, her arms outstretched so he wouldn't bolt past her and hurt himself on the fence bars. He was wide-eyed and panicked at the stranger's presence. When he saw Eppie crawl through the bars, his eyes closed a bit and he whinnied. Eppie went toward him, her hand extended, and he hopped and reared in the corner, uneasy.

"Shhh, boy. Shhhhh. I'm here. I'm here." She remembered Professor Beery's words about letting the horse come to you, and she stood in the center of his stall. He perked up, interested, and approached her, nibbling on her outstretched fingertips.

"He's okay, just started banging the hell outta the wall there, spooked every other horse in this aisle. He's a rocket, that one," the lady who had stopped him from hurting himself said.

"He's still young," Eppie said tightly. She didn't know why she felt like crying . . . that mad race down the hill . . . she thought she may have lost him! He could have broken a leg! What if he had? She checked his legs with shaking hands, the tears blearing her vision anyway.

"He's fine, really. I stopped him right away, and he hit the wood, not the metal." She pointed to the fresh dent in the plywood that was secured around three sides of the stalls to keep the horses from chewing on each other's manes and withers in the comradely fashion that horses did when left to their own devices.

"Thanks so much," Eppie managed. She tried hiding her tears and pretended to further check out Legend's hindquarters. "Silly horse."

"Take him with you, he'd probably love to come along," the woman said with a shrug before sliding between the bars on the front of the stall and returning to her own horse a few stalls down. Another weekend warrior, Eppie realized, getting as much horse time in as she could on a Saturday.

Eppie wondered if he'd behave. She was a little nervous, taking him outside of the safety of the stables. She remembered when she'd tried to lead him out before when he'd reared and put up a fight. But she couldn't leave Marta alone with that lazy Cashmere! Her insides bubbled with the conflict of what to do. She eyed his halter in the specially built box to keep it next to his stall but protected by the elements.

Without further hesitation, she haltered Legend, and put the gold stud chain across his nose and opened the gate. She led him over to the patiently waiting Kachina. He approached the mare, being a bit too forward, and Kachina pinned her ears, warning him not to make any rash moves. Legend reeled back playfully and then nosed her. Kachina snorted but seemed okay with him. Breathing fast, Eppie clambered onto Kachina's back, holding Legend's lead line tightly. Once settled, she pulled Legend into position alongside and clicked for Kachina to walk. As they went up the aisle toward the hillside it was going surprisingly smoothly; Legend seemed to enjoy having a companion. They approached the narrow gate and Eppie tried to act as if going through it was no big deal. Kachina passed through nonchalantly, but suddenly Eppie's arm was jerked back as Legend stopped. He reared straight up, looking more like a stallion than the young gelding he was, almost pulling Eppie to the ground. She loosened the line and pulled her hand all the way to the end, realizing her mistake: if she dropped the lead now there was no backup line. She'd lose him for sure. Holding her breath, she sat still, and luckily Kachina didn't move. Legend seemed to contemplate the gate before suddenly leaping through it, as though jumping it. Eppie rolled the leadline up when he neared her again and wrapped the end of it around the saddle horn for good measure. Now Legend was following Kachina; he was nervous, and the mare offered him support in a way Eppie couldn't.

Eppie got Kachina to jog and Legend trotted along beside them so that they quickly caught up with Marta's group. Marta's eyebrows shot up when she saw Legend.

"Well, that's one way to solve it. Good thinking," she said, a smile spreading across her face. "Now normally I would have thought Kachina here wouldn't have tolerated this halfling, but I'm thinking that she may have some mothering instinct in her after all." Kachina had indeed decided she was in charge of Legend; she wouldn't let him get ahead of her, and turned to reprimand him whenever he pulled to much or tried to charge in front. Eppie continued helping on the ride, happy to answer questions the trail riders had about the rather spectacular Legend, and she realized how much she enjoyed being with him on the trails under the sun on a cool fall day.

## Chapter Twenty-Four

Eppie felt beat up after the ride but this time Cashmere helped her unsaddle and unbridle all the horses, brush them down, walk them to cool them and put them away. Even though it was just one day a week, Eppie knew that Saturdays were going to take their toll on her. Cashmere was upbeat and excited when Marta handed them each $50.

"This is the first money I've ever earned all on my own!" Cashmere said. "Maybe I should frame these bills." She giggled.

"Spoken like a girl who doesn't need the money," Eppie said smiling.

"Well, yeah. But it does feel good to earn it."

Something had happened up there on the hill that Eppie couldn't put her finger on. It had to do with when she returned on Kachina with Legend and she couldn't help the riders as much. Cashmere had just risen up and taken over. Maybe because she'd been a part of all that it took bringing Legend from Colorado, or maybe because she didn't want Legend to be a problem to Marta . . . whatever the reason, Cashmere had really been *helpful.* Cashmere had even insisted that Eppie go put Legend away and then come back and help, and she'd quickly put away four horses alone while Eppie was gone. Eppie felt grateful to her in a way she couldn't express. And closer to her than ever before.

Cashmere seemed lighthearted as she hung up the last saddle. "I swear to you, I'm going to start working out at the country club. I need to build up my biceps if I'm going to keep this up! My arms are killing me!" She laughed as if in wonder that her arms would be tired from working.

"Wait til you shovel twenty stalls in one day," Eppie said. "That's even worse."

"Uh, Pauline?""

"Yes?"

"Never gonna happen."

Both girls laughed and then kept giggling, unable to stem the flow of mirth that they felt.

"I could so use a mocha frap with whip, what about you?"

"Well, yeah . . . but there's no Starbucks within walking distance, is there?"

Cashmere laughed and pulled her cell phone out of her jeans pocket.

"I have a driver, remember?" She speed-dialed and spoke quickly. "Come get me and my friend now, and then take us to Starbucks."

Eppie stared as two things occurred to her. The first was the way Cashmere just demanded a ride, not even caring about the feelings of whomever she was speaking to. The other thing that struck her was Cashmere's use of the word "friend." She had called Eppie her friend! Did she mean that, or was she just simplifying things, to not go into complicated detail with someone Cashmere obviously considered a servant? If they weren't friends, what were they now? Co-workers? Much more than acquaintances. Eppie wondered at what it could mean.

"Pauline! Close your mouth, you look like a fish."

Eppie realized she had indeed been staring, mouth agape. She pressed her lips together.

"I just can't believe we're so close to getting a Frappuccino," Eppie said quickly, covering up her shock, she hoped. "You're like a lifesaver!"

"Don't I know it," Cashmere said, flipping her hat in a 'howdy pardner' kind of way. Eppie giggled, glad to be on Cashmere's good side for a change.

Eppie woke up sunburned, sore, content, and thinking of Legend (and then Brian) on Sunday morning. She felt a little bit of guilt about not visiting her grandmother . . . and about lying to Tracey about why she had to go to the barn again today.

She was wolfing down a bowl of rice cereal when her cell phone rang where she'd left it on the kitchen counter.

Tracey was washing a pot in the sink, ignoring Lacey Bell, who was winding around her legs like a white furry rubber band.

"Your phone is ringing for you Pauline!" Tracey said, drying her hands on a blue kitchen towel. Eppie rushed to get it before it went to voicemail and picked up the phone, wondering if it was Maggie, but it said 'unknown number'.

"Hello?"

"Hi. Are you going to the barn today?"

Eppie reeled. Who the heck was asking her that? Eppie almost answered thinking it was Maggie, but then realized suddenly that it was Cashmere.

"Uh, yeah. I am going to the barn. Are you?"

"I was thinking I would if you were. Maybe we can turn out Legend and ride Cesar or something."

Eppie flip-flopped, her mind mush. What? She was supposed to meet Brian, but Tracey didn't know that, and she was right there in the room! The barn was only a cover for meeting Brian on Sundays, not a real barn day. Eppie wasn't sure what to say.

"Sure, what time are you going?" Eppie stammered.

"Um; I don't know. Eleven?"

Eppie froze. That's when she'd be climbing into Brian's car! Tracey looked busy at the sink but Eppie could tell she was listening. Crap! Carefully, raising the tone of her voice, she said, "One?"

"Oh, you're not going til one? I can go then. Maybe I'll go work out at the club beforehand, build up my muscles til then."

Eppie laughed, mostly with relief. Cashmere laughed on her end too.

"Cool. I'll meet you at the stalls at one."

"One then. Sounds good," Cashmere said before hanging up.

*Whew!* Eppie could still spend a couple of hours with Brian and get back in time for some riding with Cashmere. Today was going to be great! She smiled as she hung up the phone, proud for her sneaky move in getting Cashmere to change the time. She sat back down to finish her breakfast.

"Who was that?" Tracey asked. Eppie was right, she was listening.

"Cashmere. Beth Krause's daughter."

"Oh, on Team Cesar. You're meeting her today?"

"I help her out with Cesar sometimes."

"Are you getting paid to do that?"

"No," Eppie said, surprised at Tracey's interest as she sat back down to eat her cereal. "No. We're friends. She also works with me for Marta on Saturdays."

Tracey smiled and put her hand on Eppie's shoulder. "I'm glad you're making friends at the barn, since you spend so much time there now."

Eppie felt that lump build up in her throat but she managed to squeak out a response. "The stables are full of friendly people," she said.

"Who is friendly?" Jim asked, barging into the kitchen through the swinging door. Eppie dropped her spoon into her cereal bowl and grabbed her chest.

"Christ! You scared me!" she said, not thinking. Tracey frowned at her for cussing.

"Yeah, I'm a scary guy," Jim said in a joking way.

"I'm going to go get ready to go to the barn," Eppie said. She wanted to get away from Jim as fast as she could. He stared at her, and she could see something sinister in his eyes. She knew he wasn't done making her squirm yet.

"So where are you going today?" he asked, trying to sound innocent.

"Barn. Like I just said."

"I thought you didn't go on Sundays."

"Now I do."

"Now that you have a horse of your own?"

Eppie sucked in her breath, annoyed. "I'm training a horse there, it takes a lot of focus."

"Is it your horse?"

Eppie looked at Tracey for help, and she stepped in. "Jim, why are you giving Pauline the third degree? It's complicated and it involves a lot of people. Why are you so interested?"

"That horse is probably worth a lot of money. Seems crazy that she'd have a fancy expensive horse, that's all."

Eppie clenched her fist, wishing she could pop Jim right in the mouth. She could feel the ache for it around her own mouth, she wanted to do it so badly. Now what the hell was he up to? Damn him!

"So what time are you going to the barn?" Jim asked.

Tracey squinted at Jim. "Jimmy, what is up with you? Why are you so concerned all of a sudden about Pauline and her whereabouts?"

Jim looked sincere as he put his hand on Tracey's arm, facing her. "Look, I just learned a lot in rehab, and I feel like another adult in the house. I want to help you keep Pauline on a straight path, and not let her run free too much."

Tracey nodded as if she maybe halfway believed his crappy story. "Thanks Jim, for your concern, but Pauline is a very responsible young lady. She works, she cares for animals, she visits her grandmother, usually . . . and she's a good student. So why not just focus on yourself instead of bothering Pauline? You have enough to think about, don't you, like that C minus you're getting in physics?"

*Good one*, Eppie thought. Jim glared at her. Tracey made a shooing motion to Eppie.

"Go on, Pauline. Get dressed. I'll be ready in about a half hour to take you over there."

Eppie jetted out the door to her bedroom and dressed quickly, taking a cue from Cashmere. Now she wouldn't look overdressed, compared to Cashmere's country and western debut yesterday! Putting on a simple pair of tight blue skinny jeans and a pale flowing peasant shirt, she knew she looked cute. She slipped across the hallway into the bathroom. Jim followed her inside and closed the door behind them. She glared at him.

"Get the hell out of here!" Eppie whispered.

"I know you're meeting that Brian guy! Everyone thinks you're doing it with him."

"I'm not! I already told you, I'm not doing anything!"

"A bunch of people saw you making out at Lookout Point! I've heard about it all week. Everyone thinks Brian's a cradle-robber. And he's been bragging about it. It's sick!"

Eppie wanted to slap Jim again. "You have a lot of nerve Jim! You freaking kiss me . . . your own sister practically! And you think Brian's sick for wanting to kiss me? What is your problem?"

"I was drunk! I wasn't thinking straight." Jim's mood grew black and Eppie realized that Jim was jealous of Brian. And instinct told her that was a bad position to be in. A little voice in her head warned her to play it all down, and fast.

"Look. I'm not even that into Brian, okay? It's just fun riding in his car. This is the last time I'm going with him, I'm going to start training with another rider on Sundays. I won't even have time to see him. So just chill out, k? Don't go all macho on me."

Jim peered at Eppie suspiciously. "Promise?"

"Of course! Everything that Tracey said is true! I'm too busy for a boyfriend. It's over, really. After today. I just didn't want to tell him online. I'm going to tell him in person."

Jim visibly relaxed and opened the door. He took a peek into the hallway before scuttling out to his own room.

Realizing what a close call it was, Eppie sighed and shakily put on her makeup. Jim was getting to be a bigger problem than she knew how to deal with.

## ~Chapter Twenty-five~

It was Rich who ultimately gave Eppie a ride to the stables, because he wanted to come see her new horse. Not that he knew she really owned Legend, that information was still strictly between Eppie and Beth Krause. Eppie squirmed the whole way there; once she'd been told Rich was coming with her, she rushed him out the door, but she only had a few minutes to spare before she had to run and meet Brian at the General Store. And once Legend saw her, he would undoubtedly wipe his big nose on her clean cute pale pink blouse or somehow smudge her make-up, and then Eppie would have to sneak away from Legend to meet Brian. Eppie tapped her fingers nervously on the armrest of Rich's Celica.

"You seem nervous," Rich said, glancing over at her as he drove up the tree-lined hill. It always got so green as they entered Palos Verdes.

"Oh." Eppie didn't know what to say but noticed her own hand tapping. "I'm just impatient to see Legend, you know." She smiled weakly.

"Ah, teenage girls in love, with horses," Rich said. Eppie pushed her fingertips under her leg to remind herself to sit still. The car felt smaller than usual as the silence around them stiffened.

"So, how are things?" Rich managed. "I haven't seen you for a while, it seems like. I mean, dinner, and around, but we haven't talked in a while."

Eppie nodded, realizing it was true. Eppie had overheard Rich and Tracey fighting recently; Jim's rehab had been partially covered by their insurance but the rest they'd had to pay themselves. Rich had taken an extra shift at work every other night to help with the bills and was always "going to bed" whenever Eppie saw him. A wave of guilt passed over her; with the money she'd paid for Legend, she could have instead helped the family right now.

"You must be tired," Eppie said.

"Me? Yeah, I am. I have to admit, in this deep down, bone tired way. Like sleeping isn't even the way to get it back, you know? I don't think I've ever been this tired in my whole life."

Eppie was surprised that Rich was being so honest with her, and she looked at him; he looked older, and worn in a way she hadn't noticed before. She cleared her throat.

"Well, things are getting back to normal."

"I guess, but Jim . . ." He left the word there and Eppie wanted to change the subject. Now she felt nauseous. *Damn Jim!* He always caused problems, even when he wasn't there.

"Let's not talk about him, I know it's stressful for you. Want to hear about my Saturday job?"

Rich looked relieved and nodded. "Do tell."

"Well, there's this girl named Cashmere, see . . ." Eppie began, and she told him the story about how she'd had to get all the horses ready because Cashmere had broken a nail. By the time they pulled into the dusty stable parking lot Rich was laughing loudly.

"You must be exaggerating," Rich said. Eppie laughed too, shaking her head.

"No, seriously! You'd be amazed. I'm not kidding, not even a little." They continued laughing as they walked down the stall aisle where Legend was boarded. Legend, excited to hear Eppie coming, trotted over to the metal fence and stuck his head out.

"There he is," Eppie pointed. Rich whistled low under his breath.

"Wow, he's beautiful! Really something. You ride him?"

"No . . ." Eppie liked having Rich there, she realized as she reached for Legend. He stuck his muzzle in her hand and blew air onto her palm in greeting. "He's still a colt, a baby, not under saddle yet. I'm training him. Starting to, anyway. Isn't he amazing?"

As if it were a command that Legend was supposed to be amazing right then, he lifted his head and stood in perfect confirmation position. Eppie laughed as he trotted to the other side of his stall. His long tail, once black and now lightening to a pale gray, swished as his hindquarters moved.

"He's a character," she said.

"I can see why you'd want to spend so much time at the barn," Rich told her.

"Paulie!" A voice filled the air. It was Cashmere, walking down the aisle. Eppie's mind raced; did Cashmere have any information on her that she didn't want Rich to know? All of these secrets were making her life crazy, she realized as she tried hard to remember what Cashmere did and didn't know.

"Hi Cashmere! What are you doing here?" Eppie asked, pushing her fingernails between her teeth. Cashmere stepped forward looking like she was posing for a hunter horse magazine; she wore dark green breeches, her team Cesar polo, and her $300 velvet helmet matched.

"I'm going to ride Cesar. Did you know there's an ETI horse show coming up? I want to get back in the ring!"

Eppie was surprised. "Really? That's great, I can help you get ready!"

Cashmere came over and gave Eppie a quick hug. "I thought you couldn't come til one? Don't you have to be somewhere?"

Eppie's face grew hot. "Oh, that changed. I was going to work with Legend before we met." Her face boiled hotter with the lie.

"Oh, that makes sense, but aren't you a little overdressed?"

"I have a T-shirt in my tack cubicle." Eppie's teeth gritted as the conversation swerved dangerously.

"Oh, so we're still on at one. Who is this?" Cashmere batted her eyelashes at Rich.

"This is Rich, my . . ."

"I'm sort of like her dad," Rich cut in. They'd always stumbled on that one. Eppie had never had a father, Rich had never had a daughter; she couldn't quite bring herself to call him Dad, he wasn't technically a foster father, but a legal guardian . . . it was all so confusing.

"Oh! Nice to meet you," Cashmere said, toning down the eyelash thing. "Well, I'd better go, Alexander is saddling up Cesar for me."

"You *could* saddle up your own horse for a change, Cashmere," Eppie scolded, though she was glad that Cashmere was making her exit. Now she could go meet Brian, if she could just get Rich to leave!

"I could, but if I don't have to, and there's a cute weekender boy around to help me, why should I?" Cashmere smirked as she walked away, and Rich smiled.

"I see what you mean," he said. "Now I don't think you were exaggerating at all when you told me that story." He gave Eppie a quick sideways hug. "I'm going home to sleep some more. I'm becoming a zombie, I know. Call Tracey when you need a ride, and I'll see you at home. Thanks for showing me your little world here, Pauline . . ." Rich looked around at the young girls and adults leading their horses, brushing and bathing them, talking and laughing. "I'm glad there's one kid at home I don't have to worry about. Thanks for that too."

Eppie nodded and waved as Rich headed for the dirt lot, but the guilty lump was back in her throat. She checked her watch. Damn! It was ten minutes after eleven. She was late to meet Brian at the General store!

Brian was sitting in his Mustang talking on his cell phone when Eppie rushed up to greet him. Even though he saw her, he held up his finger to her and finished his conversation while she stood there.

"Hi!" Eppie blurted when he put his phone away a moment later.

"Hi yourself, Pretty Pauline. You ready?"

Eppie nodded and climbed in, only a little disappointed that Brian hadn't opened the car door for her. She felt red-faced and sweaty from rushing over, and was glad he was focused on driving, not her. He pulled out of the parking lot and they sped away. His hand inched toward her thigh and rested there like it belonged.

"How are you?" he asked.

"Good. Busy." *You have no idea,* she thought, thinking of how she had to rush back to the barn to have a show lesson with Cashmere.

That was the best it got with their conversation, but Eppie was enjoying her hair blowing in the wind as they drove around the pale blonde hills to San Pedro, a small fishing community perched beside the Los Angeles harbor. Brian seemed to know his way around and soon they were at a cluster of shops called Ports O' Call Village.

"What is this place?" Eppie asked, looking around at the quaint wooden buildings.

"Just someplace I grew up coming to, with my dad," Brian said. "I come here once and awhile, you know, to get away. Like a mini-vac." He sighed. "It's about to close for good, though. Thought we could sneak it in before that happens."

"Oh." Eppie could see how it was like being on vacation to stroll along the boardwalk as boats floated by in the bay, and she could hear the far-off call of seals; or were they sea lions? She didn't know, but she liked the sharp tang in the air of fish, salt water, and diesel fuel. She felt like she was on a boat, and her Rocky Mountain upbringing hadn't given her a lot of opportunities to take in the pleasures of living near the sea. She hadn't even noticed that she and Brian were holding hands until he stopped her, pulled her to him, and kissed her. She kissed back.

"What was that for?" she asked, a crooked smile spread over her face.

"Just wanted to. You look so cute, your eyes all big, looking around." He smiled and they walked on until they came to a snow cone vendor. He bought two.

"What flavor?"

"Um, cherry?"

Brian handed her the frozen treat and they sat on a gray weathered bench overlooking the teal waters of the harbor. Seagulls hovered hopefully above them, but flew off when their begging went unrewarded.

"I love it here," Eppie said, almost to herself. Brian squeezed her hand and gave her a cold icy kiss, lemon flavored.

"Me too. I'll miss coming here when it's gone."

"That's really sad," Eppie said as they sat and licked at their cold treats, watching people walk by and enjoying the late autumn sun. Eppie closed her eyes and listened to the sounds of boats hitting the docks, bells, a cruise ship horn (very loud!), and the calming chatter of people and gulls. She breathed in, and her heart suddenly tightened. She was having such a nice time with Brian. Could she really tell him that she had to break up with him? Because of Jim? Anger boiled to the surface and she opened her eyes and looked at Brian.

"I have something to tell you," she said. Brian looked surprised but nodded, urging her.

"Jim is causing me a lot of trouble. I'm not supposed to be hanging out with you . . ."

She didn't want to use the word dating, it sounded too serious for what they had together right now. "So Jim has warned me that he'll tell Tracey about us if I see you like this. He is really mad about the party thing and he's making my life miserable."

"Wait." Brian put his empty snow cone wrapper on the bench beside him. "Slow down. How exactly is Jim related to you? Is Tracey your mom?"

Eppie sighed. *Here we go*, she thought. Her life was so complicated that she hated to go into it. But today it was necessary.

"Tracey is my guardian, not my mom. My mom died three years ago." She took a breath and launched. "Tracey is related to me, she's sort of a distant cousin through marriage. Jim and his younger brother Lonny were her foster kids, but she adopted them, and then she found out I was in the Los Angeles foster care system and she pulled me out, and I moved in with them right after that."

"You're . . . a foster kid?"

"I was, for almost a year, until they figured out I had family here. I was living with my grandma but she had a stroke and I got put in the system. I didn't even know about Tracey, she's like my grandpa's other granddaughter, from his first marriage. I didn't even know he was married before or had a kid other than my mom."

"Wow." Brian seemed to take this all in. "So what's going on now with Jim?"

“Jim’s . . . mad.” Eppie decided not to creep Brian out with the fact that Jim was actually jealous of Brian. “About the party, and the fight, and he’s threatened to tell Tracey, my legal guardian, about us.”

“How does he know about us?”

Eppie looked at Brian. “Because you’ve been telling your friends, and he knows them and they told him.”

Brian looked embarrassed as his face flushed, not from the sun.

“Oh. Sorry.”

“So can we just keep this quiet, between us? I can’t afford to cause a problem where I live, it’s been hard enough with Jim being in rehab; he’s drinking again anyway. Ugh . . . it’s all a mess.”

Brian looked at Eppie thoughtfully. “No problem, Paulie.” They grew quiet and the sun was getting too warm. Brian stood up and held out his hand, helping Eppie up.

“Let’s just have fun, not let all that stupid family stuff interfere. We all have issues.” Brian paused as if wrestling with some inner thought. “In fact, it’s best for me too if we just keep this between us, for other reasons.”

Eppie was curious but didn’t want the whole time with Brian to be about intense stuff. She just wanted to have fun now, she felt so relieved that he understood and wouldn’t say anything. Now she could tell Jim she’d broken up with Brian, still see Brian on the side, and still get to work with Legend, Cesar, and Cashmere at the barn! Everything was finally going her way. She giggled at the unexpected cherry/lemon flavored mash-up kiss that met her lips.

## Chapter Twenty-six

Back at the barn, the girls' lesson with Cesar was going well, except for Legend. He was jealous and could hear Eppie calling out to Cashmere, and he screamed a high whinny and kicked at the stalls.

"You'd better just go get him, he may hurt himself," Cashmere suggested.

"I know, I will." Eppie stomped over the stall, where Legend was hanging his head out as if he wanted the railing of his gate to vanish. He whinnied a loud greeting when he saw Eppie that plainly said, "It's about time!"

"You are the biggest baby ever," Eppie complained, but secretly she was glad that Legend was so bonded to her. She quickly put on his halter and stud chain and made him stop as she opened the gate.

"Stand," she commanded. He stood, barely able to achieve the holding position, his body quivering with excitement at the outing. "Okay, good boy." Legend pushed past her and started leading her down the aisle. She had to stop him four times and make him stand until he walked properly beside her.

"He's a mess, I'm going to turn him out," she called to Cashmere.

"I'll keep doing my course," Cashmere called back. Sundays were slower paced for Eppie at the barn; the horse in the big corral was just getting haltered up to leave when she approached. Eppie was glad she didn't have to wait for the ring; Legend would have been difficult to hold, he got so excited about everything.

She led him into the long corral, carefully latched the gate, and slipped his halter from his head. "Yahh!" she called. Head up, he galloped off to the far side of the ring, his stride high as he picked up his feet and flew. Eppie caught her breath. Could she really own such an amazing animal? In her mind, she could practically sense her mother standing beside her as she watched Legend prance. A tear welled in her eye; she was in awe of the colt's power, his muscled blue-gray hindquarters bunching and rippling as he bounded away, did a sharp turn, and reared high in the air, his front feet pawing the sky. Eppie laughed, wondering how insane he must look to some of thc people around here with show ponies that stood aimlessly in the turnout waiting to be brought back to safe stalls. Legend charged full board back to Eppie and she walked to the middle of the ring. He slowed to a trot behind her, head high, and she raised the lead rope and made the familiar noise: "Yahh!"

He galloped off again, and after a sweaty twenty minutes, she haltered him up and led him down to the ring where Cashmere was riding. She was about to go in when she saw Marta rushing up. Cashmere was on the ground, and Cesar was standing near the jump he'd obviously refused. Anger welled up in Eppie: Cesar would have never refused that jump with her, was he just messing with Cashmere?

"You okay?" Eppie called out as she led Legend inside and tied him on the rails.

"I'm mad as hell, but nothing's broken." Cashmere winced as she tried to sit up. Eppie stopped her.

"Wait a sec." Eppie told her to move a few key body parts, everything seemed in working order. Marta hovered nearby.

"The body part in question is one I can't move," Cashmere said, reaching a hand up for help. "I think I broke my butt."

Marta smiled, and Eppie blurted out a quick laugh. "Ouch! Tailbone?"

"Yes."

Eppie and Marta carefully pulled her upright, and Cashmere was bent forward, holding her back.

"Can you walk?"

Cashmere breathed heavily. "Ow! I think so." She gingerly moved forward and straightened a bit, then rubbed the offending area. "I don't think it's really broken."

“You’re gonna have a honkin’ bruise tomorrow,” Eppie said.

“I probably already have one. I was supposed to go to a party tonight! Now I don’t think so.”

“A party . . . tonight? It’s Sunday.”

“We don’t have school tomorrow.”

“Oh yeah!” Eppie had completely forgotten about the long weekend, one of those random Mondays celebrating presidents or trees or something. She was glad it was still the weekend and that she got an extra day off.

“Well if you’re talking about holidays then I suppose no one’s gonna die, I’m going back to my trailer,” Marta said. She started walking away but was stopped by one of her student’s parents.

“Thanks.” Cashmere straightened considerably and could walk almost normally. “If I could get on Cesar, I’d make him take that jump right now.”

“Want me to do it?”

“Would you?”

“You go stay with Legend.”

Eppie grabbed Cesar’s reins and climbed up onto his back. He danced sideways a bit, knowing he was in trouble now. Eppie cantered him around the ring once to get the feeling of him and realized he seemed “off”.

“Marta!” Eppie called, seeing she was still nearby. “Will you check Cesar for me?”

Marta grunted audibly and shuffled back to the ring. “What’s wrong?”

“Watch his gait.” Eppie trotted, then cantered, Cesar, and the rocking horse motion she knew so well seemed lopsided somehow.

“He’s off today Pauline, you’re right. It’s his back left foot. It’s very tight.”

“Thanks!” Eppie slowed Cesar to a stop and dismounted. She checked his leg. A fine red line bridged his ankle on the offending leg.

“He’s cut,” she said. “Maybe from a jump?”

“He only had one refusal.”

“Maybe from his stall?” She grabbed Legend’s lead and led both horses as Cashmere limped along beside her. “Let’s go take care of that.”

"Should I call the vet?"

"That's up to you, but I can take care of it if you want me to."

"Sure."

"Legend's hot, I'll put him on the walker and we'll take care of Cesar first."

The day was getting complicated; one hot and sweaty horse that needed a cool down and a bath, one that needed a rinse and a wrap. The nights grew dark quickly now, and it was nearing 3:00. Only two more hours of light.

"Tell you what," Cashmere said. "This is going to take a while, can you sleepover? We can grab dinner afterward and then lie around watching sad horse movies and eating tons of buttered popcorn. You can commiserate while I mourn my sore butt bruise and the loss of my party. What do you say?"

Eppie was surprised. Would Tracey let her? That actually sounded fun. *And she wouldn't have to see Jim later.*

As if reading her mind, Cashmere said, "I'll have my mom call Tracey, and she can see if it's okay."

"Sounds good!" Eppie continued getting the horses handled while Cashmere called, and then sat on the bench by the wash racks, talking and joking with Eppie as she cared for first Cesar, then Legend. Even though Cashmere wasn't able to help much, Eppie was having fun with her. As the last light of the day vanished in the west, all plans were in place: the sleepover was on, and a warm dinner was just minutes away.

The minivan rolled through the dark curving streets of Palos Verdes in a seemingly never-ending hilly neighborhood. Eppie was struck by the lack of streetlights; like in Colorado, it was up to the car headlights to do all the work. Her belly was full from a delicious dinner at a fancier restaurant than she would have usually been comfortable with; she felt grateful she had her cute clothes from her mini-date with Brian in tow. The cream sauce pasta reminded her of a dish her mother had made her many times, and the first bite had almost brought her to tears as memories filtered through her mind. Cashmere, texting a friend, apologized for it, the glow from her iPhone illuminating her face in an eerie way, but Eppie was glad for some alone time to think. She was impressed with the grown-up way Cashmere had ordered her meal, and had even sent a water glass back because it had fingerprints around the edge. The driver, or whatever role the person had who was taking them around, was quiet and pleasant, but it was Cashmere who paid for the meal with a credit card and who scrutinized the bill and figured the tip. *She's like a mini-adult,* Eppie had thought. *But she's only a couple years older than me. That's crazy.*

And yet, Eppie felt comfortable with her. Even though she was high-maintenance, a bit spoiled, and sometimes rude, Cashmere was competent and trustworthy. People like that were in short supply in Eppie's life. Tracey and Rich were about it. And Cashmere's mom Beth, so far. A sudden feeling of rage and loss swept through Eppie. She realized that she was mad at Grandma for having a stroke, mad at her mother especially for dying, for leaving her. *Why couldn't she have been driving more carefully?* It seemed so unfair that her life as she knew it could be ripped from her, black claws plucking her mother away and pulling Eppie from her home and dropping her unconcernedly in California, away from all she knew. It was an old pain she visited sometimes, but she wiped her tears and tried to think of other things. She didn't want to be a letdown at her sleepover with Cashmere.

"Uggghhh!" Cashmere slipped her phone into her Luis Vuitton bag. "I hate being laid up."

"What's wrong?" Eppie asked, glad Cashmere hadn't noticed her tears.

"My boyfriend, Bo, he's at that party, and this snobby little PV princess is clawing her hooks into him as we speak. And is he backing off and saying, hey baby, I'm taken! No! He's pouring vodka into her vitaminwater and flirting with her!" Cashmere's eyes shone fiercely in the dim blue light of the dashboard. "I have video evidence taken by a friend."

"Wow." Eppie thought of Brian, wondering what kind of boyfriend he'd be. "That's too bad. Are you going to break up with him?"

Cashmere sighed. “No.” She shrugged. “We’re weirdly connected, like soul mates or something. Some call it ‘Twin Flames,’ like broken soul mates, but I don’t know. I’ve been with him a long time. We split up once in a while but, it’s hard to leave each other for real.”

Eppie was about to ask for more juicy details when Cashmere’s Luis bag lit up. “Hold on,” she said, raising one slim finger commandingly, a silhouette in the dark, exactly as Brian had done to Eppie earlier. Cashmere checked her texts, took a sharp intake of breath, and began typing furiously back.

Even Cashmere’s relationship was flawed, Eppie thought as she watched her reply in the dark back seat. She was wondering whether she should tell Cashmere about Brian, but were they really a couple? Sure, kissing, hand holding, car rides; but Eppie didn’t know all that much about Brian. He’d dated a “PV princess” for a while too, she remembered, and she wondered if that girl, his ex, had gone through what Cashmere was going through now with her boyfriend, if she had heard the rumors about Eppie and Brian making out in his fast car.

Eppie didn’t know if it was going to be a long cryfest of a night now with Cashmere, but Eppie decided right then and there to keep her promise to Brian and not tell anyone, not even Cashmere, about him. It was more special that way, and in the weird way that worlds collided, Eppie decided that the best way to keep all of her lies straight was to keep them secret from everyone.

## CHAPTER TWENTY-SEVEN

Cashmere's house, or more like it, mansion, was a tasteful Mediterranean that hugged the cliffs overlooking the Pacific. Though it was dark past the veranda, the ocean view out the huge glass windows was oddly familiar, similar to the one that Eppie had enjoyed with Beth that day they drank fraps and discussed Legend's future, only now with navy blue sweeping lines illuminated by moonlight. Eppie wasn't intimidated by the size of Cashmere's house though. She was used to big sprawling Colorado ranch homes, decorated differently, but this one had the same feeling. *There's nothing better than a spacious and well-mannered home,* mom used to say. Eppie sighed as she walked around the living room, admiring the fall seasonal decorations.

"This is beautiful," she said, looking up the grand spiraling staircase that sprung from the marble entryway.

"Thanks!" Cashmere limped in and tossed her bag on the sofa as if it didn't cost several thousand dollars. "Mom!"

Beth came to the top of the stairs, looking like the queen of the manor. She waved down to Eppie.

"Pauline!" She smiled. "So glad you could come stay with Cash tonight. How are you dear!" She was talking to Cashmere now. "Do you need an ice pack? We don't need a trip to Emergency, do we?"

"Nah." Cashmere was bent over slightly, her jods still smeared with dirt where she landed on the ground. Eppie had "surfer-girl changed" for dinner in the minivan, but Cashmere had no qualms about walking into a nice restaurant in horse attire complete with dusty boots.

"Well, let's get you into your room." Eppie expected Beth to sweep down the staircase and help Cashmere, but Cashmere turned to the driver of the minivan. "Thanks, Julianna," Cashmere said, and Julianna helped the hobbling Cashmere to a service elevator off the kitchen. Eppie followed uncertainly. Beth didn't even come downstairs.

They took the elevator up. Once upstairs Beth greeted them and took over Cashmere's care. She called out "Hendrick!" A man wearing a white sweat suit came out of a nearby room, which Eppie soon discovered was the gym. Hendrick helped Cashmere to the gym's massage table and without asking, pulled Cashmere's riding pants down to reveal a hot pink thong. He absently hooked the thong with his thumb and pulled it aside to examine Cashmere's tailbone. Eppie felt as if she should leave, but everyone else, including Julianna, was gathered around looking at Cashmere's butt, so it seemed ruder to leave than not.

"Oooh," Hendrick said. "Very tender." He gently probed the area until Cashmere winced, and then he rubbed a clear gel over the area that caused her the most pain and went to work on it, massaging deeply with his big thumbs. Cashmere was practically in tears but no one seemed to notice.

"Thank God it's not a break!" Beth was saying. "That could have held you up a year in training!"

"I thought I wasn't really training right now, Mother," Cashmere said. "You said I could just do small shows and have fun for a while. Earn some points."

"Well, that's true," Beth explained. "But if you had broken a bone, then you'd have no points at all, would you? And you'd be held back."

The two went on so Eppie slunk into a corner chair and picked up a fitness magazine and thumbed through it until the awkward massage was over with. Cashmere was limping less and standing taller as they went across the hallway to her bedroom.

"Jacuzzi, sauna, then facials," she said. "That's your bed." The room was large and mostly white; white carpet, comforters, huge fluffy pillows, and a lot of glass windows and mirrors. Two huge beds anchored each side of the room. All of the prints on the wall were professionally taken framed photographs of Cashmere; of her jumping Cesar, of her wearing a flowing white dress walking Cesar in the ocean, and one of her jumping high in the air in her cheer uniform. Eppie felt like she was visiting one of the Kardashians, and she liked the heady feeling of grandeur. She put her pathetic cotton zipper bag on the edge of the bed and looked around. Cashmere tossed her a bikini.

"Put this on, the guest robe in the pool house is yours, same with the slippers, towels, and the guest toiletries package." Cashmere said this all very matter-of-factly as they went back downstairs on the service elevator and out past the kitchen to the pool.

The backyard was maybe more impressive than the interior, with the infinity pool reflecting the lights of the Queen's Necklace, as the sparkling line of beach cities from Torrance to Malibu were called. A tiny corner of Los Angeles was visible toward the Hollywood Hills. "If those neighbors would cut their damn trees, we'd have a better view of the city." Cashmere pointed to two tall pine trees that hid the rest of the industrial lights. "But the ocean view is the point, right?" She pointed to the inky blue strip of Pacific to her left.

The girls climbed into the pool house Jacuzzi after they changed into their swimsuits and took off their makeup with supplies from the toiletry kit. Eppie could feel her day melting away. Steam covered her face and she put her head back and breathed in the chlorinated scent. Cashmere was quiet as well and they sat in relaxed silence until Cashmere broke the spell.

"I feel so much better," she said.

"I'm glad."

Cashmere climbed out of the steaming water and went to grab two flavored waters from the nearby fridge in the bar area. She reached into her towel bag on her way back and pulled out a bottle of clear liquid. Eppie scrunched her eyes to get a better look. It looked like alcohol.

"Don't judge," Cashmere said, handing her a pale orange drink. "I'm just taking a swig, it will help with my pain and I need to relax. Want one? It goes good with the other water as a chaser."

Eppie hesitated. She was curious, but thought of Jim. Should she? Would she get hooked, like he had? She watched Cashmere take a large gulp from the small vodka bottle and then quickly follow up with a sip of her flavored water. Eppie reached for the vodka. She followed suit after opening her own vitaminwater, and as the foul-tasting alcoholic liquid burned down her throat, her eyes watered. She wanted to spit it out but swallowed and quickly chugged a few more sips of the orangey "safe" water. She decided right then and there that drinking was not ever going to be her thing. She hated it.

Cashmere took two more shots of the vodka before hiding it under her nearby robe, sipping more water, and leaning up to look at the painted ceiling, a colorful classic cloud and star motif. She closed her eyes a moment as Eppie finished her orange drink. When she opened her eyes, she looked more relaxed and turned to Eppie.

"Want to go in the pool, or sauna?"

It was getting hot. "Pool!"

"Let's go."

The pool was warm too, but refreshing even in the cold November night. Eppie floated on her back and looked up at the stars and realized she was having a good time just experiencing this small taste of Cashmere's world. Having lived in foster homes and even in some really wretched state facilities, she could see how far she'd come since those dark dismal days after Grandma's stroke. She almost felt like her old self. Why not? She didn't have her mom, or really her grandma, but she had some family, distantly related as they were. She had friends, Maggie, LiLi to some extent, and now Cashmere. She had the beginnings of a boyfriend relationship, Brian, and she had Legend. A wave of hopefulness, an emotion she hadn't felt in a long time, for good things coming into her life swept over her. She realized that by holding onto the past, and all the bad things that had happened, she was missing the good even when it was right in front of her. She dipped her head under the water to wash away the tears of gratitude reborn on her face.

By the time the girls retired back to Cashmere's bedroom, they were ready to lounge. Eppie had never felt so clean. Hendrick had stayed and given them both massages, a first for Eppie, and while it felt a tad too intimate even with the bikini, but very relaxing. They had given themselves facials after the massage and a shower, and

Eppie felt like she glowed a thousand watts. Wearing the white cotton spa pajamas and the huge fluffy robe, she snuggled up on the bed that seemed to reach out for her.

"Wanna watch a movie in the media room? Or we can stay in here."

"In here," Eppie murmured.

"K." Eppie didn't even see what Cashmere did to make it happen, but a TV screen came down out of the ceiling. Cashmere crammed onto Eppie's bed with her and within moments a snack tray was brought up by the minivan driver, Julianna.

"Thanks so much Julianna," Cashmere said warmly, pronouncing the "J" as an "H".

"Who is she?" Eppie asked as she left the room.

"She's like . . . my mom," Cashmere said with a giggle. Eppie's eyes bugged out, making Cashmere laugh.

"No, not my real mom. But, you know, she's always been there. She picked me up at preschool, took me to all my summer camps, went to all my school activities, girl scouts, auditions for cheer, all of it. She drives me everywhere, cooks for me, takes care of me when I'm sick. She's my mom."

"What about Beth? Your real mom?"

"She pays for it all," Cashmere said with a shrug. "She's not really the mothering type. She's more like . . . my manager. But I love her, don't get me wrong. I love them both."

A pang hit Eppie. Here Cashmere had two moms, and she had none. *Don't forget about Tracey,* a small voice in her head told her. *She's like Julianna and Cashmere to me. She tries.* Eppie sighed.

"What are we watching?" Eppie asked, pulling the comforter over her.

"How about a Twilight movie?"

"Perfect."

The girls shared the bed and fell asleep watching Bella and Edward hold one another in a dangerous embrace.

## CHAPTER TWENTY-EIGHT

It was hard going back to Tracey and Rich's cramped little Lomita house the next morning but the stay with Cashmere improved their friendship, and the girls and their horses became inseparable at the barn. The entire Dursom family was invited to the Krause mansion for Thanksgiving dinner, and a somewhat harried Tracey accepted. Even Charles Krause, Cashmere's dad, showed up and Eppie got to meet him for the first time. The sit down formal affair was catered and delicious, with not a dish to be washed by any participant.

"It barely feels like Thanksgiving," Tracey said as they drove home, but they had huge platters of leftovers stacked up in the back of the minivan so that the next day, it felt like Thanksgiving again.

Now Christmas was looming, and occasional rains had soaked the dry dusty stable paths and the evening air was colder. Cesar's cut had healed and the horses were hyper in the chilly weather, and until Cashmere's backbone was completely healed, Eppie worked double hard keeping both Legend and Cesar happy.

One evening Eppie was lying on her bed studying for an algebra test when a knock sounded at her bedroom door, prying Lacey Bell from a deep sleep at her ankles.

"Come in," Eppie said, expecting Tracey, but it was Jim who entered. Lacey Bell hissed and dove under the bed.

"What do you want?" Eppie asked coldly.

"I just wanted to let you know Maggie called the house phone, I told her you were asleep," Jim said in his eely voice.

"I didn't hear the phone!"

"I was on the other line, it didn't ring."

"Are you done with the phone?"

"Yes."

"Okay, you can go now." Eppie picked up the cell beside her in her room to call Maggie, who had become much more of a "school only" friend since Eppie bought Legend and started hanging out with Cashmere. She glanced at it; three missed calls from Maggie and a text that read: CALL ME. She had forgotten to turn off her 'Do Not Disturb' mode she'd set to do her homework. As she reset her phone, she glanced up at Jim, who lingered in the doorway.

"What?" Eppie glared at him, challenging him to have a good reason to be in her room.

"I just . . . wish . . ."

Eppie's glare didn't soften.

"Never mind."

Jim left, and Eppie sighed. For the millionth time she wished he hadn't ruined everything. She dialed Maggie's number, looking at the 8 x 10 photos of Legend and Cesar on her wall. Taking a cue from Cashmere, Eppie and Tracey had printed them out and framed them. They made Eppie happy, especially the one of Legend running in the turnout, his tail straight up, his hooves captured in a mid-air gallop.

"Hello?"

"Hi Maggie, it's Pauline."

"Oh hey! Glad you got back to me, you won't believe it! I got invited to Lexel's dance party! And she said you could come too!"

"Wait, Lexel's annual thing that she has? Wow!" Lexel was renowned for her huge holiday party that she had each year in an airport hangar at the Torrance Airport. It was decorated all out, with special effects lighting and DJs. Everyone talked about it all year.

"That's the one! Can you believe it? I've been hearing about this party since 6th grade, and now we're finally in!"

"Are you sure we're both invited?" Eppie bit her lip. Lexel wasn't mean to her anymore, but Eppie wasn't friends with her like LiLi, and now Maggie, were.

"Of course. She honors you now, you know what I mean, you stood up to her, and you listened to her. She's totally cool with you."

"When is it?"

"It's a Christmas party, so it's during winter break. Friday night. I just had to tell you now!" Maggie's voice rose up in excitement.

The two talked on about the party, about what clothes they'd have to buy, and how they should rent a limo to get there, and should they do something crazy with their hair? Soon Eppie was mumbling, she was so sleepy, and she said goodnight to Maggie. She fell asleep thinking of Lexel's party, and wondering if Brian would go with her.

Eppie woke up being kissed, and in her sleep she thought it was Brian and for a while she kissed back, until the strong alcohol breath and forcefulness startled her awake. She felt a heavy body covering her. Someone was in her bed! She started to scream but a strong hand clamped over her mouth and then her pillow smothered her, forcing her scream back in. Someone was trying to kill her! Adrenaline racing, she cried as she fought hard with her fists until the pillow vanished. She gasped for breath.

"Stop!" she puffed, realizing with renewed fear that it was Jim who was on her, in her bed. Anger replaced fear and she kicked and clawed at him. "Get out!" she screamed, tears ripping down her cheeks. "Get the hell out of here! Oh my God, get out!"

The overhead light snapped on, and pandemonium broke out in the room as Tracey and Rich entered. They froze, staring, and Jim clambered off of Eppie, and she could see them clutching each other trying to take in what was going on.

"Oh my God! Jim!" Rich grabbed Jim by his bare shoulders and hauled him the rest of the way off of Eppie's bed. Eppie curled up and hugged herself and cried hard, and was vaguely aware of Rich manhandling Jim, who was only wearing boxer shorts, out of the room. Tracey sat next to Eppie and touched her arm, and Eppie pulled in to herself tighter and shut her eyes, wishing that everyone would just go away.

"Pauline . . ." Tracey's voice was shaky. Eppie kept her eyes squeezed tight.

"Pauline, are you okay? Look at me. What happened here?"

Eppie still wouldn't look or answer. Her head was spinning. Jim had attacked her while she was sleeping! Why? He had smelled like alcohol . . . drinking again. What would have happened if Rich and Tracey hadn't heard her yell? Eppie cried harder. She didn't want to think about it. Eppie shut down, Rich yelled at Jim in the living room, Tracey patted Eppie's arm, but she never looked up. She didn't want to see the look she knew must be in Tracey's eyes.

By morning, Jim had been driven back to the rehab center. Feeling safer, Eppie sat freshly showered in her clean pajamas and robe on the living room couch, sipping a cup of mint tea with shaky hands, a blanket over her middle. She had tried to sleep but couldn't. Lonny was at school, aware something was up but not sure what. Tracey and Rich sat on the sofa across from Eppie.

"Jim has problems," Rich said. "But it's no excuse. He was in the foster system a long time, his mom abandoned him, his dad is in jail and gave him up . . . he had to be the adult in the family when he was just a kid and he was the one who took care of Lonny. But now . . ." Rich's voice trailed off as he rubbed his face in his hands. Tracey tried to hide muffled sobs.

"We will take care of this," Tracey said in a quiet voice. "There's an option . . . to press charges against Jim . . ."

"No." Eppie shook her head. "No. I just want to forget this ever happened. Can't we just do that? Jim's gone now, can we just move on? Pretend it never happened?"

"It's not that simple," Tracey said. "He's been through so much. Our family was monitored closely throughout the adoption process, Jim was in counseling twice a week and we almost were unable to get both him and Lonny because he had a tendency to fight, but, we've come so far. This is a huge setback. The next problem is, now he's our son. Our responsibility. Where will he go from here? Rehab is only for thirty days. We have to discuss our options for when he comes home."

Eppie couldn't believe her ears. *Comes home?* He'd already been through the rehab program once and was drinking again! He was going to daily meetings, and he was still drinking! He now was coming after her. *He was coming home?* Tears spilled toward Eppie's teacup. She got it. Tracey and Rich were her guardians, not her parents. Jim was their son. Adopted or not, they were really family. She was a floater, someone who was just sort of there with them because Tracey and Rich had kind hearts. But who was she really? She and Tracey shared the same DNA, a grandfather, but none of the memories, none of the family experiences. Now they shared an old woman in a nursing home, Eppie's grandmother, Tracey's stepgrandmother whom she'd never even knew before she had a stroke, and that was the end of their connection. Eppie pushed her face against her bent legs, resting her eyes on her knees.

"Where do you want me to go?" Eppie finally asked.

"Go?" Tracey looked sharply at Rich. "We don't want you to go anywhere, Pauline! You're part of our family. We just have to set up the boundaries for Jim, and we have to make sure you're safe."

Eppie straightened her long legs. "How can you keep me safe from him?" she asked. "How? He has some hang-up with me, isn't it obvious? He's been lurking around me for months, threatening to tell on me when he thinks I'm not behaving, making me keep secrets for him . . . how can you protect me? He's like a stalker!" Eppie's voice drew into a wail and she put her hands over her mouth to stop herself from screaming out.

Tracey cried anew and Rich took a breath. "We didn't know that, Pauline. You should have come to us."

"He's your son! How could I?"

"We're your family too!"

"It's not the same thing."

"To us, it is."

Eppie tried to control her frenzied mind. "Look . . . he's not coming back for a month, right?"

"Yes."

"Can we not decide everything at once? Can I just go back to bed, please? I just need some sleep. This is all too crazy. I don't know what to do."

Tracey stood up and pulled Eppie to her feet and gave her a hug. "I'm so sorry," she said, handing her the falling blanket. "Go get some rest. We'll talk later."

Eppie sobbed on Tracey's shoulder. Rich kissed her on the cheek and she went back into her bedroom, scooping up Lacey Bell in the hallway as she passed the cat, who was cleaning herself and looked offended. She went into her room and saw the covers on the ground. The room stank like Jim; a heavy, sweaty, alcohol smell. Even though the weather was cold and crisp out, she flung open the windows and sprayed her ginger mist all over the sheets and covers. She shook out the pillows and carefully remade her bed. In a few minutes she couldn't smell Jim anymore, just the outside breeze and the scent of Hawaii. She grabbed Lacey Bell and drew her under the covers with her, and within minutes she fell into a restless sleep.

# Chapter Twenty-nine

While Eppie waited for there to be a lot of dialog and heartfelt conversation about what had happened over the next few days, none came. Rich was working double shifts and Tracey gave Eppie apologetic pats on the shoulder, but it seemed as if no one knew what to say to her. Eppie was disconcerted; on one hand she didn't want to mention what Jim had done ever again, but in another way, she wished they could just hash it out and be done with it. Eppie buried herself in her schoolwork and reading Professor Berry's book at home, and stayed as long as possible with the horses, her only true solace in the world.

Beth approached her as she turned out Legend a week after the Jim Incident, as Eppie now called it. She watched Legend's powerful muscles gather as he galloped around the ring. Eppie walked fearlessly to the center and held up her hand; Legend trotted toward her, nostrils flaring, tail up. As he approached she stroked him, proud of him. He nuzzled her fingers with his soft whiskers. Beth strode into the ring and stood beside them both, patting Legend's sleek neck.

"He's a beauty, no doubt. Excellent conformation. Make a wonderful dressage horse if you ask me."

"That's why my mom bred Warlanders," Eppie said. "She loved the look of them. She thought they were the most beautiful of all breeds."

"They are lovely." Beth seemed preoccupied as Eppie pressed her face into Legend's neck and breathed in his hay and dirt scent. He leaned slightly against her in an affectionate way as she slipped his halter over his head.

"You'll be putting him under saddle soon. How's he coming along?"

"Great! Well, good. I'm still having a few issues with grooming. You know, he won't always stand for a hoof picking on the back legs, and he jumps aside sometimes when I go to put a bareback pad on him. I'm trying to get him used to tacking up."

"He'll get there. He's smart."

"I hope so."

They stood in silence admiring Legend, but Eppie felt uncomfortable for some reason. Beth cleared her throat and said quietly, "I know what happened to you, Pauline."

"Wha . . . what?"

"With your family. With Jim. Tracey told me."

Eppie's cheeks flamed hot and her mouth clamped shut. Tears formed without her permission and rolled down her face. She wiped them on Legend's neck before Beth could see.

"I just want you to know I'm here for you. Not just, 'I'm here for you' in a generic way, Pauline. But if you need a place to live, a family to take you in . . . that could be us. You are an excellent influence on Cashmere, and she already loves you like a sister. And you and I . . . our desires in life are similar."

Eppie sobbed silently, wishing she could cover her ears. She didn't want to hear it! But Beth wouldn't shut up.

"We could really be a family together, and Charles, he's gone a lot, always traveling, but he has agreed that if you need us, Pauline, we are there for you. Just so you know. You have some hard decisions to make. I don't feel you are safe staying where you are now." Beth reached out and grabbed onto Legend's long mane, a rarity at the stables where most of the manes were pulled short. She absently wrapped the white, iron gray, and black strands around her manicured fingers. "I can't even imagine what you must be experiencing right now. But I want you to promise me that you won't hesitate to let me know. Promise me, that if you need me, you'll tell me."

Eppie felt lightheaded and pushed down in her boots to root herself to the spot. What did Beth think happened anyway?

"He didn't do anything," Eppie said quickly, wiping her face with the back of her wrist. "Nothing really happened."

"I know that," Beth replied. "But he violated your space, and your sense of safety in your own home. That's enough."

Somehow when she said it like that, it finally seemed like too much. Like too much had happened for it to ever be the same there again. Tears came out again and this time Eppie didn't try to hide them. Beth pulled her close to her and Eppie cried, really cried, in someone's arms, something she hadn't done since before her mother had died. It didn't matter that she was in a public place, in the turnout ring at the stables. Everything came out of her in racking sobs, but she felt safe in Beth's arms. She pulled away finally, spent, glad Beth was there to hold her up. She could not have stood on her own.

"I'm . . . I'm sorry," she sniffed, wiping her nose on her sleeve.

"Sorry? Oh honey," Beth said, tearing up herself. "You have nothing to apologize for! Nothing! Now, do you promise? You'll think about it and tell me when you need me? You will, won't you?"

Eppie nodded, looking up into Beth's eyes, surprised at herself for letting go like that. But she wasn't embarrassed. She nodded. "I promise," she said. "I'll let you know."

School was getting unbearable: Christmas decorations hung everywhere, people caroling in the hallways as they practiced for the local holiday parade appearance, Santa hats in abundance, and yet here they still were, a week out from winter break. After a long day Eppie got cleaned up and wore her pajamas and robe waiting for dinner, her hair wet from her shower. She'd worked again with Legend and still couldn't figure out the hoof problem she was having with him, and Cesar had refused two jumps for Cashmere and had almost knocked her off again. Eppie felt frustrated when even her barn time didn't go well, and she just wanted to relax and forget the whole day. During these dark winter months she was home by 5:30 and got her homework done early so she could study Dr. Beery's books. The old-timey style of writing comforted her in a weird way, and Eppie enjoyed reading the techniques Dr. Beery used in his day. She read Lesson 5:

*BAD TO SHOE*
*The reason there are so many horses bad to shoe is because of carelessness and neglect in the proper handling of them when young. Many people think that if they take their colt to the blacksmith and have it shod, it would assist them in training it, and it is a very common thing for the farmer to say to his son: "John, take the colt down to the shop and have him shod. We want to break him next week anyway: and it will make him gentle to have the blacksmith shoe him."*
*In the first place the colt's feet should be handled before it ever goes into the blacksmith shop. It is an easy and simple matter to handle the colt's feet after he has been poled and taught the lessons given in Book No. 1.*

Eppie closed the notebook carefully, and put her head on the pillow. She was handling Legend's feet all the time, so why did he always try to step down when she picked up his back foot? He didn't wear horseshoes, so why was he so twitchy about it? It dawned on her that maybe she should start holding his foot for other reasons, not just picking the dirt out. Maybe she could invent another game they could play, where she could tap his hoof and he could lift it, and if he lifted it she would give him a peppermint, his favorite treat. Then he wouldn't know when she tapped his hooves if she was going to clean them or just give him a peppermint, and he'd soon get used to her touching his hind hooves and she'd be able to pick them easily. She was devising this new training plan when a knock came at the door. Lonny walked in, and he had been crying.

"What's wrong?" Eppie reached out, expecting Lonny to crawl up on her bed like he usually did when he had a problem or was hurt. But today the towhead was gritting his teeth, and he gnashed at her.

"You did this! You're the reason Jimmy went away!"

Eppie sat up, not ready for this confrontation. "Lonny, what are you talking about? I didn't send him away."

"But it's because you live here that he left! You're the problem! Things were fine before you got here!"

Eppie flushed, and tears edged her eyes. Pain clogged up her neck. "Why are you saying that Lonny? It's not true!"

"It is true! Jim had to leave here because of you! It's your fault he's gone! Yours!"

Lonny ran out of the room and slammed the door, and within a fraction of a moment Tracey opened it again and motioned for Eppie to wait for her to return as she ran down the hall after Lonny, who had apparently sprinted to his room, crying. Eppie fumed as her tears leaked out. Again. Lonny had never turned on her before! She couldn't believe what she'd just heard. Furious, she stormed down the hall.

"What the hell is he saying that for?" Eppie said as she walked into the room Lonny and Jim usually shared. "Why is he saying it's my fault that Jim left? What did you say to him?"

Tracey looked upset, her own eyes red and water rimmed. "He was asking why Jim left, the real reason, and I was trying to explain it and it came out all wrong . . ."

"It's not wrong, it's what you really think, isn't it, Tracey? That your life was a lot simpler before I came here?" The knot in Eppie's throat loosened as she yelled. "That I'm really the problem, not Jim?"

"It's not like that!" Tracey said, shrugging. "That's not what I was trying to say!" Lonny was sitting on the window bench with his face buried in his knees, crying. "Pauline, please! I'm trying to talk to Lonny, can we please do this one at a time? He needs me right now! I can't have two of you kids freaking out at once!"

"No problem," Eppie said hotly. "I'll be in my room." She left with a slam of the door. Once back in her room, a pit in her stomach, she picked up the phone from her desk and dialed Cashmere's home phone number.

Later that evening Eppie was cried out in the guest room down the hall from Cashmere's. Her bags were strewn across the large room, decorated in beige and burgundy organza and silks. *My new home*, she thought glumly, trying to put the last couple of hours behind her so she could get some sleep. At least Cashmere's room was user-friendly and familiar; this room didn't want tears, she noticed, as large water drops stained the satin finish of the bedspread. Wiping her eyes for the millionth time, Eppie crawled under the covers. She was still in her pajamas and hadn't even changed when Beth had personally driven over to pick her up from Tracey and Rich's house. Rich had come home and the adults had a quick and quiet exchange in the driveway before Beth drove her back to her Palos Verdes mansion. Cashmere wasn't home from wherever she was and didn't even know she had a new "sister" living down the hall yet.

"Can I get you anything?" came a voice from the other side of the door. Eppie walked over and opened the door to see Beth standing there, surprised that it was Beth herself checking up on her.

"I don't need anything, thanks."

"May I come in?"

Eppie nodded, and opened the door wider. Beth walked in and sat primly on the edge of the bed, not seeming to notice the water spots on the comforter.

"Are you okay?"

Eppie sat still next to Beth on the bed, not knowing what to say. Was she okay? No, she wasn't okay. Her home had just been ripped out from under her, and she was staying in an unfamiliar place, again. Shades of the past shadowed her thoughts, as memories of those first horrid months in the foster care system rose up and took over her mind. This was just another stopping ground, wasn't it? Just another place to sleep until someone could figure out where she really belonged. She shook her head and squeezed her eyes tight. "I don't really know what's happening with my life right now," Eppie finally muttered.

"I know sweetie. But we're just giving Tracey and Rich a break, so they can deal with Lonny and Jim. Lonny's young, he's angry. He's had a lot taken from him in his life."

"So have I," Eppie said tightly.

Beth slid her arm around Eppie's shoulder. "I know Pauline, dear. I know." Beth looked around the room with its heavy drapes and expensive Persian rug. "Since you'll be here awhile, how about we redecorate this room for you? You know, make it a fun little project."

"It doesn't matter," Eppie said, wishing she could be more enthusiastic about it. "I don't even know how long I'll be here."

"You're out of school this Friday for winter break, so I told Tracey and Rich you could stay here with us until school starts again after Christmas. We'll all reassess your situation once Jim is out of rehab. Did Cashmere tell you? We're going to Vail . . ."

"Colorado?"

"Yes, and you'll come too. Just a little ski and snow weekend, it will be fun."

Eppie's spirits lifted. She was going to Colorado! Not her home town, but at least she could return to her home state.

"Okay."

"I'm glad you remembered our chat, Pauline. I'm glad you called me when you needed me."

Eppie didn't know what to say again. Who else would she call? Her grandma was in a care home, Lonny hated her now, Jim tried to molest her, and her mother was dead, and her dad: Unknown. She'd been shuffled from place to place since Grandma's stroke, and so what if Tracey and Rich had seemed like her saviors? They weren't. They couldn't protect her anymore. So who else would she call? Brian? He was just her current male obsession and occasional kissing boyfriend. She had no one.

"Try to get some rest. I'll tell Cashmere you're here but that you're asleep when she comes in. We'll talk more in the morning."

Eppie nodded. "Thank you," she whispered in a gravelly voice.

"We'll get you through this," Beth said as she walked out the door, leaving Eppie in the guest room, uncertain and alone.

## CHAPTER THIRTY

When Eppie opened her eyes the next morning it took her a moment to remember where she was. She blinked in the dim light at the shiny comforter and gold-toned walls. *Cashmere's*, she reminded herself. *This is my new room. For now.*

She threw the covers back over her head and nestled down in the safety of darkness, squeezing her eyes tight. It reminded her too much of the morning she woke up after Mom was killed, because for a brief moment that day, when she first opened her eyes, she didn't remember that her life had changed forever. She had one second where it was just another normal day in her comfortable house, where Mom was surely in the kitchen downing another cup of coffee and arguing with Nick, the ranch hand who always had opinions about how things should be run. But Mom wasn't in the kitchen that morning, she wasn't anywhere on the planet but cold and dead in a hospital morgue awaiting transport to the mortuary. And Grandma was with her daughter's body that morning, and Eppie was in the house with Nick, who was sitting in the sunny kitchen twisting his hat in his hands, not knowing what to say. This was that all over again but this time no one had died. Eppie was just homeless again, waking up in another strange place she had no choice but to call home.

Down the hall she heard an alarm clock and wondered if she had to still go to school. Was she even going to return to Narbonne Middle School? Would she still be here after the winter break? Her life had become a big question mark. She used to worry and worry about these types of things when this happened, but she'd learned that it didn't change anything. She had no say so. It was up to the Adult of the Day to make the decisions, and she just had to wait to hear what that decision was. She slipped from the warm bed and padded to the adjacent gold and black marble bathroom. *A step up at least*, she thought wryly as her stomach knotted at the fact that everything was up in the air again. *Now at least I'm living in a mansion.* Still her heart ached for her little room in Rich and Tracey's house, where her walls were covered in pictures of Legend and Cesar, and where she'd finally felt at home.

She arrived downstairs dressed and ready to go to her school, just in case. Julianna was the only one there, and she had set the table for four people and had laid out platters of toast, fruit, eggs, and sausages, the trays on heated warmers like in restaurants.

"Good morning," Julianna said in her lilting accent. "You sleep well?"

Eppie nodded, unsure of what to do.

"You eat! You must be hungry. Go on, get the plate, eat, eat!"

Eppie didn't argue and grabbed a heavy dish, warmed like the food. She put some toast and sausage on her plate and poured herself some orange juice from the pitcher. She was poking at her food, not all that hungry after all, when Cashmere walked in.

"Bon jour Julianna!" Cashmere said in a sing-song voice.

"Why you take French, not Spanish? Then you talk to me instead."

"But I'm hoping to move to France someday, that's why." Cashmere looked at Eppie and her expression changed to concern. "How are you? Oh my God, my mother told me you were staying here now! I'm so sorry things are rotten for you right now, but I'm glad you're here!"

Eppie was relieved to see Cashmere. "Thanks for letting me stay."

"Are you kidding? I've always wanted a sister, now it's like I've got one!" Cashmere filled her plate and joined Eppie at the table.

"Should we wait for your mom and dad?" Eppie asked, in mid-bite.

"Oh, Daddy's eaten. See the toast crumbs? He leaves the house at like five, and Mother isn't up yet, probably she'll eat around nine or ten."

"Oh," Eppie said, stuffing the bite of sausage into her mouth. Even though the food smelled appetizing, her throat was tight and it was hard to chew and swallow. She felt like crying but held it in.

"In the car in fifteen minutes," Julianna said. "I take you to school, Pauline. After Cashmere."

Cashmere's school was up on a hill surrounded by a wooded thicket of trees. The pupils wore preppy gray and blue uniforms and everyone looked polished, like professional students, if there was such a thing. Eppie was impressed but kept her thoughts to herself; Cashmere had been going on a tirade about her boyfriend Bo, who according to the latest text was seen at a party over the past weekend flirting with some Townie, which is apparently what girls who didn't live in Palos Verdes were called. Eppie barely listened as she tried to fathom how she'd gotten herself bumped out of Rich and Tracey's house. Tracey should be taking her to school right now! She hadn't done anything wrong! Jim was the problem, not her! It wasn't fair.

By the time Julianna dropped off Eppie, the first bell had already rung so Eppie dashed for class. She didn't get a chance to talk to anyone until lunch. She found Maggie and LiLi in line in the cafeteria. Julianna had packed her a lunch, thank God, because Eppie had forgotten to bring her money from her bedroom's secret stash place under the daybed mattress.

"Hey," Maggie said, and Eppie was so glad that there was something as normal as meeting up with Maggie at lunch that she considered not telling her about what was happening.

"Hey," Eppie said. She looked at the table where LiLi's other friends sat with Lexel; the table's bench was overflowing with people. "Where are we sitting?"

"The usual, Lexel will ditch those dweeb hanger-ons and make some room, watch."

Eppie was painfully aware that just a few short weeks ago she and Maggie *were* the dweeb hanger-ons, but she didn't say anything and just watched as sure enough, a space for the three of them emerged at the coveted Lexel table.

"We are discussing party tactics," Lexel filled them in. "As in, how are we all dressing for my party? Because this is one bash you don't want to be caught in last year's dress in, if you know what I mean."

"I didn't even own a dress last year," Eppie whispered to Maggie, who giggled.

"When are we shopping?" Maggie whispered back.

Eppie shrugged. Would she even get to go to Lexel's party? She tried to remember everything that was going on. Colorado. She would be in Colorado during the time of the party.

"I don't think I can go," Eppie told her..

"What? Why?" Maggie turned to her, eyes flashing. "My mom can get Tracey to give in."

"No, it's complicated . . ."

"Am I boring you?" Lexel interrupted. "Cuz if so, you can just move on over to the Loser Table if you want to."

Eppie looked up and saw Lexel staring at her, arms crossed in front of her.

"No, sorry," Eppie said casually, not even caring any more about any of it. Nothing mattered. Not Lexel's party, not Colorado. These weren't parts of her life.

"Pauline was saying her mom won't let her go," Maggie said apologetically.

"She's definitely not my mother," Eppie huffed.

"Well your foster mom or guardian or whatever. I can make it happen, my mom will talk to her and . . ." Maggie continued.

"I'll be out of town," Eppie announced. "I'm going skiing in Colorado that week, so I won't be around. But I hope you all have fun."

Maggie gave her a questioning look. Maggie knew that the Dursoms couldn't afford a fancy ski vacation, especially during the holidays.

"In fact," Eppie said, realizing as she said it she knew it was true, "I'm probably not coming back here. I'm moving to Palos Verdes and I'll probably go to school there after winter break, because I got kicked out of the place I'm living and it doesn't look like they want me to come home again."

As she heard the word "home" come out of her mouth, Eppie got up and stormed away. Home! As if she had one! There was no place for her anywhere. She went to the library to hide but forgot it was locked during lunch. She sat down in front of the big blue metal door and was surprised no tears fell. She was just mad, not sad. Pissed off.

"Pauline!" Maggie ran to her, alone. LiLi must have stayed behind to talk about her, no doubt.

"I'm sorry," Eppie said. "I didn't want to tell you like that. It's been a really crappy 24 hours."

"How could they kick you out?"

"It's not like that, it's just . . . they're picking Jim over me. He's coming home soon, but everyone knows that they can't keep me safe from him. Jim's become really weird and lecherous. But he's got his brother Lonny there, so they're keeping him, not me. Lonny doesn't want me anyway. He thinks it's my fault Jim left."

"Lonny loves you! You're like, his favorite person!"

"Not anymore."

Maggie sat slowly beside Eppie, and the look on her face said it all. She was dumbfounded.

"Can't you . . ."

Eppie waited but Maggie had no more words. *Useless,* Eppie thought. Sure, the Dursoms could say, come back Eppie, we love you, we want you to stay. But the bottom line was that Jim would always be first for them. Blood or no, Jim was their son. Lonny was their son. Eppie was just a happenstance bloodline based on old relationships that didn't matter to anyone living anymore.

"I'm really going to miss you," Maggie said, her eyes full of tears. "I'm so shocked."

"I know. I'm having a hard time with it all too. But guess what? We can at least text and stay in touch and stuff. You can come visit me and we can still hang out on weekends."

It sounded good but Eppie knew, she didn't go anywhere but the barn. Barn and school. It was ages ago that she and Maggie and Tracey shopped for clothes on a Saturday afternoon, like it was someone else's life. Maggie sat quietly next to Eppie and their jeaned knees leaned against one another. Maggie wiped her tears when the bell rang.

"Are you going to be here until Friday?"

"Yes," Eppie said, standing and giving Maggie a big hug. "I think so. And I have to get my stuff and move out, all of that. Awkward stuff."

"Yeah. Well, I have practice after school, so I won't see you until tomorrow. But at least we have this week."

"Yeah, at least."

It turned out to be Eppie's last day at Narbonne Middle School. By the time she got back to the Krause's mansion after school, her belongings from the Dursom's house had been moved into her new room and organized for her. Even her envelope of cash from under the mattress was in her new desk drawer, all bills accounted for. Her horse pictures were on the wall, and gone were the heavy gold and maroon curtains and bed linens. Her room was redecorated in a simple and elegant fashion, with white embroidered airy linens and fairy-like Anthropologie window dressings, the same ones she'd seen when she'd gone shopping with Tracey. The silk lamps were replaced with colorful funky chandeliers, and new cool Ikea-type furniture had been brought in. Eppie felt a little like she was in a dream, it was all so surreal. But beautiful. Her new room was lovely.

Later Beth came in and put her arm around Eppie. "Since we didn't have time to decorate before the holidays I thought I'd just do enough to get you started. You can do anything you want to this room later."

"It's beautiful," Eppie said. "Thank you!"

"It's a hobby of mine," Beth beamed, obviously proud. "I love to decorate, but there's only so much you can do in your own house. I was so glad to do it!"

"It feels like my own room now," Eppie said.

"Well, that was what I was thinking of while I was shopping for stuff. What would Pauline want? And like I said, we can change it anytime. It's just a starter room."

"I love it just how it is."

"Great! Too bad you won't be seeing it for a few days then," Beth said.

"What do you mean?"

"Oh, you didn't hear? Change of plans. Get packed, we're going to Colorado tomorrow! Then when we get home, you'll have some time off to ride before you start school with Cashmere in January."

Beth left the room with a smile, and Eppie could do nothing more than stare helplessly after her.

# ≈Chapter Thirty-one≈

Flying over Colorado, Eppie pressed her face against the glass while Cashmere listened to songs on her iPhone and zoned out. The Rockies beneath her were jagged, snowy mounds. Bits of green poked through reminding her of the town she'd grown up in, the outskirts of Evergreen. She wished fervently that they were going there instead of Vail, but she knew that strangers lived in her home now, and part of what had made it home was being there with her mother. Returning now made her think of people she'd long ago forgotten in the upheaval of her life, like her best friend in Elementary School, Rachel, and her neighbors the Meskers, who also owned horses. They had three kids and most summer nights were spent at either their ranch or Eppie's, barbecuing, swimming, hanging out, or more frequently, riding on the trails until the last vestiges of sunset would cause them to hurry back to the barn. Eppie remembered many fun days with them, what were their names? The oldest girl, Holly, the middle one, Alana, and little Joo Joo, aka Jonathan. As her breath fogged the airplane window her memories fogged up too, as she tried to recall the faces of people who were strangers to her now.

Her suite was adjacent to Cashmere's at the Vail resort, which was a combination of woodsy and luxury, with a wood-burning fireplace that was lit when they arrived, but a huge spa bathtub with all the modern amenities made the difference. Eppie was a little awe struck; it was the nicest place she'd ever stayed, and she briefly wondered how Beth had managed to pull off the second suite on such short notice during the holidays, but nothing about Beth surprised her anymore. She was the most capable woman Eppie knew.

Eppie opened the glass slider that led to a balcony and breathed in the cold Colorado air. Being here made her lungs feel less full due to the altitude, but she felt at home now, high up in the mountains. She heard a knock and looked around. Cashmere was tapping on the door that connected their suites. Eppie opened it.

"Can we just leave this open?" Cashmere asked, walking in. "Then it's like we are sharing a cute little house!"

"Sure," Eppie said. She watched as Cashmere flopped on the couch in front of the fireplace.

"Damn, it's cold here. Once I warm up we can go downstairs and go shopping, there's like a million little boutiques around here."

"I didn't bring much money," Eppie admitted with a shrug. Cashmere stared at her.

"Duh! I have Daddy's credit card, no worries."

By noon the girls were sipping hot apple cider adorned with cinnamon sticks and whipped cream by a roaring fire in a small café. Eppie felt a guilty lump in her throat about how much she guessed Cashmere had spent on her; not that Cashmere ever even looked at a price tag. The word *thousands* kept entering Eppie's mind; she remembered how much horse poop she had shoveled to earn the money she'd spent on Legend, and thinking that her new wardrobe may be the equivalent price of her horse made her feel a bit ill.

"That was fun, we really found some darling things for you. I just love shopping here, it's so . . . Americana, you know? Not at all So Cal," Cashmere was saying.

"Yeah," Eppie said, guilt washing over her further. "Thanks."

"Don't be silly, my mom insisted that we get you some new clothes."

Cashmere looked over at a table of cute boys and waved while Eppie digested this information. Beth again, watching out for Eppie. She'd arranged the whole thing.

"Well, it's getting late, let's go back and get you into some of your ski stuff and we can hit the slopes, K?"

Eppie nodded and the girls returned to the hotel, where their packages were awaiting them in Cashmere's suite. Beth had also arranged for a Christmas tree to be delivered and decorated in each girl's living room, so the place smelled like pine when they stepped inside and the ornaments glittered in the light that filtered through the windows. The ornaments gleamed with the promise of gifts to come, and Eppie was floored. How did Beth manage it? Cashmere barely noticed the trees, but Eppie spent quite a bit of time looking at the gold glittery orbs until Cashmere pulled Eppie away and made her start going through the bags of clothes they'd bought. On top of an entirely new winter wardrobe, Cashmere had also bought Eppie an entire ski wardrobe as well, a down jacket and skis included. Eppie hadn't skied in years and hoped she'd live up to the clothes.

Once on the slopes in her new baby-pink skiing outfit, however, it all came back to her, and she forgot everything as she soared over the snow. She was laughing by the time she and Cashmere landed at the bottom of the slopes, skiing up to the lodge together, winded.

"Wow! You're great!" Cashmere commented.

"I'm from here, remember?" Eppie grinned. This was the best she'd felt in a long time.

"Well, it shows. How long has it been since you've skied?"

"Over five years," Eppie told her, trying to recall her last skiing day trip with Mom. Where had they gone that last time? She couldn't remember.

"You haven't lost your touch, that's for sure."

The sky was darkening to a deep blue as orange light burnished the west. "Want to ski some more or maybe go find a club or something?"

Eppie's toes were frozen, even in her new cozy ski socks and boots. "Club?"

On they went, and to Eppie it was the most freedom she'd had in ages, maybe ever. Beth and Charles were there, dining, shopping at antiques stores, and Beth spent an inordinate amount of time in the hotel spas. But it was like there were no parents, just patrons with unlimited credit cards who didn't care what the girls did. Vail became a home away from home, with each morning spent at the spa, afternoons on the slopes, nights drinking mocktails at the nearby "kiddie clubs" as Charles called them, and even more shopping spent in between. Christmas morning arrived quickly and Eppie was glad she'd spent her own money carefully, finding little sentimental gifts for Charles, Cashmere and Beth. They opened presents after a delicious breakfast was served in Beth and Charles' suite, which was bigger than the girls' and had a large extra room with their holiday tree in it. Beth pulled Eppie aside.

"I have a surprise for you," she said. Eppie fingered the new necklace she wore from Beth, a gold horseshoe with diamonds.

"You've done so much already," Eppie said.

"I want to take you somewhere. Let's go, Cashmere is napping anyway."

Cashmere was curled up asleep on the sofa with a throw pulled over her, wearing her new Ralph Lauren slippers and robe set.

Eppie joined Beth in their rental SUV and Beth headed back toward the Denver airport along the 70. The mountain passes were cleared by early morning snowplows and the sun was shining, the bright day sparkling on crystal snow. Soon everything seemed familiar; Eppie recognized a little eatery with a wood carving of a bear in front, and a ranch with gray fuzzy llamas standing in white fields. She saw a sign for Silverthorne and her heart leapt; they were nearing her old home town of Evergreen.

"Where are we going?" she asked.

"Just up here a ways, you'll see."

Eppie hoped that Beth would keep driving to Evergreen but she slowed just outside of Silverthorne and went up a long plowed road. Soon two huge gates ended the road, and Eppie realized it was actually a driveway. Beth pressed the button on the call box.

"Yes?" Came a tinny voice.

"It's Beth Krause, with Pauline Wills," Beth said loudly.

"Come in." The gate creaked open, shuddering on its cold springs. Beth pulled up into a snowy wonderland as the SUV climbed the tree-lined hill toward a large house.

The house, however, was a barn. It was bigger than any Eppie had ever seen. She stared at the immaculate structure, ornate in design, as they entered through large open doors. Inside were at least two dozen stalls with attached corrals, and off to the side was a huge indoor riding ring.

"What is this place?" Eppie whispered as a woman in jods walked forward, hand extended.

"This is Fiona Cartwright, from the Olympic team," Beth whispered back.

"Hello," Fiona said, shaking Eppie's hand. "You must be Pauline! I was close friends with your mother. Your mom Evie was a great person. We all miss her so much. And hi Beth, it was lovely talking to you on the phone."

Eppie admired the way Fiona and Beth were so much alike, so polite and gracious. Fiona smiled at Eppie.

"Shall we visit your old friend?" she asked. Eppie looked at Beth, puzzled.

"She doesn't know why we're here, it's a surprise," Beth explained. Fiona nodded.

"Well, come along then. There's someone here who would love to see you."

Eppie's mind wandered all over the place as she followed Beth and Fiona, who were chatting as they walked. Who was it she was going to see? She couldn't begin to guess. As they approached the riding ring, Eppie stopped. Loose in the ring was a huge black Friesian, prancing and tossing his head. Eppie stared. *Could it be?*

The horse stopped, lifted his head and snorted, hot breath fogging the brisk air. He appraised Eppie, ears shot forward, and suddenly nickered, then cantered toward the ring's gate.

"Onyx!" Eppie called, rushing forward to greet her mother's favorite horse, and Legend's grandfather. Onyx curved his delicate head down as Eppie hugged him and breathed him in. Huge emotion flooded her as she held her old friend, the horse she'd grown up with, the horse that had worked in unison with her mother for years. Onyx seemed overcome as well; he broke away from Eppie and trotted away in a circle before returning for more hugs. Eppie walked into the arena and wrapped her arms around him, tangling his thick long black mane into her fingers. Onyx pulled his head up quickly and Eppie remembered their game and grasped onto his neck and bent her knees. He lifted her up off the ground and trotted as she clung to him, giving her a little ride against his great barrel chest. Eppie stood and patted him as she heard Beth and Fiona laugh.

"I've never seen him do that before!" Fiona called.

"He has a lot of tricks," Eppie said. She stood back and bowed to Onyx, and he lowered himself down on one knee in reply. Beth clapped in astonishment. Then Eppie held her hands up over her head and Onyx reared up and pawed the air. Eppie patted him when he landed and she pointed to the ground. Onyx rolled over on his back and she scratched his stomach as he stayed perfectly still.

"My mom played with him this way all the time," Eppie called, her voice cracking. Onyx had missed this as much as she had, she realized. He must have wondered what happened to the woman he'd spent most of his life with. Eppie thought that it must be even harder on him than on her; Eppie knew what had happened. What if she'd been ripped from her life at Wills ranch without explanation, like Onyx, Pixiedust the Andalusian mare, and all the other horses? Sadness for them filled her and Onyx stood up and shook off the sawdust before he nudged her with his nose as if to try to cheer her.

"I've missed you so much," she whispered as she brushed more wood shavings from his back with her hand. Onyx followed her as she returned to where the women stood and watched, transfixed.

"You can ride him if you want," Fiona said. "I have to tell you, he's the best stud horse we've ever owned. And I teach dressage on him, your mother took him to the Olympics when she went in the 90s, he's phenomenal. I've sent a mental prayer to your mother for working with him so well. I'm so glad you are able to visit him!"

Eppie looked around at the impressive stables. "I'm so happy to see him, to see where he lives! This is amazing, just . . . the best . . ." her words failed her.

"His tack is just over there. Here's his halter." Fiona handed Eppie a white leather halter and leadline. Eppie took it and slipped it over his big head. She beamed up at Beth and Fiona.

"This is the best Christmas gift you could ever give me, to visit Onyx" she said, happily leading the stallion to the tie outs to tack him up.

Her day ended too quickly, but the visit with Onyx really was the best present Beth or anyone could have given her. It filled her with hope. Fiona promised to send pictures and updates periodically. The rest of Eppie's Colorado ski vacation was fun, but Eppie's mind kept wandering back to her time with Onyx, a distraction even when she was sliding down the slopes. Eppie would cherish the memory of his smooth muscled body moving underneath her, the way he lifted his elegant dinner plate-sized hooves and carried her across the ring. His gait, so different than Cesar's, was like flying as he lifted his big body into a canter. Eppie had thrown her arms out as she cantered him around the ring; even if her body wasn't really flying, her heart was, riding her mother's favorite horse. Onyx was family. On that Christmas day, Eppie finally felt at home.

# ❧Chapter Thirty-two❧

Back in Palos Verdes after the holidays Eppie was so busy getting ready for her new school and keeping up with Cesar and Legend's training that she sort of let herself forget about the Dursoms. It was decided that she'd stay with Cashmere's family, to keep her safe from Jim, who had returned home according to Beth's last report. Now in her rooms at the Krause mansion Eppie had her own computer, a new smart cell phone, and in some ways her life was easier than it had ever been. She was more like Cashmere now; she didn't work at the barn mucking stalls anymore, though she and Cashmere both spent Saturday helping Marta on her final holiday break trail ride, under Beth's orders, since the trail rides were about to end for the season. It was time to put Legend under saddle, to get him used to the feel of a girth around his middle. As the days slowly lengthened in between cold weather snaps and occasional rains, Eppie worked carefully with her horse, the image of the amazing Onyx fresh in her mind, encouraging her to keep going.

Brian was back in her life too, and he seemed surprised that Eppie was living in Palos Verdes.

"How did all this happen?" he asked as they sat up on a hill overlooking the ocean, Catalina Island faint in the distance across a bright sea.

"It's a long story, but in general my other family, that is, my legal guardians, signed over their rights to my new family, and they live in PV. I even sort of have a sister now, she goes to a private school, not your high school though. I start there next week."

"Does she ride horses too?"

"Yes, that's how I met her family."

Brian's look was unfathomable. "Hmmm. Well, since so many adults have their eyes on you still, do you mind if we just keep our thing on the down-low? You know, just between us, like before?"

"I have no problem with that," Eppie said truthfully, because it was really her seeing Brian that had started the whole issue with Jim. For all she knew anything could happen, who knew, so she had decided the less said about *anything*, the better. Today Eppie had met Brian at the General Store again, this time because she still couldn't figure out how to give directions to the Krause home. It was nestled onto a hillside overlooking the ocean amidst some slithery roads that she couldn't pronounce. She decided they may as well keep meeting at the store, since she could always get Julianna to take her to the stables.

Spring finally showed itself, and in early February the hills had fully turned from gold to green, and wildflowers sprinkled color on the landscape like confetti candy. Eppie's days were becoming a blur, and as she made friends at her new middle school, Maggie, LiLi, and Lexel were like shiny precious stones stored in her pocket for her to take out and examine someday, not now. At the barn Cashmere was getting ready for the big April horse show that everyone was talking about.

"I need a better helmet, this one is from two seasons ago!" Cashmere complained as she trotted up to Eppie, adjusting her chinstrap. Cashmere and Cesar were finally working well together, and they could manage some spectacular jumps.

"You need to focus on keeping your legs steady and your hands still," Eppie admonished, hearing the instructors she grew up taking lessons from in her mind. "Hat schmat!"

Cashmere laughed and Eppie joined her. She sounded like such a dork! They were both still cracking up when Marta approached.

"Not a lot getting done over here, I see," Marta said, her smile belying her tone.

"Cashmere's getting Cesar ready for the show," Eppie said as she and Cesar turned toward the jumps. "And Legend is getting ready for his halter division."

"So you decided to enter him too?"

"Yes, may as well start racking up some blue ribbons now," Eppie said with a grin. Marta chortled.

"Confidence will only get you so far, dearie," she said.

"I know, but just look at him, isn't he amazing?" Eppie was so proud of the way Legend looked, and she'd been working on his hoof-lifting problem and with Dr. Beery's help, so now he was a perfect gentleman every time she lifted his feet. Seeing Onyx reminded her of Legend's bloodline, and how special he was. She wanted him to win the colt division in his halter class, where she'd lead him out to parade in front of the judges and they'd judge him on his conformation, which was basically how good he looked; whether he had a strong chest, how proportioned he was, how his head and neck arched. She'd seen her mother show their colt youngsters on the ranch before, but Mom always had one of the hands show the horse, and it was just so she could raise the price for sale time by announcing that the colt or filly was a ribbon winner at halter.

Marta was appraising Legend and she nodded. "Sure, but he's a beauty even if you don't throw him in a ring to impress the judges," she said.

Eppie frowned. "You don't like the show ring, Marta?"

Marta sighed. "Can't say I've thought it did a horse or a rider any good. I'm more an eventing type, or trails. But that's me. I just don't get this fancy ring showing thing."

"But you manage a riding ring!"

"I work here, and I live here. I just go along," Marta said. She patted Legend on the neck, who was reaching over with his nose hoping for a carrot or mint. Marta only gave him another pat before heading back to her own area, where the Western trail horses lived. Eppie stared after her. She didn't get Marta sometimes. What did she mean by that, that she never thought showing did a horse or rider good? Eppie wondered as she went back to her work with Legend, Cesar, and Cashmere.

## ~CHAPTER THIRTY-THREE~

One Friday night while Cashmere was on a date with her boyfriend Bo and Eppie couldn't find Brian online, she decided to rummage through a huge suitcase that she didn't recognize that was brought from the Dursom's house. She opened it and saw most of the contents of her desk, and her canvas floral backpack that she used for Narbonne Middle School. The jump from that school to Palos Verdes Middle School had been abrupt enough that her life stood still, and it was as if everything from her previous life had been abandoned and was now emerging, fossilized, her life before frozen in time. She dug around in her schoolbag and found some coins, pencils, pens, and her homework assignments that she was supposed to complete over winter break, never touched or even seen. She also found her school binder, and was excited to see that she had, at the beginning of the school year, written down Maggie's cell number and email address. It was like she had forgotten all about her past life, and Maggie.

Quickly she picked up the phone to text Maggie. Then her fingers froze. What could she possibly say? She hadn't seen her since that last moment they'd shared in front of the library at school. Would she even still consider Eppie a friend? They never said goodbye. Had they ever really been friends? Eppie didn't know and felt nervous. She had never gone backwards before, except for seeing Onyx. Everyone who had been a part of her life since her mother abandoned her—yes, that was the word she was feeling, abandoned—had remained part of her murky past. Taking a deep breath Eppie typed a text:

*Hi Maggie! It's Pauline. This is my new number. I hope you remember me! JK. I'm sad I had to leave so quick, but I'm good. Find me online, K? Miss you.*

That was enough. If Maggie blew her off and didn't respond, at least she tried, and at least she didn't give her too much information. She looked further through the bag before putting the canvas bag in the laundry and the rest of it, except the money and the binder, in the trash. Maggie was the only thing that she really missed, well of course the cat Lacey Bell, and Lonny too, but his attack on her had been too much. Eppie knew he was a complex kid and that he probably still believed that she was the reason Jim had left. She wondered how Tracey slept at night, and what she'd told herself to make it okay that she'd let Eppie go. A doorbell sound came from her cell. Eppie ran to check her who it was and her heart welled up with happiness; it was Maggie:

*Pauline! I'm so glad you wrote me. I have missed you a lot. Lexel's party was the bomb. I wish you could have come. The newest drama at Narbonne is that LiLi is trying to get Lexel's ex, remember Drake? But Lexel is saying no exes with besties so LiLi is OUT of the circle! But she's trying to form her own group with Lexel's castaways and I'm stuck in the middle as messenger girl. Oh well at least I'm popular, LOL. Get a Facebook and Snapchat now that you have a real phone, talk to you soon! Yay! Heart, Maggie.*

Eppie's emotions soared as she read and re-read Maggie's message. Eppie wrote her back to fill her in on the real details of her life, like her new school, and an update on her and Brian, and living with Cashmere, all of it. After a few texts, Maggie called Eppie and they stayed up late and talked about everything they could think of until after midnight, when Maggie's mom busted her and made her go to bed.

The next morning Beth knocked on Eppie's door. Saturday, but since the trails were muddy and unusable, Marta had closed down the trail riding part of her business for the season and sent all the horses that she didn't use for lessons up to pasture in Ventura county until May. Eppie looked at the clock, surprised it was after 10.

"Come in," Eppie called, but Beth was standing in the doorway.

"Let's go see your grandmother," Beth said. "She's asking for you, Pauline."

Eppie's eyes widened. Grandma was asking for her? Saying her name? She jumped out of bed and threw her jeans on and hastily ran a brush through her hair. She barely brushed her teeth and was ready in just a couple of minutes.

Beth's Bentley took the windy curves easily through misty streets and in no time they arrived at the little house in San Pedro where Grandma lived. Eppie burst through the door before Nodo, the Filipino caregiver, could tell her to come in. Beth followed and chatted with him as Eppie entered the room. Grandma was sitting in her big chair, and her eyes glistened when she saw Eppie.

"My girl," Grandma said. "My Pauline. Pauline."

Eppie got a chill that covered her whole body and she hugged Grandma's frail form. "It's me," Eppie said. "It's Pauline. Your Eppie. Grandma, I'm here."

"My Eppie," Grandma said, pulling tears from Eppie. No one had called her Eppie since Grandma had her stroke. It was the name she was waiting to hear, but had lost hope of ever hearing again.

"What did she call you?" Beth whispered as she came into the room.

"Eppie. It's my nickname."

"I've never heard anyone call you that, it's cute," Beth said.

"No one calls me that anymore. My mom and Grandma did though. All the time."

"Eppie," Beth said carefully, as if tasting a new wine. "It suits you."

"Eppie," Grandma said again, and she had tears in her eyes as she focused on her granddaughter. Eppie smiled and held her hand.

"Grandma, I have so much to tell you," she said as she settled down on the chair next to Grandma's. The old woman's eyes shone brighter.

## CHAPTER THIRTY-FOUR

Grandma wasn't fully recovered but it was as if some part of her had awakened from a very deep sleep. She still tilted her head in a strange way and she had trouble with some words, but mostly she enjoyed listening to Eppie's stories about her days at the barn. Eppie never told Grandma about what had happened to her since she had the stroke. It was too much to share, and Grandma had trouble with timelines anyway, didn't seem to be able to recall how time worked. She had mastered the concept of different meals at different times, but last week, next month; according to the new therapist, that was all part of the hazy place still in Grandma's mind.

Eppie was downstairs in the huge kitchen eating a snack when she overheard Beth in the dining room on the phone.

"Yes, I'm sure. No, it's not part of her medical insurance, I'm paying for it myself. I have been for three months. Just bill me, that's all you need to do." There was a pause, and Eppie stopped in mid-bite of her pepperoni Hot Pocket as she listened.

"The name is Emmaline Wills. She's a resident at the assigned stroke recovery home. They've been going to her and working with her three times a week. Yes, she's improved, thanks for asking."

Eppie was stunned. Beth had paid for part of Grandma's therapy? That's why she was getting better? Eppie didn't know what to say or do, but Beth ended the phone call and walked into the master foyer so she never saw Eppie sitting in the kitchen, didn't know she'd overheard. Eppie knew that thanking Beth at this point was just a drop of water in a sea of generosity. There were no words to let her know how much she appreciated everything Beth had done for her.

The month of April slipped in not on quiet cat's feet but in a blistering heat wave that dried up the trails and got the horses anxious to get out of their stalls. Eppie and Cashmere had gotten into a pleasant routine of school, homework, barn, and down time. Eppie liked being on a schedule and no longer having to sneak around to work. The only sneaking she did now was to see Brian once a week, but that was Cashmere's day to shop with her friends so no one knew.

"Eppie!" Cashmere called as she cantered Cesar around the ring. She waved and Eppie waved back as they each worked with their own horses. The show was this weekend, and all of the horses and riders were working overtime to fine tune their performances. Legend was responding perfectly to every nuance of Eppie's commands and the two of them were the talk of the stables. Legend even had a small smattering of barn girls who adored him and asked Eppie if they could feed him treats, groom him, and take him around the stable stalls on his halter. Eppie had put up a whiteboard so the girls could "sign him out". He was becoming calmer and more tame each day, though he still possessed enough of an ornery streak to keep Eppie on guard.

Friday night Cashmere invited about ten of the other riders from the barn over to their house, and in the big kitchen on the table the girls cleaned their bridles and saddles with leather cleaner, shined up mouth bits and stirrups, polished up their tall boots and practiced their hair buns and made sure their show shirts and "ratcatchers," the fake little collar they wore around their necks, were ironed and crisp. Julianna was running around bringing extra polishing cloths, more drinks, warming the pizza, and she even took over the ironing once a girl burned the edge off her fingernail. Even Beth made an appearance to check their progress. Music played and the house smelled like lemon cleaner and leather, but by the time the last girl left by 10:00 pm, Eppie and Cashmere were ready to perform the next morning.

Show day dawned crisp and then warmed slowly. Legend had never been cleaner, and Eppie found herself with two grooms, Hannah and Alison, both aged nine. The girls were Legend fanatics and they were friends who had competed in the walk/trot division early in the morning and now had the rest of the day free. They groomed Legend until he shone like pewter in candlelight. Legend looked regal in his new leather show halter, and Eppie shook with excitement as she entered the ring. There were two other colts in the three-year-old division that looked as shiny and clean as Legend, a black and a bay, but as soon as Eppie stepped into the ring she felt as one with Legend. He responded to her smallest request and it felt as if she wasn't controlling him but participating in an intricate dance, a ballet of movement and form as she led him at a trot between the orange cones. Legend was so light on his feet that Eppie imagined he was floating next to her as he trotted alongside of her. There was no agonizing minute as she finished as there used to be in the show ring when she rode dressage on Onyx and Pixiedust, wondering, hoping, waiting. Eppie nodded to the judges when she'd completed her round and stepped out of the ring feeling confident. She didn't even watch the other two horses perform. It was a nice first time out. Legend's fan club squealed enthusiastically as she brought him away from the ring, offering him peppermints and pats and even more kisses on the nose.

Legend was well cared for by Eppie's mini-grooms. He stood in his stall eating his well-deserved mash, so now Eppie had to focus on Cesar and Cashmere. Cashmere slipped her arms into her tailored eggplant hunt coat and Eppie buttoned it up for her and tied her number onto the back with yarn so that it wouldn't flap up (something the judges hated).

Eppie gave Cashmere a leg up onto Cesar's tall back. She swung into the saddle, looking elegant on Cesar, who was calmer than Eppie expected. She held onto the soft rag tightly and wiped the dust off Cashmere's boots as she entered the ring when her name was called. Cesar perked up and trotted in a slow circle, and then aimed for the course, flying easily over the jumps. It was a fences division that should have been easy enough for Cashmere, who had been practicing lately on jumps much bigger as her confidence soared. Eppie watched Cesar bunch up and realized that she should have asked him to try smaller jumps in the week leading up the show. He was definitely jumping higher than was necessary to clear the fences. He was also going faster than he should be, Eppie noted with alarm. Cesar barreled down the course for a smaller jump than he was used to and Eppie bit her lip. An over-jump could throw him off his game if Cashmere reprimanded him for it; it would confuse him. Cesar hurled high in the air and galloped off, thundering through his performance. He did well enough, although he looked a bit out of control. The judges might take off a point or two, but Eppie beamed at Cashmere as she rode out of the ring.

"You nailed it!" she said.

"Yeah, but he was high! Like I've never seen him before," Cashmere said as she reined the big Thoroughbred in. He finally stopped but lifted his legs in a standing dance.

"He's excited, he'll calm down for the next round."

"That was terrifying! I'm not even sure I want to do the next round."

"What?" Eppie couldn't believe her ears. She grabbed Cesar's reins and held him as Cashmere climbed down off of him.

"That's stupid, of course you're doing it!" Eppie's cheeks burned with fury. Cashmere had done so well! How could she think of quitting now?

Cashmere grinned. "Just kidding. That was a blast! I can't wait for the next round. I'm going to win!"

Eppie laughed, exasperated, and threw her arm around Cashmere as they walked over to Beth, whose smile equaled the girls'. The three of them hung out on a picnic blanket as they waited for their next events and by 4:00, they went home dusty, exhausted, and happy.

Cashmere was beaming as they went inside the house. She'd claimed a first, two seconds and a fourth place ribbon, and she had never been nicer to both Eppie and to Beth. Eppie had never seen Cashmere so happy. Legend won all of his events with a trio of blue ribbons and a best overall halter division winner trophy. Eppie too was beyond ecstatic. Legend had done it! Her baby was everything she could have ever asked for. *He's my perfect horse*, she thought with pride as she ran her finger alongside the golden trophy. She was so glad she'd risked so much to get him; it was paying off already. And now that she lived with the Krauses she didn't have to worry about money anymore. She could just enjoy him and have fun. Grandma was better, and Eppie felt like she was in a fairy tale as she pinned the ribbons up on her curtain rod and put the trophy in the middle of her desk so she could see it from her bed. It gleamed a sparkly gold as the late afternoon sun filtered in through the trees. Eppie swelled with pride as she took off her good boots and got ready for a much-needed shower.

## ~Chapter Thirty-five~

Eppie pulled away from Brian. His kisses were getting heavy and she literally had to come up for air. Her long hair was tangled in his hands and it took a moment for the couple to break apart. Brian was grinning.

"Sorry. Got a little carried away there."

"That's okay," Eppie blushed, wiping her lips with her fingers. Brian had been a little more . . . pushy lately. Wanting to kiss all the time, and he was like an octopus, his slippery hands often landing on her where they shouldn't. She was fourteen now, her birthday the previous week had been nice, and Cashmere had helped her set up a fabulous party with the barn girls and some of her PV school friends spending the night, and even Maggie showed up, but she didn't sleep over like the others. The Dursom's had even sent her a one hundred dollar gift card to Abercrombie and a nice note. So she was officially of high school age, even if she still had a couple more months left of middle school and wouldn't be official until next September.

But Brian was getting older too. He was about to turn seventeen. He was practically an adult! Eppie didn't know what to do when he got this way. It was too much for her. Her insides spun: part of her wanted him, and wanted more than just those sweet kisses, but a bigger part was terrified of his energy as he kissed her so passionately.

"I know, I'm bad," Brian pouted. "I can't help it. You're so damn pretty."

Eppie flushed a deeper red. "Thanks. It's okay . . . I just felt uneasy." She felt all over the place, like a spooky horse, and wished she could handle herself better.

"I'll take it slower," Brian said, putting his arm around her. Eppie nestled her head against his shoulder. They were sitting on grass at a park with a big bell as its centerpiece, a gift to the city from another country. The park overlooked the ocean, and the wind was starting to pick up. The kite fliers were out, getting ready to launch their buzzing trick racing kites.

"I've got to get back," Eppie said. "Julianna is going to pick us up at the barn at 6:00."

" . . . Julianna?" Brian looked at Eppie with a frown. "Who is that?"

"She's our house's driver. Why?"

Brian hopped up from the ground, staring at Eppie. "What?"

"The driver, she helps us at the new house, she takes care of us. Haven't I mentioned her before? Why?" Eppie felt alarm at Brian's strange behavior. He suddenly looked ill. "Is something wrong?"

"You have mentioned her, yeah. You mentioned her. But you just called her your driver. I didn't know her name so got confused. But . . . I've gotta get you back," Brian said, grabbing Eppie's elbow and rushing her toward the Mustang. "That's all. Don't worry, it's nothing. I just don't want to make you late."

After her weird encounter with Brian, Eppie fretted when he didn't show up on any of their online meeting places and he didn't call or text her all week. She wondered if her stopping him all the time from doing more than kissing her was starting to take its toll on him. *Maybe he's going to break up with me,* she thought one afternoon as she used a leather punch to push a hole in Legend's red halter, so she could tighten it. *Even though we aren't really boyfriend and girlfriend. We're sort of just kissing daters.* Brian, Brian, Brian! Her mind wouldn't let him go, it was like how her tongue used to always find the wiggly loose tooth in her mouth when she was younger and losing her baby teeth. She just couldn't leave it alone.

One day at the barn Eppie was turning out Legend when Brian showed up. She could not have been more shocked to see him as he hung on the gate while Legend raced around, tail in air. Legend was particularly hyper and Eppie was chasing him, letting him get all his bucks out.

Brian jumped down off the railing as Legend charged toward the gate.

"Whoa! That horse is crazy," Brian said, brushing himself off as a cloud of dust covered him.

"Hey!" Eppie ran over and gave Brian a hug. He gave her a quick, sort of impersonal hug back but not before looking around.

"Your roommate isn't here, right? Your foster sister or whatever?" Brian asked.

"Who? You mean Cashmere? Yeah, it's complicated, you are right about the 'whatever' part," Eppie, confused, shook her head. "She's not here today. She has cheer or choreo or something. Why?"

Brian shook his head in a mysterious way and Eppie called for Legend. He trotted to her, snorting at Brian, the stranger. She slipped his halter over his head.

"This is my horse Legend. Hey, aren't you allergic to horses? I thought you couldn't come here?"

"Nice horse. Look, I need to talk to you. Is there someplace private we can go?" Brian's eyes darted around the ring, causing Eppie to wonder what was going on now.

Eppie's thoughts eeled around in her mind as she put Legend to bed in his stall. When she was done she led Brian up to the trails behind the barn. There was a clearing under a pepper tree with big stones around it that would be out of the way. They approached the shady area just off the trail and each sat down on one of the boulders.

"This is nice," Brian said, looking around at the nearby fields, green with beautiful but invasive mustard plants. Soon the buds would sprout and it would be a sea of yellow. For now it was just knee high.

"So what did you want to talk to me about?" Eppie asked, twirling the bottom of the hem of her shirt in her fingers. *I'm about to get dumped, this is my first break up,* she thought glumly. She hadn't seen Brian in a long time and now here he was, not trying to kiss her, and acting weird.

"There's . . . a problem," Brian said. "A really crazy problem." Brian pushed his hand through his hair and then covered his eyes and then peered up at Eppie.

"First, let me just tell you, that I really like you, Pauline. You're like . . . the coolest girl I know. You're real, you're not at all fake, you're different from most of the girls I know around here. And I know you're young, but you're really mature for your age."

Eppie thought that if it was a break up, it was a flattering one. "Go on," she said.

"Well . . . there's this other girl too, that I've been going with for a long time. Like almost two years, but she's always mad at me so we're sort of off and on again, a lot."

Eppie's heart fell. Of course she didn't think that Brian was only hers; she went weeks without seeing him, and he was older, and had a car, and there were all those high school dances and things, he must have gone to those with someone else, but knowing for sure there were other girls in his life made her heart feel sad. She bowed her head, trying to hide her disappointment.

"But I just figured something out, and I'm an idiot for not figuring it out before. Pauline, it's Cashmere. Cashmere is my real girlfriend. Your roommate or whatever. You live with my girlfriend! I'm Bo. That's what she calls me."

Eppie looked up at Brian, squinting. "What?" she said, and her voice sounded hollow and far away. "That's not possible! What are you saying?"

Brian stood up and started to pace. "Look," he said. "Cashmere . . . she's hard to read, you know? And really moody. I mean, I knew she had someone new living with her and that you had just moved out of your foster home into another one, but the way she described it, I didn't know it was you."

Eppie felt dizzy. *Was this really happening?*

"What did she say?"

"Well . . ." Brian hesitated. "You know how she is. All vague and kind of snotty. She said that her mother was bringing some kid to live with them as her newest pet project or something like that, but it was a long time ago, and she hasn't mentioned it since the holidays so I sort of forgot . . ."

Eppie couldn't believe that. She and Cashmere were best friends! Like sisters almost. And Beth was almost like a mom! They felt like a family, and Cashmere was telling people Eppie was "just her mother's pet project?"

"That's kind of harsh," Eppie said quietly.

"Yeah, well, she probably didn't know you well yet then or something. Sorry. But I didn't think much of it until you mentioned that thing about Julianna . . ."

" . . . Our driver . . ."

"Yes! And I started thinking how weird, that you'd just moved in with a family in Palos Verdes, that she just had someone move in with her, and I know you're both into horses . . . I remember you said something about meeting your new family at the barn, but I've met Julianna! A bunch of times! Cashmere's driver and nanny. So that's when I put it all together the last time we were together, when you called Julianna by name."

"Wait." Eppie held up her hand. "Wait a sec. You're not allergic to horses, are you? You've been having me meet you at the store because you knew Cashmere boarded her horse here, isn't that right?"

Brian paused from his pacing and his shoulders slumped. "Uh, yeah. I admit it. I knew she was here and I was sort of seeing you while I was seeing her. In the beginning. But I had no, absolutely no idea that you knew each other! I just didn't want her to see me with you. Sorry."

Eppie shook her head. *What the hell was going on?* She felt as if she'd fallen through the earth into some kind of alternate reality.

"But wait, why does she call you Bo? I've never even heard her call her boyfriend . . . you . . . Brian! Not once!"

"Everyone at school calls me Bo. It's short for Brian Bojangles. That's what they call me on the lacrosse team."

Eppie felt her eyes begin to water in frustration. "That's a stupid name," she hissed.

"I know, it's something my coach named me cuz when we're losing I do this crazy dance on the field to psyche out the opponents. Has something to do with some old song."

Eppie covered her eyes with her hands. What she really wanted to do was cover her ears and start singing "la la la la la" but she stopped herself. Her mind was still trying to wrap itself around the facts Brian was putting before her.

She was dating Cashmere's boyfriend! Bo and Brian were the same guy! Cashmere was not an understanding person. Eppie actually felt afraid about what would happen if Cashmere found out.

"Well . . ." Eppie didn't want to hear any more details about how it had come about. "Then, we just need to end it and pretend it never happened."

"But I totally like you!" Brian said. "Like, more than I like Cashmere. I'm willing to dump her to keep seeing you."

Eppie' s mouth gaped open. She felt like slapping him.

"Don't you get it?" she asked. "Cashmere is like, the queen. And you do not date the queen's boyfriend! It's a bad idea Brian. I mean . . ." Eppie pulled in a shaky breath. "I'll totally miss you, but we just have to walk away from this disaster, right now!"

"Cashmere will have another boyfriend within nanoseconds," Brian said with a snap of his fingers. "She'll be fine!"

"No!" Eppie shouted. This time a tear eked out. She wiped it away with her finger. "It's like...she's like the boss's daughter. Don't you see? She's also my friend. It's so over. Like, completely over. Right now." Eppie got up and marched back down the trail toward the open gate that led to the stables. Brian ran after her, grabbing her arm. He pulled her into him, trying to hold her, but she wrested her arm away and kept walking.

"Just go!" she hissed. Marta was tending to her horses and looked up. Eppie kept her eyes forward and kept walking. She could feel Brian slow down behind her, giving up. She rushed to Legend's stall and slipped through the bars and threw her arms around Legend's neck, hiding her eyes in his dark fur. In the distance she could hear Brian's car rev up and leave the dusty parking lot. She kept her eyes closed, not wanting to see the dust cloud that she knew was still there.

# CHAPTER THIRTY-SIX

Eppie didn't let herself think about Brian. She'd decided to tell Cashmere about what had happened, but just couldn't bring herself to do it every time she had a chance. Her nerve failed her and she would invariably walk away, hands clenched. A few weeks after Brian's confession, Cashmere came home from a date with "Bo," a big smile on her face. She came into Eppie's room.

"Watcha doing?" she asked, flopping on the bed. Eppie put down her pencil.

"Algebra! It's wretched. Where were you?" Eppie didn't really want to know but didn't want to act any different in front of Cashmere.

"Movies with Bo. He's so much more attentive now! This is the best it's been for us."

"You never bring him here," Eppie said cautiously. She was grateful, but wondered why.

"My mom doesn't really approve of him. She wants me to date someone from my own school. Says what's the point of paying for a private school education if you're going to associate with the public school boys, especially a school with low STAR testing scores like his school has." Cashmere flashed a straight white smile. "No offense, I know you were supposed to go there next year."

"Hey, no problem. Now the high school I'll go to is way better than the one I would have gone to . . ." Eppie's voice faded. She didn't like thinking about her time with the Dursoms and she realized she was stumbling into Brian territory. She stopped herself.

"That's true, now you're going to one of the best public high schools in the state!" Cashmere picked up a *Horse and Rider* magazine and flipped through it. "I've tried telling Mom that he's a decent guy, but she never listens." Her eyes rested on a page of the periodical. “Hey; I’m thinking of getting a new hunt coat, I’ve worn mine for three shows in a row! I need a change.”

“I don’t know,” Eppie said. “The judges are starting to know you, might be a good idea to keep yours for the season, it’s the only one like it.”

Cashmere stared. “That’s brilliant!” She smacked Eppie’s arm in a friendly way. “I hadn’t even thought of that! How do you always know so much?”

“My mom used to stay stuff like that all the time,” Eppie said softly.

“She was right,” Cashmere said, standing up. “Good to represent, let them get to know me. Thanks Eppie!” Cashmere yawned. “Wow, movies make me tired! I’m going to bed.”

“Cash?” Eppie said. Cashmere stopped and looked back. Eppie wanted to try again to tell her about Brian, but the glow she had, and that new constant smile . . . she just couldn’t do it. She looked down instead.

“What is it?” she asked.

“Nothing, just wanted to say goodnight,” Eppie said.

“‘Night! See you tomorrow morning!!” Cashmere left, leaving a knot in Eppie’s gut. *Better just leave it,* she thought. But the fact that Brian might tell first was why her stomach hurt so much.

Eppie didn’t have much time to think about anything as she neared the finish line. School was nearly out for the summer, and it seemed as if the Powers-That-Be were trying to cram everything in to the last second: There was an ice cream social, an 8th grade dance, a fun run, a beach party, 8th grade Disneyland “Ditch Day,” and Movie Day, where all of her classes showed movies for the period. It was different than the other schools that she had attended. But she had barely scraped into a group of girls who had known each other for years, since elementary school. Finally graduation day arrived and the girls stood on the football field holding their diplomas.

“I’m going to miss you!” Ivanna, a pretty dark haired girl, hugged her friend Deena.

"Me too! We'll have to have to hang out every day at the beach this summer!"

"Ugh!" Steffi, a white-blonde, said. "I have water polo practice like all summer long!"

Ivanna looked over, sympathetic. "Well, we have to hang out, no matter what."

Eppie stood, swaying lightly back and forth, feeling out of place. She'd spent lunches with these girls since the first week she arrived at Palos Verdes Middle School, but she didn't see them outside of school. They all lived on the opposite side of the peninsula and she was always at the stables. She wondered if she should stay and listen or go, but suddenly the strawberry blonde, Deena, slipped her arm around Eppie's shoulders.

"You'll come hang out with us, won't you?" she asked.

"Sure!" Eppie said. She would love a decent beach day with the girls. That just seemed so . . . normal. Like when she first hung out with the Dursoms and they took her to Torrance Beach to watch Lonny surf. Relaxing on the sand was unlike anything she'd done in a long time. "I think we'll be going to the beach club too, so maybe we can meet there as well."

"Are you a member?" Deena wanted to know.

"Yes." It amazed Eppie that it was true, but now that she lived with Cashmere, they went there to use the Jacuzzi & gym for a change of pace sometimes after riding.

Deena's smile widened. "Great! Me too. Let's go there, we can hit the pool Jacuzzi and check out the cute lifeguards."

Eppie smiled. She realized that even though she would be training Legend under saddle and working four days a week at Marta's trail riding business, she would have some free time for the beach club and hanging out with the girls she would be going to high school with. She hugged Deena, glad to have a friend again.

"I can't wait!" she said.

Beth seconded the motion. "We need to have a party," she said when they dined at the country club to celebrate the end of the school year. "Next weekend. Invite all your school friends, Eppie. Cashmere, the boys too. Let's really kick summer off with a bang!"

"Cool, Mom! Good idea," Cashmere seconded.

"That sounds fun!" Eppie said, taking a mouthful of buttery carrots.

Charles cleared his throat and wiped his mouth with his pale linen napkin. "I know when I'm outnumbered. You girls do what you want with this party, but just don't let me see the bill," he admonished.

Party Night, and Eppie stood at the top of the stairs with Cashmere. Cashmere had told her to wait upstairs while she finished getting ready even though her friends were already downstairs, and they'd make an entrance together. They'd ditched the stables two days that week to work on their tans, and now, in her bright yellow summer dress, standing next to Cashmere in her turquoise one, the girls held hands and walked slowly down the landing. Their friends waited below and some even clapped; they both had spent the day at the spa and had their hair and make-up done professionally. In a word, they looked amazing.

"Oh my God!" Deena, Ivanna and Steffi crowded around Eppie, and Cashmere's friends did the same with her.

"You look so great!"

"Thanks!" Eppie wasn't used to this kind of attention, or this kind of life for that matter, but she smiled at her friends. "I missed you already." The girls all talked at once and broke away, laughing. Eppie had never been to such a fancy party, let alone thrown one. Several "kitchen helpers" as Beth called them, walked around carrying big trays of food, and a bar in the corner serving mocktails was getting a lot of action. Eppie was a little sad that Maggie couldn't come because her family had gone on vacation, but everyone she hung out with at her new school had come. She was laughing and about to take a bite of a California sushi roll when she looked up and saw Brian standing in the doorway. She dropped the sushi on her plate and looked away, but not before Brian had waved at her! Eppie made a threatening gesture with her eyes but saw too late that Cashmere was looking right at her.

"Just a second," Eppie said to her friends. She put the plate down and was about to leave the room when Cashmere came up to her.

"Do you know Bo?" Cashmere asked. "He was waving at you!" The *you* was emphasized, Eppie noticed. She swallowed hard.

"BB . . . Bo?" she asked.

"My boyfriend! Bo! That's him!" Cashmere was pointing at Brian.

Eppie nodded. "Well . . ." she hesitated. Brian was smiling, didn't look at all like the fox in the hen house. "I know Brian. Do you mean that guy over there?"

"Yes!" Cashmere's voice squeaked higher than usual. "That's Bo!"

"Really?" Eppie said as Cashmere dragged Eppie over to him.

"Hi, Pauline!" Brian said, kissing her on the cheek.

Cashmere's eyes grew large. Eppie flushed crimson. "Bo! Pauline . . . Eppie . . . says she knows you, as Brian!"

"Yeah, she was friends with one of my buddy's little sisters at Narbonne," Brian said, his voice smooth and clear. "Pauline and I go way back."

"What?" Cashmere was in shock. Eppie took her cue from her reaction and played shocked too.

"Oh, wait, Brian is Bo? The same guy? Your boyfriend? I just put this whole thing together!" she said, wondering why on earth Brian was bringing this mad drama to their party. Her face burned and she had an urge to run outside.

"Wow, that's crazy," Brian said, his voice like silk. "So Pauline is this Eppie girl that you've been talking about? What are the chances?" Brian said.

"I know, right? It's just so weird!" Cashmere said, still looking a bit unhinged.

Eppie nodded, but she breathed in, and started to relax a little. They both had other names. It wouldn't be the most farfetched thing for this info to come out here. After all, it would be more suspicious for Brian to not show up for Cashmere's party, since he was so rarely invited over. *Crisis averted*, Eppie noticed as Cashmere clutched her hands around Brian's arm and led him off to her group of friends.

"Who is the hot guy?" Ivanna asked.

Eppie shrugged. "Just some guy," she said. "Someone I knew in another life."

She watched Cashmere lead Brian across the room and they began kissing in the corner. She made herself look away. No point in making herself miserable by wanting something she couldn't have.

Eppie looked around. There were plenty of other fish in the sea; in fact . . . she let her eyes dart around the party in the backyard. Some of the best looking guys at her school were right here! She looked over to Mark, a boy she'd noticed her first day at PV. He looked like what she thought Lonny might look like in a few years but the similarity ended there. He was definitely hot. Eppie floated over to him and the girls followed her. Other boys crowded around as Eppie boldly put her arm around his neck. "Wanna dance?" she asked, as the dance floor was already full of party guests and the DJ was killing it. Eppie pulled Mark along with her and tried her best not to look at Brian and Cashmere as they danced.

*Brian can have Cashmere*, she told herself as she found herself dancing now with three boys. She'd barely spoken to them all school year but now she had nothing to lose.

The evening buzzed with the glittering hope of youth but the party was winding down as many of the guests left mumbling about curfews. Eppie and her friends, including some of the boys, sat in the Jacuzzi. It was hot and crowded and their bodies were pressed together, steam rising off bare skin.

Steffi rubbed her hands together. "Hey, let's play Hide and Seek!" she called out. The boys, about six in all, nudged each other in the ribs, and the girls giggled.

"Sure, the girls will play," Ivanna volunteered.

"The boys too!" said super-blond Mark. Eppie stared at him, and her insides purred. It made her realize how lost in Brian she'd been, not even giving guys at her school a second look. Mark was *cute.*

"Want to play Hide and Seek?" Mark whispered next to her. Eppie nodded and smiled; she was confused though;

here they were, going into high school, and they were going to play Hide and Seek like a bunch of kids?

"Send Pauline first, since it's her party. Pauline, you pick a boy to go first."

This wasn't the same game she'd played growing up, but she thought it must be different rules in California.

"I pick Mark," she said.

"Ooooh," said one of the boys as Mark stood up, steam rising up off of his tanned body. Eppie stood up too, carefully wiping steam from her face so her make-up wouldn't smear. Her new yellow bikini matched her dress, and she knew her tan made her look good as the boys peered up at her.

"Do we hide or count?" Eppie asked, thinking Mark must be her partner.

"You hide, and Mark finds you. Mark, pick the next girl."

"Ivanna," Mark chose Ivanna. Eppie realized she didn't know how to play this game at all. Steffi seemed to understand how lost she was.

"Look," Steffi said. "Here are the rules for those who don't know. Pauline hides, and Mark finds her. When he does, they kiss until Ivanna finds them. Then Pauline comes back and tells us Ivanna's choice, and then that guy goes, but Ivanna and Mark have to kiss until the next guy comes and replaces Mark. Got it?"

Eppie got it. She was going to have to kiss Mark! She wanted to back out. This was starting to remind her of Maggie's party. But everyone was now excited about it, so Eppie said, "Okay, since we're wet, the house is off limits. Just pool house, gazebo, and back yard. Ready?"

She knew right where to hide; the gazebo had a curtain she could hide behind, and there were a bunch of pillows on the chaise lounges in there; she'd be comfy until she was found, and later while she and Mark were waiting to be found at least they wouldn't be under a bush or somewhere icky. Mark and everyone else turned around and counted to 100 while Eppie snuck out of the hot pool. She left through the garden exit, noticing her watery footprints could be seen, so once outside she backtracked toward the gazebo which was closer to the front door of the pool house. The night air was getting nippy but she doubted her goosebumps had anything to do with that. She slipped quietly behind the curtains after grabbing some pillows and sat down on them, waiting anxiously. Soon she heard breathing and footsteps; Mark was coming! She held her breath as he suddenly flung the curtains back. In spite of herself, she squealed.

"Shhhh!" Mark said, sitting down next to her. "Ivanna will hear us and find us quicker." His body was still warm from the Jacuzzi, and his breath smelled like the peppermint he was chewing on. He leaned against her in a familiar way and smiled at her. "I'm going to kiss you now, k?"

"K." Eppie was surprised at how gently he leaned over and began kissing her. She let her thoughts go, aware that while it wasn't the same as with Brian, kissing Mark reminded her of him. She quickly pushed the thought of Brian out of her mind and started to enjoy herself, even though occasionally they'd start laughing quietly because they were strangers after all, in an intimate circumstance. Soon they heard footsteps coming up the gazebo path. Mark began kissing her in earnest, as if trying to get all the kisses in that he could before Ivanna caught them and he'd have to change partners. The curtains flew back again, and their little pillowed alcove against the back gazebo wall was uncovered. Eppie looked up expecting to see Ivanna, but Cashmere and Brian were standing there looking down on her and Mark. Eppie suddenly realized how bad it looked, both of them in bathing suits, kissing and hiding like that. She stood up, mouth open, unable to find words to explain.

"Eppie!" Cashmere said, but she had a smile on her face. Brian had the opposite, he looked miserable.

"Oh! We were just . . ." Eppie mumbled, as miserable as Brian looked.

Mark laughed. "This probably looks bad, but it's innocent," he said. "We're playing Hide and Seek."

"Don't ask, don't tell," Cashmere said with a shrug. She led Brian away by the arm, giggling, just as she had earlier at the party.

"Dang!" Mark whispered, unaware that Eppie felt like someone had just drained all the life out of her. Her knees were weak but Mark had his arm around her, so she didn't crumble. He whispered, "we can hide still, but maybe we should move, Ivanna's way over in the garden, I heard her talking."

The guilty lump in Eppie's throat was huge as she thought of Brian's face.

"Okay," she whispered.

Mark grabbed her by the wrist and led her around the side of the house. They hid together in an alcove, and Mark continued to kiss her. Eppie kissed back a little fiercely, so many emotions were churning around inside of her.

"You're pretty intense," Mark said quietly, pulling her back and looking at her in the dim garden light. "I like it though."

"Sorry," Eppie said. She almost wanted to just do more with Mark, to get back at Brian for coming to her party, for making her so miserable whenever she saw him. She knew she'd regret it if she did, but could tell Mark would probably go along with her, as his hands were starting to wander around her belly and arms, wanting more. It was only seconds too soon when Ivanna found them.

"My turn!" Ivanna said, falling dramatically into Mark's arms. He looked at Eppie in a disconcerted way.

"All yours," Eppie said. She was shaking as she made her way back to the group. The hot Jacuzzi never felt so good as she climbed in.

"That took a long time!" Deena whispered.

"Tell me about it," Eppie answered. She dipped her body backwards, allowing the hot water to engulf her as she disappeared under the bubbling surface.

## Chapter Thirty-seven

The next few days were a numbing combination of trail riding with Marta and working with Legend at the stables, but Eppie's heart wasn't in it. Although she was always glad to arrive at the stables, where the smell of the hay and manure greeted her each day like an old friend, being with Cashmere most of the day as they took the trail riders out in the mornings and evenings, and then working with her again in the ring on Cesar made Eppie feel sick to her stomach. Cashmere was in a good mood these days, and loved to share little stories about Brian/Bo, and how wonderful a boyfriend he was. Eppie thought she would puke if she had to hear it one more time. Faking nice to Cashmere was wearing her down.

At least Mark became mild distraction from the "couple in love" in the evenings when Eppie talked to him online or sometimes on the phone. The nagging question on Mark's mind was, when can I see you again? And Eppie knew what that meant. He probably wanted more than just the kissing they'd shared at the party.

"I'm over men," Eppie told Maggie on the phone one night. She flopped onto her bed and let her hair hang down over her face as she talked.

"I doubt that!" Maggie replied. "I mean, come on, you're fourteen! You're just starting to date. Hell, my mom won't even let me date til I'm sixteen. You're spoiled rotten that Beth would even let you date so young. And what about stuff like proms and all that in high school? You can't really be over men yet."

"It's so complicated all the time!" Eppie wailed, glad at least there was one person who knew what she was going through. Maggie had become the perfect friend. While Eppie didn't see her much, at least Maggie knew all the parts . . . about Brian being Bo, about how much Eppie had liked

Brian, about how Cashmere would react if she had found out about Brian and Eppie. Eppie was grateful that she didn't have to explain anything or, more importantly, defend herself to Maggie.

"Just let it go, this new guy Mark sounds cool, and I've seen his picture so I know he's a hottie, why not just go out with him?"

"I told you, he's going on a cruise for a month starting next week," Eppie said. "I think I'll wait til he gets back and see if he's still interested."

"That's stupid. See him before he leaves, then you'll be sure he's still interested. What are you going to do, Rapunzel, stay locked up in your tower and wait for your prince to come rescue you? Get out there!"

Eppie laughed in spite of how tight her insides always felt now. "Maybe," she said. "I'll think about it." Eppie rolled over onto her back. "I guess I do like him, but it's just that I still like Brian too." There, she'd said it.

"No!" Maggie said. "Don't even say that again. Brian is completely off limits, are you crazy? He's a two-timer, a complete jerk! You can do better. Go out with Mark."

Eppie was surprised that her admission to Maggie made her feel like crying, but she'd become an expert at keeping her tears at bay over the months. "I guess you're right," she said. "I mean, I know you are. Brian bad. Mark good. I got it."

"Great!" Maggie said with a sigh. "Because seriously, Paulie, where are you gonna go if Cashmere finds out about you and Brian and she gets you kicked outta that mansion you're living in?"

It was something Eppie had thought of, but not seriously. "She can't kick me out, only Beth can. I mean, they wouldn't kick me out for that."

"Hell, are you crazy? You lost your last home because your second cousins whoever-she-is guardian's son tried to molest you. You, the victim. I'll tell you something, moms are weird. The weirdest ever. They'll sometimes do anything to protect their kids. You'd better watch it."

Now Eppie really felt like crying. She hadn't had a mom in a while, for years now. She didn't remember that.

"Well I'm not going after Brian, and so Cashmere won't find out. There's no problem. I'm just gonna work, train Legend, and stay out of trouble this summer."

"Then you'll need a distraction to keep your mind off Brian," Maggie said. "And Mark seems like a perfect and rather hot distraction, don't you think?"

Eppie flushed. "I guess you're right." She could picture Maggie sitting in her pretty Pottery Barn Teen decorated room, her red hair pulled off her face in a neat ponytail. Eppie felt a pang of loneliness and wished she could see her in person. "Wanna come for a sleepover tonight?"

"It's 11:30! Just who do you think is going to wake up and drive me? My parents? I think not."

"What about your beloved brother? He's driving now, right?"

"Kyle? Are you kidding me? Kyle only does anything for one person, and that's Kyle."

"Oh." Eppie sighed. "Oh well. At least we can still talk on the phone."

"Actually I have to go. I have to wake up early tomorrow, we're going to Santa Barbara this weekend for a wedding."

Eppie couldn't believe it, it seemed like Maggie and her family went someplace every weekend. "You're always gone on weekends!"

"I know, but you always work on weekends anyway, so what's the diff?"

"I know it doesn't matter, we can still text and stuff while you're gone. Again."

Maggie laughed. "That's the payoff for being from a big Irish family on my mom's side, there's always a wedding, baby shower, or a funeral to go to."

"K, well I'll text you later, I'm gonna go to sleep now too. May as well, there's nothing to watch on TV and no one else is around to talk to."

"Cashmere's out with Brian?"

"Yep. Now that Beth knows him better she's letting him drive Cash around. As if my life weren't hard enough! He's coming around here now! I bumped into him in the kitchen the other day."

"Ranting again Paulie, and I'm hanging up now. Go to sleep. It will help."

"Maybe I'll dream about Mark."

"That will help too!" Maggie laughed as she hung up. Eppie looked around her room. There were no chores here, no laundry, no cleaning to do, ever. Eppie pulled her covers back off of the big bed and climbed in, and her thoughts did go to Mark as soon as she turned off the light.

Cashmere couldn't come to work for Marta at the barn the next morning, she had a cheerleading event for her club team. Eppie felt a little abandoned going to the stables alone, even though being with Chatty Cashmere had been hard on her too. Deciding it was better to be lonely than to listen to Cashmere gush about Brian, Eppie went to work getting the trail horses ready for the first ride of the day. She was deep in thought about her Brian heartache as she saddled up the horses when Marta came up behind her, startling her, which in turn spooked Kachina, the Paint mare. The horse jumped sideways, pulling hard on her lead rope and causing the other horses to prance.

"Whoa!" Marta said, instinctively reaching out and grabbing the horse's head to steady her. "Girl, what's up with you?" Now she was talking to Eppie.

"Sorry! Didn't see you there."

"Well I've never seen a girl spook like a horse before, gotta be something wrong."

Eppie smiled in spite of how miserable she felt. She didn't want to lie to Marta but full disclosure didn't seem right either. "Boys," she finally said.

"Oh, them." Marta smiled too, and tightened Kachina's cinch; the horse had bloated, holding her breath to keep the saddle girth from hitching too tight, and it had loosened some when the horse finally breathed out. "I remember boys, even though the last time I had one to bother with was a million years ago. Tough customers, boys are. They can make you soar up into the sky like a rocket and leave you as a burn mark on the ground just as fast."

Eppie blinked in astonishment. That was exactly how she felt! How did Marta know so much? Eppie couldn't even picture Marta with a man, she just seemed so much like only a horse person. "That's just how it feels," Eppie said, her voice raspy.

"Don't I know it. Best to focus on other things then, like how good your life is now Beth Krause has adopted you up."

"Well, she didn't adopt me . . . " Eppie wanted to add, *and that's the problem*, but she didn't know if Marta was just making idle chatter or really interested in trying to help Eppie so she didn't say more.

Marta continued. "Maybe not official-like, but Beth's your guardian now, and she's taking good care of things, looks like to me. Your horse's place is secured here, and let me tell you, Beth pays for all the extras, that expensive hay, the blanketing fees, the turn outs . . . all of it. Legend is living like a king, just like Cesar, so that's something better to focus on than silly boys. You're a lucky girl."

"Lucky." The word sounded strange on Eppie's tongue. How could she not have seen it before? She was so busy worrying about Brian, that she had barely noticed that she'd been "living the dream" ever since Beth took her in. She quickly calculated how much in stall fees she would have had to pay for Legend by now if she hadn't been scooped up by Beth. Almost five grand. And that was the bare minimum; Beth had dumped more than double that into Legend's care since she had taken in Eppie seven months ago. Eppie didn't have to pay for a dime of it; she suddenly realized that she hadn't picked up a manure rake since before Christmas. A churning feeling erupted inside of her.

"I know I am," Eppie said. "Lucky, that is. I could have been living in a foster home, that's where I was before they found out I had distant relatives in LA a couple years ago, and the Dursoms took me in. And even though that didn't work out, now I have Beth."

"I hear a 'but' in there somewhere," Marta nodded for Eppie to go on.

"But . . . it's like I'm Cinderella at the ball, you know? At midnight, everything could go to shit. There's no guarantee."

Marta chortled, as if surprised by Eppie's comment. "Well girl, that's probably true enough. But there are no guarantees in life. I know all about how rough you've had it before; hell, you were one runaway puppy away from a country song, but for now you're golden. So focus on the positive, and the boy . . . dump him if he's twisting up your heart. That's my advice. It hurts a little for a while, but then you'll heal up, good as new."

Eppie nodded as the first of the trail riding customers pulled up. Marta went to greet them and show them where to park. Marta's words echoed in Eppie's head. *Dump him.* But dump who, Mark? Or Brian, from her heart? Eppie didn't know and maybe didn't want to know the answer. It was all too confusing. Maybe Marta was right, and she should just focus on the good things that had happened in her life and not worry so much about boys.

Marta's horse Big Red stomped impatiently as if in agreement. Eppie buried her nose in his neck and hugged him before checking his girth to make sure it was tight.

# Chapter Thirty-Eight

Eppie stood nervously waiting in the movie theater lobby with Deena, Ivanna and Steffi. The girls were all dressed in shorts and tanks, and they'd just perfected their makeup in the public restroom. As if on cue, a group of boys walked in through the main lobby doors and Eppie felt warm all over. There was Mark, walking in with his friends, a smile lighting his face as he saw Eppie. Eppie didn't know what to do, if she should rush over to him or wait, but Deena held onto her arm so she waited for him to come up to her. He did, pulling her into his chest for a hug.

"Hi," Eppie said.

"Hey. Good seeing you." Mark hugged her again and Eppie let her chin linger on his shoulder.

"Good seeing you too, Mark."

He felt so . . . comfortable. Somehow more than she'd ever felt with Brian. Maybe it was because he was her age, but Eppie felt as if the hug had broken away all the awkwardness and now they were just going to have fun.

"We all got tickets to the same movie right?" Eppie asked. Someone had bought all the tickets together, and she didn't even know what movie they were seeing.

"Well, it doesn't really matter," Mark told her, throwing his arm around her neck and leading her with the group toward the theaters.

"What? Why?" Eppie was confused. Once they handed their tickets to the usher and she ripped it and gave them half back, they rushed in toward the theaters. She noticed her ticket stub was for the romantic comedy with the puppy that had just come out as she stuffed it in her front pocket.

"Because, we're not really going to the movie we bought tickets for. We're seeing the ripper movie instead."

"Ripper? You mean, the R rated one about that serial killer?" Eppie gulped. She had never seen a movie like that, but she'd heard all about them in the foster care homes she'd lived in; her roommates (she'd never been able to call them *foster sisters*) there had loved sharing the blow by grisly blow as she tried to fall asleep at night. Part of her now wanted to stamp her foot and walk away, but she gripped Mark's arm tighter, hoping that maybe she could sway him toward the puppy movie. But no such luck.

A master plan was hatched and suddenly Eppie felt herself being towed by Mark into the dark theater while one of their "decoy" friends pretended to lose a contact lens to distract the security guard. They found a seat next to Ivanna and the boy she liked, Cody. Those two were holding hands and sharing a drink. Eppie couldn't help remembering the old school nurse's speech at the end of the school year about mono and sharing straws, but she thought it was sort of romantic too. Ivanna had her hand in Cody's and Eppie took Mark's, trying to prepare herself for the blood bath. He smiled at her and squeezed her palm. *This is easy, being with Mark*, Eppie thought. In fact, she told herself, Brian had been a good experience for her. Now she could be confident about boys her own age and not always be so edgy. She settled down into her seat, glad she'd brought a lightweight sweater. She planned to use it to cover her eyes during the really scary parts.

"Eppie!" she heard her name like a hiss from behind. She turned, expecting to see Steffi or Deena with their 'dates', and she was so surprised to see Cashmere in the row behind her that she stood up. Brian was with her! She groaned but it couldn't be heard over the roar of the movie previews.

"What are you doing here?" Eppie blurted, more to Brian than to Cashmere. Could this be happening?

"What am I doing here? What are you doing here? I saw you come in here earlier!" Cashmere's look in the dim light was unfathomable. Eppie squinted against the projector glare.

"I'm just out with friends tonight," Eppie said.

"Come to the hallway a minute with me," Cashmere said loudly.

Eppie crossed her arms over her chest. Why was Cashmere treating her like a baby? "What for?"

"I need to see you. Pronto."

Cashmere handed Brian her drink and said to Eppie just loud enough so Eppie could hear, "I'm waiting to talk to you!"

Brian avoided looking at Eppie, but stammered, "You want to just see this film instead?" to Cashmere, who shook her head and glared at Brian. Cashmere pointed toward the exit and Eppie leaned over to Mark and whispered, "I have to go talk to my sister for a minute, I'll be right back."

Eppie could feel all eyes on her as she walked back down the dimly lit stairs, feeling like a kindergartner in trouble with the teacher. She gritted her teeth as the theater's hall glow hit her when she swung open the door.

"What's going on?" Eppie asked, her arms still crossed. She didn't want Cashmere to know how mad she was and was pinching the underside of her arm to keep herself focused on staying calm. Brian ducked into the men's room to avoid the scene.

"Maybe you should tell me what's going on?" Cashmere said, looking Eppie up and down like an inspector. *Did she know something? What was up?*

"I'm just seeing a movie with friends," Eppie said. She wanted to add *got a problem with that?* but she knew better.

"Why are you in an R rated movie? You're just a kid!"

"You're not allowed in there either," Eppie pointed out.

"I'm not seeing an R rated movie! I'm watching that new one about the puppy."

"Oh." Eppie flushed hot. Why was Cashmere suddenly like a little mother?

"I didn't even pick the movie," Eppie explained, "those guys did. I'd rather not even see it. I think that the ticket that they bought for me was that one you're seeing, but they all snuck in . . ."

"So you didn't want to be left out. I get it, Eppie, but really, I thought you were above this sort of thing. Those kids shouldn't be in there watching that movie. Do you have your ticket stub?"

Eppie dug into her jeans shorts' pocket and found the stub. Cashmere smiled. "There you go, see, it is the same movie! Want to come to it with Bo and me?"

"What?"

"Want to ask your little date . . . what's his name again? Mike?"

"It's Mark."

"Mark then, to come to the other movie? Because I really don't want you going back in there."

Eppie sighed. She hadn't really come up against Cashmere like this before. Would Cashmere tell Beth? Would Eppie get in trouble? She didn't even know. The rules were sort of murky, like the ocean on a cold winter's day. She had no idea what was really expected of her. She went to school, worked, rode Cesar, trained Legend: what were the boundaries? She was a fourteen year old on a date. But she couldn't see an R rated movie. Not that she wanted to. She fished her phone out of her pocket and texted Mark *Meet me in the hallway for a sec, k? sorry.* She and Cashmere leaned from foot to foot while waiting in silence, and since it was getting awkward standing there and not talking, Eppie found a nearby bench and sat down. At this rate they'd all miss both movies. Finally Mark, who looked quite red in the face, probably from being harassed by his friends, appeared. Cashmere walked up to him and put her hand on his shoulder. His eyes widened.

"I'm Cashmere . . . "

"I know who you are, my brother Jonas used to go to your school."

Cashmere squinted. "Jonas. Oh, right. We went to middle school together before he transferred to public. You were at my house at that party, right? Well . . ." Cashmere launched. "I don't want Pauline here to see that film you're about to watch, but I'm going with my boyfriend to the other movie. Would you join us? I don't want her to have to feel like a third wheel, if you know what I mean."

Eppie cringed. She had never been so embarrassed! Cashmere was worse than a meddling parent! She looked at the bathroom door across from where she stood rooted, and felt an impulse to run inside and hide in one of the stalls. Her feet failed her.

Mark looked as uncomfortable as Eppie felt and found a sudden interest in his shoelace. He stared at it, then shrugged his shoulders. Finally he looked up at Cashmere.

"I don't really care which movie I see," he said. He looked at Eppie, a small grin inching its way up the side of his face. Eppie was startled to see him smiling and realized he was trying not to laugh. It made Eppie want to laugh too, and suddenly the two of them were trying not to bust up while following the prim and uptight Cashmere to the next theater over.

The movie had just started as they took their seats. Brian joined them carrying a huge bucket or popcorn. Cashmere snuggled in next to him, Eppie took the spot next to Cashmere, as Mark sat on the end next to Eppie. Eppie was keenly aware that she was sitting between Brian and Mark at the movies! Sure, Cashmere was in the middle, but it was still awkward. As the screen illuminated them she could see Brian out of the corner of her eye. He was slouched in his seat as if he was trying to disappear.

Bo, Bo, Bo. It made Eppie want to hurl. And now he was pushing his body as far away from Cashmere (and Eppie) as he could, eating popcorn with his hand up near his face. *Coward*, Eppie thought.

She tried to focus on the film. Mark held her hand and then put his hand on her thigh, just above the knee. He was a gentleman compared to that octopus Brian. Cashmere scuffled around in her seat and got Brian to sit up and put his arms around her. *If they kiss*, Eppie thought, *I will leave and call Julianna to come and get me early*. She tried hard to watch the film but finally she had to leave to get her bearings, scooting out toward the bathroom after telling Mark in a whisper that she'd be right back.

After splashing cold water on her face she went into the stall and sat down. Brian was still a thorn in her side, that was for sure. Here Mark was sweet, nice, funny, and as comfortable as her slippers and yet . . . Brian still made her heart beat faster, and sitting near him with a girl between them was more than Eppie could take. She took a couple deep breaths and headed back out toward the movie, telling herself for the tenth time that she could get through it without spying on Brian out of the corner of her eyes.

Brian was waiting for her in the empty hallway. Eppie tried to huff past him but he grabbed her and pulled her close to him. Eppie's instinct was to start hitting him to let her go but then his scent sort of washed over her and she let herself melt into him. It felt good. Too good. Tears fell and she didn't even know they were coming. Small spots of water wet his shirt.

"I'm sorry," he said. He kissed her on the forehead. "I didn't plan this. What a disaster!"

"Tell me about it." Eppie didn't want to talk. There was nothing to say. Brian held her again and she closed her eyes. She heard a theater door open and giggling behind her and she looked up. Ivanna was standing there with Steffi, an amazed look on both of their faces. Eppie straightened up and stared at them. She had no idea what to say, and her face turned so red she could feel the heat. She felt exposed, but then realized those two probably didn't know what any of this meant; her tears, his wet shirt, the hug, no Mark. A question mark was etched on Ivanna's face. Of the two of them, she was the instigator of everything, and Eppie could see her trying to put it all together. Had Ivanna met Brian at the party? Did she know who he was? Eppie couldn't remember the party details; it was all a fog and jumble of dismay, until Mark had rescued her later on with distracting kisses. Brian squeezed Eppie's arm gently and looked into her eyes, mouthed the word 'sorry,' and moved on back to the movie theater, leaving her raw and open right there with her two friends on her like hyenas.

"What the hell was that?" Ivanna asked.

"Yeah!" Steffi piped in.

Eppie shrugged. She walked back into the bathroom, not wanting to make her crazed love life public. Any more than it already was. The girls were on her heels, watching as she adjusted her makeup with a shaky hand, after finding her eye pencils in her purse pocket. The tears had washed part of the color away. Ivanna hovered in close like a vulture waiting for some animal to die already. Eppie tried to ignore her but it was as impossible as ignoring Brian.

"Strike two," Ivanna said.

"What does that mean?" Eppie asked.

"It means, that this is the same guy that you were moping over at the party. What gives?"

Eppie tried again to remember her encounter with Brian at the party. They'd barely spoken. Had they even? How did Ivanna know that? She was surprised . . . and worried. Somehow Ivanna knew too much.

"It's nothing. Just an old crush."

"Crush? Def of a crush, Pauline, is when you likelikelike someone but they don't know you exist. This is not a crush, it's positively steamy."

Steffi nodded, letting Ivanna go in for the kill. She'd take her leftovers later. "What I don't get is why you're so busy leading Mark on. He really likes you, you know. Like really likes you. Thinks of you as his girlfriend, or his soon-to-be-girlfriend once he gets back from his cruise."

Eppie didn't know that and was happy to hear it, but now . . . she didn't trust the look in Ivanna's eyes.

"Okay," Eppie said. "Here's the thing. That guy and I, we had something once, it's over, it's been over for a while, but it's still hard. That's it. We can't be together but it didn't end well and we're tying up loose strings."

"Tying up loose strings? Could you be any more vague?" Ivanna scoffed.

"I don't know what you want me to say!" Eppie roared, surprised by her own anger. "I told you, it's over! I like Mark! That's the end of it!" Eppie stomped out of the bathroom, done with feeling cornered, and hurried back to her own movie theater. Damn! Why had she yelled at Ivanna, who by now was back in the other theater telling everyone what she'd seen and what had happened? Eppie gnawed on her nail as she rejoined Mark. He was a warm solace as she leaned up against him.

"You okay?" he whispered. She nodded, still shaky. She twisted her body away from Cashmere and Brian, determined not to look over at him or let her thoughts go his way. Mark was what she wanted, and what was best for her. She tried not to let her thoughts race about what Ivanna might do as she sat curled up next to Mark in the darkened room.

## Chapter Thirty-nine

Eppie braided Legend's mane, glad for the plywood boards that surrounded his stall so no prying eyes could see her. She needed time to be alone to think; Mark was safely on his cruise, and if Ivanna was causing problems by texting all of their school friends about her hug with Brian, Eppie hadn't heard a peep about it. She felt different in the daylight, as if she could maybe start to let it all go and move on. *Is this relief?* she wondered briefly. *Or stupidity?* Legend stood still, allowing his mane to be her plaything though he stamped his front foot impatiently after a minute.

"Sorry boy," Eppie whispered to him. "I know you're bored. Let's try something new today." Beth had bought Legend a driving harness, and had left it on Eppie's bed without a note or explanation. Eppie had barely seen Beth for nearly three weeks; she and Charlie had been to their time share in St. Tropez, and then she'd been busy heading up a fundraising group for a local children's theater. Cashmere told Eppie rather bitterly in June, "Don't expect to see much of Mom during the summer," and that prophecy was proving to be true. In a way Eppie missed Beth. While Julianna was more like the caregiver, Beth made Eppie feel safe. The two girls were practically living alone in the house with Julianna driving them around and cooking for them, but there was no "in charge" adult to anchor their days, just a list of phone numbers of people to call if problems arose. *Tracey was always home, always there,* Eppie remembered. *She was strict, but she was always on top of what I did, where I went.* Eppie realized with a start that she missed Tracey. A sense of deep loss permeated her to the core, eliminating her earlier feelings of moving on. She felt like she couldn't afford to lose even one more thing, not even Mark. She hugged Legend tight.

"You're my best friend," she told him. "I'm the luckiest girl alive to have you." Legend nudged her with his face in reply, and Eppie felt like crying but it was a luxury, one she was determined not to allow herself anymore. In a practiced way she shut down the waterworks and focused on being numb, a condition she was starting to master. She groomed Legend, using the colorful brushes in the purple plastic grooming box, and then showed him the harness. He sniffed it, ears perked forward, and snorted. Eppie laughed. She'd looked up in Dr. Beery's book how to handle a horse that was "Bad with Harness," but it merely said to punish the horse with the bridle, something she didn't agree with and couldn't see herself doing. She tried a different approach.

"Silly, it won't hurt you. See?" She gently petted his neck with the long leather reins. He pranced sideways. "Legend! This is fun! Don't be scared!" Eppie continued to run the reins around his neck and shoulder until he could ignore the contraption, and then she carefully put the harness on him, slowly unfolding the unwieldy stiff leather straps and placing them across his back. He snorted a couple more times but stood still and let her put the contraption around his girth. When she figured out all the tight buckles and attachments she stood back to admire her work. "You look adorable!" she said, and hugged him again. Legend gave her a doubtful sideways glance but the dark brown leather complimented his silver-gray coat and he stood erect and proud as Eppie went behind him to show him how she would pull on the reins to guide him. After a few minutes, Eppie cautiously let him out of his stall and tried walking behind him up and down the aisle of stalls. At first Legend didn't get it at all; weren't you supposed to *follow* the human? But after a couple of attempts he had figured out driving; to Eppie it seemed almost not as if he was learning something new, but remembering something he already knew how to do. A few of the barn locals poked their heads out of their horse's stalls to comment and smile. As she tried turning the corner, Legend almost ran right into Marta.

“Holy smokes!” Marta said with a chuckle. “You don’t expect a horse to come around the bend with no person beside him, do you?” She reached up and grabbed Legend’s headgear to inspect the new harness. “Nice, real nice. Beth get this for you?”

“Yes, but I don’t know why. We don’t have a carriage.”

“It’s just a way to keep the horse well rounded, you know,” Marta explained. “Good for a young horse to know how to wear all kinds of tack. You never know, he may be a Budweiser horse someday.”

“He’s no draft horse!” Eppie laughed.

“No, I don’t suppose he is.” Marta chuckled and gave Legend an affectionate pat. “He’s too much of a beauty, aren’t you Legend? What a gorgeous boy.” Eppie had never, in all the time she’d known Marta, heard her compliment a horse so much. Marta usually didn’t play favorites but Eppie could tell she really liked Legend. Eppie smiled.

“He’s being great today,” she said. “He’s really coming along.”

“He’ll be ready to ride soon enough. Are you putting weight on his back yet?”

“He’s in a weighted saddle, an English hunt saddle,” Eppie said.

“I have a Western one you should throw on him too, just to get used to the different types of girth. What about a bit?”

“Egg-butt snaffle,” Eppie replied.

“I have a Western curb bit on an old bridle you can use, too,” Marta said. “Let’s make this boy a solid, anything-goes kind of horse, Pauline. He has so much potential, but only the horse knows what he’s best at. Let’s let him tell us, what do you say?” Marta patted his neck and then saw one of her stable workers. “Francisco!” she called. “Ven aqui!” She waved to the hunched little man carrying a halter in his hand as he stopped and turned. “I have to go see Francisco,” Marta said, looking at Eppie intently. “You okay though? I know Beth isn’t around much.”

“Fine,” Eppie said automatically. She forced herself to smile.

“Okay, but if you want to talk about anything, I’m around.” Marta patted Eppie on the shoulder much as she had Legend, and rushed off to catch up with the horse hand. Eppie clicked for Legend to move on and wondered what she would tell Marta. *I'm tired of being left by the people who say they'll care for me? Even though I'm grateful for Beth and Cashmere and Charlie rescuing me, I'm lonely? I really miss my mom? Grandma is better now but it's not the same as having a real relative who cares for me?* That was it, she realized. As much as she felt protected and cared for, she didn't really feel "cared about." She felt the threat of internal rain again so she tightened up her mind and clicked again to Legend, walking forward and pushing those confusing thoughts away as her black barn boots kicked up a fine powdery dust.

Work, training Legend, visiting Grandma, and going to the beach club rounded out Eppie's summer, and soon enough Cashmere was joining her for most of these things again ("Bo has summer training in Lacrosse," she'd told Eppie). It felt more like family time and Eppie was glad when suddenly in late-July, it was Beth driving the girls to the club, not Julianna, and the three of them would order drinks (faux Mai Tais) and sip and sunbathe and swim. Eppie felt deeply relaxed at the end of each tiring day and often fell asleep in the chaise lounge chair, the sound of children splashing in the pool and the melodious sea beyond her lullaby. Then Mark came home from his cruise.

Eppie was nervous about seeing him again but as they met at the mall on a Friday evening, the sight of him made her heart soar; he, like her, was deeply tanned and looked like he'd had a great summer of sun and shore (and time well spent on the Lido deck). He hugged her and Eppie breathed in, realizing she missed his scent.

"How have you been?" she asked as he grasped her hand and they walked in the soft pink light of the sunset, the store fronts in The Promenade cheerily lit. They stood and looked at the fountain a moment, the illuminated dancing waters mesmerizing.

"Good! We had a great trip, but it's better to be home. I got to surf some but not enough, I need to get out there."

"I've heard the waves aren't that good," Eppie said, to keep the conversation going.

“Well, not in summer, but you know . . . just want to get in the water and surf a little.”

“Can you teach me?”

“I thought you were more of a beach club kind of girl,” Mark said with a small laugh.

Eppie thought about her lounging around at the club all summer and giggled. “Well, you’re right about that, but I’m game. I’d like to try surfing again.” She nearly mentioned Lonny but stopped herself.

“Early morning the waves are best. Sometimes in the evening too if the waves aren’t too blown out.”

“Isn’t that . . .” Eppie hesitated. “When the sharks feed?’

Mark laughed. “Um, there are no sharks in the ocean, Pauline. That’s just a rumor, you know.”.

Eppie smiled. “Oh! Well in that case, tell me when, and I’ll be there.”

As it turned out, Eppie was pretty good at surfing and was standing on the board and taking small waves by the end of her third lesson with Mark. Now she was trying to fit in surfing with Mark into her schedule, and she managed to a couple times a week, but it was just so she could splash and play around with him in the ocean. Some days when the waves weren’t worth the walk down the long hill to the beach Mark would join her at the beach club. Even though they’d kissed a lot at the party, it was a couple weeks in before she was kissing him hello and goodbye, and soon they were relaxed and comfortable together. Life was good.

As summer waned everyone came back from their vacations, and soon Eppie’s friends were all hanging out at the mall weekend nights, getting caught up. Ivanna and Eppie were at Starbucks getting Frappucinos when Brian and Cashmere walked in to the espresso-scented hang out.

“Hi!” Eppie said, nearly dropping her just-purchased drink at the sight of them in line behind her.

“Oh, hi!” Cashmere said cheerfully. “What are you all up to?”

“Movie at nine.”

“We’re meeting friends to go to a Collier’s party,” Cashmere said with a flashing smile. She said *Collier’s* with emphasis, to show that it was a snooty prep school party, not for the public high school locals.

"Sounds fun," Eppie said hastily, realizing that Ivanna was giving Brian an intent look. She could almost feel Ivanna's mind churning and her heart pounded. Uh oh, Ivanna remembered seeing their hug! Eppie had to get Cashmere out of there.

"See ya!" Eppie grabbed Ivanna's arm to lead her away but Ivanna turned back.

"Oh, hey, aren't you Pauline's ex?" Ivanna said to Brian in an even voice.

Brian turned dark red and looked flustered.

"Uh, no," Cashmere said forcefully. "Bo is my boyfriend, not Pauline's."

Eppie's thoughts raced. She was afraid to open her mouth.

"No, I'm sure of it, this is that guy you were hugging in the theater hallway, you know, that night we all saw that killer movie and you saw the puppy one with Mark, remember?" Ivanna said, her eyes wide as she looked at Eppie. Eppie shook her head, still not able to think of a thing to say.

"What are you talking about?" Cashmere asked Ivanna as Brian and Eppie stood by helplessly.

"Let's go, Cashmere, we're gonna be late," Brian attempted to pull on her arm, but she wrenched it away.

"Um, no, I really want to hear this."

Ivanna looked like a diva on stage as she puffed up and began her story about what she'd seen, and even included the part about how Eppie had been huffy in the bathroom about it and said that Brian was her ex that she was having trouble getting over ("Well, she implied it," Ivanna said). Cashmere's face reddened as the tale continued. Her fists clenched and when Ivanna ended triumphantly, neither Brian nor Eppie moved or said a word.

"She's crazy," Brian said finally, breaking the silence. "Let's go." But Cashmere turned on Eppie.

"So is this true? Have you been sneaking around behind my back dating Bo?" she hissed, her mouth set tight.

"No!" Eppie said in an explosion of emotion. "I would never do that to you!" she lowered her voice, hating the pleading sound she was making, wishing she could punch out Ivanna and knock that smug look off her face right now.

"Then explain to me why we're even having this conversation? Why were you hugging my boyfriend at the movie theater?"

Eppie couldn't help but notice that all of Cashmere's attention was on her, not Brian. *Because she feels most betrayed by me*, a small voice in her head told her.

"Can we not discuss this here?" Eppie said. She recognized a few kids who had wandered in and were watching the confrontation with interest.

"Yes, take it outside," called out the barista behind the counter, who had apparently noticed a scene was commencing.

"No," Cashmere said loudly enough for everyone to hear. "I want an explanation right now about why you were hugging my boyfriend and why this girl . . ." she said the word with distaste as she looked at Ivanna ". . . is saying that you two are seeing each other."

Eppie wanted to run outside and wondered if she'd make the door before Cashmere took her out. Deena and Steffi walked in right then with Mark, Cody, and some other boys from school. Eppie looked around, desperate, knowing how a wild horse must feel when caught and brought into captivity.

"I'm not having this conversation right now," Eppie whispered fiercely. "We can talk later."

"What's going on?" Mark intervened, grabbing Eppie around the waist to comfort her. "Is there a problem?"

"Oh yes, there's a problem. Apparently my boyfriend and your girlfriend are seeing each other secretly behind our backs," Cashmere announced.

Mark dropped his hands and stared at Eppie.

"That's not true!" Eppie said. She realized, as all eyes scrutinized her, that she would not get out of Starbucks without an explanation. "I dated Brian last year, before I even lived with you," Eppie told Cashmere. "I had no idea he was your boyfriend, and as soon as I found out, I broke it off."

Some people went back to their business, bored with the story now. It wasn't going to be the drag-out fight they'd hoped for. Deena and Steffi tactfully pulled their friends out of the building. But Cashmere and Mark were still very interested in more details, and Ivanna was practically panting, she was so excited. Eppie realized her hand was wet and numb from gripping her ice cold Frappuccino so tightly. She set it down on a table nearby and pulled the small group away from the line.

"This is private, between the three of us," she said, pointing to herself, Cashmere, and Brian. "But Mark, this has nothing to do with you, that hug was just . . . a goodbye kind of hug, before you and I were officially dating. And Cashmere, I promise, the second I made the connection that Bo was Brian, I stopped all contact with him. I swear."

"It's true," Brian said.

"But you were still dating another girl behind my back," Cashmere pointed out slowly to Brian, which Eppie knew from experience meant she was aiming for the kill. "So you're still a two-timing asshole, aren't you Bo? Or is it Brian? You have to keep changing your name around to keep your girlfriends quiet and confused?"

Ivanna smiled broadly at that one.

"We were broken up when I started seeing Pauline, and it was casual. I met her when she lived in Lomita, it had nothing to do with you Cash. I didn't even know you knew her! It's just a big coincidence."

Cashmere swung around, dismissing Brian, eyes locked on Eppie. "And you . . . you lived in my house . . ." her voice was quavering with anger now . . "you ate our food, let my mother spend a fortune trying to heal your sick grandmother, we bought and took care of your horse, we rescued you from that hell hole in Lomita . . ." she said the city name with great distaste. "We even took you on our family vacation, and all the while, all that time, you couldn't have told me that you even knew Brian? Didn't you ever think that maybe if I'd known he was two-timing me, I wouldn't have kept dating him? I thought we were like sisters! How can I ever, ever trust you again?"

Cashmere's face twitched with rage, and Eppie felt the crushing blow of her words. When she said it like that, it seemed so simple. Yes, of course, she should have come clean and protected Cashmere. She should have told her about Brian, or at least told Beth. What had she been thinking? Why hadn't she? The truth outed itself.

"I was afraid I'd lose you, and lose my home with you, and end up back in foster care," Eppie said quietly. So many more thoughts ricocheted around in her brain but they were like flies buzzing around and she couldn't nail them down. Tears leaked out the corners of her eyes but she brushed them away.

Cashmere's eyes narrowed. "And now what, you think lying to my family all this time will save you from foster care? Fat chance." Cashmere turned and walked away, leaving Brian, Eppie, Mark and Ivanna standing there in the coffee house. Ivanna turned away and began texting madly. Brian stood awkwardly in front of Eppie, a panicked look in his eye. His eyes wandered to Mark and he shrugged his shoulders, turned, and followed Cashmere. Mark put his arm around Eppie's shoulder. She turned her face into his chest and cried as he led her out the door. She barely felt the relief of the warm summer night air as she realized that her worst fear had come true. Knowing how vindictive and ruthless Cashmere could be, and how Beth would go along with whatever Cashmere wanted, Eppie realized with a sense of devastation that she had probably just lost everything, including her beloved horse, Legend.

# Chapter Forty

Eppie was silent as Julianna navigated the minivan through the dark curving streets toward home, home at least for now. Her mind raced wildly as she tried to figure out what to do. *I'll go and talk to Beth,* she told herself. *If I get to her first, she'll understand that I didn't mean to hurt anyone.* Eppie jumped out of the car with a quick thank you to Julianna and ran into the kitchen through the garage door. The house was quiet, as it usually was. Eppie raced up the stairs two at a time to Beth's master suite. She knocked lightly on the door. It was slightly ajar; she saw movement inside.

"Come in," Beth's voice called. Eppie slowly opened the door and her heart sank when she saw Cashmere sitting on the edge of the bed beside Beth, leaning against her, crying into her arms.

"I . . . I . . ." Eppie sputtered. It felt so private, this moment. She'd never even seen Beth hug Cashmere like that, didn't really think that they were close. And yet here she'd stumbled onto a major mother/daughter moment, and she felt like an interloper, an outcast.

"We need to talk," Beth said evenly, her tone unfathomable. Eppie nodded, but didn't know what to do. Beth had the answer for her. "Why don't you wait in your room, Pauline, and I'll be in soon."

*Pauline.* Beth called her Pauline. She hadn't called her anything other than Eppie since she'd learned about her family's nickname for her. Now she was Pauline again? Her foster home and school name, her non-family name? Heart heavy, Eppie trudged down the hallway to her room. She sat against the pillowed headboard, missing Laceybell, Tracey's white cat, who she would have held, and she would have cried into her long fur. She grabbed a pillow instead and held it against her cheek. Looking around the room she realized that everything in here wasn't really hers, it was Beth's. There was nothing, except maybe the big portraits of her and Legend, that she would be allowed to take with her. Beth certainly wouldn't want to keep them. Why had she let this place feel like home? She'd fallen right into it, like a trap, and claimed it as her own. Now all of her familiar things, from her lamp to her bedspread to the white fuzzy rug under her desk, were going to soon be a memory. Where would she go? Back to the Dursom's? What about Jimmy? Grandma? Thoughts reeled in her mind like a spiraling wheel with no beginning, no end, just a circle of endless questions. She closed her eyes tight and shoved her face into the pillow and finally, the tears she'd held in for days sprang from her. She sobbed.

Beth came in and shook Eppie, who realized she must have fallen asleep, because she was unsure of how much time had passed. It was over an hour ago that she'd gotten home, she saw as she looked at the clock over her TV set. She sat up and smoothed her hair, embarrassed to be awakened by Beth.

"Is Cashmere okay?" Eppie asked, her voice groggy.

"No," Beth said. "She isn't." It wasn't the answer Eppie wanted to hear.

"There are two sides, Beth. I promise you I didn't hurt her on purpose. I just . . . I was trying to protect her."

Beth regarded Eppie as she sat down on the edge of the bed. She looked up at the pictures on the wall, at the bedroom she'd decorated for Eppie. She rubbed her eyes in a tired way.

"You know, I really like having you here," Beth said. "You've been so good for Cashmere. She's showing her horse again, she's having fun on Cesar, she's working, and she's even enjoying the beach club when last summer I had to bribe her to go. She's enjoying life in a way she hasn't in a long time, and she's more engaged with her father and I, and I owe thanks for that to you, I think. You've brought her out of her shell."

Eppie nodded, not trusting words to come out of her, barely breathing, hoping not to break the spell.

"And now we have a problem," Beth continued. "And to be honest, I have no idea where we go from here."

Eppie was startled. Beth always had an answer. She always knew what she was doing.

"Just so you know, I met Brian—Bo—when I lived in Lomita with the Dursoms," Eppie said quickly. "I didn't know he was dating Cashmere at all, not for a long time. And the second he told me, I told him it was over, and I haven't seen him since, except when he's with Cashmere, and we haven't even talked or anything since I found out."

"I know," Beth said with a sigh. "That's what Cashmere told me that you said."

Eppie's heart lightened. At least Cashmere wasn't lying to Beth about things, that was a good sign.

"Cashmere has considered you to be like a little sister," Beth said. "She's trusted you. In a deep way, and she's let you into her life in a way that she's not accustomed to doing."

"I know."

"And now you've broken that trust with her."

Eppie couldn't swallow past that damn lump in her throat. Warm tears dripped again without her permission.

"I don't think she can trust you again, Eppie. Which puts us all in a bind. At this point, she's so upset that she's threatened to leave our home . . ." Beth's voice wavered. "If I keep you here, she swears she'll run away and we won't see her again." Beth wiped a tear from the corner of her eye. "I think she may be bluffing, but she could do it, she has resources. And I can't risk it. Not for you. Not for anyone. I'm so sorry." Beth reached out to hug Eppie, but she was wooden. She stayed stiff, her arms crossing her chest, holding back the tidal wave of tears that were on the way up.

"Eppie . . ."

"Don't call me that! That's a name reserved for family," Eppie said coolly. "I hear you, Beth. You're kicking me out. I get it. I'll pack my things."

"I'll have Julianna do it, you don't have to do anything," Beth said quietly. "And not this second, we have to make arrangements. I've talked to Tracey, but Jim is living at home again and he's stayed sober and things are good, so she's a little concerned about bringing you there right now."

“She is technically my family,” Eppie said defensively. “I could go back there if Jim is sober.” She didn’t want to go back there at all if Jim was living there, but Eppie was aware that the hated known was often better than the unknown.

“Yes, Tracey should take you back in, but I’m not sure I trust Jim,” Beth said. The ironic words hung there. Eppie was losing two homes, one because she couldn’t be trusted, and the other because Jim couldn’t be trusted.

Panic rose up in Eppie. “Beth . . .” she said, her voice forceful, “Please Beth, don’t send me back to foster care! I’ll lose everything! I can’t go there again! I can’t!” Her tears fell freely again, her face a wet mess. She covered her eyes and let herself cry into her hands. If she went back into the foster care system, Legend would be sold and lost to her forever. There was no way she’d be able to keep him, or even her job at the stables.

“Well,” Beth said. “No, that’s not something I would consider an option until every other avenue was exhausted. But, maybe you should prepare yourself, just in case that becomes a temporary solution. We’re on a tight timeline, school starts soon.”

“I can’t go back into the system! Don’t send me there, I’ll lose everything! What about Legend?” Eppie asked, feeling now that he was her only true family.

“We have an agreement,” Beth said. “Don’t forget, Legend is now only officially yours when you turn eighteen, Pauline. Legend is the least of our concerns at this moment. Legend has a roof over his head right now. You’re the one we need to think about.”

Beth looked lost in thought, and Eppie wanted to talk more about Legend and what that meant. She knew that Beth technically owned him now, but she’d said that was to protect Eppie from losing Legend! What would Beth want with an untrained young horse that was costing her hundreds of dollars a month if her daughter wasn’t getting free lessons? Would she sell Legend out from under her? Eppie’s eyes widened in fear and the only solace she could find was her already damp pillow. She threw herself down on the bed and felt an overwhelming darkness cover her. She barely heard Beth tiptoe out of the room.

Eppie was in a daze at work the next day, so much so that she didn't react when one of the horses in the rear spooked, scaring a customer.

"Just pull back on the reins," Marta called out, trotting from the front of the line of horses to the back to guide the Paint gelding that had jumped off the trail and was now standing stock still in the dried up brown mustard field. Marta was taking over for Cashmere, who didn't go to work with Eppie and was nowhere to be found that morning. Eppie's stomach was a tight ball when Beth had mentioned that Cashmere was "staying with family friends temporarily". Eppie knew that meant Cashmere had moved out until Eppie was gone, to ensure her mother didn't falter in her promise to get Eppie out of the house.

"You look a million miles away," Marta said after rescuing the horse and rider. "First Cashmere's a no-show, and you're just not here. Anything you need to say?"

Eppie had come to work determined not to say a word about her personal problems, mostly because she was afraid of crying in public, so she resolutely bit her lip and shook her head.

"You sure?"

"Let's for now just say that I'm in the market for a new place to live, and leave it at that," Eppie said in a low voice.

Marta looked stunned. "That's some pretty serious news. What could have brought that about?"

Eppie hesitated, but the word left her lips anyway: "Cashmere."

Marta nodded. "I see." Her own lips were drawn into a thin line. "Tell you what, we're going to have a sit down chat sometime soon, okay? Just you and me."

Eppie nodded, not trusting her words. She assumed that Marta might want to make her a deal, Eppie working at the stables in exchange for Legend's stall fees, and she started worrying again about how to hold on to Legend when Marta saw her wrinkled brow and tactfully changed the subject.

"I was thinking, we should start ponying Legend out here with us, let him get used to the trail again."

"You think so?" Eppie was glad to think of him instead, although now with so much uncertainty in the air, it felt impossible to make any future plans with Legend.

"Sure. Kachina is a great pony horse, I'll lead him on Big Red until he gets used to things, then you can bring him along with Kachina once he remembers it's all good out here and nothing will hurt him. Then every time you take a trail ride you can bring him and be working with him at the same time."

Eppie actually smiled in spite of everything that was so wrong. "You've got to be the best boss ever," she said.

Marta harrumphed. "I was thinking that I was more than that to you, girl, but it's a start." She clicked to Big Red and trotted back up to the front of the line where a scenic spot was approaching. Eppie watched her, glad to let her mind wander to Legend. She imagined him with her now and wished that he was part of the group; she vowed to keep him close as long as she had him, since the clock was now ticking and she had no idea what their future held, or if she'd even own him much longer. She watched the long summer shadows of the walking horses and recognized that school would be starting soon, and she didn't even know which school she'd be going to, or where she'd be living. *Just breathe this moment in,* she told herself as she looked up into the pepper trees, seeing the blue sky beyond. *This could be the end of all things good. I need to just enjoy this time that I have out here.*

Determined not to think of anything scary or negative, Eppie allowed herself to just feel Kachina's solid sway under her, the leather of the saddle against her jeans, the quiet stillness of the pre-sunset air. The herd climbed up a steep hill and at the top the riders saw the entire Los Angeles basin, the ocean aglow like flame as the sun lowered into the sky to the west. *I promise,* Eppie told herself, the sky, that gleaming ocean, and the universe, *that no matter what happens, I will not let anyone take Legend or this life away from me. This is where I belong, the only place left where I can find peace. And this is where I will stay. Somehow, I will make it work, and I will stay.*

## Chapter Forty-one

Eppie woke up and stretched, momentarily forgetting her problems until the black cloud moved back in and covered her senses. She propped herself up on her pillows and looked around her beautiful bedroom, hating that it was the best thing she'd had since her mom died and she was about to give it up. Part of her wanted to just leave now and go sleep in the hay room at the stables, just to get away from the pain of being in this house where she knew she wasn't wanted. That was the worst part, that feeling that she had no one to care or take her in. She wished for a miracle and the old niggling thought like a loose tooth dawned; what about her father? He was a fantasy who always popped into her mind whenever she found herself in transition; but she only imagined him to be that guy in the picture, Mom and Grandma had never admitted a thing. Daddy Dearest was off the radar and unavailable to come and rescue his homeless orphaned daughter. And homeless was the word Eppie didn't like to think about. Eppie squeezed the confusing thoughts from her mind. Forget about an imaginary parent she'd never met. What she needed now was to not have any parents, to get all of the adults out of her life so she could just live.

She sat up straight. *Emancipation!* She remembered one of the foster kids had gotten a gratis lawyer who had helped her become emancipated, which meant she was free from parental control. That girl had become a legal adult at age sixteen. Well, she was almost seventeen, but she had a job, a place to live, and she was taking her GED to get out of high school. Could Eppie do that too? Sure, Eppie was younger, just fourteen, but she had a job, she could probably do it! She got up and freshened up, found a bathrobe, and went downstairs.

Charles and Beth were sitting at the sunny kitchen table over coffee, scones, and the newspaper.

" . . . and she's still not taking my calls," Beth was saying.

Charles shrugged. "She's a spoiled brat. You shouldn't let her rule your life like that, Beth."

Eppie cleared her throat. Charles smiled broadly at her when he saw her.

"Eppie! Come in, dear. Have some scones." Eppie was glad he at least seemed glad to see her, and she didn't mind at all that he was calling her Eppie. She'd always liked Charles, even though he wasn't around that much. She looked at Beth to make sure it was okay.

"There's juice, and milk," Beth said in a friendly way. Charles stood and pulled a chair out next to him, and squeezed her shoulder as she sat down. She was hungry and took two scones, some jam, and a glass of milk.

"I want to apologize for my family," Charles said as Eppie ate. She looked up at him, surprised, but was taking a sip of milk and didn't say anything.

"Charles, please don't . . ." Beth said, putting her hand on his wrist.

"No, I need to say something, Beth. I never, never would have agreed for Eppie to come into our home if I knew that Cashmere was calling all the shots. That's unfair to Eppie, gives Cashmere a sense of entitlement I don't think she deserves, and proves that it's a sixteen-year-old girl that runs this place, not her parents. It's pathetic, upsetting, and I'm against this entire thing. As far as I'm concerned, Eppie should be able to stay here as long as she likes."

Eppie was grateful for the words, and for a moment she thought Charles was going to put his foot down and make Beth and Cashmere let her stay there.

"Pauline doesn't want to stay here with Cashmere hating her for it," Beth pointed out. "I wouldn't, at any rate, and it will bring conflict into our home. Cashmere only has two more years here before she goes off to college. Why make those years difficult?"

Beth's voice was so smooth, and she talked as if Eppie wasn't sitting right there.

"I'm giving my opinion, Beth. This is your project, your thing with the horse and Eppie . . ." Charles looked at Eppie and gave her a sad smile. "I'm not happy at all about this decision, and I want everyone here to know it." He stood up, put his cloth napkin on his plate, and left the room.

"Poor Charles," Beth said to Eppie. "He really doesn't handle conflict well."

Eppie was disappointed that Charles had only given a little speech and then left. *What a chicken*, she thought, and she was reminded briefly of her conflict with the Dursoms, of their son preying on her, and wondered what Charles would have done about that. The conflict in this household was that Cashmere was off vacationing with friends and apparently not answering Beth's calls. It was distant and sterile, and Eppie was somewhat outraged that Cashmere was lording over everyone with her antics.

"Don't worry, Beth, I have an idea," Eppie said stiffly. "I want to be emancipated. That way I won't end up back in a foster home."

"Emancipated?" Beth tried the word on for size. "Really? You're a little young, Pauline. I'm not sure it's legal."

"Can we find out?"

"I'll certainly put a call into my lawyer for you, and we can see."

Eppie nodded, her scone seeming too dry in her mouth to chew, her appetite gone. Aside from Charles' words, there was no plan to save her, no one was realizing how drastic it was that they were really going to let her go. Eppie had hoped that a couple days of thinking things over would have changed everyone's minds, but time hadn't changed a thing. It was as if she were the cute puppy from the pound that they'd brought home, loved up, but then she'd misbehaved, chewed up the good furniture, and now they were sending her back.

Eppie choked down her breakfast and watched out of the corner of her eye as Beth looked at the newspaper. The phone rang, and Beth, who usually didn't answer it, got up and picked up the kitchen line. She walked into the dining room chatting.

Alone again, Eppie turned her mind to emancipation. She decided her morning would be best spent online researching what it meant to be an emancipated teen.

⁂

The lawyer's office was full of shiny leather furniture and bookshelves. Eppie sat on the edge of her expensive chair, afraid it would swallow her up if she leaned back.

"Fourteen-year-olds have been emancipated in California, but it's rare," said the lawyer, Mr. Sawelson. He peered at Eppie through his square glasses. "You say you have a job, but do you have a work permit? Your current employment isn't necessarily a legal job, you realize."

Eppie's insides jumped. *Uh oh!* Could she lose her job at the stables now too?

"It's akin to babysitting," Beth said in her silky voice, who was sitting in the chair next to Eppie. "She doesn't make nearly enough to file taxes with the government."

"Then she doesn't make nearly enough to be an emancipated teen. Are you willing to work enough to cover your expenses, including a place to live, and to provide for yourself? Because while you may be 'working' for Marta Greeves at the stables, that is an 'under the table' job and not one we can use in your emancipation case."

Eppie slowly realized that the answer she thought would save her was dissolving before her. Her mind did cartwheels. If she couldn't claim her job, she'd have to get one that she could claim, but if she got a 'real' job, then she couldn't work at the stables and she might lose Legend. But if she went back into foster care, then she'd probably lose him anyway. It was beginning to look like Legend's life with her was the thing on the chopping block. Eppie fixed her lips into a tight line, determined not to lose her horse.

"What about her family?" Mr. Sawelson asked Beth.

"They aren't in a position to take her back. It's a delicate matter involving Pauline and their oldest boy." Beth looked at the lawyer in a pointed way. He cleared his throat and nodded.

"Are the Dursoms her only remaining family?"

"She has a grandmother who is incapacitated."

"I see." Mr. Sawelson stared at the folder in front of him as if he expected the answer to Eppie's dilemma to magically fly up and present itself to him. "I see there is an estate but that there are complications because the grandmother is now incapacitated, and Pauline is not yet of legal age." After a moment he closed the folder and stared at Beth. "That will take some time to resolve, certainly."

"It was only recently discovered," Beth said.

"I see that you tried to help Miss Wills here by taking her away from her previous untenable living situation, and I'm sorry for you both that it didn't work out for the long term. However, if you don't find a place for her, Beth, the only option will be for the state to take over until her inheritance issues are resolved. She is not a candidate to become emancipated, I'm afraid. She's just too young to provide for herself at this time without her estate monies. Maybe in a couple of years we can revisit this option."

"It was our first option," Beth said coolly. "Just something that we wanted to look into. I won't let Pauline here go back into the system, I owe her that much."

"I'm glad to hear that, but in today's economy, you may be hard-pressed to find another family willing to take her. No offense to you, my dear, you're a lovely girl," he shook Eppie's hand. "I wish you the best of luck."

Eppie nodded blindly, keeping all of her emotion inside of her. "Thanks," she managed.

"We'll start looking into other options now," Beth said. "I appreciate your time, Gerry."

"Let me know how things turn out," Mr. Sawelson said as they left his offices.

Out in the parking lot the morning ocean breeze was a refreshing change from the leathery office air, but it did little to improve Eppie's mood. She had to think of something! As Beth drove her back into the hills of Palos Verdes, Eppie put out an SOS text to all of her friends in her phone's address book, asking if they knew of anyone willing to take in a hard-working fourteen year old girl.

## Chapter Forty-two

The next two days were quiet at the mansion but Eppie's phone remained lit from the time she woke up until she went to sleep. Her Facebook page also had a lot of comments and suggestions about what she could do. Someone's aunt outside of Houston, Texas, offered to take Eppie and her horse in, but with her own grandmother in San Pedro nearby, Eppie had to decline that rather unexpected offer. She checked her texts one last time before leaving in the minivan to visit Grandma.

"I'll be right back," she told Julianna as they parked in front of the house.

"I'll wait here, don't hurry," Julianna said. She'd been extra nice to Eppie since she learned that she would soon be leaving the Krauses.

Grandma was in the living room in a big chair facing out into a small backyard complete with a bird feeder hopping with wild birds.

"Hi, Grandma," Eppie said, bending and kissing her. Grandma smiled, a weird twist on one side of her face.

"Eppie Girl," Grandma said. She patted Eppie on the head using her good arm. She was so much better, almost like her old self, except she wasn't really walking yet. The nurses said she could shuffle around some but she mostly got moved from room to room by wheelchair. Still Eppie was glad to see her out in the main room, not in the small bedroom she shared with another tenant.

"How are you today?" Eppie asked as she sat down in a folding chair beside her, suddenly so glad to see her. She held her frail old hands gently.

"Good, good."

"I'm glad you're better."

"How's school?" Grandma asked in her slow, peculiar way.

"I'm not in school right now Grandma, it's still summer, but school starts in a few weeks. I'm going to be in high school."

"Fair Oaks High School," Grandma said.

"No, Grandma, that's the one mom went to in Colorado. I'm going to a high school here, in California. Peninsula Hills High School." Eppie stopped short. Or was she? That's where she was enrolled, but if she didn't get a place to live in the school district, who knew where she might end up? Lomita High School with Brian? Wouldn't that be ironic, if she moved back in with the Dursoms and went there with Brian, Maggie, and Lexel and the Narbonne Middle School gang? But Jim would be finishing his senior year there. That would be a disaster.

"Um . . . what?" Eppie had to ask. Grandma had said something but she'd been too lost in thought to hear it.

"Did you ride Onyx today?" Grandma asked. Eppie shook her head. Grandma was still confused about timelines, the doctors had told Beth.

"I only rode him that one time, around Christmas, Grandma. Remember, I told you? I own a new horse named Legend. Remember I showed you his picture?" Eppie knew there was a little photo album of her life in Palos Verdes that she'd given to Grandma in July; it had labeled pictures of her friends, of Eppie at the stables on Kachina and Cesar, and of her leading Legend around. But often Grandma would also ask to see the pictures of Evie, Grandma's nickname for her mother, Evangeline. In a way, Grandma had found a great way to block out the pain of a dead daughter and husband. She'd checked into the La-la-land Hotel in her mind, where everyone was alive and everything was just as she remembered it in the good ol' days. Eppie wished she could be so lucky.

"We're having spaghetti for dinner," Grandma said suddenly. It seemed that she could keep stuff that was going to happen in her nursing home straight in her mind, if not past events.

"You like spaghetti," Eppie said, remembering the nurse that had told her to always remind her of things that she already knew.

"It's messy, but I like it," Grandma agreed. Eppie knew that was as deep as her conversation with Grandma was going to get, but she tried a new tact.

"I may be moving, Grandma. With some new people. Remember when I was living with Grandpa Bud's other granddaughter Tracey for a while, and then I moved in with the new people, Cashmere and Beth? Well now I'm going to move again."

"Who are you going to be moving in with?" Grandma asked, stopping Eppie short. She shrugged.

"I have some new roommates, Grandma. Real nice people. I'll tell you all about them next time I see you, but for now I don't want to tire you out too much." Eppie stood and kissed Grandma's forehead, feeling more like the adult than the kid in the situation. "I love you."

"I love you, Eppie Girl," Grandma said. "Say hi to Evie for me."

Eppie nodded. "I will," she said, not up to reminding her again that Evie Dearest had bailed on them both by dying. She clenched her teeth and her purple Vans carried her quickly out the door to where Julianna was waiting to take her back to the mansion in the hills, the place Eppie could no longer call home.

# ~Chapter Forty-three~

Eppie sat across from Marta, who'd poured her a Coke over ice and pushed it toward her on the small trailer's coffee table. Mrs. Tibbles the cat had already found Eppie's lap, and was painfully kneading her thighs with sharp claws. Howser the dog was loudly sniffing the door in the other room he was locked in, occasionally whining to be let out, but he was all jumps and dangerous tail when company came so Marta ignored him.

Eppie launched. "So I'm going to ride Cesar. I can't stand to see him cooped up like that, sure he's getting turnouts and hot walks, but then what? No contact with anyone who cares about him, none of the attention. Beth doesn't come here, and Cashmere is God-knows-where. I just wanted to tell you. I have to Marta. I can't take seeing him like that anymore."

"My lips are sealed. I do what's best for horses, not people. You know that about me. As far as I know, you're supposed to be riding Cesar still."

"Beth hasn't told me not to, but Cashmere did." Eppie grimaced as she remembered the impolite note she found outside on the hallway floor by her bedroom door, left by Cashmere before she scurried out of her own house in the middle of the night like some cockroach: *Don't you touch my horse.*

"Well she didn't tell me a thing, not even, 'hire someone else because I'm leaving, and that horse needs a work out'. You'll be starting from scratch, he's a wreck. I saw Francisco leading him to the turn out, he was jigging so sideways that he knocked Francisco down."

"Damn." That's what Eppie feared. Horses needed constant attention and work, love and most of all, commitment. She still sort of hated all these stuck up PV girls who owned horses like skis, taking them out when they felt like it, and not bothering with them the rest of the time. Girls who had never lifted a manure rake or cleaned out a hoof or saddled up a horse they owned themselves. To think all Eppie did to get Legend, and all she would do to keep him, she just couldn't stand the thought of it.

"We should probably be discussing Legend's future here as long as we're discussing Cesar," Marta said grimly as Eppie took a sip of her drink.

"I know. I have to figure out how to pay for Legend. Beth hasn't mentioned it yet, but do you think she's planning on letting me keep him?"

"She hasn't talked to me, and there's a 30 day cancellation agreement, so I'd say you're good through September at least. Beth pays about $850 a month but we can get you down to about $350 if you put in some work around here in exchange for part of the keep and you move Legend to one of the stalls off the main road."

Eppie nodded. She loved where Legend was boarded now, right across from the trails where he could see the green grass emerging in the springtime and all the horses coming and going, but the road stables weren't bad, as someone had planted a row of wind-blocking trees long ago and it was green there too, and the traffic on the main road leading into Palos Verdes was a good ways away on the other side of a tall chain link fence. Eppie wondered at herself, worrying about her horse's view when she should be worried about whether she would end up having a home at all. She sighed.

"I wish she'd just tell me already what's happening. She keeps telling me she 'owns' Legend, but what does that mean? She's never even worked with him before. And Cashmere still hasn't been home yet and it's been over two weeks. Cesar isn't getting ridden at all, Cashmere is missing work and refusing to take her mother's phone calls, and I'm too distracted to do well at work for you and Legend . . . well, he's just like one giant hanky right now, all I do is cry on him and wipe my nose on his mane."

Marta smiled at that last part. "Glad to see you've kept your sense of humor," she said.

"I wish I could say I have, but there's not much funny going on here Marta. This is damn scary! I need to know what's happening so I can make plans for Legend, and for me, and fast."

Marta looked deep in thought. "Don't lose hope, okay? I'm willing to work with you about the board for Legend, so let's take that worry off your shoulders until we find out what happens next."

"I did overhear something, Beth asking if there was a bed available . . ." Eppie didn't even want to say it. She'd heard Beth on the phone two mornings ago asking that question, but the word "bed available" rang the warning bell that it was a foster home, maybe even a state-run facility.

Marta frowned. "Well, don't jump to conclusions, Paulie. Nothing's nothing until it's something."

Eppie managed a weak smile. "That sounds like lyrics from one of those country songs you always listen to."

"It very well may be, it's something my daddy used to tell me. And it's good advice. Now go get those horses saddled up, I've hired Leane to come help you until Cashmere comes back, if she ever comes back, that stuck up little princess."

"She's more like the queen," Eppie said with another sigh, remembering her discussion long ago with Brian about Cashmere's "royal rule." She took a long swallow of her Coke and wiped her mouth with the back of her hand, then wiped her hand on her jeans. "I'll see you later. You want Howser to come with us?"

"Nah, I'm going to come too to break Leane in, but I'll be in charge of Legend. Let's get him ready to go out on the trail today, shall we? He could use a good outing, may help dry up some of that snot you've been leaving on his mane."

Eppie cringed. "Good idea. Thanks, Marta!" Her heart lifted some, knowing that Legend could start spending the day with her out on the trail. If she was really going to lose him, at least her last memories of him would be fond ones, she thought as she sprinted toward Marta's trail riding stables.

Eppie's spirits lifted as they brought Legend again on the trail ride. He was more curious than spooky, and navigated the terrifying gate to the trail without any fuss. She felt better as the barn became her therapy center again. Eppie spent every day there. When she arrived at the barn, she turned off her cell phone and secluded herself; she just wasn't up to seeing friends and answering their questions about her plans, as she didn't have a plan yet. In fact she was waiting, again, for an adult to tell her what her future would hold.

One night she returned to the mansion exhausted from work. Surprise was hardly the word for it when a gentle knock sounded on her bedroom door just after she had showered. She was reading Marta's horse manual on her bed wearing a tank top and her boy shorts that she wore as pajama bottoms when a huge bunch of colored balloons came through the door.

"Surprise!" came several voices, and behind the balloons she saw Deena's face, and then suddenly her room was full: Deena, Steffi, and even bitch-on-wheels Ivanna stood there, looking sheepish, and before Eppie could react Mark stepped out from behind them. Eppie squealed in excitement at seeing her school friends in spite of herself.

"Oh my God! What are you guys doing here?"

"Well, if you're going to just fall off the planet, we had to come to you," Deena was saying as Eppie hugged everyone in the doorway. She had an extra-long hug for Mark, and a barely-there air hug for Ivanna. Balloons and tears intertwined.

"You are so sweet, come in!"

Mark hesitated at the door but Eppie grabbed his arm. Soon they were all crammed onto Eppie's big bed with the pink, gold, and blue balloons hovering like parents above them, although Ivanna sat as far off the edge of the bed as she could manage without actually standing.

"Wow, so what's been happening? No one has heard from you in like, a week!" Steffi said, her cute little nose twitching like a rabbit's.

"I don't know what to say."

"You could answer your phone once in a while!" Deena chimed in. "I mean, seriously, I sent you like . . . a billion texts and even voicemails."

"I know," Eppie said sadly. "It's just . . ." she sighed.

Mark grabbed her hand. "You're even ignoring me? We're your friends, we can help!"

"I wish that were true," Eppie told him. "I have tried everything to stay here, I mean everything. I even tried to get emancipated. Nothing is working."

"Well, I have good news, my mom says you can stay with us for a while. I mean, not permanently . . ." Steffi flushed red as Eppie perked up with excitement. "But for a few days if you need too."

"Thanks," Eppie said, mad at herself for not playing it cool. "But while that's totally great, I need something more permanent. I don't think Beth would go for my bumping around like that."

"Oh." Steffi sounded disappointed.

"What about that Texas lady?" Deena asked.

"My grandma is here, I can't leave the area."

"We'd miss you anyway! I'm glad you have to stay here."

"What about getting an apartment?" Mark asked. Eppie smiled at him, he really was clueless about the real world, nice as he was.

"I can't manage it," Eppie said. "But let's not talk about me, what have you been up to?" She had missed her friends, and she felt so happy that they hadn't let her slip away. *That was probably my secret plan,* she told herself. Instead of a million sad goodbyes, Eppie had wanted to just sort of fade away. But sitting here on her bed with her friends (except Ivanna, whom she still hadn't forgiven), Eppie was glad that they'd found her.

Cesar twisted his body into a tight U, refusing the jump so abruptly that Eppie nearly lost her seat. She gripped hard with her thighs and dug in, grabbing his thick neck so she wouldn't get pitched sideways. He galloped toward the gate, causing another jumper in the ring to have to pull up her horse into a crazy stop.

"Hey!"

"Crap! Sorry!" Eppie yelled, feeling like an amateur. The big bay stomped angrily, snorting, as Eppie regained composure and gathered his reins. She cropped him on the rear. Normally she didn't use a crop but today, it was Eppie or the horse. So far, the horse was winning.

“It doesn’t seem possible you stayed on for that ride,” Marta called out from where she stood by the ring’s fence. She’d agreed to supervise Eppie’s riding of Cesar, not only because he was becoming uncontrollable but also because they’d agreed that if Cashmere had a spy at the barn and found out, an adult would be able to witness that it was the best for the horse.

“I can’t believe she abandoned him!” Eppie replied in anger. “Look at him! He did so well for Cashmere in those shows just a few months ago and now he’s like a green horse!”

“An angry green horse, the worst kind,” Marta said as Eppie trotted Cesar toward her. The morning air was warm but the lather on Cesar’s coat had nothing to do with the heat. Marta grabbed his reins and stroked him while Eppie got her boot back in the correct position in the stirrup.

“The more I work with him the worse he is, what’s up with that?”

“He’s Cashmere’s horse, he probably misses her. What’s it been, almost a month since they’ve ridden together?”

“Five weeks.”

“He’s despondent. I’ve seen this before with backyard ponies, families forget them, toss them a half flake of hay every day, clean out their water troughs once a week, and that’s it. The result is a mad ornery horse. He just needs attention.”

“I want to turn him out with Legend,” Eppie said suddenly.

“I don’t know,” Marta said. “Why?”

“Because Legend has excellent manners in the turnout, and Cesar needs to have fun.”

“Well . . .” Marta frowned.

“I know what you’re thinking, you should ask Beth, but I have a good feeling about it Marta. Cesar never has fun like Legend does. You’re the one who taught me that lesson, that horses like to play and have fun! When was the last time Cesar had fun?”

Marta smiled. “He has fun when he’s jumping in the show ring with Cashmere, but that’s about it, and it’s been awhile.”

“I’ll take full responsibility.”

"No . . ." Marta paused. "I'll take full responsibility. I think you're right, Eppie. You have damn good instincts. You go get Legend, I'll take Cesar, meet you up there."

Like a storm cloud the two horses, one dark blue-gray, the color of granite, the other dark bay, like well-oiled leather, raced toward Eppie, tails high in the wind, ears forward, heads high. Right before they would have bowled her over they stopped, skittering sand all around, and a film of dust covered Eppie entirely. She smiled, ignoring the grit in her teeth, as Legend reared and directed Cesar away from her, and they galloped off toward the other end of the ring. Soon they moved into a trot, and then they were walking together, heads hung in a tired way. Cesar dropped down and rolled to itch his back in the warm sand while Legend sniffed nearby, and once Cesar stood up again the two horses nuzzled next to each other, grooming each other's necks with gentle teeth. Marta walked up and put her arm around Eppie.

"You're a genius, I'd yell it from the rooftops if I had to," Marta said.

"Well, yep. I kind of am," Eppie said with a laugh. They watched "the boys" as they frolicked and nuzzled each other more, until Eppie stood in the center of the ring, palm up. Legend broke away from Cesar and came to her, and Cesar followed, calmer now, a contented look on his face. Eppie let him sniff her fingers.

"I won't abandon you either, Cesar," she whispered as she slipped his halter over his head. "I've already made my promises to Legend, but I owe one to you too, I think. I promise, I'll won't leave you. I won't let this happen to you again."

# Chapter Forty-four

Eppie ate breakfast while thinking about Legend and Cesar, feeling anxious to get to the barn. The heat of summer had culminated in a wretched combination of thick hot air blowing across Southern California with the onset of dreaded Santa Ana winds. Terrible for horses and humans. She wanted to settle Legend in case he was uncomfortable.

Beth walked into the kitchen. She poured herself some coffee and sat down.

"I found a place for you," she said in an even voice. "It's certainly not my first choice, but it's here in Palos Verdes, it's a foster care home, but it's above average, really. The best we can do and still keep you in the school district."

Eppie stared, finally realizing her mouth was open. She closed it, unsure which messy question to ask first.

"Can I keep Legend?" was the only question that mattered.

"We will work something out, these people are agreeable to you being on the school's equestrian team for PE, so your time at the barn would count toward school work."

"But I can't ride Legend yet!"

"You'll be riding next year and you can still show him without riding him, or you can ride Cesar for shows."

"Cashmere would never let me ride Cesar again!"

"I'll deal with Cashmere," Beth said tightly. "I've spoken with Marta, and it's apparent that Cesar needs you."

Eppie relaxed a little. The rest of it, whatever happened, barely mattered now. Legend would still be her horse. She realized she didn't even care about the rest of it, she would sleep on a cot in someone's garage if it meant keeping her horse.

"Your new home is near the school, so you can walk. There are four other foster girls at the home now. One is a senior and will be eighteen during the next school year so you'll take her bed when she moves out, she's getting her GED now. They are a nice family, Pauline. I've met the wife, their home is respectable . . . immaculate; really, and you'll be comfortable there, and you can keep your friends, your life at the barn, and the life we gave you here in Palos Verdes."

Eppie appreciated the way Beth was able to spin things; Beth had found a way to make it seem like all she'd done for Eppie was one big favor, except for this kicking her out thing.

"Thanks." It was all Eppie could think of to say.

"School starts next Tuesday. So we're going to move your things over today so you can get situated. Can you be ready by noon?"

Her head began to spin but she nodded. "Sure."

"Excellent. Pack, and I'll have your things delivered later. Julianna will drive you there for lunch, which starts promptly at 12:30, according to Mrs. Yao, your new foster mother."

"Okay," Eppie said. The other questions she had rose up but Beth was already heading for the garage door dressed in her Juicy sweats, her gym bag over her shoulder and her Bentley keys in her hand. She exited, leaving Eppie alone in the kitchen. She didn't say goodbye. Eppie carried her breakfast dishes to the sink (she was the only one in the house who did) and slumped upstairs to pack.

The Yao household smelled like fish and brown rice as lunch was presented to Eppie. She sat down at the worn laminate kitchen table in the dark wood-paneled ranch-style house, awkwardly glancing up at the other girls around her. One was tall, Black, and skinny and reminded her of Lexel. Two were Asian and were sisters, and the other was a younger girl of about nine. Mrs. Yao clapped, her hands small but strong.

"Hurry, lunch over soon, must start homework!"

Eppie wondered, were they in summer school? Wasn't summer school over? Eppie had prematurely given Beth her cell phone back by leaving it on her bed at the mansion, and now she realized she was trapped here. No one knew where she was living, or had her new landline number, and she had no access to her social media or email or texts. She cleared her throat.

"Um, excuse me?" Eppie said.

"What is it Pauline?" Mrs. Yao said in her quick way. She wasn't mean, it didn't seem like. Just very abrupt.

"I need to get to work."

Mrs. Yao stared at Pauline. "What you mean work?"

"I have a job, at the stables. I'm supposed to go at 1:00 today."

"No, no, no," Mrs. Yao said in her fast way. "No work. You do not work, you stay here, do homework, help at the house. No job."

"But . . ." Eppie gulped. *What?* She hadn't asked enough questions, stupidly she'd heard that she could keep her horse, and hadn't bothered to ask if she could keep her job to pay for the horse, or even get a lift to the barn to ride! "I need to tell my boss."

"Phone time at 7:00 to 8:00 pm. Only then. No phone. Go to room, unpack bags. Girls will show you where."

Frightened and now feeling as if a dark cloud had filled her soul, Eppie got up blindly and followed the other girls into their big shared bedroom.

Eppie's bed was in fact a cot in the corner of the room. The room was unusually clean, very sparse and organized. Eppie's bags and boxes, including Grandma's trunk, had been brought by the delivery service and were strewn all around her cot. The pile was an eyesore in the pin-straight room.

"God she's such a bitch!" The tall black girl, Kianna, said.

"OMG, did you hear her? *No you can't work.* I hate her!" chimed in one of the sisters named Ashley. The other sister, Chelsea, giggled nervously. The younger girl she'd heard one of the girls call Prissy climbed up into her top bunk and curled up into fetal position. Mrs. Yao came down the hallway and the room grew silent.

"Get to work! Homework, homework! Go go!" she said, and left. She glared at Eppie. "You, clean that up! No mess!"

"How can you have homework?" Eppie asked as Mrs. Yao scurried back down the hallway, confused and now even more worried as she looked at her pile of bags, not knowing how to clean them up to Mrs. Yao's standards.

"She makes us study all summer long, homework four hours a day, we have to have As to stay here or we get kicked out."

"This place has high turnover, and the second you're eighteen, boom, you're out." Kianna said. "I have to leave here in February when I turn eighteen, and she's making me get my GED first so I will at least graduate high school."

"What will you do?" Eppie asked, glad for the first time that she was only fourteen.

"I've been planning on going to school, I've got a scholarship at Dominguez, but I have no idea where I'll live or how I'm gonna make money. It's damn scary. Getting free college money is easy if you're poor with good grades but I'll probably be the first person ever to be homeless while working on a PhD."

Pain seared through Eppie's abdomen. She wished she could go back to Beth's house. She'd never tried pleading with Beth, not really. She hadn't stood up for herself. With a weird fascination it dawned on her that all of her friends' phone numbers were in her cell phone. She hadn't thought to write them down, things were happening so quickly. She had no way to contact anyone, even during 'phone hours'. She was truly alone. Why hadn't she put a final message on her Facebook or told someone where she was? She felt like a prisoner.

"Do you have a computer here?" Eppie asked her new roommates hopefully.

"Yes, in the office. Why?"

"No one knows where I am," Eppie said in a meek voice.

"Oh, it's for studying. There's no access to the outside world, it's all blocked. You can't contact anyone," Ashley told her.

"You can use the home phone," Chelsea said as she smoothed her long black hair. "If you don't mind Madame General listening in."

Eppie nodded, missing her other world, wishing she could hug Legend right now, and call Marta and tell her she couldn't come to work. She looked at the sorry pile of her belongings, a pile that looked so huge in the small room, and began trying to find a way to stash it all (neatly) in the tiny cubicle that was allotted for her personal space.

By Day Four, as Eppie called it in her mind, Eppie felt like she was going out of her mind. She had tried finding Marta's phone number but was only able to leave a brief message on the stable answering machine, which wasn't even answered by Marta but by one of the city's Parks and Recreation employees. *Marta,* she'd said as Madame General Yao listened, *I'm in my new foster home and they won't let me work. I'm sorry I couldn't tell you, I didn't know ahead of time. Please hug Legend and Cesar for me. I'll see you when I can.*

Her belongings presented a bigger problem. Mrs.Yao made her get rid of the big framed pictures of the horses, but Eppie gave up the frames and hid the photos under her sleeping bag on her cot. At night she was careful to hide them when Mrs.Yao came in for what was called "Night Check". She had to give up over half her clothes so they would fit into the cubby; she sneaked some to the other girls, who hadn't had new clothes in a long time, before Mrs. Yao took away a trash bag full of shorts and spaghetti strapped tank tops and cute miniskirts and all of her summer sandals, which weren't allowed (and neither were bikinis, so now Eppie didn't even own a bathing suit). She had two pairs of tennis shoes and her riding boots left to wear. Mrs. Yao had almost taken away Eppie's Team Cesar gear when Eppie, figuring out Mrs. Yao's motivation, quickly told her it was "for school".

"No room!" said Mrs. Yao. "Messy, messy! It's no good!"

Eppie had to get rid of a few other things to make room in the tall cupboard for her bulky riding boots and helmet. The hardest item to part with was grandma's trunk.

"No stay here, too big, too ugly, too old," Mrs. Yao said when she saw it under Eppie's cot.

"But, it was my grandmother's, it's . . . special," Eppie told her, nearing tears.

"No good, no good, I throw it away. You keep what fits in the cupboard, the rest goes. No room."

Eppie cried silently when Mrs. Yao left the room, and Chelsea, who was the friendliest of the girls, put her arm around Eppie's shoulders.

"Sorry Pauline. That sucks. Want some help moving it outside to the trash?"

"I . . . can't. I can't part with it."

"Well, there's no place to hide it here, trust me."

"I . . . I have a place to put it, but . . ." She thought of her tack cubicle at the barn. With Cashmere gone, she could stash the trunk in her tack unit and put Legend's harness and weighted saddle in Cashmere's bigger tack room until Cashmere came back. But how would she get the trunk there? Her mind spun with ideas, none of which would work.

"How far is it?" asked Kianna.

"Just about five minutes away driving," Eppie calculated the distance to the barn. "But it may as well be five hundred minutes away, if we don't have a car."

"Maybe I can help you," Kianna said. She looked lost in thought. "I'll see what I can do, okay? But for now, let's not talk about it." She put her finger to her lips, indicating that the walls had ears.

It must have been about one am when Eppie felt a cold hand on her mouth. She tried to scream but the hand held her down. Eyes opened wide, she looked around, seeing a shadowy human form above her in the room.

"Shhh." It was Kianna whispering. "Shut up and follow me."

Eppie did, wearing the long stiff cotton pajamas Beth had put in her suitcase without telling her, and grabbing a jacket she'd left on the chair. Chelsea moaned in her sleep and Prissy snored lightly. Kianna stuffed pillows under Eppie's sleeping bag to make a human looking decoy, and the two girls tiptoed out. Kianna went straight for the back door, tiptoe exited, and they crept quiet as cats alongside the house. Out front they turned left and walked down the sidewalk past dimly lit homes, Eppie's heart galloping in her chest.

"Where are we going?" Eppie whispered as she trotted alongside the long-legged Kianna.

"You'll see."

Soon they saw a truck with headlights on around the next bend, and as they approached, Eppie was shocked to see her grandma's trunk in the back of the truck.

"Oh my God! You got it out! Thanks so much!"

"Well, we're not free yet. Let's go."

Eppie climbed into the truck where a long-haired teenaged boy smiled behind the wheel.

"Hey, I'm Freddy."

"Pauline." Eppie was really embarrassed at being caught outside in her jammies but she grinned and shook his hand.

"Thanks!"

"Where to?

"The stables."

"Okay." Freddy seemed to know where he was going and drove on, Kianna and Eppie squished together in the passenger seat. Now Eppie had a moment to think. The stables were closed at night and they would have to sneak in. The gates were locked though. She would have to wake up Marta. She didn't want to surprise her in the middle of the night, but it was the only way she could get her grandma's trunk into the cubicle without the National Guard getting involved.

Eppie shivered as she knocked at the door to Marta's trailer, having slipped between the chain linked gates to get onto the stable lot. Howser barked, the bloodhound in him apparent as he woo-wooed from across the stables. Soon he was at Eppie's feet, doing a happy dog dance, and Eppie was glad she'd had Freddy and Kianna wait in the car.

"Better be something on fire at this hour!" Marta grumped from behind the door. When she opened the door, a wave of emotion ran through Eppie. She clutched onto Marta and held her close.

"What? Why, girl, what in tarnation is going on?" Marta asked. Eppie stood up and wiped her cheeks, flustered.

"I'm so sorry, I had to bring my grandmother's trunk here, they wanted to throw it away, but I couldn't get it here, so we had to sneak out, and I really have to go but I want to put it in my cubicle, but the barn is closed so . . ."

“Whoa. Easy, Pauline. You okay? You’re racing down the track here, just settle down.”

Eppie realized she was a blathering mess and she nodded, and took a breath. Marta grabbed the interfering Howser and threw him in the trailer bedroom and shut the door. She held her hand up as Eppie opened her mouth.

“I called Beth Saturday, she told me you got a new place to live and you didn’t have a new cell phone yet and you couldn’t call, so I forgive you about not showing up for work . . . for a week.”

*Cell phone?* “Oh, Marta, this new place is so different, I’m not allowed to use the phone, they won’t drive me to the barn, and I have to walk here during the school year if I want to come after school for my PE credits, it’s 2 miles one way, but I’ll do it, I’ll come back when school starts.” Eppie’s words raced again. “But for now, I just need to leave this trunk in my tack cubby, so do you mind if we drive in? Can you unlock the gates?”

“What is this trunk you keep going on about?” Marta saw the truck Eppie was pointing to in the truck bed and walked toward it.

“My grandma’s!” Eppie said, huffing alongside of her. “All of her stuff, and my mom’s, they want to throw it away, but I can’t do it! So I’m just going to keep it here in my tack cubicle.”

“Whatever it is, you can keep it in my place, hell, my dog has his own room, he can share a corner for your things. Come on, let’s pull it up here.”

With Freddy and Kianna’s help they lifted the trunk into Howser’s room, who was now pushed out the door as people came in. Kianna and Freddy stood awkwardly by in the doorway as Eppie hugged Marta in the trailer’s living room.

“We really have to go, we’ll be in big trouble if we get caught out Marta, but I’ll see you . . .” Eppie didn’t know when. “I wish I had time to see Legend!”

“I’m caring for him personally until you get back,” Marta assured her. “But I’m not liking what I’m hearing, with them wanting to throw your belongings away. Here.” She opened the roll-top desk drawer and handed something to Eppie. It was paper, envelopes and a sheet of stamps.

“This thing called letter writing has worked since long before there were phones, write me a note and tell me what’s happening, since you can’t call me to tell me.” She scribbled her own address on the front of one of the envelopes. “Fill me in. You make it sound like prison where you’re staying.”

Eppie was shaking as they drove away back up the hill, the dark shadows of night all around them in the tree-filled community. Her mind was full of everything she would tell Marta. Mrs. Yao wasn’t a mean person really, it wasn’t like she was beating Eppie, but she was super strict. It was like being in the military or something; Eppie had been horrified for poor Prissy (which she’d since learned was short for Priscilla) when the girl had to clean the entire bathroom floor with a toothbrush for missing one problem on her math homework. And on Sunday when Eppie had asked Mrs. Yao for a ride to grandma’s, Mrs. Yao had said it was once a month, not once a week, that she could take her, for one hour, including drive time, which was twenty minutes each way. And Eppie had to do extra chores that day to make up the time it took to take her. Eppie was used to hard work and had been in worse facilities; this one was clean, her roommates were nice, but now she had her beloved horse that she could never see, and if she couldn’t work she couldn’t earn the money to keep him. In her mind, that was the worst torture of all.

## CHAPTER FORTY-FIVE

*Dear Marta,*

*School started today so things are better. Thanks again for taking my grandma's trunk! It's just a bunch of old stuff no one else would care about, but I really care about it so thanks. It means a lot to me, my family's memories are in there. It's all I have. I feel safe knowing you have it and Howser is guarding it!*

*There was a lot I couldn't tell you but the main thing is that Mrs. Yao, who is my new foster parent, won't let me have a job. I will be able to come to the stables starting next week for my PE credits at school but I have to walk and it's far but to see Legend I will do it. I need to ask you for my old job back of mucking stalls because I need to earn Legend's stall fees again so can we talk about that? It will have to be a secret between us that I'm working there though because Mrs. Yao can't know. I'm adding my address where I live now so you'll know where I am. I don't know the phone number here though.*

*Love, Eppie*

Eppie spent a lot of time trying to decide whether she would write the name Eppie or Paulie, which was what Marta called her, and decided Marta was the best adult in her life right now, so Eppie it was. At the last second she added (Paulie) underneath just to make it less confusing.

She mailed the letter with a stamp Marta had given her, sticking it into an empty mailbox on her way home from school so Mrs. Yao wouldn't know about it, because Eppie wasn't sure where the post office was in her new neighborhood. Her insides gave a thrilled turn; soon she would see her beautiful Legend again. Her PE class was only in the discussion stage on the bleachers in the gym for now, but would start for real at the stables the next Monday. Soon. Soon.

Eppie found it painful that her short walk to school was up a steep hill the whole way, but because she walked with Chelsea, Ashley and Kianna, it wasn't so bad. She found all of her PV friends her first day at her new high school, though it felt a little weird eating lunch with them while the other girls in her foster home ate together. She also had Mark at school, not that Mrs. Yao would approve. Eppie knew she wouldn't be able to see him anywhere but school. No more movies, parties, or dates. The fact that her high point of her day was being on her high school campus that first week was something Eppie couldn't quite believe.

Finally Monday came and Eppie felt grateful Beth had already arranged for Eppie to take Independent Study for her high school physical education credits. Marta would sign the paperwork and she had to ride or work with Legend instead of going to a regular PE class, so Eppie got out of school an hour early and walked the long downhill trudge to the stables. *The walk itself should give me a PE credit,* Eppie thought as she arrived at the stable nearly 40 minutes later with stinging feet. She breathed in the smells of the barn and rushed to Legend's stall. He wasn't there! There was a gaping space on the wood where his sign had been, *Owned and Loved by Pauline Wills.*

*Oh no*! Had Beth taken him after all? Fear clutched at her heart. After everything she'd been through, had she lost Legend too? Where was he? She raced toward Marta's series of stalls where she kept her trail horses.

"Marta!" she called in a panic. "Marta!"

Marta poked her head out from Kachina's stall. "Eppie! What are you screaming about? You're going to wake the dead, and worse, scare the horses!"

"Legend's gone!" she called. Marta opened the gate and exited the stall as Kachina nickered at Eppie.

"Well, Beth did finally call, she gave me that month's notice. I had another tenant come in so I had to do what I had to do, you know . . ." Her voice trailed off.

"You let her take him? You let her sell Legend out from under me? No Marta, how could you?" Eppie turned toward the barn door and hit it with her fist, causing Akron, a big chestnut, to spook. Marta took Eppie's hands.

"No, girl, no! I *moved* Legend. He's here. He's in the street stalls, remember, we talked about that less than a month ago. I just moved him. He's here, he's here."

Eppie calmed herself and mouthed "I'm sorry" at Marta, then raced toward the last row of stalls and called for her horse. "Legend! Legend!" she cried, and she heard his high-pitched whinny in answer. She found his stall and slid through the bars and hugged him, wishing she could hold all of him at once. She would never let go, never again. She held him for a long time, feeling his body next to hers, the coarse hair of his mane against her cheek. This was her home, her being here with Legend, and it didn't matter whether he was in the fancy expensive stable or the cheap stall by the road, or whether she could ride him or if they would just stay like this forever, but here he was, hers again. Forever. Marta approached and gave her a minute before talking.

"Beth said that her custody over the horse was designed to be in effect only while she was your legal guardian, so he's all yours now."

Eppie looked over and saw the sign, *Owned and Loved by Pauline Wills,* had been attached with wire to the metal bars. She smiled in relief.

"I liked your nickname, by the way, that you signed on your letter. Eppie. Is that short for Epona?" Marta asked.

"Epona?"

Marta shrugged. "Epona, the goddess of horses. You know, I think there's a line of horse care products by that name too. I thought that the goddess Epona maybe was the connection with your nickname."

Eppie's smile broadened. "It's something my family called me. I didn't know that about the goddess of horses, but I like it. Epona. Eppie. Kind of funny how they are almost the same, right?"

"Right. And now that you are the true custodian of one of Epona's greatest gifts to mankind, we'll have to do some fancy footwork to make it so you won't be afraid of losing that horse again. The way I see it, if you can't earn money on the weekends, you will have a hard time keeping that horse. There has to be a way around this mess."

"Whatever it takes Marta. Really, whatever it takes. I'm in."

"Great, because I have something in mind."

Eppie walked home from school. It was a long walk but she didn't mind it, in fact, she felt grateful for it. She approached the barn and went straight over to the far stalls and called out Marta's name.

"Marta! I'm home!"

"Go put your backpack away and let's get Legend out to roll, shall we?" Marta looked at her watch. "You're later then usual, it's gonna get dark soon. Change up and I'll head over there now."

"Okay!"

Howser bounded over and gave Eppie a big waggly greeting, and Eppie reached down and patted his brown head. He followed her to the little trailer she now called home and went inside with her. Now painted a cheery pale yellow over the once dark-green walls, the place was bright and sunny. Eppie opened the door to Howser's room—now hers—cleaned up and painted pale pink. Inside was grandma's trunk and some of the furniture she'd used from Beth's house; Beth had it delivered when she heard that Eppie was moving in with Marta, and that Marta had agreed to be her guardian until she turned eighteen. Mrs. Tibbles the tabby stretched her long feline body across her bedspread from the mansion in that stretchy way cats do, and Eppie rubbed her fingers along her belly.

"Hey Miz Tibbs," she said, "I'll be back soon and we'll get some serious snuggles in, k?"

Eppie put her backpack on her desk next to the white phone that actually had a cord attached that went into the wall, totally old school but functional. Beth had even given Eppie the computer she'd used when she lived at the Krause estate. Her beloved horse photos, newly framed, adorned her pink bedroom walls once again. With a soulful sigh, Eppie changed into her riding clothes and was zipping up her boots when there was a knock at the trailer door.

Eppie opened it and Cashmere stood there, looking impatient in her riding helmet and boots. She rolled her eyes. “Do you *have* to walk home? It takes forever and I TOLD you Julianna would be happy to pick you up after school, you know.”

“I know, sorry I’m late,” Eppie said. “Let’s go get the horses ready. Maybe I will take you up on that offer to get picked up from school now that it’s getting darker earlier, k?” She followed Cashmere toward Cesar’s stall; Legend now lived right next door to Cesar.

Eppie didn’t bother to explain it to Cashmere, but she liked the walk home. She liked seeing how the landscaped flowers came into bloom and then faded, how some neighbors were having things done to pretty up their houses, and how she could feel the day, and think about her life as she walked home to the barn from school. But mostly she liked it because each step reminded her of how far she’d come, and how damn lucky she was that Marta had rescued her from Mrs. Yao’s strict regime, and how close she’d come to losing everything that was important to her. And now that she could relax and reflect, her heart was filled with deep gratitude and love for all those adults who had helped her get to this place in her life: Tracey, Rich, Charles, Beth, and her sweet grandma Emmaline. And best of all, every step toward home was a step she had earned, each step bringing her closer to Legend, her own horse Legend who was the reason for everything. He had saved her, and she wouldn’t mind walking across the earth in gratitude for that horse every single day.

## About the Author

Raised in the semi-rural community of Rolling Hills Estates in Los Angeles County, California, Cat Spydell grew up riding horses and has owned four ponies over the years. While writing *Epona's Gift*, Cat spent a great deal of time at the barn with her teenage daughter Cassidy, Cassidy's friend Cori, and their beloved ponies Dale and Cappucino, two pygmy goats, a potbelly pig, and a giant white dog named Drinian, guardian to critters and people alike. Like Eppie, Cat once dreamed of owning a Warlander colt named Dunedain, who became the inspiration for Legend in this book.

Cat holds a master's degree in English Literature & Creative Writing from California State University, Long Beach, and now lives off-grid in the deep redwoods in Medocino County. In addition to *Epona's Gift*, her Young Adult novel *The Time Traveler's Apprentice at Hollywood High* and fantasy novel *The Fairies of Feyllan* are available on Amazon through Mischievous Muse Press. Her popular dog training book, *The Wolf Pack Guide to Dog Training,* can be found as a free pdf download online on her blog, https://catspydell.wordpress.com/.

# ~Thank You~

It is said it takes a village to raise a child, and in my case, I have a village of people to thank for their help in creating *Epona's Gift.*

My dear friend and business partner Gineve shared her photography skills, editing tips, and book-cover-making-skills to help give *Epona's Gift* its identity. Thank you so much Gineve, for your unwaivering support in my authorship endeavors.

My daughter Cassidy and her friend Cori were thirteen when they met at the barn while I was first writing *Epona's Gift.* They both helped inspire the story into being. All the horse girls we met helped formulate the scenario and the setting. Thanks to my 'other horse mom' Lisa Glazer for all the fun times we shared while teaching our girls to ride and taking ponies, goats, kids, and the big white dog out on the trails with us. Special thanks to Mackenzie for modeling for the cover, and blessings to our wonderful friend Annamay, who passed away in 2011, for her 'horsegirl" expertise. These girls all helped develop the character of Eppie, and I am appreciative for every beautiful moment we all shared.

I am exceptionally grateful when people go out of their way to help, and that help came through from my pre-publication readers, including animal communicator Meredith Whitney; mustang rescuer of LaRoux, Stephanie Petra; and Tiffany Chiu, owner of the magical Mystic Canyon Ranch/Tiffany's Red Barn. All gave great insight to the character of Eppie and excellent input to improve the book.

My uncle, Chester Traynor, showed me and my cousins the world of horses at a young age. The photo of me on the previous page was taken in my grandparents' backyard, and that lovely horse was named Sissy. Every Sunday our family would drive to Santa Fe Springs, CA and visit my grandparents, and we would first stop at the nearby barn where Chester lived as a stable master. These early childhood impressions followed me my entire life! I was in love with horses from an early age and learned much of what I know about them from Chester. My parents, Joe and Billie Leach, gifted me with a pony at Christmastime my ninth year, and I will forever be humbled for that spectacular opportunity, to love a sweet Shetland pony named Baby Duchess. Later, my next-door neighbor on Ranchview Road, Jenny, who owned a thoroughbred horse named Spicy Alibi, taught me the rest of what I came to know about horses and ponies during my childhood days.

I would like to thank Wendy Francisco. She is the breeder of the horse that inspired the character called Legend, the Warlander colt named Dunedain that I began the process of purchasing, even though as an underpaid mom raising two kids there were some months we barely made ends meet. My attempt to buy a horse was a secret extravagance few knew about. Dunedain's photo was on my wall in my room. I channeled the character of Eppie out of my desire to own a Warlander horse. It wasn't meant to be, however, as we ended up being gifted with a wonderful local show pony named Dale instead. I let my dream of owning Dunedain go for the 'greater good' of letting my daughter learn the fine world of horsemanship. Looking back, it would have been a hectic thing to bring an untrained colt into my life at that time. But I love the passion I found for baroque horses, the dreams that kept me motivated, the inner 13-year-old girl in me coming alive through words, based on myself at that age, when I rode my pony all over the Palos Verdes Peninsula, gaining the freedom and wonder only life on the back of a horse can give a girl.

## Online Resources

Author Cat Spydell has rescued wild and domestic animals out of her home for years. Her rescue ranch is a magical place called Pixie Dust Ranch.

Here are some online social media pages and hashtags available to follow the animals of Pixie Dust Ranch, and Cat's other book pages.

Facebook:

Pixie Dust Ranch
Cat Spydell, Author and Animal Communicator
Rad the Peacock
The Fairies of Feyllan
The Time Traveler's Apprentice at Hollywood High
On the Road with Rad the Peacock
The Wolf Pack Guide to Dog Training

Instagram:
Rad the Peacock

Twitter:
Rad the Peacock

Hashtags:
#Dalethebigredpony #RadthePeacock #athenathekitten
#drinianthebigwhitedog #buttercupthecurseslayinggoat
#fernthenubiangoat #daisythepygmygoat #lilythepig
#thefairiesoffeyllan
#thetimetravelersapprenticeathollywoodhigh
#Ontheroadwithradthepeacock
#soulshinebus

Coming Soon: A Memoir by Cat Spydell

*On the Road with Rad the Peacock*

MISCHIEVOUS MUSE Press

READ • DREAM • MUSE

www.ingramcontent.com/pod-product-compliance
Lightning Source LLC
LaVergne TN
LVHW091035080826
845145LV00002B/502

* 9 7 8 1 9 3 8 2 0 8 4 2 3 *